Prais
and the Ma

"Absorbing and edgy, ——— ——— ——— ——— ——i-
pire romance should ——— ——— ——— ——— ——g
read.... Laura Wright turns up the heat and takes you
on a wild ride. I can't wait to see what's next!"
—Lara Adrian, *New York Times* bestselling author
of *Darker After Midnight*

"Grabs you by the heartstrings from the first page and
pulls you along until the cliff-hanger of an ending....
[The] complexity of emotion is what makes Laura Wright's
books so engrossing.... One of the best new series and
authors around, [and] I highly recommend *Eternal Beast*
to all lovers of paranormal romance."
—Sizzling Hot Book Reviews

"This has been a series I love to read and seem to fall
more and more in love with."   —Paranormal Reads

"Laura Wright did my two favorite characters justice and
gave them an awesome story.... *Eternal Beast* is the best
in the series!"   —Under the Covers

"An incredible installment to the series.... If you haven't
experienced this series yet, you are totally missing out."
—Literal Addiction

"Laura Wright has done it again and totally [blown] me
away.... Laura Wright has created an original and extraordinary world, and I am her fan girl for life."
—Book Monster Reviews

"I'd put Laura Wright's level of world building and char-
acter development in with Black Dagger Brotherhood
and Immortals After Dark."
—Scandalicious Book Reviews

continued ...

Eternal Captive

"Riveting. . . . There are plenty more stories to be told in this fascinating universe." —*Romantic Times*

"An action-packed read . . . enough twists that leave one anxious for the next in the series."—Night Owl Reviews

"Very sexy. . . . The emotional strength of the story elevated this above other paranormals I've read of late."
—Dear Author . . .

Eternal Kiss

"The perfect book for anyone who likes sexy, dangerous vampires with dark secrets." —Fresh Fiction

"Complex and riveting." —*Romantic Times* (4 stars)

"A super urban romantic."—Genre Go Round Reviews

"I fell in love with book one in this series, but this second edition moved me from innocent love to full-blown love addiction. . . . [I] could not put it down."
—Shameless Romance Reviews (5 stars)

"A great ride where a sweep-off-your-feet romance ignites within a high-risk plot. Laura Wright has found her niche in the paranormal romance genre with her larger-than-life Roman brothers!" —Leontine's Book Realm

Eternal Hunger

"Just when it seems every possible vampire twist has been turned, Wright launches a powerful series with a rich mythology, page-turning tension, and blistering sensuality." —*Publishers Weekly* (starred review)

"Dark, delicious, and sinfully good, *Eternal Hunger* is a stunning start to what promises to be an addictive new series. I can't wait for more from Laura Wright."
—Nalini Singh, *New York Times* bestselling author of *Tangle of Need*

"Action, passion, and dark suspense launch a riveting new series. Laura Wright knows how to lure you in and hold you captive until the last page."
—Larissa Ione, *New York Times* bestselling author of *Lethal Rider*

Also by Laura Wright

Mark of the Vampire Series

Eternal Hunger
Eternal Kiss
Eternal Blood
(A Penguin Special)
Eternal Captive
Eternal Beast
Eternal Beauty
(A Penguin Special)

ETERNAL DEMON

MARK OF THE VAMPIRE

LAURA WRIGHT

A SIGNET ECLIPSE BOOK

SIGNET ECLIPSE
Published by the Penguin Group
Penguin Group (USA) Inc., 375 Hudson Street,
New York, New York 10014, USA

USA | Canada | UK | Ireland | Australia | New Zealand | India | South Africa | China

Penguin Books Ltd., Registered Offices: 80 Strand, London WC2R 0RL, England
For more information about the Penguin Group visit penguin.com.

First published by Signet Eclipse, an imprint of New American Library,
a division of Penguin Group (USA) Inc.

First Printing, May 2013
10 9 8 7 6 5 4 3 2 1

ISBN: 978-0-451-23975-4

Printed in the United States of America

PUBLISHER'S NOTE
This is a work of fiction. Names, characters, places, and incidents either are the
product of the author's imagination or are used fictitiously, and any resemblance
to actual persons, living or dead, business establishments, events, or locales is
entirely coincidental.
    The publisher does not have any control over and does not assume any respon-
sibility for author or third-party Web sites or their content.

If you purchased this book without a cover you should be aware that this book
is stolen property. It was reported as "unsold and destroyed" to the publisher and
neither the author nor the publisher has received any payment for this "stripped
book."

To those who are searching for their true mate:
Keep your eyes open, your heart ready,
and your blood warm.

ETERNAL
DEMON

Mark of the *Balas*

Erion landed on the familiar cobblestone street, not giving a shit who saw him flash, who saw him feral. The rage within him was raw, painfully uninhibited, and strangely uncontrollable. Only minutes had passed since Cruen had taken the *balas* from them—from *him*—and yet every breath he drew felt heavy and prolonged.

He moved down the street, letting his nose, not his memory, guide him. He needed information, and the male he sought had better be there to give it to him. Evening was dropping down in blankets of shade over the tops of the antiquated buildings and stores in the small French village, but Erion knew the *mutore* male stayed in his shop well past closing time. In fact, it was possible he lived in the rooms above.

Erion pursued the weak scent at a quicker, irrepressible pace, almost as if an invisible wire were pulling him. Every human he passed was an inconsequential blur. Every storefront the wrong one. The dire need to know if the boy his adopted father—the mad vampire Cruen—had stolen was breathing and well consumed his mind and his focus. It was insane to think that Ladd had been snatched right out from under him, the child's large, liquid eyes wide with fear as he was sucked back into Cruen's flash. Erion growled at the thought, at the vibrant memory. It was more than diabolical anger he felt. It was as though a limb had been ripped from his body. And gods help anyone who got in his way, he would not rest until it was returned.

He came to a halt outside the *mutore* shifter's shop, his keen sense of smell alerting him to what he had already suspected—to the male inside. Just as he'd hoped, Raine was still at work. He entered the dusty space in a rush of manic testosterone, his gaze taking in every inch. He'd been inside the antique-furnishings shop only once before with his twin, Nicholas. The Roman brother had purchased a home about thirty miles away. Not far from where they had been born—born and thrown away, in Erion's case. Nicholas had wanted to put down some roots. A concept Erion had never considered before, not until the boy he'd never known he had was introduced to him.

Ladd.

His guts ached like an infected fang. He had to find him, get him out of the clutches of that cruel vampire before any permanent damage was done. Dammit, he should've had an inside track, since Cruen had raised him, but that cagey bastard moved from one secret location to the next as often as a pair of rabbits fucked.

He shouldered his way through masses of antique furniture, rolled rugs, and ornately framed landscapes and up to the front of the shop. But before he reached the massive desk and the brass bell atop it, a humorless voice stopped him.

"That's far enough, Beast." In the far-right corner of the store, Raine appeared behind a thick wood table that lay on its side. The reptilian *mutore* skulked toward Erion, his brown eyes wary, his mouth a thin, grim line. "I hope you're here to purchase something."

"I am," Erion said. He was a good foot taller than the *mutore* shifter and had no problem using it to his advantage.

As he approached, Raine's gaze moved around the store nervously. "What is it you seek, then? Love seat? Chaise? Whatever it is, make it quick."

"The location of your uncle."

Raine froze halfway to his desk, his eyes blinking rapidly as he stared at Erion. "Get out," he uttered tersely.

Erion forced a cool smile. "Your customer service leaves much to be desired, *mutore*."

"You are no customer here," Raine said fiercely, "only a pest that wishes to infect and destroy." Eyes down, he made a beeline for his desk, but Erion shot past him and blocked his way.

"Why do you protect a monster?" Erion growled.

Raine's gaze lifted and his eyes narrowed. "I see only one monster, and he stands before me."

"Then you are a fool."

"Perhaps. But I remain alive, and that is all I can hope for now." He started forward again, and this time Erion allowed him to pass. "I'm surprised you came alone," Raine continued, rounding his desk. "Without the added muscle. Where is the other one? Like you, but Pureblood?"

The sting of the male's words found their mark. Erion was as pureblooded as his twin, but, unlike Nicholas, he had been born a *mutore*—a mutant vampire with strains of other creatures' DNA. Granted, the Romans and the *mutore* were all children of the Breeding Male, the genetically altered vampire monster, but mistakes like him weren't used, weren't even deemed worthy of breath. Erion and his beast brothers and sister—Phane, Lycos, Helo, and Dillon—had been luckier than most, though only if you call being rescued from the trash bin by a mad vampire and raised in a laboratory lucky. Erion wasn't sure what he called it. Or whether the life he'd led thus far had been worth saving.

Jury was still out, as Alexander said.

"My brother is searching for Cruen as well," Erion told the nervous-eyed male. In fact, now that the moon and stars provided the only light to brighten the sky, all the brothers, *mutore* and Roman, were spread out searching for the vampire and for Ladd.

Raine clucked his tongue. "A fool's errand. Whatever you want him for, you would be best to forget it. My uncle wouldn't hesitate to kill even the ones he calls family if they get in the way of what he wants."

"I will take that chance," Erion stated flatly.

From behind the counter, the *mutore* laughed softly. "How brave you are, *mutore*. I, however, have no interest in baiting a rabid shark with my blood. My death weighs heavily on my mind—and my family's—at all times." He flipped through a file of papers on the table. "Speaking of which, where is my elixir? The one you promised me.

The one you believe Cruen may have. The one that may prolong my life."

Erion grunted. "I must get to Cruen to find it."

"Then we are at an impasse," the male said sadly. "I don't know where he is. He has not contacted me in some time."

Erion's eyes narrowed. "You know something. I can feel it, smell it."

The male lifted his head, locked eyes with Erion. For one moment, he looked the true reptile his shifter genes carried. Scales appeared on his face and neck, and between his teeth a forked tongue darted out.

"Yes, you know something," Erion hissed.

The reptile retreated on a gasp, and left the shell of a bereft-looking male with deep fear in his eyes.

The demon inside Erion, the lionlike animal that clawed to get out, growled with possessive ire. "Cruen took something that belonged to me."

"What? Your dignity?" Raine sighed. "Welcome to my universe."

"A *balas*."

Raine stilled, his gaze holding Erion's tightly, curiously. "Why would he take a *balas*?"

"It belongs to me."

The words took a moment to sink in. "It?" Raine looked horrified.

"He," Erion said gruffly. "A boy. He belongs to me."

The words were strange on his tongue. It had been a mistake, the boy's conception. After learning of Nicholas's existence, Erion had been watching his twin for some time, was so curious about his brother's strange relations with women. Now Erion knew that Nicholas had only been carrying out a long stretch of torment from his past, a pattern of prostitution that his mother— their mother—had forced upon him as a young vampire. But Erion had seen only pleasure, connection, the bliss of being touched, in Nicholas and the females he mounted.

He'd wanted that too.

Fuck, he'd wanted that desperately.

He'd met with one of Nicholas's females, allowed a mating to take place between them. It had been a good union, comforting. He'd had no idea she'd bore a child from their coupling. Hadn't known until several months ago. He'd thought such a thing impossible, as Cruen had told him and all the *mutores* that they were unable to breed.

A growl escaped his throat, rumbled through the dusty air of the *mutore*'s shop. Another of Cruen's many lies. For too many years the bastard *paven* had pretended to care about them all, pretended to be a father, when in truth he'd used them. They were nothing but tools. Heavily muscled lab rats that Cruen had deemed unworthy to breed.

Erion's face and body language must've taken on a raw, hostile air, because Raine had inched back, shaking his head and looking fearful.

"I am sorry he has taken your *balas*," he said in a careful voice. "I wish I could help."

"You will help," Erion said, retreating from the blips of his past with barely suppressed rage. "I don't wish to harm you, but if you keep something from me—something that would help me find the *balas*—I won't hold back my beast from ripping you apart."

Abject fear glittered in Raine's eyes. "It is only rumors, rumblings."

"Whatever it is, I want it."

Behind the desk Raine crumpled into a chair. He looked utterly miserable. "It is nearly too fantastical to be believed. I don't want to send you on a wild, impossible ride."

Ah, the male did know something. He had been wise to press. "Nothing is impossible when Cruen is involved."

"This is true, but . . ." Raine's jaw tightened. "If I give you the information I have, you must promise me something. My daughter is in *swell*. I wish to live to see this child. If you find it, this elixir you believe Cruen possesses, will you bring it to me?"

Making promises, making deals; they suggested weakness. But Erion could relate to the need this male had to see his line continue. As it was, they were both concerned fathers. He nodded. "I give you my word."

Raine's eyes closed and he released a weighty breath. "Believe it or not, I have heard he is to be mated."

"What?" Erion roared.

The male flinched but managed to nod. "Cruen is taking a bride."

1

"**A** re you listening to me, Your Highness?" Hellen drew back her bow, aimed it at the streaking ball of pale yellow light ten feet in front of her, and let the arrow fly. She waited for impact, for the impish little rogue demon to drop, but it didn't. It ran away, cackling.

She turned and glared at Eberny. "You must cease talking while I hunt."

The ancient demon, a male/female hybrid, was undaunted. "You will be leaving us very soon, Your Highness. Your father has instructed me to make certain you understand your duties."

Under the haze of auburn daylight, Hellen grabbed another arrow from her quiver and said in a dangerous voice, "My duties."

"Indeed," said Eberny, following Hellen as the young female demon suddenly took off, jogging along the perimeter of the Rain Fields. "How you are to conduct yourself."

That little bastard, thought Hellen, her eyes searching for the lost rogue. *Ah! There.* It was ducking in and out of a cloud, grinning its toothless grin, toying with her.

With one easy movement, Hellen drew back her arrow and sent it straight for the cloud. It whizzed through the Rain Fields like a bolt of lightning.

Flash! A hit.

Hellen grinned as the rogue demon creature exploded.

"A worthy shot, Your Highness," said Eberny in a contained voice before picking up the topic of discussion from a moment ago. "It would be wise to recall the lessons learned in the Academy. The ones dealing with a female's obligations to her male counterpart."

Scanning the Rain Fields for more rogues, Hellen snorted. "Unfortunately, I do not recall it. A much-needed nap was taken during that bout of instruction, I believe."

"Your Highness, that is not at all amusing," stated Eberny, the hybrid's mud-brown eyes narrowing with disapproval.

Girlish laughter sounded behind them. Hellen looked up to see her two younger sisters skipping down the black-earthed hillock toward them, long, pale yellow hair at their backs and yards of fuchsia and gold skirt trailing behind. Levia and Polly looked like a painting, so demure, so female. Perfect demon royalty. While she—if not for her disagreeable red coils of hair—looked like their brother.

"Hellen, dear."

"Pray don't shoot at us. We come in peace."

Each female gave her a kiss on the cheek. They smelled

of fireflower, the only flower allowed to grow in the Underworld. It was rarest, picked and bottled the moment it flowered, then made into a perfume oil for the daughters of the Demon King.

Hellen preferred the scent of ashes, of the black soot beneath her feet—of the death of each rogue demon.

She was strange that way.

She had been told many times that she was named for her place of birth. But over the years she had come to wonder if her mother had known what grew inside her womb, what she would be unleashing into the Underworld. A true hellion. Had the female demon had a premonition about a fiery gust of flaming hair and a defiant disposition, then come to a quick decision about her name?

A sudden flash of light, bright blue and practically spitting off rogue energy, caught her peripheral vision, and she whirled around, grabbing for an arrow.

"Your Highness, please," Eberny implored. "Listen to me."

Hellen shifted the bow and arrow, following the muted blue light deep in the Rain Fields ahead. "My eyes may be on my target, Eberny, but my ears are open. What is it you think I need to know?"

"The male you are to be given to will expect certain behaviors."

"Indeed. I spread my legs when instructed, yes?"

Behind her, Levia and Polly gasped. Hellen drew back her bow and grinned. She could practically see the girls' wide blue eyes, their gloved hands covering their mouths. She would miss them terribly, miss their sweet ways and perpetually outraged reactions. But, then again, she was glad to be going. Her sacrifice would be their safeguard always.

Eberny's voice dropped to a whisper. "Sexual relations are only a small part of being a submissive partner, Your Highness."

Submissive.

Hellen's urge to kill amplified and she narrowed her eyes on the acres upon acres of Rain Fields where the rogue demons, the excess magical energy her father, Abbadon, released within the Underworld, loved to hide.

"Do not look him in the eyes when he speaks to you," Eberny continued.

"Where shall I look, then?" Hellen asked with an emotionless tone. "Between his legs?"

Again, her sisters gasped. "Oh, Hellen, you are wicked," said Levia, her voice muffled through her gloved hand.

Eberny turned to them and sniffed. "She enjoys giving me pains in my head."

Very true. Hellen chuckled and drew back an arrow, waited for the flash of blue, and sent it flying. It missed by a good ten feet. The little bastard's subsequent cackling killed her laughter.

"If you could just be more like your sisters," Eberny said on a sigh.

Hellen glanced back at the lovely specimens of female demon and shook her head, her gaze affectionate in the extreme. Yes, she would miss them terribly. "I know. It would be easier all round."

Levia and Polly laughed, rushed forward, and embraced her.

"You are perfect as you are, Hellen," Levia crooned.

"Yes, indeed," agreed Polly. "Except for the hunter attire ... Perhaps if we had something made in a soft shade of pink—"

The mute button was pressed on Polly's appraisal of her clothing as Hellen spotted the blue rogue staring at her through a thin layer of cloud. It grinned. Hellen's blood heated and she gripped her bow tightly. She had been hunting demon rogues ever since she could hold a bow, and they knew how to play with her. Pure, soulless energy, they weren't afraid to die or to be hunted. On the contrary. Abbadon's excess magic loved risk and chase and the possibility of being extinguished.

And so did Hellen.

Sir Ugly and Blue widened his yellow eyes and made a disgusting noise at the lot of them, then took off.

Hellen smirked. "I'll be back."

"No, Hellen. Wait," Levia called.

But Hellen refused to be deterred from the hunt. She raced into the Rain Fields. Drops of water as hot as ash fell from gray clouds only feet off the ground. She'd been inside the Fields hundreds of times, and knew how to maneuver through them without getting burned. Bow and arrow at the ready, she kept her quick pace, her eyes narrowing each time she lost sight of the blue flash of light.

It came as sudden as a breath; a rush of intensity, a familiar scent. Hatred and disappointment, sadness and intense power.

Hellen stopped short and dropped her weaponry. A forced and familiar action. As the bow and quiver sat in a small well of collected water, a tornado ripped through the Rain Fields and came straight for her, stopping just a foot away. The blood of excitement, of chase, that had been rushing through Hellen's veins a moment ago turned to black ice.

He was before her.

The Devil himself.

The Demon King, Abbadon.

Hellen looked up. "Hello, Father."

In his present state Abbadon looked the very essence of a demon. Ten feet tall, red skin pulled tight over heavy, impervious muscle, eyes the color of the clouds that only moments ago parted for him. As Hellen stared up at her sire, she saw nothing of herself in him and yet knew that she of all the sisters was the most like him.

"What are you doing?" he asked in a voice unworldly and growlingly low.

Unlike her sisters, Hellen felt no fear when standing in her father's presence. Only a desperation within her mind to be cautious and thoughtful with the words that came out of her mouth.

"Preparing myself for wedded bliss."

His scaly-skinned eyebrow lifted. "With a crossbow?"

"Perhaps this male you have sold me to will appreciate my hunting skills."

There was a flicker in his gaze, a momentary flash of fury, but he contained it. "I allow you to hunt the rogue demons for me because, frankly, you are a far superior shot to any of the male hunters I possess, but it stops the moment you leave my Underworld. Do you understand?"

Hellen nodded, but her fingers flexed, ached to hold her weapon.

"You will not shame me."

"I am rather good at it, though, Father."

Again the flash of fury clouded his already pale eyes. "Yes," he hissed. "But after today the consequences will be dire."

Hellen's muscles tensed. "Today?" She'd thought she had more time.

The Devil's grin made the black scorched earth below her feet tremble. "The time has come, daughter. You will leave us and take your place aboveground—"

"With the bloodsucker," Hellen finished for him, unable to restrain her acerbic tone.

Abbadon's nostrils flared and he coiled over her like a snake. The air went silent and the rain ceased to fall. It was his attempt at intimidation. There was nothing the Demon King appreciated more than fear in his offspring. Especially from the one before him.

But Hellen remained cool under his taut, red-faced glare. This was never the way to get her to cower, get her on her knees, eyes down and shoulders trembling. Unfortunately, over the past few years Abbadon had found the way in to her fear center.

He cocked his head to one side. "Is that your sisters' carefree laughter I hear?"

Hellen heard nothing but the deadly silence and the threat that hovered next on her father's thin, reptilian lips.

"I will do as I am instructed," she said in a quiet, noxious voice.

In a shock of movement and hot wind, Abbadon rushed toward her. Matching her height now, his face the color of rich, thick blood, he placed one long finger under her chin and lifted. "You had better."

Or the two lovely demon females waiting for you on the bank of the Rain Fields will feel my true wrath, he didn't say.

He didn't have to say it.

Hellen pulled her chin from his sickeningly warm touch and said in a firm voice, "I will be the perfect little demon."

Abbadon grinned and gave a wave of his hand to the fields around them. "You will be the perfect little female."

The clouds instantly released their torrent of hot rain, sound returned to the air, and out of the corner of her eye, Hellen saw a flash of blue light.

"Now," Abbadon said, his gaze sweeping over her. "Get back to the Dwelling. You leave within the hour, and you must be bathed, combed, dressed, and prepared."

Prepared.

Hellen clung to the word as the Devil turned and dissolved into the hot, misty air. She had sacrificed herself, would give herself to this bloodsucker her father had sold her to, but that's where it would end. And her most important bit of preparation would make it so.

The flash of demon blue hit her peripheral vision once more and she reached for her weapon. Without taking another breath, she stretched back the bow and released. The arrow hit the target, and Hellen reveled in her final kill as she walked out of the Rain Fields and toward her sisters for the last time.

Erion's lip curled as beneath his feet, the earth rumbled. It was a soft, uncomplicated movement, just a hint of warning to the animals thereabouts. *Flee, little ones. Get out of the way before you're run down by an ill-fated traveling party.*

And a *mutore paven* who would kill anything and anyone who got in his way.

As he stood there, the earth's easy tremble intensified. Granted, he was still able to hold his ground without issue, but the manic shudder made him not only cautious, but also suspicious. *Is this truly it?* he mused, his fangs descending, his muscles flexing, tensing. Had Raine been truthful with this location? With the arrival of the parcel Erion had come to steal?

The *bride* he'd come to steal.

Cruen's bride.

Erion's gaze narrowed on the length of dirt road ahead. For Raine's sake and the future the *mutore* wished to see, he hoped so.

Suddenly, the shudder escalated into a severe shake that reverberated up through Erion's feet and calves to his gut, into his chest, and all the way to his jaw, making his teeth rattle inside his mouth. Around him, the trees creaked as their weight was redistributed and the birds took to the air en masse.

Erion dropped into a fighting stance and unsheathed his blade.

This is no wedding party approaching, he thought blackly, slowly rotating so he could see in every direction. This wasn't Cruen's bride. Couldn't be. This was belowground, nature's doing, inconvenient though it was, a cry of—

The thought died inside his mind as a massive shudder nearly sent him to his knees. Before him the earth cracked, one long seam, splitting apart with a jarring lurch. *Christ!* Erion jumped back as the plaintive wail of breaking rock and shifting plates stole the forest's air. An earthquake—had to be. He was on California land, after all.

A few feet away, a mega blast of dirt shot into the air, raining down sharp, black pellets onto his face and body. He should flash. Get out of this particular line of fire. Return to France and demand a new location from Raine. Or maybe a strip of flesh from the male's lying hide.

He was on his way, his cells nearly transferred, when suddenly from inside the dust geyser came a wail, a shriek so intense Erion felt it deep within his bones. Like a wave crashing against the shore, he heard it again and again. The sound boomed through the forest, pinging against the battered trees, then slamming back into Erion's ears. He shook his head, attempting to clear the sound. As he did, his gaze caught on the crack in the earth. In the very center, where the sound seemed to emanate from. Though any sane *paven* would've gotten the hell out of there at that point, Erion drew closer. He couldn't help himself. He saw something.

But what? What the hell was it?

His blood pounded in his veins, every muscle inside him tense and ready.

Then he saw it fully, saw *them* fully: two horses, pale as paper, with see-through skin, emerging from the ground. They were snorting and sighing as they pulled something, their hooves scrabbling for purchase on the crumbling rock face.

Steeled and ready for a fight, Erion stared, unblinking at the scene before him, nearly thinking himself mad as a gleaming, bride-white, pumpkin-shaped carriage crawled out of the hole in the earth, legs moving like a gigantic white spider.

Erion's mind squeezed.

No.

Impossible. Perhaps even insane. This couldn't be Cruen's bride. Inside this Cinderella carriage from hell?

As the ghostly team cleared the split in the earth and found solid ground, the carriage came to a halt. One of the horses turned its head and eyed Erion. Its nostrils flared in warning as it pawed the ground.

Erion's hand tightened around his blade, and in that moment he remembered what he was doing there.

Whom he came to steal—and why.

As if they sensed it too, the transparent beasts shifted their gazes and took off, bolting into the now-still woods, dirt kicking up around them.

Erion exploded forward, his blood fueling his pace. This female, whatever she was, belonged to him. She was his bargaining chip—the ransom he would keep at his side until Ladd was returned. Returned to the ones who knew how to love.

He ran through the black, cool woods, keeping pace with the carriage until it burst forth into an open field. Moonlight poured down overhead, spread its ethereal shards out over the overgrown expanse.

No farther, my lady.

In a burst of speed, Erion shot forward, made a quick right, and stopped dead in front of the horses. The beasts screamed as they came to a halt, rearing up, nearly braining him with their massive hooves. The demon inside Erion pulsed to get out, tame what was snorting and hissing in front of him, muzzle what was letting loose a cacophony of terrified screams inside the bride-white carriage.

He smiled grimly. The terror was only beginning for his parcel.

He leaped onto the footrest near the carriage door and gripped the handle. A flexible wall of dark magic pushed at him, tried to buck him off, tried to convince his mind that he was seeing a mirage, but Erion mentally shoved back at the sensation and yanked at the door.

It wouldn't budge.

Not a problem. He enjoyed tearing the gift wrap off a parcel.

Reaching up, he grabbed the metal bar on the roof of the carriage, swung back, and crashed his feet into the door. It went down with a thud. Another feminine scream pierced the night air, and the horses panicked and took off again, barreling across the field. Erion's gaze was razor sharp now, but all he saw was a red blur with electric green eyes before he was hit in the chest and thrown backward.

He landed on the ground with a teeth-shattering slam, something fierce and flooded with layers of skirt on top of him. He heard the horses scream and snort, saw out of his peripheral vision the coach clattering past, abandoning the meadow for the dark woods beyond.

The Layers of Skirt spoke. "Before I kill you, I want to know just who the hell you are!"

Wet grass and cold earth at his back, Erion's brows descended over his narrowed gaze. The female sat astride him, had his arms pinned at his sides as though she were under the impression she had some kind of control in the situation. In truth, he could not only flick her off like a bothersome fly, but stretch her arms over her head and slit her throat with one fang, all in under a breath. But then he wouldn't be able to feel her weight atop him. So for a moment he let her remain where she was.

Miles and miles of shocking red hair, illuminated by the moon overhead, draped either side of his shoulders, and those inhuman eyes the color of emeralds in the brightest sunlight gazed down at him with equal parts scorn and I-want-to-rip-your-head-off.

This female, Erion mused, the organ between his legs pulsing with curiosity, *may be sixty-five inches of soft, round, sexual pleasure wrapped up in a hundred irritating layers of creamy white wedding costume, but she is clearly one fierce bitch.*

He had no doubt that she would kill him if he gave her the chance.

If he gave her even an inch.

With one smooth, swift roll, Erion reversed their positions. On her back, her arms pinned above her head by one of his hands, her hair splayed like a sunrise around her face, and her eyes flashing in the moon's light, she hissed at him, struggled against him like a caged animal.

"You have made a grave mistake, Male," she said, her voice as deadly as her gaze.

"We shall see," Erion answered, his tone smooth and resolute as he slipped the other hand around her waist.

She kicked at him, tried to get her knee up between his legs. "I am to be mated this night, you fool!"

Erion chuckled softly. "It may need to be postponed."

"My betrothed will not look kindly on having his bride accosted," she said through gritted teeth.

"I am counting on it," Erion said, releasing her pinned arms and yanking her closer to his body. His gaze traversed the moonlit landscape one last time. "Let us hope that Cruen cares enough to come after you. For if he does not . . . well, we are both doomed to a fate worse than death."

And from the cold, moonlit ground, Erion flashed away, his parcel still struggling like a feral cat at his side.

2

He moved through the city like the ghost he'd once been called—like the ghost he could've been if the ruddy gods had been merciful instead of perpetually cruel. The cover of night did little to shield him from the eyes of the millions who lived and worked in Manhattan, and so he took to the airways, flashing in and out of the crowds until he reached the quieter, less-populated parts of town.

SoHo, and particularly the street on which the Roman brothers lived, was devoid of pedestrian traffic, almost suburban in its cleanliness and drawn-curtained windows exposing the warm lamplight from inside. *The brothers have done brilliantly well in choosing this location for their compound,* he thought, abandoning all flash progression and heading toward his destination at an easy jog. Though the building they lived within wasn't difficult to find, if one was looking.

And he was definitely looking.

He rounded the corner of the warehouse, dropped to

the ground just before the fence line, and planted five of his strongest military-grade magic deflectors. Minutes ticked by as he let the deflectors do their job, pulling in and defusing the magic. Then he gingerly stepped across the line and leaped over the fence.

They didn't know he was coming. Well, he'd never given them a bloody save-the-date card, had he? But the Roman brothers had offered him their allegiance that night in Cruen's laboratory nearly seven months ago, when the world had gone to rubbish—when his first love had been murdered by Cruen. He'd gone there to find Cruen, but had found his love in a cage, nude, starving for sex. Believing her a Breeding Female, Cruen had abducted her, kept her until he could bring Lucian Roman, the Breeding Male to her. Cruen had wished to force them to breed.

The thought, the memory, of her in that cage, in sexual pain, made his blood churn and heat in his veins. He was ready to call in his marker. For months he'd been trying to find Cruen, take him down, but that ancient bastard had managed to block him at every turn, using deeply powerful magic that both repelled him and destroyed his mind and body.

He didn't like having to ask for help, but it was becoming dire. He needed backup before Cruen's repelling magic killed him.

He beat his fist hard upon the wood, and in moments, the door opened. Lucian Roman stood there, framed in the wide entryway. The tall, near-albino Pureblood gave him a curious, fascinated, and annoyingly familiar assholelike glare.

"Been a while, Brit Boy?" Lucian said. "You look like hell."

"'Course I do, Frosty. I've been living in it for the past seven months." Synjon Wise nodded at the white-haired *paven* who had mated his good friend, Bronwyn, and was his chuffed equal at imparting insulting pet names. "Seven months and I've yet to capture the devil." He moved past the Roman brother and stepped inside without being asked. "Don't like asking for help, but it seems I have no other choice."

Hellen landed with a jolt, her feet smacking against hard earth, her teeth knocking together, and her hand automatically reaching back for her bow. But it wasn't there.

'Course it wasn't there.

She wasn't home. She wasn't in the carriage. And she wasn't in the arms of the bloodsucker she was promised to.

Her heart pounded hard and fast in her chest, but she forced herself to calm. Think. Assess.

Her eyes took a moment to adjust to the darkness surrounding her. She was still outside, but the landscape had changed. Beneath the cool moon, she saw rolling hills dotted with trees, and beyond, miles and miles of what appeared to be brown, spindly vines. Where was she? Flowing up through her nostrils, the scent of earth was strange and lovely and begged her system to calm, but that wasn't about to happen. She'd been stolen, ripped away from her destiny. And the thing, the tank with arms, who had done it was holding her still.

In fact, one of those arms was clamped around her

middle, keeping her tight against the wall of muscle that was his chest.

Who is he? And how is he connected to Cruen? What did he want from the bloodsucker? And how far would he go to get it?

Every muscle inside her screamed to flex, to fight, but the shift of space and distance had slowed her reaction time. Her mind and body weren't as tightly fused as they normally were. It was only the years of disciplined battle in the Rain Fields that allowed her to push past these new and frustrating limits and begin the process of a competent struggle.

As the male moved forward, up the steep incline of a gray-green hillock, Hellen kicked and wriggled to get free. As she did, her body slowly realigned. Moans, grunts of pressure escaped her throat, and she slammed the back of her head into whatever she could make contact with. But instead of releasing her, the male cursed, then yanked her even tighter against him.

Panic threatened to waste her energy, make her muscles tired and useless, but she ignored their need, their protest. She hadn't given up everything: her life, her freedom, her future—shit, *everything*—for some asshole with a grudge to come in and take it away.

Gathering all the rage and heat and determination she had in her guts, she cried out in battle, arched her back, and slammed her elbow into the male's belly.

The pain came quick. But it wasn't his pain. "Shit!" she hissed as her bone met the granite wall of his abdominals.

"Cease fighting, woman," he growled, completely unfazed by her assault. "You will injure yourself."

His voice, a rough timbre of equal parts death and intrigue, echoed in the cold air he dragged her through. But she refused to heed his warning. Again, she screamed out her battle cry, again she thrust her elbow back, then twisted and snarled and fought like the demon she was to get free.

"Your struggle is useless," he said, his breathing unfettered, as though he carried an irritated child, not a fully grown, feral demon female.

"It will be of great use," she sputtered, refusing to stop fighting, "if I can get one good shot to your crotch."

He grunted as he moved swiftly down the steep slope of the hill. "Tell me where your betrothed is and perhaps I will release you."

She would sooner believe a rogue demon. "Bullshit." She swallowed the urge to ask him why he wanted Cruen. Had the bloodsucker she was to mate done something heinous to this male or his family? And did she care? "You're not about to let me go. You've risked too much in stealing me."

She could practically feel his satisfied grin. "True. But I could ease my hold on you."

"Oh, what a wondrous bargain," she spat out caustically. "And one I would certainly make, for your stench is most foul. But alas and once again, I do not know where my fiancé resides."

"Perhaps a few days as my houseguest will cause that information to surface."

"Not a chance," she returned, then whipped her head to the side and hit his cheek with a resounding smack. It hurt like hell, but she didn't care. She reveled in his quick and pissed-off curses. She had to get away from him, get to Cruen, or get home. "I demand you return me to the forest! To my coach!"

A growl vibrated against her neck and the male came to a fierce halt at the bottom of the verdant valley. He released his hold on her waist, only to grab her shoulders and whirl her to face him. Her breath caught in her lungs as she hung there, a good foot off the ground.

"Demand?" he repeated caustically. "You *demand* from me?" His voice dropped to a deadly whisper. "Let's get one thing very clear, woman. There will be no demands and very few opportunities to bargain. From now until I decide otherwise, you belong to me. You are my prisoner and my bait. Only when I have back what was stolen from me will I even think about releasing you."

She stared at him, forced herself to hold his gaze. It was all she could do, as her throat and tongue refused to work. Gods, she was pathetic. She hung there, immobile and stunningly fearful. She had been raised by the most hideous of beasts—the king of all beasts, in fact. Abbadon was the Devil himself, massive, ugly, feral, and he loved to strike fear in every cell of everyone he encountered. But this male . . . this male was somehow worse. This fearsome creature with long black hair, severe catlike features, and silver eyes that smoldered with determined passion wasn't interested in intimidation or arrogant threats. No, this male's motivation for abducting her and holding her hostage was fueled by something far more dangerous. Deep emotional stakes. Cruen had taken something the fearsome creature desperately wanted, and Hellen knew down to her very core that he would stop at nothing, not even the promise of his own death, to get it back.

The male watched her, knew her mind raced with assessments and questions and perhaps even unhatched plots. His fingers dug into her skin as he stared at her. His lip curled and the muscles in his neck bulged.

"Shall we end this, woman?" he growled. "This dangerous game you're playing?"

Letting him know how fearful she was would be foolish at best. Forcing an attitude of confidence had always served her well in the past.

"I play at nothing," she said through gritted teeth.

He glared at her as if she were something to consume. "I will give you one chance. Tell me where your beloved is, where the location of your soon-to-be mating bed resides, and I will return you."

She shook her head, nostrils flaring. "I can't help you."

Fury glittered in his diamond eyes. "A liar and a hellion."

She didn't deny the latter, but he was kidding himself if he thought she was lying to him. "Do you really think I want to remain here, captive and treated like a rag doll? I have nothing to gain in that."

He sniffed arrogantly, as though the answer was as obvious as the sneer on his face. "If you would mate with Cruen, you would also protect him."

"You think Cruen needs protection?" she said with a trace of black humor. "Clearly you don't know him intimately. He is far more powerful than you can even imagine."

The corners of the male's full lips curled up into a demonic smile. He pulled her closer. The scent of him entered her nostrils, made the skin on her arms tingle, and perhaps something in her belly as well.

"You have seen this power up close, have you?" he asked, his face a mere half arrow's length from her own.

"Of course," she lied. She had no intention of letting him know she'd never met her fiancé — that, in fact, she'd basically been sold to the bloodsucker. "And if you don't return me this very instant, that power shall be released on you. Are you and those you love prepared to die for this cause?"

His face turned to stone in an instant. His nostrils flared as he pinned her with a look so still, so cold, she thought her breath would be visible when she exhaled.

"Yes, woman," he said. "I am prepared to die."

Hellen didn't say another word. She never had the chance. Without warning, the male tossed her over one shoulder and started up the rise. Panic shot through her and she continued to fight, using every part of her body that wasn't contained. But even as she fought, she knew it was no use. He was impossibly strong and determined to have his way. Her chest grew tight, the air fighting to get in and out. If she didn't find her way to Cruen, mate with him, her father would punish her sisters, perhaps even force one of them to wed the bloodsucker in her stead. She'd sworn to their mother before the female died that she would care for her sisters, protect them from Abbadon, the male her own mother had been forced to wed. And Hellen had—she'd done everything she could to keep that promise. She had become the sacrifice. And now this bastard was getting in her way.

Facing backward, nearly immobile within his grasp, Hellen craned her neck, attempting to glance over her shoulder. She wanted to see where he was taking her. Under the bleak light of the mist-coated moon, a gray stone castle spread out across the land, its four turrets rising up to the clouds. With its slit windows and acres of grapevines in ruler-straight rows, it was impressive and oddly welcoming. Not at all what she thought her prison would look like.

An iron gate surrounded the property, and a pair of massive wooden double doors announced the entrance. When the male stopped before them, Hellen wondered if this was her chance to escape. Though her field of vision hadn't been optimal, during the quick surveillance over her shoulder, she'd seen no guards. The male would have to release her to open the gate, wouldn't he? She waited, slowed her breathing, and combed the landscape behind them for the best route once she broke from him—the thickest stand of trees, the darkest spots within the small forest.

It was in that moment, the moment she spied a heavy growth of trees in the distance, that her ears caught the sound of quick pain, and her nostrils the scent of blood.

She gasped, flinched, thinking that it was her own blood she scented. He had cut her. How had she missed it? How had she not felt it? She craned her neck again as her mind searched for the point of pain on her skin. But this time, what she saw over her shoulder killed the cool, thought-based awareness she was striving for and sent flares of sick panic coursing through her.

The male had bit into his wrist. He was lifting the wound toward the gate, blood dripping from the twin fang pricks onto the ground.

"You're a bloodsucker!" she cried, as he pressed the wound against the lock.

He hissed, perhaps at the pain of it or the coolness of the metal. Perhaps at her.

"You're a vampire," she continued, true fear within her now. How hadn't she guessed this? He wanted Cruen. It stood to reason whatever issue they had would stem from the fanged world.

"You sound horrified," he said with mild amusement.

There was a sharp click, and the double doors drew back at a slow, even pace.

"I am!" she said, feeling suddenly queasy. "Your fangs. The blood. You bit into your own flesh."

"Get used to it," he said, carrying her toward the front door of the castle. "The *paven* you are to wed will be biting into far more than his own wrist. If you get my meaning."

She didn't want to get his meaning, even though she saw it clearly in her mind. It was the one thing she feared about her mating. Not the sex; she could blank out and open her legs easily enough. But the bite of a vampire. The fangs breaking her skin, blood being sucked out of her. It sickened her. She began to struggle once again as he moved up the stone steps and entered the castle.

The space was solemn and, unlike the exterior, aesthetically unwelcoming. Barren of all furnishings, the foyer had only sparse light provided by a few candles. This was far more like the prison of her imaginings.

True panic gripped her, and the male must have felt it, for he tightened his hold on her as he left the foyer and headed down a long hallway. A few servants appeared out of nowhere and rushed toward them, but the male grunted something at them and they fell back immediately. Hellen assumed they were servants, but who knew? Whatever they were, they kept their eyes down and off of her—afraid to look, or maybe they'd seen such barbaric behavior before and had been warned against interfering.

Bloodsucking bastard.

How many times had he taken a female here?

How many times had that female been released?

Her lip curled. When she got free, he would die for this.

They traveled for many minutes deep inside the castle, through doorways and down one lonely corridor after the next. Hellen had ceased her struggle and curbed her panic after leaving the foyer, and instead was using her energy and keen awareness to keep close watch on which way they turned, which hallways they went down, and which doors they entered so she could find her way out again.

It seemed like forever before they finally stopped. As painful as it was in the hold he had her in, she craned her neck to see what was going on. The door they stood before was black wood with what appeared to be two streaks of blood crisscrossing in the center. Hellen's belly clenched with nerves and with the feeling one gets when one's soul-lifting plans for escape are suddenly drowned by a few head dunks into an icy bath of reality. This was bad. She wasn't sure what awaited her behind this door, but she was willing to guess it involved torture of the most gruesome kind.

Her skin tightened around her muscles, and she forced her mind to think beyond the immediate. Panic was out of the question; fight too, for she had no weapon that could match his brawn. What she did have were brains and—

The male yanked open the door and headed down a set of stairs. With each step, cold infused Hellen's skin, a dark, mean cold that threatened those brains she had been relying on a second ago. But she pressed against it. Again she craned her neck to see where they were going. It was brighter than it had been in the foyer, and when the male hit the last step, she could see the room that met them far too well. It was circular and damp, with stone walls that looked anything but clean. Her heart pounding against her ribs, she noticed that there were three doors cut into the rock, thick torches in ancient holders bracketing each. *What the hell is behind those?* she wondered. But the question floated away, became absolutely insignificant, when she saw what was bolted into the remaining wall.

A rusty set of shackles.

For both hands and feet.

Terror like she'd never known surged through her. But she forced it back. Fear would serve no purpose except to aid him. She had to remain calm and plot, plan.

"You think that's where you're going to put me, ass-hole?" she said, purposefully adding a hint of confident humor she didn't feel into her tone. He would not know how her belly clenched and her heart raced.

"If you don't play nice." The bloodsucker grabbed her shoulders and whirled her around, then set her on her feet. He called to someone to her left, "Take her—hold her, Cayman."

A large, pale-skinned, thin-lipped male crept out from the shadows near the base of the stairs and moved toward her. *Shit.* She tensed. What the hell was this? Were there more? More hiding in the shadows? Hellen hissed at him, flashed her demon eyes. Immediately, he slowed his pace, looking wary.

Wise male.

And if she was willing to venture a guess, not nearly as powerful as his master.

Hope snaked through her blood. Perhaps they were all this meek; perhaps she could manage an escape after all.

The bloodsucker whose chest brushed against her back growled at the male servant. "You hesitate over this insignificant female?"

Yes, she mused, staring at the guard, giving him her ugliest glare, her most fearsome expression. *Come here and I'll show you insignificant.*

The male backed up a foot.

"You embarrass yourself, Cayman, and me," the blood-sucker said tightly. "She is only a female. Do you wish the rest of the guards to know your shame?"

His words hit their mark with perfect accuracy. The guard's pale skin flushed with heat, and though he kept his eyes below her chin, he strode forward and took her by the shoulders. He yanked her against him in a display of masculine assholery, holding her far tighter than the brute male had. So tight, in fact, that she could feel his private parts against her belly. She glared at him, growled low in her throat, hoping he would take the hint and loosen his hold, but he didn't.

Satisfied that his servant had control, the bloodsucker walked away from them. He opened the door to one of the rooms cut into the stone wall and entered.

Now. Do it now.

Shit. Do something or you're done for. Make a move or you're not your father's daughter.

Hellen scoured every inch of the dungeon with her gaze. As she'd thought, this male, though he held her tightly, didn't have near the strength of the bloodsucker. She could sense it. But she would let him think he did. She would press against his inferior hold, make it seem as though she were attempting to fight, then sigh with frustration at being caught.

She studied each door, the stairs. She'd have to be quick. Who knew when the bloodsucker would be back? Her gaze caught a patch of pale light behind the stairs, and her heart pumped furiously. The light, it moved, changed. She started to struggle, inching them toward the light so she could get a better look.

The male gripped her arms shockingly tight.

"Move again, and I'll knock you out," he warned, though beneath his threat lay a tremble of insecurity.

The pain was nothing. She saw it fully now. A small

window and the strange, erratic light. It was rain. Hope flared. Rain would make it harder for him to track her.

It's now or never.

Whimpering as if she was in pain, she sagged against the guard. When he loosened his hold to get a better one, she grabbed his arms and pushed herself back. Silent and fierce, she struck. Three solid moves: head butt, elbow to the neck, then her knee slamming up directly into those less-than formidable male parts she'd felt earlier.

The male was stunned, his face a drastic shock of pain, before he dropped to one knee on the stone.

Hellen didn't wait to see anything more. She bolted past him, sprinted across the floor, and leaped at the window, shoulder first.

The bargain had been struck centuries ago. Magic, powerful blood for a promise. Unsatisfied by the meager power of his race, Cruen had wanted to create the ultimate vampire. Something he could use and control. But his attempts to blend DNA within the vampire community had failed. He'd needed something more, someone who had what he lacked.

He'd found the Devil, Abbadon.

The trip into the Underworld so long ago had nearly cost him his life, but it had been worth it. The blood Cruen had consumed from Abbadon's veins had made him unstoppable, and the blood he'd extracted from himself, then mixed with shifter DNA, had made the Breeding Male. For decades it had been a happy bargain.

Until he'd accidentally infected himself and become *mutore*.

And until the Devil had called in his marker.

Inside his chamber, Cruen's nostrils flared with disgust. She was here. Abbadon's firstborn. The thing he had promised to mate. The creature he would take to his bed until the first child of both hell and earth was born.

The child Abbadon had never been able to create himself — the child he believed would have just the right magical balance in its DNA to be able to remain on either plane. A gene the Devil would extract and use to finally be able to remain on Earth.

Cruen gazed up at the portrait in his bedchamber, at the female he would kill to have in his bed. Yes, the *veana* who gazed down at him, Pureblood, pure vampire, ripe and beautiful, intelligent and wicked. He would do anything to possess her again. And, in fact, he was.

Mating with the demon female Hellen would grant him all the power of the Underworld, and once she bore the heir her father so desperately wanted, Cruen would finally be free to seek out the *veana* he'd always wanted.

Celestine.

They would live together, love as he'd always known they were meant to. As he continued his work with the Breeding Male and Female, she would be at his side. She would encourage him, support him, love him. And in return he would tell her of the daughter they'd made together — the daughter Celestine had always thought had died at birth.

Movement at the door drew Cruen's attention away from the portrait. "What is it, Gale?"

His servant hovered, his eyes not meeting his master's. "She has arrived, my lord."

"Very good. Bring her to my antechamber."

Cruen forced good humor as he left his private room and went next door to his offices. He would steel himself for what would come, both female and the power her presence brought forth. For if he failed to mate with her, Abbadon would cut him off completely. As it was, the demon king was granting him blood only sparingly until the match was made.

Cruen scented the demon female as she approached his office, scented her blood—after all, her father's blood was within him too.

A hooded figure appeared in his doorway.

"Come," Cruen said, keeping his tone amenable.

The figure did as she was instructed, stepping into the room. But once inside, she removed her hood and stood before him with a worried frown.

Cruen sneered. "You are not she," he uttered, his gaze running the length of her. This demon female was beautiful, demure, and nervous. He knew what awaited him, and this was not it.

The female paled. "No."

"What is this?" He stood, glanced behind her to his guard. "Where is the one I'm to mate?"

He could not risk Abbadon's wrath or his refusal to give his blood.

The guard stepped forward, but it was the female who spoke. "The coach brought us here, but without Hellen." She bit her lip. "My sister was taken, my lord. As we traveled. The coach was waylaid, and she was taken by . . . by—"

"By what?" Cruen said venomously, moving toward her.

Someone was about to die for interfering with this grand bargain.

"I'm not sure," she continued. "It was a male. Dark, powerful—something akin to the ones in the Underworld." She looked pained. "That cannot be possible, I know."

The room began to vibrate, and Cruen felt his blood, Abbadon's blood, heat in his veins. No. This could not be, and yet . . . How would the *paven* know about his demon female?

His gaze narrowed on the female. "Was this male dark-haired, with eyes like stars?"

"Yes! You know him, then." She seemed relieved.

Cruen's jaw tightened, and he said through gritted teeth, "I know him."

He is my son.

"Then he will bring her to you."

Yes. He will bring her. "For a price." Cruen cursed his foolish and impetuous decision. Taking Ladd from Erion had been meant only as a way to bring the eldest *paven* home to him, where he belonged. He could never have imagined the male getting his claws on Cruen's power source.

"I do not understand," the female before him said, her brows drawn together, her claim on relief gone.

Cruen gestured to the guard. "Take her away."

"No! Please. My sister."

Time was precious, and Hellen's sister was not. He owed her nothing. As the guard removed her, Cruen shut the door on her anxious pleas. *Erion.* How had the *paven* known about his impending nuptials? It was impossible. And now he had taken the demon female and was holding her ransom for the *balas.*

Cruen cursed and paced the room. He wanted his *mutore* children back home, but keeping his fangs inside the vein of the demon king would always come first. If he wished to regain his power, and the love of the *veana* he desired most, it must.

3

The epic sound of glass shattering and hitting stone brought Erion bolting from the room that was to be the female's cell while she remained with him. His gaze went first to the guard who was staggering to his feet, cupping his balls, then to the window. That small, inconsequential window that had just allowed his prisoner to escape.

"Shit!"

No female, no *balas*.

Erion ignored the guard. Every predatory instinct inside him had ratcheted up to high. There was no way he could make it through the tiny crawl space; he was going to have to get outside the old-fashioned way. He tore up the stairs and down hall after hall until he reached the entryway. The light was dim, the candles nearly burned down, but he could see everything. His diamond eyes were useful in the dark. They would help him find her. They must. There was no way he was allowing his bargaining chip to escape. Panic flared inside him as he burst out the front door into the gentle rain. The boy needed him.

He sniffed the air. It wasn't easy to locate her direction in the mist. His nose was good, but it did not have the strength of Lycos's. That wolf *mutore* could scent a rabbit at a thousand feet in a tornado.

Scent pushed into Erion's eager nostrils and his body tensed. *Ahhhh* ... There she was. His prisoner. He growled into the night and took off into the rows of sleeping grapevines. He wasn't sure what the female was—human or otherwise—but she couldn't flash; he knew that. And she had no vampire blood in her. Not yet anyway—not until she was reunited with her beloved.

He flash-ran, one stop to the next, row after row of vines, and toward the hillside, following her scent. The woman was running to Cruen for protection and mating. Cruen! Making Erion seem like the evil one. What a sick joke. In the valley between the hillocks, he stopped at a tree and ran his nose down the bark-covered trunk. What female in her right mind would agree to wed that bastard? Granted, she was a vile-tempered creature, but she was truly the most beautiful female he'd ever seen in his life. A face to die for, and a body to live for. She could stake claim to any male of her choosing, surely. Why that *paven*? A male so incapable of love?

Catching her scent again, he flashed over the hill, then to the outskirts of town. He stood atop the rise, his gaze panning the landscape, buildings, homes, and churches. This was human territory, and he needed to be cautious. The rain fell harder now, soaking through his clothes, causing his hair to lengthen and grow heavy, but it didn't mask the intense scent that shot up his nostrils.

It wasn't the woman, and it reminded him of Lycos.

Canine. Dammit! He whirled around, flashed into the woods on the far side of the village. Where the hell had she gone? She couldn't have gotten far. He flashed again. Then again. He was dripping wet and spitting ire when he dropped down in a dark alleyway behind a pub in the village. He leaned back against the stone, cursing himself, cursing Cruen, when suddenly he caught her scent. It was mixed up in the scents of other animals, but he instantly took off toward it.

The village was quiet and dark, everyone tucked away, escaping the rain. Erion's insides shook as the woman's scent grew thicker, sweeter, inside his nostrils. He came to the edge of the church grounds and slowed. This is where she hid. He moved out of sight quickly, down the alley behind the church. He would have to come upon her without detection and attack without pity. He couldn't have her running away again.

Her scent continued to thicken with every step. It was a heady, delectable aroma that made his lower half stir, but he forced that disturbing realization away. She was bait, his bargaining chip to have Ladd back where he belonged, and he was nearly upon her. He rounded the corner, flashed ten feet ahead to the steps of the church, where he believed she took cover. But no woman stood before him, no female scream met his ears. There was only the yip of a canine whose tail was now lodged under Erion's boot.

"Damn it!" Erion stepped back and waved away the little brown-and-white beast who'd no doubt escaped his home in the village. "Get."

But the dog didn't run. He crouched down and growled.

Erion's gaze shifted to take in the churchyard beyond, then returned to the canine. "I have nothing for you, mongrel. Move on. Go back to the humans you belong to."

The dog growled again, then barked—three times in succession.

Something fell from its mouth. It was white against the black pavement. The rain quickly soaked it through, but Erion could tell it was a strip of fabric. He bent down, reached for it, but the dog snatched it back up and stood a foot away, his eyes wary.

Erion glared at the mongrel. "Come."

The animal growled again, then started to back away.

"Now, Beast," he ordered in his darkest, deepest voice. "Come to me."

The canine's eyes flashed before he bent his head and dropped the fabric into a growing puddle.

Erion watched the white strip disappear into the murky depths. *Impossible,* he mused. And yet . . . He glanced up, locked eyes with the dog. "You know where she is?"

The dog cocked his head to one side and yipped, then turned around and ran.

"It's like a bloody church service in here," Synjon said as he followed Lucian through the quiet, dimly lit house. "Where is everyone?"

"We've had a bit of bad luck recently."

Synjon grunted. "Welcome to the club."

"Where have you really been, Brit Boy?"

"Trying to off myself."

Lucian glanced over his shoulder, one pale eyebrow lifted sardonically. "Didn't take?"

"Sure it did. I'm a hologram."

Lucian chuckled and led Synjon into the library. "Well, you still have some fight left in you. That's good."

"Just enough for one kill." *If I can just get to him.*

Lucian dropped into a leather armchair and gestured for Syn to take the one opposite. But he didn't want to sit, couldn't sit. He had too much pent-up energy inside him. His hands clenched and unclenched, hungry for a weapon, and his mind urged him to plan, plot . . .

"I think I know the target," Lucian said with a grunt of satisfaction. "Mastermind, master manipulator, master fucking murderer. Cruen?"

Just the ruddy bastard's name set Syn's fangs on edge. "An easy guess, mate."

He paced back and forth in front of Lucian, his adrenaline at a fever pitch. Just like it had been for the past seven months. Ever since he'd left the South American rain forest, given Juliet's body over to the sun, then allowed himself to grieve in the arms of the *veana* who had saved his life when he'd wanted to end it and follow Juliet.

The *veana* who had left him while he slept.

Petra.

Crickey, just bringing her name to the surface of his mind made the guilt pulse inside him. Juliet's murderer was still out there, breathing . . . his only thought should be on how best to take that breath away.

"I've been in South America," Syn offered as he

moved from one side of the room to the other. "I buried the one he killed."

"Juliet," Lucian said softly.

Pausing for a moment near the armchair, Synjon nodded. "Now it's Cruen's turn to be laid out in the sun. But I'm having a hard time getting to him."

Lucian nodded. "As are we."

"Is it revenge you seek for your imprisonment? Your Breeding Male status?"

"It is for the abduction of Ladd, the young *balas*."

Syn stopped pacing, his brows knit together in a frown. "He took a *balas*?"

"He would take, torture, or kill anything to further his cause," Lucian said, menace flashing in his almond gaze.

Cruen was truly a bug that needed to be crushed. "We will find him, Frosty. If we work together."

Lucian's mouth spread in a wicked grin. "I like when we're on the same side."

"Enjoy it. Who knows how long it's going to last?"

"You going to crash here? You're welcome."

Syn grunted, moved away from the Roman brother and toward the picture window. "I won't be sleeping, but yeah, I'll be here for a while. Until the deed is done and the blood is spilled."

"You going to be all right around my *veana*?"

Synjon turned to look at the *paven*, his head cocked to one side. "Maybe the question should be, Are *you* going to be all right with me around your *veana*?"

"I'm no charitable bastard, London, but you look like you could use all the friends you can get."

"I don't need friends," Synjon said, returning to the picture window and the view of a pair of late-night lovers sucking face across the street. "I need warriors."

Hellen's lungs expanded as she moved quickly through the dark village, the pain and pressure begging her to slow, but she ignored it. By this time, her sisters had to have arrived at Cruen's compound. The enchanted coach would've seen to it, made sure they reached their destination. Her fiancé had to be pissed, and Hellen prayed the male wouldn't take it out on Levia and Polly. She had to get there, and her only chance now was returning to Hell and to her father.

She hadn't made the mistake of thinking the vampire wouldn't come after her. She knew he would. That male was determined to have her, determined to use her to get something back from Cruen. Or maybe it was just to punish him—the black-haired, crystal-eyed bloodsucker seemed to hate her betrothed.

Whatever the reason for his thievery, Hellen hadn't been about to wait around and see if he and her new mate could work things out. With a knee to the balls, she'd gotten her chance, and ran away from the castle as fast as she could manage. Rain soaked, she'd slipped through a cracked section of the gate, ripping her dress before heading for the hill and into the woods.

It had been a moderately rugged terrain and the rain and lack of light were no help, but she'd managed. Her only regret was that she didn't have her longbow. If the bloodsucker did manage to find her, it would come in handy. She'd make sure she got off a perfect shot.

Between the eyes.

No. Through the heart.

Did bloodsuckers have hearts?

Avoiding homes with lights blazing and heading back into the shadows, Hellen kept her body on high alert, her eyes, though relentlessly coated with rainwater, searching for the way back, the way home. Finding her way back to the Underworld and standing before Abbadon wouldn't be met well, but the Devil would be hard-pressed to blame her for the abduction—and if she was very lucky, maybe even praise her for escaping and returning home.

She hated the feeling that bloomed inside her when she thought of her father. He was the Demon King, vile and hated and cruel and without compassion—had sold his child to the highest bidder—and yet the need to feel his pride, even his love, had always been strong within her.

All of it was moot, though. She wasn't going anywhere if she couldn't find a portal, and she'd been searching for quite a while. The portals into the Underworld had been created by Abbadon in case one of his citizens found themselves aboveground. No one knew exactly where they were. There were many, and they were undetectable by humans—by anyone other than a demon. They released heat, attracted a demon's DNA, but so far Hellen had felt only the cold night and rain.

She wondered where the dark-haired bloodsucker was, how close he was, and if he would punish her greatly if he got his hands on her again.

A pinprick of lust shot through her.

Idiot, she thought, pushing on. Attracted to anger and power and unpredictability. Her father had raised her to respond to such prized qualities.

The small village was dark and quiet, except for the constant patter of the rain. She kept moving, down the streets, keeping to the shadows, desperate to feel the heat of home. After rounding the square for the third time, she started to think about the impending daylight. Perhaps she should go now, before dawn, abandon this village for the next.

But her thought, her burgeoning plan, dissolved in the sudden onslaught of warmth at her back. She whirled in its direction, sighed at its safe, familiar feeling. Rain continued to pelt her head, keep her clothes stuck to her skin, but she ran toward it, toward the small church and its graveyard beyond.

The closer she drew, the hotter the air and the rainwater became. *It will be good to be home,* she thought, entering the graveyard, *even for a short time.* No matter how horrible the place where you grew up, it still bore a strange comfort. She'd start afresh, acquire new vials of the draught that kept her sexual desire frozen, and have her father deliver her to Cruen in person.

Yes. It would all work out.

She would be what she was meant to be.

The willing sacrifice.

She wove in and out of the headstones, following the heat like a beacon. Her sisters would be safe and happy. Poor Polly and Levia. They had to be so frightened.

Sudden and nearly painful heat shocked her, and she came to a halt before a massive blue glow. Hellfire. It erupted from the grave of one Pierre Contrale. Relief moved through her and she rushed to the grave and nearly leaped inside the blue fire when a gritty, feral voice halted her.

The bloodsucker's mouth hovered close to her ear as the jagged tip of a knife met the small of her back.

"Take a step inside that flame, bitch, and you will know a slow and pain-filled death."

4

"Just so we're clear," she spit out, as Erion strapped her to the dungeon wall, snapping the ancient cuffs on her wrists one at a time. "My name is Hellen. Not 'bitch,' not 'woman,' not 'female,' 'ransom,' or 'prize.'"

"I'll try to remember that," Erion said, dropping down on his haunches and fastening the ankle shackles that would keep her from running away again.

"No, you won't," she said, her tone as coolly pissed as when he'd found her and stolen her back. "You have no feeling, no care for a poor, innocent female."

He grunted. "Perhaps I would if I saw a poor, innocent female."

Her lip curled. "You're a monster."

"Indeed."

Erion inspected his work. The ancient cuffs had come with the house. They were solid and would hold her well without being too irritating on her wrists. The chains at her feet, however, were new. They weren't attached to the wall, so they would grant her some movement, just not enough to get her anywhere near the window or staircase. Escape was futile. He would not allow it again. Right now, he could walk away and wait for Cruen to contact him without worry. The problem was, he didn't want to walk away. Her scent bothered him. Made him snarl, made him hungry—made him more aggressive than normal. It was a good thing her attitude, personality, and verbal ways were so irritating, or he might be tempted to taste her.

"Why is that beast still here?" she said.

For a moment, Erion thought she meant him. But she spoke of the brown-and-white dog who lay on the floor behind him, the dog that had followed them into the woods, the mutt who had shown up at the castle gates twenty minutes after they'd flashed home. Erion wasn't sure what the canine wanted with him or with his prisoner, but at the very least he owed the mongrel a good meal for assisting him in her capture.

"I have a kindred spirit in that canine, I believe," he said, stepping back to admire his work.

She sniffed her irritation. "Fangs, fur, and a penchant for licking your own balls?"

His gaze roamed over her, the captive bride. "You have quite a mouth on you."

"So I've been told."

"By whom? Cruen?" He chuckled disdainfully. "Has he sampled your mouth already? Isn't that against the rules of engagement?"

"There are no rules in this engagement."

Erion's eyes met hers and he frowned. What did her words mean? And why did her voice grow quiet, morbid even, as she spoke them?

He moved closer, his nostrils flaring as her scent begged entrance. It was a diabolically wondrous scent, but it gave no clue as to her species.

"What are you?" he asked.

She smiled. "Cruen's woman."

"No. That is an unfortunate state of being, not an origin of blood."

"Whatever it is, it's all I'm giving you," she said, cocking her head to the side, exposing a long, pale column of neck. "Unless you choose to disclose your true species."

He shrugged gently. "I already have. The bloodsucker, remember?"

She shook her head. "No, you're more than that." Erion had no idea what she was talking about or what game she was playing, but he could continue to watch her mouth move for hours. In fact, if he leaned in one more inch, perhaps two, he could take it, taste it. That full, pink bottom lip between his teeth.

"Maybe I should guess," she continued, interrupting his thoughts. "You are part bloodsucker and part . . . hmmm, let's see . . . A very foolish little prick who has no idea what he's stolen."

Erion returned to reality with a jolt. "Little prick?" He burst out laughing. "That's amusing."

"Oh, of course," she said with obvious disdain. "I'm sorry. You are a big dick whose tiny brain resides in his ass. How's that? More accurate?"

Moving in, Erion reached for both her hands, pressed

them flat against the dungeon wall with his weight. "The proof is in the pinning, female."

He heard her breath catch, felt the pulse at the base of her neck quicken. His hunger flared.

"The warden likes it rough," she uttered blackly.

"Yes, he does." He faced her, his eyes locking on to her emerald green fire. He would teach her not to goad him.

"Do you think Cruen likes it rough as well?" she asked.

"Probably. Most assholes do."

"Good to know." One pale auburn eyebrow lifted pointedly. "Asshole."

His eyes narrowed and he shook his head. "Such disrespect."

"Always."

"I will gag you, if I must."

"Try it," she said dangerously, leaning toward him, struggling against the cuffs and his hands and his body. "My father will wipe you from the face of the Earth when he finds out what you've done."

"Stop squirming," he growled, but released her and eased back. "You will rip into your flesh."

She snorted. "As if you care."

"Oh, I care." His skin was on fire, the lower half of him responding to the nearness of her body, the scent of her. "I must have you exactly the same as when I stole you."

"You fear him," she said, her gaze searching his, looking for any whisper of weakness. "You fear Cruen."

Erion recognized a bright, quick, and possibly savage

mind within this female. He would not underestimate her. Or his own attraction to her, for that matter. She was no blushing, sweet-hearted bride-to-be, just as he was no kind and compassionate jailer.

They both had reasons for being in their situations.

But his were far more dire.

"Make no mistake, female," he said. "I will do whatever I must to get back what was stolen from me."

She lifted her chin. "And what was that?"

"Not your concern."

Her eyes flashed with interest. "A woman?"

Erion chuckled.

"Jewels?"

He angled his head. "Do I look as if I wear jewels?"

She leaned back against the wall, her lips thinning. "It must be something of great value."

In that moment, Ladd's face appeared before him. Frightened yet hopeful. Erion ground his teeth. Cruen would pay dearly for taking his son.

His lids flipped open and he narrowed his gaze on his bargaining chip. "What I must have returned is priceless."

For the first time since he'd taken her, the female appeared worried. "You won't tell me what it is?" she asked.

He remained silent.

The worry in her eyes intensified. "And how do you expect Cruen to find you? To make this trade?"

"I believe it was you who called him all-powerful. By now he knows you were taken and knows who has taken you. He will come for you. Have no fear. Very soon you will be in his arms, and he will make you his." His voice dropped to a whisper. "In every way."

Erion watched her closely, watched for her look of worry to morph into a look of desire or fear or contempt. Something he could understand, something that gave him a clue as to why she'd entered into a lifelong mating with that bastard. What he saw was ruthless determination. The woman was pure fight, pure venom—like her name, *Hellen*. She was giving nothing away but a battle, a struggle, and as much as he wanted to dislike that quality, he found her internal drive and strength most appealing.

He would have to watch that.

"In the meantime," he said. "You will find comfort down here."

She raised her arms as much as she was able. "This your idea of comfort?"

"When compared to the other scenarios I had in mind for you after you ran from me, yes."

Her gaze mocked him. "How romantic. The women must just swoon over you."

He ignored her jab, ignored the way his blood continually threatened to pool lower every time her scent pushed into his nostrils. "You will be clothed and well fed."

"Perhaps I will starve myself so you have nothing to negotiate with."

He shook his head slowly. "Don't make threats. I will force-feed you if I must."

"You don't even know what I eat."

"Baby animals?"

She shook her head, her eyes flashing.

"The souls of innocent children?"

She grinned. "Close."

"Not to worry," he said, trying not to stare at her mouth. "We'll find you something that not only keeps you alive, but also keeps your mouth occupied."

Her eyes widened and her nostrils flared. "Barbarian," she uttered.

Grinning, he turned to leave, the dog scrambling to his feet and trotting after him.

He barely reached the stairs when she called out after him. "Are you truly one of them, Male?"

He paused, glanced over his shoulder. "One of whom?"

"A bloodsucker."

"If the vein beckons."

"Then how did you see it?" she demanded, pressing forward, straining at her ties.

"See what?" Erion asked brusquely, forcing his gaze from her jutting breasts to her flashing eyes.

"The light by the gravestone," she said.

Erion hesitated, one foot on the bottom step. Thoughtful, he searched his mind for the scenario that had prompted such a question. Then it hit him. The light she'd nearly walked into before he'd captured her. He shrugged with the noncomplexity of the answer. "Because it was there."

Her eyes narrowed and her lips parted. She looked as though she were about to say something, but decided to hold her tongue.

"Is that it?" he asked.

She nodded. "For now."

"Then welcome to my home, Hellen. May your stay be fruitful and short-lived."

He was up the stairs, had his hand around the door handle, when he swore he heard her voice on the air behind him. She'd uttered only one word, but a word that had him concerned.

"Demon."

Bronwyn had just put her infant daughter, Lucy, down for a nap and was going in search of Lucian. She wanted to see if her mate had returned, his brothers too, and if anyone had discovered a lead on Ladd's whereabouts. She was just entering the library after hearing voices down the hall when she stopped abruptly and backed up. If she had a heartbeat, it would be pounding like a jack-hammer in her chest right about now. *What the hell?* She flattened herself against the wall outside the door and listened.

"You and Bron are happy, then?"

"As happy as I know how to be. But I try to make her happy—that's all that matters to me."

Bronwyn shook her head. What in the world was he doing here? The last person she expected to be sitting in the Romans' library was the *paven* she'd shared a Vera-cou ceremony with nearly a year ago talking to the *paven* who now owned her blood, her breath, her body.

This wasn't good.

"And the *balas*?" Synjon asked. His voice was different than she remembered. No longer jovial and confident. Now it rang cold and empty.

"My little bloodsucker, Lucy." Lucian chuckled. "She's beautiful and sweet. Shit, she's perfect."

"Who's the father, then?"

"Fuck you, Brit Boy."

Syn laughed, but the sound was anything but merry. "You know I'm bloody chuffed you're happy, Frosty."

"No, you're not," Lucian said, though his tone held no malice. "But I don't give a shit what anyone feels or what anyone thinks except for my *veana*."

Synjon grunted. *"Your veana."*

"Don't go there, man."

"Haven't you gone there? Over and over in your head?"

"Don't know what you're talking about. Kinda don't want to."

"That's rubbish and you know it," Synjon said. "What happens when her actual true mate shows up? When he claims her? No matter how she fights it, doesn't want it, she won't be able to stop her body's attraction to that chap. She'll be *his veana*."

The growl that blasted out into the hall made Bron jump. "No one will ever touch her," Lucian raged, sounding ever more the Breeding Male beast he carried within him. The beast that would never have a true mate, but loved his *veana* and *balas* more than his own life. "No one! I don't give a shit what calling card the male sports. I would kill anyone who laid a hand on what's mine."

Refusing to allow fear to anchor her, Bronwyn leaned in and glanced into the room. She found both males on their feet, aggressive in their stances. But it wasn't Lucian she worried about or even took the time to look over. It was the sight of her once close friend, the *paven* she'd protected when they were young and the *paven* who had agreed to mate with her when she was so afraid she'd be given over to the Breeding Male.

Oh, the irony. Now she was with the Breeding Male, her blood able to keep him sane, her unbeating heart filled with the hope that her real true mate would never find her.

Her gaze ran the length of her friend. In the seven months since she'd seen him last, Synjon Wise looked like a shell of his former self. He was tall and still shockingly handsome, but far too thin and pale. And his eyes . . . they were dark and sunken, and though they'd always flashed with a deadly fire, now they just looked dead, empty.

"What are we looking at?"

Bronwyn jumped at the whisper near her ear and whirled around to find two bright blue eyes staring curiously at her. "Jeez, Sara. You scared me."

Alexander's mate grimaced. "Sorry." She gestured to the library door with her chin. "Who's in there?"

"Lucian and Synjon."

Sara's eyes widened. "Synjon? Really. What's he doing here?"

"I don't know." She felt tired all of a sudden. "I didn't even know he was here."

Sara glanced past Bron's shoulder, her growing belly pressing against the *veana*'s flat one. She gasped softly. "Oh, my gods. What's wrong with him? He looks like he hasn't fed in weeks."

More like months, Bron was willing to bet. That was long-term starvation. "I have no idea."

"Well, don't you want to go in and find out?"

Bronwyn couldn't blame the female for asking. Alexander's true mate was a psychiatrist who was used to getting to the root of people's problems, then fixing them. But Bronwyn didn't know if she wanted to go there with Syn. She cared for him deeply, always had, but the guilt she felt for mating him, then succumbing to her desire, her love, for Luca was still so strong within her. She'd never had his forgiveness — and she knew she didn't deserve it.

"Maybe later," she told Sara, who looked as though she were waiting for the right answer but had just gotten the wrong one.

"He's your friend, Bron."

Yes, exactly. Gods, Sara couldn't possibly understand this. Synjon Wise was her friend, had been her best friend, and she'd taken advantage of that friendship, betrayed him in every way possible.

No doubt seeing her internal struggle, Sara put her hand on Bron's shoulder and softened her tone. "You look miserable. What's wrong?"

She glanced up into her sister-in-law's gentle, encouraging face and crumpled. "All he went through, all that I put him through, and then the *veana* who died in Cruen's compound . . ."

"Synjon's *veana*," Sara finished for her, knowing the story. "The female he was in love with, thought he'd lost, thought was dead."

Bronwyn nodded. "It's my fault."

"Okay. Come here." Sara took her hand and led her

down the hallway, away from the library and the *paven*s. "What you just said." She shook her head. "No, Bron. Not true."

"If I hadn't brought him into my drama, asked him to mate with me, he would never have known the truth." Tears pricked behind her eyes. "Juliet would still be alive."

"You don't know that."

"I know that, Sara. Just like I know he looks that way because he's consumed with hatred, is desperate for revenge. And maybe after he gets it he'll want to follow his *veana* into death."

Sara looked horrified. "Bron . . ."

Bronwyn couldn't stay under that microscope of shame. She didn't want to talk anymore. She turned away from Sara and ran down the hall toward the stairs. She needed her baby, needed to see Lucy, smell her hair, bury her face in the tiny one's neck, know that the one thing she'd created in this world was right and good and worth everything—even the slow death of the *paven* who at that very moment was standing in the Romans' library with the *paven* she'd left him for.

Day began in shards of pale light through the window across from her. In those first moments of dawn, Hellen didn't question how the glass she'd shattered so thoroughly the night before had been repaired or when. No. As she took in her first golden sunrise aboveground, she could think only about the heat that had been coming on slowly and continuously over the past several hours. It was a heat she hadn't felt in years, prayed she would never feel again, and it was going to ruin her if left unchecked.

At that moment, it remained focused on her feet and calves, but soon—very soon—it would travel upward. And once it hit her inner thighs, she would be a slave to it.

Terror filled her as she pulled against the chains that held her. Where was Cruen? Why hadn't he come for her? She was in such desperate trouble. The draft that had kept her cool, kept her chaste for so long, was bleeding out of her. She didn't know how to handle the shock of need that would hit her. Her body was used to the steady, even coldness the draft gave her. Relied on its protection from the insatiable need for sex, the sexual heat of the Underworld. This need was only one of the things her mother had called Unfortunate Gifts or Unwanted Inheritances for the Devil's firstborn. But the loving female had always made sure Hellen knew how to handle each one, while keeping Abbadon in the dark.

Through the window, the sky lightened to a pale blue. The true dawning of a new day.

If Cruen didn't come for her soon, bring her to his lair, where her draft sat cushioned within her clothing bags, she would need sexual gratification just as she needed air—and, gods help her, she wouldn't be able to stop herself from begging for it.

As a bubble of sweat trailed from her forehead down to her cheek, her lip curled. She would die before she was forced to ask that male—that strange, mixed-up bloodsucker who could see demon fire—for help.

She would beg him to kill her first.

She heard a door open and movement on the stairs. Her eyes instantly followed the sound and saw a male guard descending. He wasn't the same one she'd unleashed her fighting skills on the night before. No doubt the bloodsucker had requested a more powerful, less timorous guard to attend her. And this one certainly fit the bill. Tall, skull shaved, and bulging with muscle and a cocky attitude, he was the very model of intimidation.

As he neared, Hellen caught sight of the tray he carried and the scent of food within.

Her stomach lurched. It was the last thing she wanted—the last thing she wanted to fill her.

"Get out," she uttered without care. "And take that slop with you."

The guard didn't pause, didn't look wary in the least. Instead he kept coming, his gaze raking over her as he sauntered forward.

Hellen despised her body for reacting even in the slightest to his obvious and offensive perusal.

"You will eat," the male insisted, placing the tray on the floor beside her feet. "The master has given me strict instructions."

The master. That bloodsucker was one arrogant bastard. He'd get along with her father swimmingly. She tipped up her chin. "And did your master tell you how I am to consume this meal?"

The male appeared momentarily confused. It wasn't a good look for him.

A low growl escaped her lips. "No? That would be far too logical."

Unfortunately, the guard understood sarcasm, and he didn't appreciate it. "You would be wise to not insult Master Erion, female."

ERION. She perked up. Finally, a name. *It suits the bloodsucker,* she thought. Overpowering, dictatorial, and mysterious—the name of a male who lived by his own code of conduct. The heat licking at her toes and ankles seemed to flare in agreement. She pressed against the cool metal chains, trying to get some relief.

"Perhaps you could go and ask him," she said in a pained voice. "Maybe grab a knife and fork while you're at it."

"Master Erion is not at home." The male was staring at her intently, his nostrils flared.

A slow stream of unease went through Hellen. His master was gone, leaving him in charge of a creature who would tempt him in ways he couldn't possibly understand. His eyes raked her and he was sniffing.

"We don't need any help or implements," the guard said, a grin forming on his thin lips. He moved a foot closer, continuing to inhale. "I could feed it to you."

Panic prickled her skin. Was she really going to have to deal with this right now? With every guard her jailer would send her way?

She steadied her gaze and her breathing and recalled everything her mother had told her, taught her, begged her to use if she had no other choice. "Or you could just untie me."

The male's grin widened to the point of maniacal. "That would be the illogical choice. Don't you think?"

"So you wish to feed me like an infant?" she said quietly.

He chuckled. "You are far from an infant."

You have no idea how far.

His gaze pinned to her breasts, which were barely contained by the ravaged wedding gown, the guard moved closer, the tray at her feet all but forgotten.

5

Erion was Pureblood vampire, but he was also a *mutore*. And while that moniker took away many of his rights, stripped him of all respect, it had granted him the ability to live in sunlight—unlike his Roman brothers.

He flashed into the alley across from the Roman and Beast compounds, which were situated next to each other on the moderately quiet SoHo street, and if all went according to the construction plans they'd devised, would be one massive home in just a few months.

Erion liked the idea of the entire clan living together, but it hadn't stopped him from wanting his own space as well, something that was just his—something he could pass down to a future generation.

He bypassed a decent amount of daytime traffic and headed for the *mutore* compound first. Getting through his own enchantments was simple and quick, and when he entered the house, he was glad he'd chosen this side of the lawn first. Devoid of any of the afternoon's sunlight, the main living space was lit with lamps and the flickering glow of the fireplace, and it was packed with the entire Roman and Beast crew. Erion heard them before he saw them—male and female, serious and aggressive— but Lycos, with that damn nose of his, was on Erion before he even crossed the threshold into the huge circular space.

"Where the hell have you been?"

"I'm well. Thank you, Lycos." Erion gave the wolf beast a surly glare as he walked into the room.

"Well, shit. I'm glad to hear it," Lycos said, his eyes ripe with irritation. "But I want to know where you were. You can't be out of communication. We need to be able to reach you."

Erion cared deeply for his *mutore* brothers and had grown fond of his Roman brothers as well, but right now all he cared about was his boy.

"Have you found Cruen's whereabouts?" He addressed the query to the room, to all who sat and stood and stared at him.

"Not yet," Nicholas told him, his expression grim.

Erion noticed Kate wasn't in the room. A soft ping registered in his chest. The *veana* was like a surrogate mother to Ladd. She loved and cared for him deeply, and was no doubt hurting, fearful.

"Nothing on the walls?" he asked, his gaze still on Nicholas.

"The Order hasn't contacted us," Nicholas said quietly. "There's been nothing."

Phane stood up, anger flaring in his mismatched eyes. "You're just going to ignore Ly's question?"

"I've been searching for the boy," Erion said on a

growl. He hadn't told anyone about the house he'd purchased. It was his private business. He didn't want questions, didn't want to have to explain why he'd bought it,
his hope for who he might give it to someday.

"You've been gone twenty-four hours, Erion," Helo
said calmly, though with marked pointedness. The water
beast was perched on the edge of a chair. "We have
enough to worry about without having to send a search
party out for you."

Erion knew they meant well and that everyone was
jacked up on worry for the boy, but Helo's last words
really pissed him off. "I will be gone for as long as I wish
it, brothers. I am no *balas*; I need no *tegga*. I came here
only to see what information you have gleaned." He
looked around the room and snarled. "Which seems to
be nothing. Christ, have you even moved since I was
here last—since the boy was stolen?"

Alexander and Lucian cursed, Phane and Helo stood,
growling, Sara tried to speak civilly to him, but Lycos got
in his face and pushed.

"What the hell is wrong with you?" he shouted.

"Just don't appreciate doing the work of ten."

"You run off, don't stay in contact, then presume once
you deign to come back here that we've just been sitting
on our asses all day drinking blood?"

"You have nothing!" Erion shouted. "No information,
no trail to follow."

"Neither do you, asshole!" He looked around, behind
Erion. "You got the *balas*? You brought him home? Is he
hiding under your fucking shirt or something?"

A fierce snarl escaped Erion's throat, and he headed toward his wolf brother. "Screw you, Lycos."

Phane stepped between them. "Ease up, Erion. You're acting like a—"

"Nutcase!" Lycos called, his beast out and snarling.

"No, an idiot," Phane said.

Lycos snorted. "Fuck, no! A—"

"A father."

The air in the room seemed to flatten. All aggression and seething, testosterone-laden fire bled from each male, who a moment ago were ready to kick the shit out of one another.

"He's acting like a father."

All heads turned to Nicholas. The *paven* stood by the wall, alone, his eyes tired and sad as he watched Erion.

"You think you're the only one feeling like this, brother?" he said.

"Like what?" Erion returned, not fierce but fearful. "Disappointed in the lack of work that's being done to locate the boy."

Nicholas shook his head. "You know that's not true. You know every vampire in here is doing all he can to locate Ladd. What I mean is that you're not the only one worrying about him, wondering if he's hurt, if he's scared." Nicholas's hands balled into fists and he slammed back at the wall that he was leaning on.

Erion didn't want to see the *paven* emotional, afraid. He couldn't afford to feel any of that. He had to stay detached and clearheaded and vicious.

"We've all been out searching, Erion," Alex said, his tone as calm as he could make it. "Until the very last moments of night."

"We all want the boy back," Sara said, moving into the crook of her mate's arm. "We must work together."

"The Eyes are looking into Cruen's whereabouts," Lucian said. "But those fanged street rats aren't being even remotely helpful. I swear Cruen has stolen their minds from them, made them think they are no longer informants for hire but his personal servants. We've offered them insane amounts of money, and they're not even tempted."

"Dillon is working with the Order now," Sara added, "She's trying to find out what they know, and Gray is seeing if the Impure warriors can obtain a mental link."

Alexander turned to his brother. "How is Kate?"

Erion flinched, then hated himself for it. He didn't want to fall into the sad warmth of their emotional connection. He watched as Nicholas shook his head, his eyes weary. "Frantic. She tried to go with Dillon to the Order."

Alexander snorted. "Went over well, did it?"

Nicholas's mouth lifted. "Like a jackhammer on a tin can."

"Mating hasn't mellowed that *veana* one bit."

Erion's skin tightened around his muscles and bones, and his chest rumbled with the beginnings of a growl. If he remained here, listening to this, he was going to explode.

"You can continue socializing," he said. "I have work to do." He turned on his heel and started for the door.

"Where?" Helo called after him. "What work is it? What's your plan?"

"One of us will go with you," Phane added. "Wait, brother."

"No." Erion didn't slow.

"Goddamn you, Erion!"

Lycos's frustrated outburst followed Erion out the living room door and into the hall, but the only one who actually followed him was his twin.

Nicholas caught up with him near the kitchen and blocked his way. The *paven* looked tired, older, but in his dark eyes a fire smoldered.

Erion bared his teeth, flashed his demon. "Move."

"I don't like this, Erion," Nicholas said, undeterred by the show of brawn.

"Not my problem."

"He is mine too, and Kate's."

Erion's jaw worked, a quick and irrational anger surging within him. "You think that's what this is? That I would steal him back only to keep him for myself? I am no father." His eyes narrowed. "He is all yours, brother. I would never attempt to claim him."

Nicholas's dark gaze turned sympathetic. "You know what I mean. I respect the fact that he is your biological—"

"He is nothing but a missing *balas*!" The words were like cut glass in his mouth. "Now get out of my way before I help you."

Nicholas didn't move. "If you want to prove something, it would be better served to work together."

"Not this time."

"I know what you're doing. You think you owe him, that you're making up for not knowing about his existence."

The rumbling in Erion's chest exploded into a full-fledged growl of warning. "Don't tell me what I'm feeling."

"I know—"

"You know nothing," Erion hissed, something tightening in his chest, something he wanted nothing to do with. "You and I have no understanding of each other, our histories, our perspectives."

"Is this about the past? About our mother and what she did to you?" Nicholas shook his head. "If so, you have nothing to make up for. I truly believe you were better off."

"That *veana* may have used you, brother, hurt you, but at least she wanted you."

Nicholas laughed bitterly. "Oh, she wanted me. She wanted me for my mouth and my ass after she could no longer service those pieces of shit herself." He turned away for a moment, his nostrils flaring, trying to catch his breath. "What does any of this have to do with Ladd?"

Erion could barely feel, barely think, he was so pumped up on adrenaline and anger and fear. "I cannot . . ."

"What? What, Erion?"

His gaze lifted and his eyes found his twin's. He shook his head miserably. "The *balas* will not think, will not believe—*ever*—no matter where he ends up—that I did not want him."

There was a moment of silence between them, and Nicholas's eyes softened. "You don't have to do this alone for him to know that."

Erion straightened his shoulders, shoved away the sentiment and emotion. "I must find him. *I*. Must find him."

"You are being irrational. And it's dangerous for the boy."

"My passion, my drive, will bring the boy home. You will see."

Nicholas released a grave sigh. "God, I hope so."

Erion bit into his wrist, then grabbed his brother's and bit into his flesh too. Nicholas cursed, but he allowed Erion to press the two bloody gashes together.

"Now we are connected," Erion said, his eyes locked on his twin. "Feel for me within yourself if Cruen contacts you."

Without waiting for an answer, Erion ripped his arm away and pushed past Nicholas to the door. He had to get back to his search, to his prisoner. The moment he stepped out of the house, the moment he felt sun on his face, he flashed.

In seconds, he landed on another lawn, in another country. It was night and the rain had stopped. Erion ran his bloody wrist along the lock, then waited for the gate to draw back. It had barely swung two feet before he saw the front door to the castle burst open. One of his servants came running out, followed by the brown-and-white canine. Both barreled down the small incline and through the vines.

Breathless, the dog on his heels, the servant halted before Erion. "Your prisoner, sir."

Instantly alert, Erion said, "What about her?"

The servant's mouth formed a grim line and his eyes were wide with anxiety.

"What?" Erion demanded, a sudden caustic panic gripping him. "Has she escaped again?"

The male shook his head.

He grabbed the male by the collar and said in the deadliest of voices, "Tell me before I gut you."

"She has eaten Timothy," the male squeaked.

At first Erion didn't believe he'd heard the servant correctly. But one look at the male's utterly terrorized face and he knew it was true.

"Christ!" he uttered, tossing the male aside and immediately flashing up to the house.

Goddamn female! What the hell had she done? And, more importantly, what the hell was she? Humans didn't eat flesh, and vampires drank only blood.

He stalked into the house and down the many hallways that led to the door and the dungeon stairs. Whatever she was, he wouldn't tolerate her making meals out of his staff.

Return . . .
Return her to me—
Cruen opened his eyes and snarled at the plants surrounding him in the rooftop greenhouse. He couldn't

even send a message to the walls of the Roman brothers' compound. He couldn't get through their enchantments.

He grabbed at a violet bloom and ripped it from its stem. For too many years to count he had been all-powerful, divine, feared, and formidable. Sending a message to anyone, anywhere, took only a brief thought, such little effort.

Now he was . . . what? Like all the other vampires? Limited powers. He didn't know how to exist in the realm he now found himself in.

Erion had taken his key to continued power, his key to unlimited life, and to his work developing the ultimate vampire.

Erion had taken the key that would finally unlock the door to Cruen's true love.

Celestine.

He had to find the female. But how was he to get to his *mutore* son? He couldn't use any of his advanced magic. And he couldn't go to the source of his power and ask for it.

He crushed the flower in his fist. He couldn't bring Abbadon into this. The demon king would make Cruen pay, make him go without a feeding until Hellen was found. Abbadon would consider her abduction Cruen's incompetence, but the fact that Cruen's adopted son had done the deed . . . well, that might just make the Demon King forget their union altogether.

And Cruen couldn't allow that.

Without Abbadon's blood, he was a worthless *paven*.

"Gale!" he shouted.

The male came at once, had no doubt been hovering near the door. "Yes, my lord?"

"Are the Demon King's daughters comfortable?"

"Yes, my lord." The male cocked his head. "Should we continue to make them so?"

Cruen's lip curled in pure menace and warning. "You will treat them as the royalty they are while I am away."

The male nodded, his gaze sweeping low. "You are traveling, my lord?"

He tossed away the broken and battered bloom. "It seems I must."

"I have tied you up! Is that not enough to contain your wickedness? Do you need a muzzle as well?"

Hellen watched the male, Erion, pace from one end of the dungeon to the other, his black hair hanging to his hard jawline, his diamond eyes fixed on her, his lips forming a sneer. His wide shoulders were rolled forward. Every thick muscle she could see outlined in the jeans and black T-shirt he wore flexed and bunched as if he was ready to attack. He was a fearsome sight, and she licked her lips, tasting the blood of his guard.

Metallic and unsatisfying.

"You seem tense, Male," she said, her gaze trained on him, wondering what he would do next, how he would deal with her. "Hasn't my fiancé contacted you yet?"

Erion's nostrils flared, but he didn't stop moving. "You should be the one who's concerned. Perhaps Cruen doesn't value you as you believed."

She refused to even contemplate that. "Or perhaps he doesn't want to give back the prize he took from you, bloodsucker."

A fearsome growl erupted from his throat, and he whirled on her. "I swear to all that is unholy, if you eat another member of my household, I will bleed you out and you'll see my bloodsucker tendencies firsthand."

She plastered on a false expression of trepidation. She knew he wouldn't kill her, his leverage. "A vile threat indeed."

"You push me too far, woman."

"Hellen."

"Whatever," he growled, turning away from her and resuming pacing.

She pulled at the cuffs encircling her wrist. "I was hungry, okay?"

"The guard brought you food. Did he not?" Erion said through tightly gritted teeth.

"It wasn't fresh."

He growled again.

"And how was I supposed to eat it?" she continued. "With my toes?"

He was in her face in under a breath. Nostrils flared, chest heaving, he towered over her. Hellen had been around males her whole life, and as she'd grown and bloomed into womanhood she'd seen how some males began to regard her. Not like they did her sisters, but there were the ones who had found her attractive, the ones who made her laugh and fought rogue demons beside her. But never in all that time had a male looked at her like this

one did. Hate and fear and sadness and hunger and . . .
lust?

She drew back as far as she could go, her shoulders
hitting the wall.

Who was this bloodsucker? And what did he want
from Cruen? She knew Cruen had to be a fiend in his
own right—after all, who would pay for a mate but
someone who craved power, someone without empathy?
Someone very similar to her father, Abbadon. Did this
male who looked as though she were something he
wished to unwrap and discover only desire the power of
her being?

Should she care? Should she even wonder? After all,
her main objective had to be escape. Or . . . if given the
chance, this male's demise.

His gaze was moving over her face. Only when he
came to her eyes did he speak. "My guards are not on the
menu. Understand?"

She couldn't help herself. She breathed him in, cold
air and hot skin.

"Do you hear me, woman?"

Hear you, scent you . . . Her ankles flickered with heat.
Gods, she needed her draft. "When they are perverted
little fucks who attempt to touch me, they are."

Erion's eyes widened and a feral growl vibrated from
his throat. "What did you say?"

"Seriously, I have to repeat it?"

He cocked his head to the side and uttered in the
deadliest of voices, "He touched you?"

"Above the waist. If he'd tried to go lower I would've
had to play with my food first before I ate it."

His gaze cut to her chest.

Just the quick look made her demon heat flare an inch higher. *Shit.* "I may not be all that hot in the face department, but I do have killer tits."

The bloodsucker's eyes lifted and he appeared confused. "You believe yourself unattractive?"

"Does it matter?"

"I find it curious."

She shrugged. "My face. The shape, the features. It's not all . . . It's—"

"It's beautiful," he said. "You're beautiful."

Silence fell between them, and Hellen wasn't at all sure what to say, what to think. She was locked up in a dungeon, prisoner to the male before her while her skin grew hotter with each breath she took.

He had called her beautiful. He stood before her, watching her, guarded, yet clearly confused on what had just transpired between them—what he had allowed himself to say.

It wasn't good.

They were prisoner and jailer. No bond was to be formed, no matter how many compliments were tossed her way.

She forced her gaze from him. "Look," she began in a tight voice. "Your guard thought the best course of action was to feed me with one hand and cop a feel with the other. And, well . . . Hellen don't play that."

"I understand." His voice was stone and ice.

Her gaze seemed to drag itself back to his.

"I apologize, Hellen," he said, his mouth grim, his eyes flaring with anger. "It will not happen again."

"Why should I believe anything you say?"

"I do not keep you here for my own sadistic amusement. It is because I have no choice."

She laughed softly. "You have a choice."

"Have you ever cared about someone, Hellen?" His eyes burned into hers. "So deeply, so desperately you would sacrifice everything for them—including your code of honor?"

Yes. Yes, she thought. Her sisters. She would give anything, everything to keep them safe. But she couldn't tell him that. She couldn't risk the possibility that he would use the information to get back whatever it was he so desperately wanted.

Before she was forced to say something, anything that was not the truth, there was noise on the stairs behind them.

"Sir?"

"What?" Erion said, irritated, ripping his gaze from Hellen and turning around.

The guard reached the bottom step and stopped. He eyed Hellen and blanched, then slowly backed up the stairs.

"You have turned my guards into pussies," Erion muttered.

"Maybe you'll be next," she said, then added, "Erion."

He glanced over his shoulder. "You know my name."

Your name, yes, but not your game.

"Sir?"

"What is it?" Erion grumbled, turning back to the guard.

"There is a message from your brothers."

"He has brothers," Hellen said softly. *Are they a part of this deal?* she wondered. *This abduction? Has Cruen taken them or hurt them? Is that what the bloodsucker wishes to get back?*

"That's not possible," Erion told the guard. "I was just with them."

"He said it was urgent, sir." His voice lowered. "About the boy."

Hellen's blood jumped in her veins. *Boy. What boy?*

Erion walked toward the guard, his large, powerful body tense. "*He* said it was urgent?" His voice was lethal. "Who is *he*?"

Hellen's eyes cut between Erion and the guard as the temperature in the room seemed to drop twenty degrees.

The guard's nostrils flared with nerves. "The courier at the gate, sir."

Hellen heard Erion curse, then suddenly take off up the stairs.

"What boy?" she yelled after him, but he was gone, the guard with him.

6

There were three stages of fire in target shooting: slow, timed, and rapid. Synjon had been at it for an hour and every round he went ended up rapid. He had no patience for conventional practice rules. Removing magazine after magazine, reloading again and again, aim and shoot—that's all he was after. Hit after hit until he saw the battered wall behind the face on each of his target papers.

He set the semiautomatic down and went to change the target. Shooting used to give him some form of release, some feeling of control. It was like the bite into flesh before the suck—the initial action that drew blood.

But there was no relief inside him anymore. No matter what he did. All he felt, all the bloody time, was manic darkness. And it was growing blacker every moment Cruen continued to breathe.

"How many rounds you go?"

The Roman brother's deep, concerned voice didn't

make Synjon start. In fact, Syn had known the male was coming, catching his scent as it had drifted in from the hall.

"Not nearly enough," Syn muttered, crushing the target paper in his fist as he walked back toward Alexander. "Glad you stopped by."

"I think it's you who's stopping by."

"Yes," Syn said. "At long last. I'm sure Frosty's told you what I'm after." He picked up the semiautomatic and started to reload. "A reminder of what was promised more than seven months ago."

Alex leaned against the wall, crossed his arms over his chest. The *paven* was big, his Breeding Male genes showing in every thick muscle, every predatory movement. "Vengeance."

The word made Syn pause, look up. His eyes narrowed. "I could say 'justice,' but why bother? I hope there's no problem with that."

"None whatsoever. Except for the fact that we're having some trouble—"

"Locating the bastard yourself," Syn finished.

"Right." The skull-shaved *paven*'s eyebrows drew together. "But I think I may have stumbled upon a way."

Syn lowered his weapon. "Tell."

"Can't. Not yet." He released a breath. "It involves my mate."

"You think she knows how to get to Cruen?"

"No. But she will be affected, perhaps even hurt, if I use this possibility."

The urge to throttle Alexander Roman until he revealed his thoughts, his plan, was almost impossible to repress. "I understand your caution, but the *paven* must be taken down."

"I know," Alex said calmly. "I just need a little time."

"Time's up, Roman," Synjon said, turning from the *paven* and lifting his gun. "For you, me, the *balas* who lies in wait of a rescue, and that *paven* bastard who killed my *veana*."

Without another word, Syn aimed at the target and fired ten rounds without blinking. All shots landed right between the eyes.

Erion burst through the front door and flash-ran down the hill toward the gate like a *paven* possessed. What the hell would he find waiting? *Who* would he find waiting? And if it was a trap, how badly could he rip the bastard apart before the male spilled the details of his plan?

His final flash brought him right to the gate's entrance. He'd already bitten into his wrist as he traveled, and he ran it over the lock. He sprang forward as the gate allowed him access. At first he saw nothing, no one, his gaze tracking every movement the moonlight favored him with. Then a sound caught his ears, a scent too, and it was one he knew well. One that was normally accompanied by irritating wafts of dust.

"What the hell are you doing here, Raine?" he called out.

Nothing. Just wind through the trees met his query.

Erion cursed through clenched teeth. "Get over here before I'm forced to hunt you down. Your beast is a midnight snack for mine."

He heard a whimper, then saw a flash of pale skin. Raine had stepped out from behind a wide bush and was slowly moving toward him. "I'm in deep trouble because of you."

"You came here for an apology?" Erion said on a growl. "Truly?"

The *mutore*'s terrified features intensified as he drew nearer. "He knew I told you that I could be the only one."

Cruen had contacted him. Erion's skin prickled with hope. "Good."

Raine, however, looked shocked at his response. "You are pleased."

"I want to meet with him, exchange our goods. It is all I want."

Raine stared piteously at him for a moment, then he sighed. "Then meet him, you will."

He moved quickly, leaped forward, and grabbed Erion around the waist. Before Erion had a chance to react, they flashed from the castle grounds. But it was a flash unlike any Erion had ever experienced before. It was slow and strange and rendered him utterly immobile; even his mouth refused to move. Panic snaked through him, but it hardly had time to take hold. In an instant, he touched down, his feet sinking into warm, gentle sand as his gaze searched his surroundings. When he realized where he was, his bowels tightened. He despised this place, hated what he'd done on this beach, who he had manipulated, who he had humiliated.

"We have spent many hours here, my son."

The words, *that* voice—it broke the spell over Erion's

muscles and his ability to speak. He lifted his upper lip and flashed his fangs at the *paven* who stood beside him. "Call me that again and I will devein you."

Cruen laughed, but it wasn't a light, frothy sound. It carried the weight of worry within it.

"There was a time when you begged me to call you son, when you reveled in my parental care."

If only I had the ability to kill here, Erion mused. "It was the desperate need of a desperate child," he stated flatly. *One who only wanted to be considered worthy of love.* "That desire was over the moment you lied to me about being able to produce a *balas*."

"It was for your protection, Erion."

"Was it?" Erion turned and regarded the ancient *paven*.

"Of course. I have always protected my children." He looked out at the ocean, the waves so calm, so serene— so unlike the *paven*s who stood before it. "All of my children."

"Then you will understand that I must protect mine."

Cruen turned to him, a strange gleam of optimism, perhaps even hope, lighting his eyes. "Come back, come home, bring the female, and I will give you the *balas*. He can remain with you in my home—"

Erion interrupted the *paven*'s worthless words with mirthless laughter. "I will be happy to trade the female for the boy, but you will never have me. I don't belong with you anymore. I am no soldier to fight for you and your ugly cause, no specimen for you to study."

"You think you belong out there in the world?" Cruen said with a trace of sadness in his voice. "Look at you.

You're a beast, something the Order would kill on sight. You can't have a real chance at life in that world, Erion. Neither can your brothers."

Erion wouldn't believe that. Refused to believe it. He already had a life—the beginnings of one, at any rate. He had his brothers and the Roman brothers, he had a home ... maybe even a child. He fixed the *paven* with a resolute glare. "They will not return, and neither will I."

All traces of melancholy left Cruen's expression and his mouth formed a hard line. "Your transition will be coming soon. You won't be able to handle it alone. You will need me, my medicines, and my expertise. If I could see your blood, study your cells, I may be able to predict the exact time of your transition."

Desperate threats were lost on him. His transition wasn't for several years yet, and he would deal with it when the time came. His answer was simple. "Never."

Around them the wind picked up, made the ocean water stir. Cruen's gaze stirred too. "We will see."

"I want the *balas*," Erion said, going to stand in front of the aged *paven*, blocking his view of the seawater he loved so much. "Bring him here, and I will bring the female."

Cruen's face lit with a strange combination of relief and irritation. He wanted Hellen, perhaps needed her, but he didn't like her. That realization should've washed off Erion's back. The boy was all he cared about; the female was nothing more than a bargaining chip.

And yet ... it bothered him.

"Not here," Cruen said, interrupting his thoughts. "You will come to my compound."

"So we are surrounded by your guards and you can take the female and the boy? I don't think so." Erion nodded at the *mutore* who had brought him here, the *mutore* who hovered a few feet away. Raine looked terrified, exhausted, like he wished he were anywhere else. "We will do the exchange at Raine's shop."

"No!" the *mutore* cried out, backing up a foot.

Cruen put a hand up to silence him. "Agreed. Twenty-four hours."

Erion growled and grabbed his adopted father's wrist. "We will do it now, *paven*. This very moment."

Cruen made no move to force his hand away. In fact, he appeared slightly less confident than a moment ago. "It is not possible."

"Why?"

A shadow of humiliation moved over the *paven*'s face. He shook his head. He wasn't going to answer.

"Your delay is suspect," Erion said, tightening his hold. "I warn you not to attempt trickery. If you hurt the *balas* in any way, your bride-to-be will have the life's blood sucked out of her every orifice."

Cruen's nostrils flared. "Twenty-four hours."

Erion cursed and released the *paven*'s wrist. Not because he wanted to, but because his hand was on fire. *What the hell?* He stared at his palm, red and stinging. It was as though he'd been burned. His gaze ratcheted up just in time to see Cruen's image flicker on and off before him like a faulty lamp. He seemed to glow for a moment; then he disappeared altogether.

Erion rounded on Raine. "What was that?"

"An illusion," he offered weakly.

Realization dawned. He had been tricked.

He cocked his head to one side and growled. "He was never here."

Raine looked terrified. "His mind was here."

"Why not his person? What the hell is going on?"

The male rolled his lips under his teeth and shrugged.

Erion stalked toward the *mutore*. "Continue to hold your tongue, and I will cut it out." With the *mutore*'s fearful gasp, Erion continued, "Is he contained somewhere? A prisoner?"

Looking around himself, Raine whispered, "I don't believe so."

"Then what?" Erion demanded, his feral voice echoing down the beach. "He blazed with heat, with color at first; then he looked as though he were fading, like he'd lost power before he . . ."

Raine looked up, blinked at him.

"His power?" Erion said, pouncing on the *mutore*'s reaction. "What about it? Is there something wrong?"

"It is all the time we have here. All I was allotted. If you are determined to cut out my tongue, it will have to be done back in France."

He grasped Erion around the waist again, and in a flash they were airborne.

The heat inside her had risen maliciously. It was no longer contained at her feet and ankles, where thinking rationally and breathing in and out was manageable. Now it surged above her knees, licking at the very edges of her thighs. Hellen internalized a frustrated whimper. Whatever was left of the cooling draft was quickly exiting her veins. If she didn't get to her supply soon, she would need to find relief another way.

She lifted her lids and narrowed her gaze on the guard who stood directly in front of the window. The male hadn't looked her in the eye once since he'd come on duty after Erion left. He was clearly wary of her. And she hardly blamed him. After all, she'd eaten his coworker.

"Hey, you," she called out.

The male's eyes swept the floor.

"I know you hear me," she said, forcing a calm, gentle tone into her voice instead of the raging frustration she truly felt. "You need to be afraid of me only if you say no."

His gaze flickered upward. "Say no to what?"

She forced a smile, hoped she didn't look too maniacal—or maybe that was a good thing in this situation. "If you do as I ask, I promise I won't hurt you. If you don't, I will kill you." His eyes widened. She continued, "Most likely in your sleep." His mouth dropped open and his nostrils flared. "I'll wake you up first, of course, just so I can get your heart pumping quickly before I rip it from your chest and devour it."

The guard turned fish-belly white and shook his head over and over. "I can't release you. I won't."

She nodded her understanding. "You fear your master more than me?"

He didn't answer.

"Fool." She sniffed, attempted to look impish.

"He would kill me."

"Yes," she agreed, still keeping her tone even. "But he would kill you swiftly. Me? Not so much."

"I could remain where I am," he said with a moment of confidence. "I won't get close to you."

She laughed. "Perhaps not. But there will come a day when your master releases me. If you refuse to help me now, I will come and find you. And I will bring friends."

She watched this news settle over him, watched as he shifted away from the stone. But still he remained where he was. His gaze, however, did flicker toward the ring of keys on the wall.

She lowered her voice conspiratorially. "If you like, I will kill him. Then you needn't worry about his wrath or mine."

The thoughts inside the male's head, the visions of being eaten and/or tortured like his colleague versus being killed by his employer stirred his features. His body rigid, he slowly moved toward the wall with the keys.

"You will jump through the window again," the male said. It wasn't a question.

Her skin hummed with anticipation. "I will run straight past you, Male, and dive for the glass."

"You will wait outside for the master and kill him before he returns." Again, his words were not a question.

"I am very good at hiding." *And running,* she mused. There was no way she was sticking around to deal with Erion. All she wanted to do was get home, get her draft, get herself under control, and get to Cruen.

Hellen's breathing changed as the heat within her surged upward, flaring between her thighs. She needed this to happen now. While she still had control. While the desire was manageable.

The male continued toward her. His hands shook as he fiddled with the keys he'd snatched from the ring.

Erion would beat this male senseless when he returned, but leaving a ring of keys on the wall had to be one of the more foolish choices the *paven* had made of late. Perhaps he'd never dreamed one of his guards would be stupid enough to take them, much less get close enough to her to use them.

She licked her lips, leaned forward. The male was getting closer. She could smell his fear. Hear the pounding of his heart. He kept his eyes below her chin as he raised his hand. He had the key held out toward the lock at her wrist when all of a sudden something rushed into the room. Whatever it was, it moved so fast, it was impossible to see or detect its action.

Until the guard fell to the floor at her feet, his neck snapped, the keys gone from his hand.

Erion glared at her, his breathing uneven. "You just cost me another servant!"

Hellen couldn't speak. She was too shocked, too angry. Her chance of escape was gone. She'd never get this opportunity again. The master here would see to that.

What the hell was she going to do?

Erion paced back and forth in front of her, huffing and puffing like a wolf. "What did you promise him, Hellen? If he released you? More than what the other guard got a feel of? A trip below the waist this time?"

"Screw you."

"I can't believe I fell for your 'I'm so unattractive' lament." He growled at her. "You know exactly what you have and how to use it."

What she'd had was a terrifying reputation that had given her a chance of escape. That was gone now. As the heat surged up between her legs again, she bit her lip, bit back the groan of need that was only going to intensify. She'd never been one to wish for something she couldn't make happen, but right now she was wishing like hell for her mother's wise words and comfort.

"Make no mistake," Erion continued on with his rant. "Punishment will be severe."

"I'm shaking."

He stopped in front of her and flashed his fangs. "What did you say?"

"Look at me!" she yelled, her fists clenching and un-clenching in their shackled cages. "I'm shackled, Erion! What more punishment is there but death!"

His nostrils flared as he ran his gaze down her body. "There is so much more I can do."

Her skin went tight. Her stupid, disloyal skin actually went tight at his threatening words. How was she going to manage this? With him around her, with him standing so near, his mood so volatile, his scent making her in-sides churn and the heat between her legs inch ever closer to hell? The draft was nearly out of her system. She was so screwed.

As if he sensed her panic, or perhaps scented her growing arousal, he advanced on her. Hellen drew back against the brick, but it wasn't far enough to stop the heat of his body from curling around hers or the spici-ness of his skin from playing inside her nostrils.

She pulled in a breath and held it, just as she held his gaze. He was inches away, his crystal eyes predatory, curious.

"What's wrong with you?" he asked.

She shook her head.

"You look afraid, and yet—"

"Yes." She released her breath with the word. "Yes, that's it." Her tongue darted out to wet her lips. She tried to tamp down the pain of desire snaking through her veins. "I'm scared."

He inhaled deeply. His eyes narrowed. "No. That is not fear I scent."

His voice, the low growl of his voice, sent another wave of intense heat between her legs.

He inhaled again. "That's desire. Arousal."

"No."

"What the hell . . ." Shock lit his eyes. "You desire me."

"No!"

"You want to fuck me."

She glared at him. Why couldn't he get out of here? Walk away? Why did it matter to him what her body was crying out for? "I think you were dropped on your head as a baby, bloodsucker."

He didn't rise to her insults. Instead he drew nearer. "But why? You should despise me."

"I do."

"Your body says differently."

Her mind scratched and clawed for a reason, an excuse, anything to stop this line of questioning. "I am thinking about the one I'm to mate. My body burns for him, is excited to be joined with his." She gritted her teeth and locked eyes with him. "Perhaps if I force my-self to think about you, I will grow blissfully cold."

Only a few inches from her body, her face, Erion's expression tightened. He said nothing for a few moments, then a slow grin appeared. "You know, I've just met with your fiancé."

Hellen gasped. "Cruen!" Her entire body flared with hope, a possible end to the nightmare raging through her. "When? What did he say? Is he coming for me?" She would be released, saved. She would have her draft; the pain would ease. No one would ever have to know.

Erion watched her, took in her jubilation, his expression nothing less than disgusted. "You truly wish to be mated with that monster."

"With all my heart."

"You love him?"

"I agreed to mate him, didn't I?"

"That's no answer."

"And that is a pointless question coming from some-one who wishes only to trade me in for what he truly values."

Erion looked startled. When he spoke, his voice was low and caustic. "Not to worry, little hellion; by tomorrow you will be in his arms and his bed. Forever after, he will take care of that painful heat I scent between your thighs."

Hellen's stomach rolled. She couldn't stop it. It was the truth, what Erion had just said, but she had rarely allowed herself to think on it. Yes, she wanted to be free, wanted to ease the pain and heat within her, but the thought of the male who had essentially bought her from her father taking her to his bed made her shudder with revulsion.

Perhaps she should've held on to that reaction until Erion had stepped back, left the room.

His nostrils were flared wide and his head was cocked to one side. His eyes were changing color as he drew in breath after breath. "Your scent changed. From desire to disgust in one second flat."

Again, her stomach rolled. "I don't know what you're talking about, bloodsucker."

"Oh, I think you do. You're hiding something."

Hellen stared at him, her insides warm and trembling, her skin tight around her muscles. "Maybe we're both hiding something. Your eyes changed from vampire to something else entirely." She leaned forward and whispered. "What are you? You're not just a vampire. You're something more."

Inches away, his shoulders flexed, his neck tensed, and his gaze moved from her mouth to her cheek. Then he leaned in and whispered in her ear, "Pleasant dreams, Hellen."

Hellen's entire body flared with lust and she bit her lip so hard she tasted blood.

When she lifted her head, the dark-haired male was across the room, taking the steps two at a time. She stared after him. What had just happened? And what the hell was he? She knew it shouldn't matter to her — nothing should matter except getting free. And soon she would be if the male was telling her the truth.

Yes, she had to hold on to that belief. In a few hours she would be home, the draft at her lips, her heat repaired, her life sacrificed to the one cause she believed most worthy: her sisters. And this nightmare, this male who held her captive in more ways than she was willing to admit, would be a distant and despised memory.

As if the heat within her had a mind and a plan of its own, it snaked up between her legs and exploded maliciously inside her cunt.

7

Kate quickly dried off from her shower, then made her way out the bathroom and straight into the closet. She barely looked at the racks of clothing, just tossed on anything that smelled clean and appeared comfortable. She didn't have the time or care for how she looked. The misery inside her was palpable. Worse than her time spent in Mondrar, the vampire prison. There she'd been held for a crime she hadn't committed but had taken responsibility for. It was time she'd served to protect her mother, her only family. And she would've done the same for Ladd if that bastard Cruen had allowed her to. But he didn't want her sacrifice, didn't care about the boy's well-being in any way. He'd snatched the poor innocent *balas* right out from under her care, and now she lived in a different kind of prison, one she'd never truly escape.

She slipped on a pair of black boots and went into the bedroom. She wasn't surprised to find Nicholas there. Her true mate, her family, the one *paven* on Earth who understood her and loved her unconditionally, was standing against the closed door of their room. He was darkly beautiful as always, but as he stood there, arms crossed over his broad chest, he carried the same sadness in his eyes as she did.

"You left the meeting," he said.

"Yeah."

He shook his head. "Didn't tell me. Didn't say goodbye."

"I didn't want to interrupt anything," she said, heading over to the desk where she kept her cell phone. She stuffed it in the pocket of her jeans with her small pocket knife.

"We were strategizing," he told her, his voice gentle but firm. "I would think you'd want to be in on that. Unless you have other plans."

She paused, looked up at him. She sighed. "Baby, listen . . ."

"What are you doing, Kate?"

"I'm going out."

"Then I'll come with you."

"You can't. It's day."

"Then wait until the sun recedes."

She walked toward him, toward the door, waited expectantly. He didn't budge. In fact, his jaw went rigid, his expression too.

She shook her head, tried to swallow the hitch in her throat. "I can't just sit here and do nothing, Nicky. Would you really want me to?"

His eyes, his dark, soulful eyes, searched her own, and after a moment or two his body relaxed. "What's your plan?"

"Going to the Impure *credenti*." She would never lie to him. She was going to the *credenti*, but it wasn't the only place she was going. She had a few vampire acquaintances who were no longer in Mondrar and who might be willing to help her. Nicholas didn't need to know that; he'd only worry about her safety.

"Please, Nicky."

Still, he didn't step aside. His eyes were penetrating as he stared at her, tried to search inside her mind and her soul. "We will have him back, my love."

"I know."

"Then what is it? I know you fear for his safety. I do too. But there is more inside you than fear." He reached out and touched her chin, lifted it so he could see her eyes. "Before I can let you walk out this door, I need to know what's in your head."

Kate knew her mate was deadly serious, and knew as well that when he looked at her that way, that intensely, she could only tell him the truth. No matter how dark it was.

"Even if we get him back . . ." Her voice broke for a second. She shook it off. "Even if we get him back, I fear it will only be to lose him again."

Nicholas sighed. "You speak of Erion."

She shrugged. "I speak of his true parent, Nicky."

"Oh, baby." His hand dropped to her shoulder. He squeezed gently. "We always knew this could be a possibility. That Ladd didn't belong to—"

She didn't want to hear any more. She certainly didn't want to hear that. Not now. Not yet. She eased herself from his grasp. "I need to go. I'll be careful, and I'll be home soon."

This time when she tried to get past him, he let her.

It's unfortunate I don't sleep, Erion thought as he stood inside his bedroom—the one he'd claimed after purchasing the home. The room was mammoth, and at the very highest point of the castle. It was circular and sported floor-to-ceiling windows and a panoramic view of the forest, vineyards, and village. Thick rugs over dark hardwood blanketed the floor, and the cream inlaid fireplace, though unlit, reminded Erion of the fairy tales Dillon had told him and his brothers back when they were *balas*. An antique writing desk took up one wall of windows in the south corner, an unopened MacBook atop it, and a claw-foot bath sat in the north corner, overlooking the gardens below. But the true set piece on the stage that was his room was the four-poster bed in the very center. The incredible frame carved from one solid piece of wood, or so it seemed, was lifted several feet off the ground and sported four sumptuous black silk curtains that hung to the floor on every side but one, allowing the master of the house to take to his bed.

Or, at the moment, the mongrel.

The small brown-and-white dog had refused to leave after being fed. Anywhere Erion went, the dog trotted along behind. Just to keep himself from tripping over the tiny beast, Erion had placed him in his room, allowed him access to his bed. At least until he decided to whom to feed the beast. His mouth drifted up in a grin.

As if hearing his new master's thoughts, the dog lifted his head, cocked it to one side, and barked.

"Go back to sleep, lazy canine," Erion growled good-naturedly. "Someone should get use out of that massive thing."

The dog barked once again, then dropped its head and placed its muzzle on its paws. In seconds its eyes were closed.

Lucky beast, Erion mused as he paced in front of the unlit fire. No doubt the mattress the dog slept atop was extremely comfortable. He wouldn't know. He hadn't slept in it once. In fact, he'd never slept in a bed in his life. But the room was his; it was the best and he'd claimed it. And if he did need to rest, he would simply pull back one of the rugs and take to the floor.

The thought brought forth a memory that involved Ladd. Not long ago, the *balas* had been in his room at the Romans' house in SoHo, asking about his weapons, telling Erion of his wish to stand with the brothers and fight. Erion grinned. The boy was of his blood, most certainly. He was a robust child, persistent and ready to learn the ways of battle. Perhaps Erion could teach him. There were many good weapons to start with in the dungeon . . .

The dungeon.

Erion cut his gaze to the door. The dungeon, where he now housed a different weapon entirely.

Without forethought, he moved across the room, curled his hand around the door handle. He hesitated. The female was dangerous to him. Her scent and her secrets, and the fact that she seemed thrilled to lie beneath that monster.

His beast growled, and he gripped the door handle until his knuckles went white. Perhaps he should reverse course and take to the window, flash to New York, let his brothers know of the trade the following day. Let them know what had happened in the beach reality with Cruen.

But did he want the Romans and the *mutore* involved in his business, his dealings with Cruen at this time? His brothers would want to set a trap and capture the Pureblood *paven*. And as much as Erion wanted that bastard in a cage under guard, he couldn't risk Ladd's life.

Tomorrow, if all went according to plan and his bait was well and unharmed, he would have Ladd back. He opened his door and stepped out into the hall. Instantly his thoughts of his brothers and Cruen died. No, were drowned out. A tortuous, agonizing sound—or was it screams? He couldn't be sure—filled the air around him.

He snarled, his beast springing forth, ready. But for what, he didn't know. It was her, the female—Hellen. She cried out. She wailed. He slammed the door, keeping the mongrel inside, and tore down the hallway. His teeth ground against one another as he moved toward the pain-laced wails like a weed toward sunlight. If he found anyone touching her, hurting her, he would rip them apart. She was his—his prisoner, his bait.

His only way to Ladd.

He nearly slid down the stairs, jumped to the bottom, and took off toward the dungeon door. Hallway after hallway, he counted guards. All were stationed in their proper places, eyes forward, bodies rigid. Why had no one reported her calls to him? Were they all so terrified of her that they didn't give a shit?

Cowards had no place in his home. He would have words with them after he found out what was wrong with Hellen. Perhaps he would have fists and fangs too.

When he arrived at the dungeon door, he nearly ripped the thing off its hinges, cringing at the intense wailing that met his ears. It was like a bird, a wounded, tortured bird, and his body readied for a fight. Whoever was touching her would soon find himself without hands.

Then the scent hit him.

He staggered on the steps, gripping the railing until it nearly crumbled under his palm. His entire body shuddered. Not because the scent repelled him. Not because he didn't want to run like a starving animal toward it, breathe it in, and find the spot it emanated from with his tongue. But because he was afraid he might do far more than that.

The scent of female arousal surrounded him, infused him like a hot bath, and his cock erupted to life inside his jeans. A feral need to take what writhed and whimpered against the wall before him was unbelievably overwhelming. He'd never felt anything like it in his life—this obdurate pull to take and feed and fuck—and he didn't know if he could stop with just a taste, much less force his ass back up the stairs.

He gripped the banister until his knuckles turned white, his dilated eyes pinned on the woman he called his prisoner. Under the pale light of the torches bracketing her, Erion saw that her head hung down, her masses of fire-red curls falling in a curtain against her chest. Her white mating dress was drenched in sweat, and her captive hands were clenched into fists.

She was crying. Softly. Pitifully.

Erion's jaw clenched so tight, he was in danger of breaking a fang. *This has to be another ploy,* he thought through his haze of black desire. A trick, a ruse by his precious bait to get him to set her free. This female wasn't the leaky type. She was hard, mean, delectable, and *ahhhhh* ... his nostrils flared ... *shit* ... scented with his perfect brand of ambrosia.

A guard came running down the stairs, took one look at the female, and cursed. "Sir?"

Erion couldn't stop himself. He was jacked up on her scent, felt way too protective. Where a few minutes ago he was planning to terminate the guards for not coming to him with Hellen's cries, now he wanted them nowhere near her.

"Return to your room and don't come out," he growled softly, his throat dry. So dry ... His fangs descended. His eyes narrowed on Hellen. His mind blank, his beast screaming to emerge. She had much for him to drink; her blood, her cream ...

The guard at his left hadn't moved. Erion cocked his head at the male. Nostrils flaring, skin flushed, and a tent in his pants.

"Get the fuck out now!" he roared, rounding on him, ready to pounce if the male took one step farther into the room.

The guard jerked, seemed to wake. "I'm sorry, sir," he stammered, then turned and retreated up the steps.

Erion focused on the female again. His beast was just below the surface, but he was trying like hell to get his mind to work, to question.

"What is this?" he said, his voice sounding strangely otherworldly to his ears. "What is happening to you?"

Her head still down, she only whimpered.

Erion moved toward her, his hands curling, desperate to touch, grip, squeeze. "Answer me, woman. What is happening to you?"

What's happening to me?

Her body twitched and she groaned.

Christ. Through gritted teeth, he asked, "Are you hurt? Did someone hurt you? One of the guards—"

She lifted her head then and locked eyes with him. Erion stilled, his entire body flooding with desire. From her wild red curls to her beautiful, flushed, and sweaty face, the woman looked as though she'd been fucked good and hard and wanted more. Erion had to force himself to remain where he stood, but it was nearly impossible. Her green eyes were huge and heavy with tears—just as he imagined her cunt to be.

Suddenly, her eyes clamped shut and she tossed her head to the side, muttering something in the most pained of tones.

"What is it?" Erion said, barely able to think straight as she was casting off so much heat. "What's wrong?" Even as he spoke the words, his mind warned him to walk away, get out, in the fresh air, away from her scent.

"Help me!" she cried out. "Please help me!"

Christ. Why couldn't he make his feet move?

"Release," she hissed. "Please."

"No," he ground out. Just the word—that one word—was torture on his tongue.

Her eyes fluttered open and she found his gaze,

searching, begging him through her sexual fog. Erion saw the desperation within those green orbs, knew whatever she was feeling was real and not a ruse to gain his sympathy as he'd believed. But how could he help her? He wasn't letting her go. No matter what pain she was in, she was his ticket to Ladd.

He growled.

Why was he standing here? Why did he care if she was in pain or not? All that mattered was keeping her alive.

"I need release," she whimpered.

But alive and well. Would Cruen hold on to Ladd, harm him, if Hellen was not returned in fair health?

"You will run from me," he uttered tersely. "I cannot take that chance."

"Just my hands," she cried, her gaze dropping to her belly. "Goddamn it. Feel me. Feel where I burn."

Confused, Erion followed her line of vision. Her stomach. Was it pained? No . . . no. Lower. Her hips . . .

He froze, finally understanding her meaning. Where she hurt, why she whimpered, and why the scent of her heat, her desire was making him insane. And it was worse than her wanting to escape him. She wasn't asking to be released from her chains, but from the climax that was building inside her. His lip curled up and his fangs dropped low. What was this? Why was it happening?

Fool, he called himself as he moved closer, as he reached out and palmed her stomach. Her breath hitched and she released the most delicious of moans. Christ. She was fire-hot and coated with sweat, and his fingers, which were pointed down toward her sex, felt the blaze that raged there as well. He knew he should back the hell up and get the fuck out before he pressed himself against her, let his hands search, let his nose nuzzle her neck, his tongue lick the sweat from every inch of her skin—then put her out of her misery.

"What are you?" he demanded, releasing her belly and leaning in, placing both hands on either side of her head, sniffing her, drinking her in. "A witch? A shifter?"

She whimpered again, moaned.

"This heat you are in . . . you must be animal."

"No . . . I am Hellen," she said through gritted teeth. "Only Hellen."

"Lie," he whispered, his lungs crying out for more of her scent, his cock a column of marble against his belly.

"Just let me go," she begged. "Just for a few minutes."

"You're going to have to tell me what you are first."

"Nothing to tell."

"We're going to keep playing this game, are we?" he whispered against her cheek. "Holding back?" Whatever she was keeping from him could affect his dealings with Cruen. He wouldn't allow himself to be blindsided when the time came. No matter how badly he wanted to ease her from her bindings, get her on her back, and feel her release around the cock that strained against his zipper. He moved his thigh between her legs until he felt heat surge through the fabric of his jeans. "You'll find that holding back from me will come at a cost." Ever so gently, he nuzzled her ear, licked the shell.

She whimpered and tried to get closer, get his tongue deeper.

But Erion eased back from her face, his resolute gaze

locking with her desperate one. "Who are you?" he said again.

Her lip curled and she said, "Cruen's female."

Anger surged through him and warred with the sexual desire. Nostrils flaring, he leaned closer, his hip pressing against the apex of her thighs.

She cried out. "Damn you!"

Erion knew he'd crossed a line with her, knew he was acting like the beast who paced restlessly inside him, but he couldn't stop himself. He wanted everything from her in that moment—her origin, her species, and her sex.

He lifted his thigh, the muscle making contact with hot, yielding flesh. Shit, she was wet. His fangs dug into his bottom lip, drawing blood. "Is this what you need, Hellen?" he said, his face close to hers.

She moaned, tried to lower herself, grind her sex against his leg, but the bonds wouldn't allow it.

"Don't fret, female," he whispered near her mouth. "I'll give you what you need if you tell me who and what you are."

Her chin lifted, trying to get at his mouth, and yet she uttered a terse, "Fuck you."

He laughed softly. "My dear little witch, it is you who is crying out to be fucked. And I could be persuaded to assist you in your pain, if you tell me who you are and why the hell you're mating with that bastard."

"I've already told you," she cried out, fresh tears pricking her eyes, her hips swinging to find a lock on his thigh.

He nipped at her bottom lip, and she moaned. "You love Cruen. Do you, Hellen?"

"I am mating him."

"Not what I asked."

"If you're not going to release me or touch me, get out!"

"Shouldn't it be your mate who touches you? Shouldn't you wait for his hand to touch you . . ." He lifted his thigh another inch and growled when she moaned. "Here?" He leaned in and kissed her cheek. "What about here?" He couldn't help himself. He lapped at her neck. "And here?"

"You bastard," she whimpered. "You are the most vile creature I've ever encountered, and I've seen much that is evil."

"You haven't met Cruen, then." He eased back and found her gaze. "What. Are. You?"

For a moment, her eyes blazed emerald fire and she looked ready to bite him. Instead, she drew in a breath and spit in his face.

The thread of control Erion had been holding on to since he'd entered the dungeon snapped. He dove at her, crushed her mouth under his until she moaned, and ground her pelvis into his leg again. His tongue pushed past the barrier of her lips, and she responded instantly and sucked it into her mouth. He ripped his hands from the wall and gripped her head, raked his fingers into her curls, and kissed her hard. She was the sweetest thing he'd ever tasted, and he knew he'd never recover from what was happening between them right now, what he'd allowed. Shit, what he'd taken. He was an animal, a brute, and she was crying out for him to take her. It was all a lie, a fantasy of the worst and most delectable kind, but in that moment it didn't matter. Nothing mattered.

That one thought echoed through his mind. *Nothing matters.* Nothing matters?

Shit. What was wrong with him?

He pulled back and roared.

Her chest heaving, her eyes heavy with passion and need and ire narrowing into pinprick slits. Panting, she raged at him, a sound that held acute misery. "I fucking hate you!"

"Well, stop," he growled. "It makes your scent stronger, your body wetter, and your mouth impossible to resist."

Her body trembled and she whimpered again. "You will pay for this, you bloodsucking bastard!"

"I already am." He shook his head, rage and lust flaring, warring, inside him. "Do you think it pleases me to want to touch and taste the female who's going to mate with that worthless animal? I despise my desire for you."

"Get out!" she screamed. "Just get out and let me be!"

His jaw tight as steel, Erion turned to go. His body raged with the pain of arousal, and he prayed he could remain under the same roof as her scent without losing his mind or going after her again. He should get out, flash to New York. Or maybe he'd wait outside Raine's shop until daylight. But that would leave the female here alone, with just the guards, who could also scent her. He growled low at the thought of her allowing one of them to touch her.

He was at the bottom stair when she called him back. "Wait!"

His teeth grinding against one another, he turned slowly. "You have only to wait until tomorrow, female.

Then Cruen will take care of this little problem himself."

"I can't wait. The pain is too much . . ." Her face glistened with sweat, and shame coated her wide-eyed gaze. "Release one of my hands?"

His brow lifted.

"Please," she begged.

Erion knew exactly what she was saying, what she was asking for, and it made the blood within him rush to his cock. His skin ached, burned, it wanted her so badly. His gaze narrowed on her. He wanted to let her suffer, at least until she told him who she was.

For several seconds, he watched her whimper, watched her eyes close, and watched her suck air through her teeth. It was only when she looked up at him with tears in her eyes and a strange expression of longing that he grabbed the ring of keys from the wall and stalked toward her.

He tried to breathe through his mouth as he snarled at her. "You touch anything or anyone but yourself with that hand, and I'll cut it off."

She watched him, panting as he shoved the key in the lock of her right hand and snapped it open.

She clenched her fist, shook her wrist, then lifted her chin to glare at him.

"Leave. Now," she uttered.

Erion took a step back, but that's as far as he went. "I don't think so."

Hellen felt insanity lick the very edges of her mind. Back when her mother had first given her the cooling draft, she never would've believed her body capable of such an extreme sense of need. Intense arousal, yes. But painful, debilitating, reason-threatening, would-beg-plead-and-kill-for release kind of arousal? Never. If she had known what could happen to her, she would never have jumped from the carriage. Leaving behind not only her sisters, but the dozens of vials of draft.

She wasn't sure if she would ever recover from this. If touching herself, bringing herself to release, would slow the pain, or, gods help her, intensify it.

Perhaps the male standing before her was wondering the same thing.

Erion the brute. Erion the beast. He would remain near, watching her get herself off, while he . . . What? Would he do the same? Would he touch himself too? Or would he attack her, try to get inside her? Ruin her for her mate?

Desire flooded through her, pooled between her legs at the thought. She was truly lost to reason. And he . . .

She glared at him. "You're one sick bastard."

"Perhaps," he said, his eyes glowing with silver fire. "But that is not why I remain."

"Then why do you?"

"I will not leave you alone. Not with your scent that heady. I won't have the other males in this house watching you or feel tempted to touch you."

She sneered. "How honorable."

"Hardly," he said. "Cruen will want his female back unharmed and chaste."

A shock of heat plunged into her sex and her clit hummed. She couldn't wait any longer, not when she had access to herself, a way to ease the pain inside her. Her fingers flexed and she lowered her hand down her body until she cupped herself through the material. Confusion, panic gripped her. She couldn't do it, not this way. How was she to touch herself?

She started grabbing the fabric, yanking it up, collecting it in her fist. Her breasts tingled and her nipples tightened in anticipation. Saliva pooled in her mouth, and she didn't care about Erion anymore, didn't care that his eyes raked her or that a soft growl emanated from his throat. She was in pain and she could actually do something about it. Her hand shifted from the material to slip past the white silk band of her underwear. Her fingers shook as she met hot skin and soaking-wet heat, and her eyes drifted closed.

Her fingers slipped easily through the seam of her pussy and she wasted no time in circling the swollen ridge. She released a moan, her teeth gritted. Yes. This was good. This would help. Sweat broke out on her forehead, and she moved down the ridge for a moment, then plunged one finger inside herself. She gasped at the heat there, at the juices that flooded over her knuckle. It was too good a feeling to stop or even slow, and she kept at it, finger fucking herself until her clit screamed for attention.

In the back of her mind, she heard him, Erion, heard his breathing, his low, frightening growl, but she was too far gone now. She sensed the relief of release and she rushed toward it.

She flicked her clit, feather light, as her breasts swelled painfully and her nipples ached. She would've given anything to be naked in that moment, her hands free and able to grope and spread and squeeze. But this was enough. For now, here, it had to be enough. She clenched her muscles and thrust her fingers in and out of herself while her thumb played her clit like a violin's bow.

It was coming, her climax, reaching up from the floor to grab her and swallow her whole. And she welcomed it.

"Hellen . . ."

Shaking uncontrollably, she cried out at his call. She didn't want to see him, knew that once her eyes met his she would be weak to the desire in his own gaze. He was already in her head. In her mind, it was his hand that worked her, his mouth that sucked at her clit. Her legs threatened to lose their purchase. She didn't want him in her head. But the more she thought of him, the more her mind kept up the fantasy, the more her cunt wept.

"Look at me, Hellen."

No. No. She worked her clit harder, fucked herself deeper. Waves were crashing against her, inside her.

"Look at me, damn you!"

Her eyes slammed open, and the moment they did, the moment she connected with his face, she came. Hard, shattering blows of pleasure seized her cunt, and she doubled over. Her lips parted, and she may have uttered his name as she screamed.

"Yes, Hellen," he whispered, his voice racked with desire and pain and deep frustration. "Oh, gods, yes. You are . . . shit, the most beautiful thing I've ever seen."

She gasped, air caught inside her lungs and she convulsed with the final torrents of climax. She sagged against the wall, reveled in the relief of a satiated body. For moments, minutes, she hung there limp and weak, her breathing slowly returning to normal, her body temperature regulating.

And then she saw him. Really saw him. For the first time.

Erion.

A few feet away and pulling in air through his flared nostrils stood a beast. Erion had always been a good-looking male, but in that moment, as his diamond eyes glowed and his face contorted into a lionlike creature, she realized why she felt so drawn to him—why he made every inch of her spark with desire. He was like her, like her kind.

"You . . ." she uttered, wetting her dry lips.

His gaze reached into her own and pulled out her very soul.

"You are a demon, Erion."

His eyes raked over her. "As are you."

8

The words, the confirmation, had come out of Erion's mouth without his consent. It was as if the beast inside him had spoken. But what beast was that? He knew what his sister and brothers' *mutore* sides represented. Lycos had the wolf, Helo the water snake, Phane the hawk, and Dillon the jaguar. But Erion, though he had some catlike features during his shift, was no feline. In all his long days, he had never known what he was—besides vampire and a descendant of the Breeding Male.

Until now?

His gaze narrowed on the female. Whatever he had seen in her as she'd climaxed, the change in skin color to a pale green, the ethereal glow from inside her, the electric jade eyes, was nothing compared to what he'd felt from her. The demon, her demon, had called out to him, and he'd wanted to run at it, jump inside her skin, and get lost in that strange though familiar power. It was as if he'd been branded. Her demon wanted to take and contain the part of him that understood, that connected, that desired it.

Christ, none of this made sense. He didn't know his history, and clearly he didn't know his DNA. He was *mutore*, a descendent of the Breeding Male gone wrong. He knew that Cruen had created the Breeding Male and that he had added in some animal DNA during the process.

But demon?

Was that even possible?

Hellen was staring at him, her face flushed, her eyes wide and glassy, her demon now hidden from view.

Erion wanted it back.

"You said you were a vampire," she uttered, shaking her head.

"I am."

"You have demon blood. How is that possible?"

"I know nothing of demons."

"I do. I am one," she said, straightening up, coming back to life from her haze of need. "You wanted to know what I am—well, now you do. And what came out of you just now, that is demon."

As her gaze roamed his face, Erion wondered if she'd liked or despised what she'd seen come out of him. "I have no answers," he said. Then added with more than a touch of derision, "I'll have to ask my adopted father."

"Who is that?"

"Cruen."

Shock registered on her face. And if he wasn't mistaken, fear. "What?"

"The male who raised me, fed me, clothed me, and

ultimately betrayed me is none other than your soon-to-be mate." The words were bitter on his tongue.

He watched her process, watched her confusion—watched her pretty brow crease with concern.

"How did he betray you?" she asked in a soft voice.

Erion hesitated, feeling grim. Cruen had betrayed him in so many ways, but keeping his true identity, his lineage, from him was the worst yet. But it wasn't something he was willing to share.

"That is my secret," he said tightly.

She watched him closely. "I knew I wasn't the only one who kept them."

"Yes, but yours is a secret no longer, demon girl."

"Which means you will release me."

He forced his bleak mood back and he moved toward her. Cruen would not have control over him anymore, not in body or in temper. "I know what you are now, but I don't know where you come from, why you've come—"

"You know why I've come, Erion." Her gaze flickered away from his for a moment.

"I don't think I do. You are too special, too exquisite to have given yourself to that manipulative, heartless, soulless vampire." He shook his head. His words, the compliment to her being, had been impetuous. And yet it was true. She was an intriguing female, and beneath her needles-and-pins exterior, lay something glorious and fiery—something he'd never experienced in any female he'd encountered. There had to be more to her engagement to Cruen than a forced claim of love.

He came to stand before her and made great effort to soften his tone. "Are you in trouble, Hellen?"

As an answer, a pained whimper escaped her. She clutched her stomach. "No," she whispered, her face scrunching up as she turned her head to the side.

Concerned, Erion reached out to touch her, but she flinched and drew back. "What is it?" he said. But just as the word exited his mouth and he inhaled the scent around him, he knew what made her moan.

"It's returning." He brushed a hand across her cheek. "This strange, problematic heat."

She turned her eyes on him, and they glittered like polished gems. Another wave of arousal tantalized his nostrils and he breathed it in and swallowed it down. What the hell had he found himself caught up in? This was supposed to have been a simple transaction: the female for the boy. It was turning out to be anything but simple. In fact, it was impossible and startling—and a potential key to his DNA, who he truly was.

She leaned in to his hand, and heat surged into his palm. He wanted to devour it. He asked, "Why is this happening to you?"

"Genetics," she uttered, pulling in her air through her nostrils. "I was born with an unfortunate destiny."

"What destiny?" he asked, knowing this was foolish, this closeness, this care. She was his bait, his ticket to Ladd. Nothing more. And yet he couldn't stop himself from asking. He couldn't turn away. "Have you had this problem, this heat, since birth?" His hand refused to draw back from her face, her skin. Her warmth.

"It happened when I shifted from girl to woman." Her gaze held his. "But I've kept it under control for a long time."

"How?"

She shook her head. "No more," she begged, her nostrils flaring. "I must get to Cruen."

As she stared into his eyes and silently implored him, Erion's chest tightened. The struggle within him to protect her, touch her, hold her, breathe her in, warred with the cruel understanding that she was his currency. She didn't belong to him. It wasn't his duty to help her. Cruen would ease her torment, ease the heat that was once again spreading through her like wildfire.

Erion's nostrils flared, and he ripped his hand from her cheek with a growl.

Just the thought of Cruen touching this female made him involuntarily irrational, made him murderous, and yet he couldn't act on those possessive thoughts in his head because if he did, he would be risking the life of the *balas*.

And that he would never do.

"Just a few hours, now," he said, moving back, away from her, away from her scent. "You will be in the arms of your lover."

When the sadness bled from her emerald gaze like paint in the rain, and was replaced with hope, Erion wanted to shove his fist through the wall behind her and roar.

But instead he turned around and headed for the stairs, leaving her to care for herself again.

This time, without an audience.

Cruen watched them, the demon females play with the *balas*, Ladd. They were taking turns teaching him a game

Cruen did not know, but the boy's laughter irritated him. It spoke of a brave, fearless heart. Much like his father's. And right now, that kind of internal strength made Cruen feel even weaker.

It reminded him of Titus. That washed-up Breeding Male who'd used him, used his blood, relied on him until he'd decided to abandon his goal, his work, and go soft. Helping the Roman brothers, pretending to be the father they'd always desired, when in truth he was perpetually clinging to the edge of Breeding Male status.

Where was that *paven*? Cruen wondered with displeasure. Where had he run to when the well had dried up? Was he a Breeding Male once again? Or was he being cared for by his children?

One of the females looked up from her game with the *balas* and gave him a tentative, worried smile. Cruen had assured them both that their sister would be coming home—that he'd located her and was soon to retrieve her.

What he did not tell them was that he needed to rest first. It was why he'd told Erion twenty-four hours instead of immediately. He was too weak to flash. His lip curled. He despised weakness.

One of the demon females stilled suddenly, confusion creasing her features. Then her eyes clamped shut and her lips started to move. Cruen leaned forward in his chair, nervous tension flickering to life within him. He didn't know what was wrong with her, but whatever it was, it didn't look good. Her body jerked, spasmed, and her sister gripped her arm and called her name.

Cruen fought his fear, his ire again. He couldn't have

one of Abbadon's children hurt or falling ill in his care. It was enough that the Demon King's eldest, and Cruen's bride, was missing.

As quickly as the episode had come on, it retreated. The female's eyes opened and she seemed to relax. Cruen did as well, leaning back in his chair. That was until she looked up at him, her expression a mask of terror.

Cruen arched a hand over the glass and it disappeared. The action cost him big, but he knew there was no choice. He dropped back in his chair and sucked in a breath.

"What is it?" he called out in a hoarse voice.

"My father," the female called up to him. "He has just spoken to me inside my mind."

Cruen felt the blood drain from his face.

"And what does he say, female?" he ground out, utterly exhausted.

But he knew. Even before he asked and even before the female's words lifted up to scratch at his wounds.

"He knows Hellen is missing," she said, her gaze retreating. Not to her sister, but to the *balas*. "He is coming."

Quiver at her back, bow at the ready, Hellen ran through the Rain Fields, her bare feet pounding the ground, her vision acute, her heart determined. She was shooting at the rogues. One kill, two, three, four—ha! She wouldn't stop until they were all dead.

An arrow shot past her ear and she grinned, motioned for the one who ran just behind her to catch up. The male had missed his target, and growled his irritation as he ran beside her. Clouds rolled in at knee level, but they barreled through the moist puffs, kept pace as the male tracked, a fresh arrow in his fist, the rogue that had gotten away.

Hellen reveled in the male's company. He was a fine hunter, and they moved well together; a true partnership. And, hell, he wasn't bad to look at either.

In one fluid movement, he dropped to one knee, narrowed his gaze, and stretched his bow, flexing his impressive muscles. The arrow released, and the squeal and pop of death curled into the air.

Hellen grinned at him.

Erion grinned back. "Another round?" he asked, excitement, thrill in his tone.

Her body hummed. He was so handsome, so impassioned, his black hair falling to his naked shoulders, his diamond eyes piercing into her, his full mouth ready and willing to possess hers.

"We have hunted for more than an hour," she said in a teasing voice. "Are you sure you have more to give?"

His eyebrow lifted. "Do you challenge my stamina, demon girl?"

She laughed. She loved when he called her that. She grabbed his bow and tossed it into the Fields. Hot rain broke from the low clouds, instantly soaking them from the hips down. Hellen flashed him her demon and pushed him up against a nearby tree. He staggered back, growled at her, then grabbed her ass and lifted her to his waist. Hellen wrapped her legs around him and squeezed, then dipped her head and kissed him.

She moaned against his lips. He tasted of the Under-world, spice and heat and wickedness. Her hands wrapped around his neck, delved into his midnight-black hair, and fisted. There was a low rumble in his chest and he yanked her closer, his tongue plunging into her mouth. It wasn't a simple kiss or even a passionate one. It was survival, not being able to breathe or function unless they consumed each other's essence.

His hands dipped under her shirt, cool fingers raked up her back, and she rocked her hips against his.

"Shit! You're burning up." His voice sounded faraway instead of a few inches from her ear.

"Don't stop, Erion," she murmured, gripping him tighter. "We're just getting started. I need you."

There was another curse. "Wake up, Hellen. Wake up now before my entire household descends on this dungeon and feasts on you."

She came out of the dream on a gasp. Sweaty and confused, she opened her eyes to both the pain of desire and the face of the male who'd just held her close and kissed her fiercely.

It was a dream, demon girl, she told herself, trying to push the fog from her brain. Oh, gods, she was weakening—every inch of her, including her mind, which was conjuring up fantasies, insanities.

"What are you doing?" she said, realizing he wasn't standing in front of her anymore, watching her, studying her as he normally did.

He was at her side, keys out. One already in the lock at her left wrist.

"You're being released."

"It's time?" she said, her tone rising with happiness. "I'm going to Cruen now?"

"Your anticipatory glee disgusts me as much as it astounds me," he ground out against the click of the lock. "Perhaps save it for your mate."

She didn't care if he was angry. She was so relieved that there was an end in sight for her misery. She would have her draft soon, she would see her sisters and finish this bargain once and for all. She rubbed her wrists as he dropped down and swiftly took care of the shackles on her ankles. Her destiny would be realized, Polly and Levia would be safe, and she would never have to know or access or deny the ultimate power of being her father's firstborn.

"Hey!" she called out as Erion stood and gathered her up in his arms. "I'm capable of walking."

"You've had your limbs caged. I'm sure you're weak."

She tried not to think about how good his chest felt against her side. "My limbs were caged because of you."

He nodded. "Exactly. It is only right that I care for you as punishment for my crimes."

His crimes. Was he actually trying to make nice here? Humor and chivalry? "That's really sweet and obnoxious and all, but I'm not weak, Erion. I don't get weak." *My beloved and protective mother saw to that early on.*

Erion chuckled softly as he carried her up the stairs. "Doesn't scent that way to me."

"That's a different kind of weakness," she clarified.

"Yes, it is, but I cannot assist you in taming that heat," he said, shifting her in his arms, pulling her closer. "So this will have to do."

"So, I'm a demon in distress."

"Stop being ornery and just relax. Enjoy the ride."

The ride. His words brought back the dream she'd just had. Him against the tree, her straddling his waist.

As she'd revisited that foolish fantasy, she hadn't been noticing where they were going. Or where they weren't. Not outside as she'd assumed, but up several flights of stairs.

Her hot skin prickled and her muscles tensed. "Where are we going?"

"I asked you to relax."

"You said it was time."

"No, *you* said it was time. I said I was releasing you." He reached the top of the staircase, breathing easily as if he carried nothing at all. "Before we go we need to clean you up a bit. Don't want your lover seeing you like this, do you?"

"Like what?" she said, suddenly indignant.

"Ravished."

"I wasn't ravished."

"Yes, you were. I saw it with my own eyes." His voice dropped to a ragged, husky whisper. "Don't think I'll ever forget it."

She didn't speak. Couldn't. It was one thing to push against the need, the heat, the desire snaking through her system, but having Erion remind her what had happened in the dungeon—what he had witnessed, what his eyes and mouth and skin had looked like when she'd claimed her orgasm, was something else entirely. It not only inflamed the already debilitating heat, but it made her yearn for something she should never want.

She just had to keep reminding herself that soon she'd be with Cruen, soon the draft would cleave to her veins, cooling her blood and making her rational once again.

"It wouldn't help either of our causes if you met him looking like a woman of the streets," Erion continued, stopping before a heavy wood door.

"I don't know what a woman of the street is," she said as he carried her inside a large, well-lit room. "But I don't think I like the sound of it. I'm sure I look decently presentable—"

She stopped speaking because he'd crossed the room and placed her in front of a mirror. Her sisters used mirrors in the Underworld, but Hellen never had. It had always seemed like a waste of time and, frankly, just another reason to feel bad about her appearance. *Kind of like now,* she mused, her eyes moving from foot to face in a slow progression.

"Oh. My."

Erion grunted. "Indeed."

She whirled on him, the vision of her wild hair; tear-soaked face; and dirty, wrinkled gown still weighty in her mind. "Let us not forget whose fault it is that I look so improper and so . . . ugly."

The violent look that crossed his features made her heart stutter, and she drew back.

"Call yourself that again and you will be back in chains," he said. "Do you understand me?"

She gaped at him, stunned at his words, his passion.

"You need a bath, yes," he continued, "your hair combed, and a new gown, but your beauty is irrefutable and not to be insulted."

Hellen had said but minutes ago how weakness was not a part of her person. She had been schooled by her mother to not only never show weakness, but to smile in the face of fear. That advice had served her well in the Underworld. It had kept her clearheaded and brave when dealing with her father, while allowing her to look at her future without resentment. But this male and his impassioned opinion regarding her appearance was not something she could smile at or write off. Perhaps because instead of making her feel weak, his words filled her with a strange new sense of strength.

She caught his gaze, resolute yet concerned, and knew it was vital that she get to Cruen as quickly as possible. This demon bloodsucker who kept her prisoner, scolded her for self-flagellation, looked at her as though he'd never seen anything so intriguing or so desirable, could be her downfall if she allowed him to be.

If given the opportunity, he could do great damage to the house of cards she'd built. He could have the power to make her see herself differently, change her opinion of herself. Want for more than she believed she deserved.

"We don't have much time," he said, yanking her from her thoughts as he walked over to a white oval structure that stood about five feet off the ground. "I have had this drawn for you."

Hellen stared at the oval and at the steam that rose from its center. It was filled with hot water. "What is it?"

"You're not serious."

She looked up at him blankly.

His mouth lifted at the corners. "It's a bath. For washing."

She shook her head. "I've never seen such a thing before."

Erion looked amazed. "How do you clean yourself in the ... ?"

"Underworld," she provided, then shrugged. "We have rain, hot rain, and a fragrant flower that grows and provides us with a powder to wash with. It's all we need."

"The Underworld," he repeated, looking thoughtful. "That's where the coach emerged from, and the horses, their skin as thin as paper. That is where you live?"

Hellen felt a bite of pain near her heart. "Where I used to live," she corrected. "This is my world now."

His gaze narrowed and his nostrils flared. "You should wash while the water is heated." He gestured to her. "Remove your dress."

Her eyes shot to his. "No."

"You cannot bathe with clothes on."

She lifted her chin. "Then perhaps I will not bathe at all."

His fangs dropped all the way, and as they stared at each other, the room seemed to grow very dim, as if the sun were afraid to emerge.

"If you do not wash yourself," he said in a soft, deadly voice, "I will be forced to do it for you."

Fear and heat fused inside her. "Do you enjoy humiliating me?"

His jaw tightened, but his eyes held no ire. "No."

"Then why this brutish, caustic, egotistical way of yours? The inappropriate demands?"

He stepped toward her, invading her space. "I only

want what's mine returned, and I will do whatever it takes to make sure that happens without incident."

Her hands went to her hips. "Cruen will be fine just to have me returned."

"I will not risk it."

"You will not risk your treasure!"

"No, I will not!"

Hellen bit her lip, bit back the wave of heat that was assaulting her. His treasure. What was it? Who was it? And why did it make her hurt and angry and jealous that it meant so damn much to him?

"If you want to see your beloved today or ever again," he said with quiet vehemence, "you will do as I say." He nodded at her feet. "Shoes first, then stockings, then your dress."

Hellen fought with the idea of telling him to fuck off, telling him she wasn't about to get naked in front of him—that if he wanted her clothes removed, he was just going to have to do it himself. But she knew her words meant nothing and her threats gave him permission.

Gods, she needed to go home. She needed her draft. She needed to seal this bargain with Cruen. And this was her chance—probably her only chance. Lest she forget, Erion had seen her touch herself, cry out in orgasm. What was a few feet of skin compared to that humiliation?

She hissed but began to undress. First she toed off her shoes, then tossed them over her shoulder. A canine yelp sounded, and she glanced over to the bed where the mongrel slept. Her shoe now lodged in his mouth, the little beast jumped from the bed and tore across the room and out the door.

"The canine is still here?" she said, staring at the open door, her feet bare.

"He refuses to leave me."

She turned back to face him. "Perhaps you do have a soft heart beneath all of that battle armor, Erion."

"No, demon girl," he said. "Never be foolish enough to believe that."

Hellen looked at him curiously, but he wouldn't allow her to study him. He pointed to her feet. "Stockings, please. We waste time."

She heaved a breath, pulled off one stocking, then the other, and deposited them in a little pile on the rug.

"Now the dress," he said.

This was madness, and yet what choice did she have? She gave him an impertinent glare. "I need help with the laces."

He made a circle with his index finger. "Turn around."

"You are getting entirely too much pleasure from bossing me around," she said, giving him her back.

Pleasure.

Erion growled softly. Pleasure was the last thing he was feeling in that moment. Pain, frustration, desperation, concern, desire . . . nothing even remotely close to pleasure.

He came to stand behind her and tried like hell not to breathe her in, but it was impossible. His lungs had tasted her scent in the dungeon and ached for more, ached for their fix. His nostrils flared and he pulled her in. *Ahhhhh . . .* Her scent was intense, intoxicating, and the heat poured off her body in waves. He wondered if it had been wise to draw her a hot bath. Perhaps cool water was needed to soothe her skin.

She was nape to waist laces, and he made quick work of them, easing them out two at a time with his index fingers until her back was exposed. Erion hated Cruen more every second, every pale, smooth inch that was exposed to his greedy gaze. But though his hands itched to touch her, encircle her waist, rake up her stomach and ribs until he captured her breasts, she wasn't his prize to claim.

His cock strained against his zipper and he forced himself to remember what they were doing in his room. Getting her clean, getting her perfect for the one who held Ladd.

She stepped away from him then, turned, and held the bodice of her dress to her breasts. "You can go."

"No." He was foolish, reckless, but unable to deny himself.

"Dammit, demon! My body is not for your eyes."

"I know perfectly well who your skin belongs to," he ground out. "But I won't allow you the chance to escape."

She looked nonplussed. "Why would I escape now? You are bringing me to Cruen."

His head cocked to one side and he had to force himself to remain still. "I wouldn't dare to guess what goes on in your brain, female. What games you play, what tricks you pull. Now remove the gown. We don't want to be late."

Her cheeks flushed. "You are acting like an animal."

"I believe I am acting like a demon."

Her jaw went tight and Erion wondered if she would fight him on this—and how he would respond if she did. But just as he took his next breath, she lifted her hands and let the gown fall. Perhaps it pooled at her feet, a great puff of white. Erion didn't know. He didn't care. His eyes were nowhere near the floor. They were wide and hungry and feasting on every inch of her creamy white skin. He'd suspected she was utter perfection beneath her gown, and he'd been right. Her legs were long, her hips round and ripe for a male's hands to grip and guide toward his own. Her waist was small and flared upward to a set of the most beautiful, mouthwatering breasts he'd ever beheld.

His hands no longer itched at his sides.

Now they ached.

"All of it, demon girl," he said quietly.

He heard her swallow and take a quick, nervous breath as she hooked her fingers in the waistband of her white silk underwear and eased them down over her luscious hips. The moment she stepped out of them and stood before him completely and gloriously naked, Erion lost his mind. He turned and roared, stalked toward the open bedroom door, and slammed it shut with a bone-clattering bang that was meant as a grave warning to all who dwelled within his castle.

Come near this room and die.

When he rounded on her again, Hellen was standing there, staring at him, tall and beautiful, her chest rising and falling, her nipples beading in the cool air.

"What now?" she asked.

His jaw clamped shut, his molars grinding with frustration. He chastised himself. *You did this, foolish male. You brought her here, made her undress, and now you can barely breathe for wanting her. Remember your purpose—remember her purpose.* He had to get her clean, had to deliver her to Cruen just as he'd found her, as he'd taken her. Unharmed, untouched.

"In the water," he growled. *Now. Before I bend you over the side of my bed and finally make use of it.*

She gripped the side of the tub and stepped in. Her hiss as skin met hot water drove blood to his groin and heightened his foul mood.

"Sit down," he demanded.

"No."

His gaze ripped to her and narrowed. "Why not?"

She stood there, a goddess, a demon goddess in white skin and flaming curls both on her head and between her legs. Erion licked his lips.

"I don't like the feeling of sitting in water," she said. "I won't."

"You are trying to be a pain in my ass," he growled, crossing the room and grabbing a small towel and a bar of soap from the table beside the bathtub. He knelt down and plunged the washrag into the water, scrubbed it with the soap until he created a substantial lather, then uttered the terse command, "Don't move."

Her hands fisted at her sides, but she stilled, remained silent as he reached down and dragged the hot, soapy cloth over her calves, then behind her knees. When he moved up her thighs, avoiding the red curls that called to him like a lover, she gasped and his cock pressed hard against his zipper. She was so close, heat surging from every pore of her skin and entering the atmosphere around them. He gritted his teeth against the growl of desire that wanted to escape his lungs and throat. He wanted to go slow, hours if he could manage it, explore every inch, let the cloth be his excuse to know her. Shit, this was madness. Though his nostrils were heavy with her scent and his tongue ached to be heavy with her cream, he forced himself to remain on task.

That is, until the rag brushed against her belly and she moaned deep and pained and sensually, and she stepped wider apart, granting him a perfect view of her pink pussy lips.

He fisted the wet rag and cursed blackly, violently.

"I am holding as still as I can," she said, mistaking his desire for irritation. "You are rough. I can't help shifting to keep my balance."

His eyes lifted to meet hers, and he knew they were pitch-black and untamed. "Your scent makes me insane."

"Your scent does the same to me," she said, her breathing gently labored, her skin flushed.

Erion watched as one lone teardrop of sweat fell from her forehead onto her cheek. He licked his lips. The bead continued to move over her jaw, down her neck and collarbone, until it rose and fell over her nipple. His throat was so dry. That bead of sweat would quench his thirst; he was certain of it. It continued, building speed as it trailed down one side of her ribs, made a gentle left near her navel, then dropped, disappeared, into the arousal-soaked curls of her sex.

Erion cast the washcloth into the tub and brought his hands around her hips to cup her backside.

"I need it, Hellen," he groaned, filling his palms with hot, plush skin. "I need to taste you, bury my tongue inside you." He looked up, flashed her his fangs. "Just once."

She stared down at him, her mind working, desire and panic and uncontained heat making her limbs tremble. "You won't hurt me?"

"Never," he said passionately. He couldn't. He knew that weakness within himself now. He could contain her, quarrel with her, desire her, and miss her, but he could never harm her.

Her eyes darkened and she raked her teeth over her bottom lip. "Then wash me, Erion," she breathed, her eyes mirroring his desperation. "Use your tongue and lick me clean."

It was all he needed.

His hands left her soft, taut backside and came around to where she truly ached. He spread her open with his thumbs. Pink, so damn pink. Saliva pooled in his mouth and he growled at the wetness leaking from her cunt. He'd never been so hungry, so desperate to taste anything in his life.

"Erion, please," she begged, her knees flexing slightly.

He leaned forward and licked her. The honey that met his tongue made his cock pulse, while the scent of her unrelenting heat made the tip bead with come.

"You are so beautiful, demon girl," he whispered. "So hot I'm desperate to get burned. So wet I want to drown."

His tongue lapped at her again, tended to both sides of the hard, swollen ridge before coming home to her clit. He circled the hot, tight pearl until her moans reached a fevered pitch. Then he eased back and looked up at her.

"Touch your breasts, Hellen," he commanded as he pressed a finger inside her and stroked the tight velvet passageway of her sex. "I want to see you squeeze your nipples as I suckle your clit."

"Oh, gods," she moaned, grasping her breasts as her hips swung forward and back.

Erion eased another finger inside her cunt and fire-hot juices spilled around both his digits. *Shit, I'm going to come just from touching her,* he thought, as he watched her release her breasts and pinch and flick her nipples.

"Please, Erion," she begged as the room filled with the luscious scent of her heat. "Please. I need to come. Right now, before I lose my mind. Please."

Erion would never admit to it later, but in that moment, Hellen owned him. Her scent had taken up residence in his lungs, her moans directed the swell of his cock, and her pussy possessed his tongue. He eased his fingers from her tender cunt, spread her lips as wide as he could manage, and suckled her. Her clit instantly swelled in his mouth and he couldn't help himself: his fangs elongated and they bracketed the hot bud. Just those tiny pinpricks combined with the rhythmic sucking of her clit made Hellen cry out. But it was no ordinary cry of pleasure. It was a scream, a sound so high-pitched, so otherworldly, the glass in the mirror by the bed moaned, then shattered.

The violent crash made Erion growl against her flesh, made him so deviantly hungry he slid his mouth all over her, dipping his tongue inside her, pressing his fangs closer, suckling her swollen clit until her legs shook, her back arched, and she came hard and uncontrolled.

For several moments, she rocked her cunt back and forth against his tongue, his mouth, his wet jaw, until her breathing began to slow and her moans turned to whimpers. And then she pulled back from him, sighed, and sat down in the water.

Erion stared at her, watched as she picked up the soap and the cloth he'd discarded and began to wash herself in earnest. Confusion commingled with the intensity of his desire and the raging hard-on in his jeans. She was in the water. Sitting in the water. She'd said . . . She'd said she wouldn't sit in the water, wouldn't wash herself . . . She'd forced his hand . . . She'd made it so he would have to—

His gaze narrowed and he growled, his anger another being in the room. "You lied to me."

"Yes." She sounded calm, clearheaded.

"You lied to me so I would touch you, lick you, get you off."

She looked over at him, her red hair a mass of wild curls, her cheeks stained with pink from her climax, and her green demon eyes a little glassy. "It wouldn't do to have me arrive sexually charged. Cruen might suspect something happened between us."

Erion couldn't believe what he was hearing—what he was seeing.

"You could've touched yourself," he snarled, coming

to his feet. His fucking cock was like granite. "You didn't need me!"

"Yes, I could have," she said coolly, then shrugged. "But you wanted to, and I wanted you to."

He pointed at her. "Shut up!"

"Don't be angry. Think about it. If he suspected you touched me, he wouldn't give you what you're after." She gave him a tight-lipped smile. "It wouldn't have helped either of our causes. Now, would it?"

Erion's nostrils flared and he slowly backed up, his hands fisted. "You are a . . . a . . . DEMON!" he roared.

"Yes."

And with that, she slipped down beneath the water.

9

Night bled into the last seconds of daylight as Kate watched the four members of the Impure Resistance try once again to break into Cruen's mental communication link. Gray, Piper, Rio, and Vincent had managed this feat with the Order not long ago, using their combined mental gifts to hack into the ten vampires' telepathic mainframe to gain information. But for some reason, Cruen was proving a difficult subject.

They'd been at it for hours, first inside their compound, then on the beach near the water. The newly constructed Impure *credenti* was situated near the Atlantic Ocean and housed not just the Resistance members, but Impures who wanted to gain leadership roles within the new vampire ruling structure.

Kate hadn't come looking for a new home, but to find and bring her fostered *balas* back home, where he belonged.

"I'm sorry." Gray glanced over his shoulder, his eyes pale steel under the light of the moon. The leader of the

Resistance, and Sara's brother, stood shoulder to shoulder in a tight circle with his allies. "We can't locate him. We hear rumblings, static, like someone talking on a cell phone, but locking on isn't possible."

Vincent, the dark-skinned Impure who was all broad shoulders and masculine swagger, gave her a grim smile. "We'll try again, *veana*."

"Absolutely," Gray confirmed. "This continued and dangerous break with sanity will not go unchallenged."

"To take a *balas*," said Piper caustically. The third member of the Resistance opened her eyes and sighed. "He is a true monster."

"We shouldn't be surprised. He has committed atrocities for ages," Riordan James added, his dark, narrowed gaze hitting each of them in turn. He moved out of the circle with the natural grace of a military killer. "Another sin to add to the list. Another sin we will be sure to remind him of when we strip him of skin and make him scream."

A wave of grief moved over Kate, and she turned away from the group and walked down to the water's edge. She understood Rio's violent words. She felt them herself. But the idea of making Cruen pay didn't soothe her. It only made her fearful, made her miss Ladd more. Made her desperate to have the *balas* safely back in her arms.

The gentle waves licked at her bare feet, the cold water making her shiver.

"I met a very insistent Nicholas Roman at the gate."

She turned to see Dillon, Gray's Pureblood mate and the first *mutore* she had ever met, come to stand beside her. The newest member of the Order shrugged with feline grace. "I wasn't in a position to stop him. You know *paven*s and their mates. Even with my jaguar out and growling, your true mate would not be denied access."

"Damn right." Nicholas moved to the other side of Kate and took her hand.

Though his palm felt good against her own, safe and warm, Kate pushed back against the feeling of being cared for.

"If you've come to take me home ..." she began coolly. She wasn't ready to leave. She'd already met with two of her acquaintances from Mondrar, paid them well to dig, find out anything they could from within their circle. Now she would remain here, watch as the Resistance attempted once again to find Cruen. And again. However long it took.

"We're not going home, *veana*." Nicholas lifted her hand and kissed it, his eyes locking on to hers. "We're going to see Erion."

Kate gasped, hope surging as she rounded on her mate. "Did he find Ladd? Does he have him?"

The light in Nicholas's eyes dimmed as he took her other hand. "Not yet. But I think he knows something he's not telling us. I want to find out what that is." He lifted one dark eyebrow. "You in?"

Kate tried not to feel the heaviness of disappointment, the unending scratches of fear on her unbeating heart. Nicholas was trying so hard to help her, to help Ladd—they all were. And maybe Erion did know something. He'd been so secretive.

But leaving the Resistance. Would they continue? Would they push as hard to get through Cruen's impressive mental bindings if she wasn't there standing over them?

"We'll keep trying, Kate," Gray said behind her.

She glanced over her shoulder to find Gray once again shoulder to shoulder in a tight circle with the members of the Resistance. She'd forgotten the brave Impure male could hear the thoughts of all but his true mate.

"Promise?" she said, looking at each one of them in turn.

Rio clipped a nod; Vincent and Piper too.

"Every hour," Gray said, then turned to Dillon and smiled gently. "And my kitty cat here will return to the Order and dig deep while we do."

Dillon growled and flashed her jaguar. "They all fear my beast. I will put it to good use."

Though she felt less than confident about leaving, Kate nodded, then wrapped her arms around Nicholas and whispered, "Let's go."

Cruen stood on the balcony overlooking the desert and attempted to access his balance, his power, but he had nothing in reserve. The male who stood beside him, who had entered the compound in a flurry of green robes and overt condescension, was in his most human form, but that didn't fool Cruen into thinking the male was weak. Cruen knew what this male was, what he was capable of when he was angry or felt betrayed, thwarted, or threatened.

Or when his daughter was missing.

"She never arrived, Abbadon." He despised the curl of fear in his own voice.

"Unfortunate." The Demon King spoke with deadly calm.

"This is not my doing," Cruen said, turning his head but not looking directly into Abbadon's eyes. He knew what lurked there, knew it could make even the bravest of males lose their bowel functions.

"And what have you done to recover her, Cruen?"

"I have searched, both in my mind and on foot." He spoke too quickly.

Abbadon glanced around himself with an expression of false confusion. "Yet she is not here."

"I will get her back," Cruen ground out.

The Demon King made a soft grunt, like someone who was applying little effort in cutting off the airway of an enemy. "You know where she is?"

Sudden exhaustion blanketed Cruen and he gripped the railing. "I know who has her." What an unfortunate turn of events. Not at all what Cruen had planned, had hoped for. Erion had better come through, or it was going to be a bloodbath for all.

Abbadon's inhuman snarl slapped him out of his reverie. "You know where my daughter is, and yet you are still standing here." The male ran his forked tongue over his dry lips. "Perhaps I have chosen foolishly. Perhaps you are not the one who will bring about my heir, my foothold on this Earth."

"I am the one," Cruen said with as much aplomb as he could manage.

Abbadon's nostrils flared. "I wish to all that is evil that

I could create this child myself, that my bitch of a mate hadn't tricked me with her pleasing tongue and rendered me vacant of seed."

"Truly, there is no one more fit for this task than I. But . . ."

That last word had Abbadon changing, growing, morphing into his most demonic state.

There was nothing Cruen could do about it, nowhere he could go. He couldn't flash, which meant he couldn't get to Erion. His gaze traveled the length of the scaly, red-faced, and terrifying Demon King.

"I regret to say I need your assistance. Again."

Nervous energy rolled through Hellen as she stepped inside the furnishings shop that would soon contain her fiancé. She wasn't afraid of Cruen, of seeing him and binding herself to him—no, that she counted on, that she was glad for, because it would bring her the draft and it would save her sisters from a future of handpicked males and hell-born children. What made her nervous was her appearance. She was bathed, combed and presentable, but dressed in new, modern clothing that Erion had procured for her. They were similar to his own jeans and sweater though tighter fitting.

Will Cruen accept me this way? she wondered. *Question why I no longer wear my wedding gown?* She couldn't afford to have him reject her.

Erion stalked forward, leaving her near a mustard-colored chaise. The male had barely glanced her way since the bathtub incident. Not to give her the clothes, not even when he'd escorted her here. His eyes refused to connect. It was clear he hated her for deceiving him, for making a fool out of him. And she didn't blame him.

She watched him move to the counter, inspect a few items, then slam his hand down on a small brass bell. He'd thought she'd used him just to ease the continual heat that raged inside her. She reached out and touched the top of the chaise, so cool under her hand. Maybe she had, but not in the way he was thinking. Not as a power play, not to shame him for wanting her. She'd manipulated him slightly because she'd wanted his touch—believed that he wouldn't give in to what they both desired without that ruse regarding the water. The truth was that she was inexplicably attracted to him, had been from the first moment he'd touched her. She couldn't help herself, her mind, from wondering what it would feel like to belong to such a male as this one. Brutally handsome, savagely loyal, with a touch that burned and cooled and soothed and possessed.

But she would never know. Beyond one moment of sexual bliss. She was destined for Cruen. She was destined for a life without love, without true passion, heat, fire, or lust. Erion was appalled and offended by what she had done, but, truly, could she be faulted for constructing a moment where she got to experience all those glorious feelings at once?

"You're late."

Hellen heard the voice before she saw the male it belonged to. The curtain behind Erion rustled, and a strange man appeared. He was short and meek, but he didn't seem human. Although he certainly didn't come across as vampire either.

"Where is he, Raine?" Erion said, his tone thick with impatience. "I'm more than ready to return this package to its rightful owner."

When the strange male glanced her way, Hellen tried not to show her melancholy at Erion's words and frigid tone. Frankly, it was better that he treated her like the ashes of the Underworld. If he didn't, if he showed her his care again, his demon side, or his untamed desire in those rare diamond eyes, it would be harder to walk away and do what must be done.

"I don't know," the male told Erion. "He should be here by now."

"That *paven* can never be trusted." Erion turned those diamond eyes on Hellen, and they were hard as stone. "You two will make a perfect mating."

Hellen nodded and forced out the words, "I think so."

The strange male was looking her over as if he were assessing Cruen's choice, his words overpowering Erion's low growl. "So, you are his intended."

"Yes."

"If he shows," Erion said with a grunt.

"He must." Hellen said the words quietly, almost to herself.

"If he doesn't, he will pay dearly," Erion said, his eyes narrowing on her. "He will wish himself dead."

Hellen shivered, both from fear that Cruen would not come and from the look of the demon male before her. How would she forget such a face, such intensity, such power? Her own demon cried to get at him.

Gods, she needed her draft.

A flash outside the door to the shop drew everyone's

attention. Hellen's chest constricted and painful pin-pricks of nervous energy rushed through her. Erion practically flew past her for the door, his hand wrapping around the handle with unmasked aggression.

Hellen wet her lips.

This was it.

Her gaze searched the space for the one thing—the one person—she was looking for. But it wasn't Cruen who walked inside the shop.

"Hellen!"

"Levia!"

Hellen ran to her sister, but Erion stopped her seconds before they could embrace.

"Who are you?" Erion demanded of Levia, his grip tight on Hellen's ribcage. "Where is Cruen?"

Hellen growled at him, beat at his arm with her fists. "Leave her alone. She's my sister. Can't you see she's scared? Damn it. Let me go, demon!"

At that, Levia, who was all beauty and innocence, looked up at Erion with wide eyes. "Demon?" she repeated before turning her curious gaze back on her sister.

With a frustrated grunt, Erion loosened his grip on Hellen and she pushed past him, diving into her sister's arms.

"What's wrong?" she demanded, looking the female over, every inch of her lovely face. "Why are you here?"

It was with this question that the mood inside the dusty shop turned from relief and quick happiness to deep unease.

"I was sent," Levia told her, releasing Hellen and regarding her with fearful eyes. "Oh, Hellen. It's awful.

Father came. He was very angry when he found you gone. Cruen told him everything. He had no choice."

A deadly growl echoed through the shop.

Everyone turned to stare at Erion. He looked ready to attack anything that moved his way. His eyes were a soulless black, and his fangs dropped below his bottom lip.

"Where. Is. The. *Balas*?"

Levia's eyes filled with tears and her voice trembled as she spoke. "Our father took him—him and Cruen."

The sound that ripped from Erion's throat was something that could come only from a demon—and a very dangerous demon at that.

Hellen watched in horror as he whirled inward, flexing his hands. Long, sharp nails shot out of the tips, and in under a breath, he ripped apart the ancient couch to his right.

Levia gasped, and Hellen pushed her away, back toward the door. "What is it?" Hellen whispered to her sister. "What is a *balas*?"

Before Levia could answer, Erion rounded on them, his demon fully emerged. "Where did he take them?"

Levia shook uncontrollably, and Hellen hated him for scaring her like this. It wasn't Levia's doing. It was Abbadon's. The male was cruel and vile and deserved to know what true torture and pain felt like.

But now wasn't the time to wish it upon him. If she didn't help Erion, who was acting terrifyingly unreachable and irrational, she would be risking her sister's safety.

"Where are they, Levia?" she asked her sister gently.

The young demon licked her lips, looking as though she wanted to cry. "Our father has taken them home."

"My *balas* is in the Underworld?" Erion raged, his chest rising and falling rapidly.

"Yes," Levia uttered on a cry.

Hellen faced him, blocked her sister from his snarl. "What is this thing you deem so valuable?" she demanded. "This . . . *balas*?"

"A child," Levia answered.

Hellen gasped. *No. Gods, no.* It wasn't possible. *Why would Cruen take a—?* Her eyes snapped up to lock with Erion's.

"The *balas* is . . ." she began.

"My child," he told her.

Wave upon wave of despair rushed at her from his gaze, and for the first time since they'd met, Hellen saw what he had been masking all along under the guise of anger, lust, fear, and frustration.

The crippling pain of a missing child.

10

"You have a child?"

Erion's jaw was so tight, his teeth pressed so firmly together, that no words, no answer to the female's query, would pass through his lips. He'd never felt such epic rage, and the control he'd been relatively adept at wielding over the past several years had all but dissolved.

Still blocking her sister from his verbal wrath, Hellen looked at him as though she'd never truly seen him before. This demon female who had manipulated him, lied to him, now seemed to hold pity within her gaze.

He didn't want it.

The only thing he wanted was answers.

"That was the boy you and the servant spoke of," she said, her green eyes thoughtful, intelligent, as she mentally reviewed the past several days.

"Yes," he ground out, moving toward her.

She inched back, pushing her sister with her toward the door. "Why didn't you tell me?"

He laughed softly, scenting fear in the room. "So you could feign your concern?"

"No." She shook her head with emphatic denial. "I wouldn't have pretended anything if I'd known a child's life was involved."

He stopped a few feet away, his nostrils flaring. "How magnanimous. It is good to know you have a moral code for some things."

She pointed her finger at him. "Don't pretend you are some pious renegade, Erion," she said with venom. "You also took an innocent who didn't belong to you."

"I did what I had to do to bring the *balas* home."

"We all did what we felt we had to do," she said. "Whatever it took to bring about our goals, be it a child back to his father, freedom to be with the male of our choosing . . ." She raised one auburn brow. "But choices have consequences; good, bad, regret, pleasure. In that, we are all the same."

Erion's lip curled. He hated the rationality of her words. Fine. Agreed. He was no better than any of them.

But Ladd—he was better than all of them.

As she sensed his mood changing, his ire shifting into something thoughtful, Hellen's eyes softened and she asked, "Why did Cruen take him?"

He hesitated telling her. She may have looked genuinely concerned, but as he'd come to know, her expressions could not be trusted. He decided to skim the surface only. "He wanted a trade as well. Something I refused to give him."

"What?"

Erion shook his head. It was all she needed to know,

all that was safe to offer her. "We waste time with questions. How do I get to this Underworld?"

"You don't."

He lowered his head and growled at her.

Her sister whimpered beside the door, and behind him, Raine's breathing quickened. But Erion didn't care. No matter what Hellen had said, what truth lay bare in her words, all the wrong he'd done to get to the right, he would have his boy returned.

And then the female did something most unexpected, something that made Erion's entire being jolt with electricity: she reached out and took his hand.

Startled, he glared down at her pale fingers wrapping around his large hand, the thumb unable to reach its four other digits.

"What are you doing?" he demanded.

"You can't get into the Underworld," she said. "Not without an escort."

"Oh, Hellen, no!" the sister shrieked.

"This isn't wise," Raine offered behind them, his tone thick with fear.

Erion locked on to the strong, level gaze of the female he knew he couldn't trust—but wanted to so desperately, he ached with it.

"What are you saying, demon girl?" he said, his tone a soft, deadly thread.

She ran her thumb over the top of his hand and offered him a weak smile. "I will take you into Hell, Erion."

Synjon shoved the male who got in his way and continued down the street. He heard the human bark out an irritated response, and grinned. *Yes, come after me, you wee shite bastard. Try to get an apology out of me, maybe teach me some manners.*

I have a terrible thirst.

"I can hear you."

Grinning, Synjon flashed another passerby his fangs.

"What the hell are you doing, Syn?" Alexander said with irritation as they moved down East 27th Street. "You're drawing attention to yourself."

"Do I look as if I care, mate?" he ground out.

"If you wish to provoke a fight tonight, I will return to my home and my mate, mate."

"Go on, then," Synjon replied, growling at a particularly lovely human female who winked at him as she passed. "I'll follow that female back to her apartment, and you can spend the evening looking for your bullocks. No doubt your Impure mate has hidden them from you."

With a foul snarl, Alexander jerked out in front of Syn, blocking his way. "You tempt me, *paven*. But I won't use my fists street side. I'll haul your needling ass into one of those alleys, drop you into a puddle of fresh piss, and teach you what happens when you speak of my mate."

Synjon hit him with a look of mock confusion. "Is this show of brawn for your female or for your balls, then?"

As the city moved around them, neon and sirens and conflicting scents, the pair remained locked in a battle of wills. Alexander looked ready to attack, nearly did before he was distracted by the squeal of a human child crossing the street with his mother.

He backed up a foot, shaking his head slowly, warily at Syn. "You've changed."

"Have I?"

"You were always a bit of an arrogant asshole like Luca, but now . . . you've turned into something far worse."

"An honorary Roman brother?"

"A bully."

Synjon's gaze didn't falter, and his ire didn't pique. His insides were coated with ice and steel. Precious little managed to get through. "You know," he began, "I think this visit to your contact's club might be a wasted effort. Perhaps I am going about finding Cruen the wrong way."

"What does that mean?"

Synjon watched Alexander, watched a muscle below his eye and just above his facial brands twitch.

"The *paven* is smart," Syn said, his tone even, deadly calm. "When he wants something or someone, he builds a trap for it. Like with the *balas*, Ladd. He took something you all love."

Another twitch.

What is this? Synjon's eyes narrowed. "Perhaps we should be looking for the one thing that Cruen loves."

"That *paven* is incapable of love," Alexander said with a shrug. "Forget it."

Synjon narrowed his eyes. "Why do I feel as though you aren't really trying to help me, Alex?"

The Roman brother shrugged again, his face a cool, composed mask now. "Trust issues, apparently."

"And why would that be?"

Alexander sniffed, then spoke inside the male's head. *"Oh, Synjon Wise. You have no idea how much I'm trying to help you."*

Then he turned and continued down the street.

*   *   *

Hellen weaved in and around the headstones, her hand still clasping Erion's, with Levia making her way on the left. Hellen didn't know if this was going to end well, if all that she had worked for, sacrificed for, would come to pass now that she was taking this intruder into her father's territory. But she did know it was the right thing. There was a child in the Underworld, held by her father—who, incidentally, didn't possess an ounce of either sympathy or empathy—and before anything else was ironed out, she would make certain he was released.

Erion's child.

She still couldn't believe it. Not that he had given life, but that he had gone so far to preserve it and bring it home.

She felt a pull in her chest. It was hard to understand unselfish acts such as that. After all, Abbadon's care for her return wasn't out of love but out of greed for furthering his domination on the world, on its population.

"We have been here once before," Erion remarked as they stopped before the familiar headstone. He turned to look at her. "You were about to step into fire."

Hellen nodded. "The flame is a portal."

"Our gateway to Hell," he said.

"He saw the flame?" Levia exclaimed, her voice rising above the whisper she'd held on to since the furnishings shop.

Hellen answered them both, her gaze returning to the headstone that had yet to blaze with blue fire. "Only a being of demon blood can see it. It is our way home."

"Our way into the Underworld," Erion corrected with ill-disguised menace.

Hellen didn't bristle at his ferocity. She merely shrugged and stated simply, "No matter what comes from there, what comes out of there, what is done there, it is my home."

Erion fell silent for a moment; then she heard him release a weighty breath.

"Why are you doing this?" he asked, his voice a low rumble.

She turned and looked up into his extraordinary face. "Helping you?"

He nodded, his eyes searching hers almost violently.

She bit her lip, then swiped her tongue over the indentation. *The boy,* she wanted to say. *I want to help you find your son.* But the truth felt far too intimate, too rife with a passion she didn't understand or want to claim, to utter aloud.

"It will help us both," she said at last. "You want to get to the boy, and I must get home, get to . . ."

"Cruen," he finished for her. Nostrils flared, lips thinned, he lifted his head and looked around the place of death, of long-term rest. "I still have a difficult time believing that you love that male."

"I don't love him."

Hellen flinched at the words that had slipped from her mouth unbidden. *Fool. Stupid fool.* What was wrong with her that her normally impenetrable common sense continued to lapse? She saw that Levia was staring at her, gaping—Erion too, but his eyes were filled with confusion.

"It is a bond between families," she explained quickly. "Between powers."

"You do not love him?" Erion said.

"No, but—"

"You do not want him?" he pressed, his confusion fading into something far more worrisome.

Was that satisfaction she noted in his diamond eyes?

Before anything more could be said or questioned, a burst of blue fire erupted from the ground a few feet away. It rose high into the air, then settled into a gentle blaze next to the headstone. All eyes followed its heat.

"Are you ready, demon?" Hellen asked him, gripping his hand tightly.

He nodded at her.

"I cannot detect it within him," Levia said, her gaze running over his face. "He is a demon? Living aboveground? Really and truly, sister?"

"Let us hope so," she replied. "Otherwise he'll burn up like a rogue the moment we step into the portal."

Hellen grabbed for Levia's hand too, and all three of them jumped into the fire.

11

Erion hadn't burned.

In fact, for ten seconds he wondered if he'd been sent home to his castle in France, and more specifically to the dungeon. The room he was in looked exactly like the one he had kept Hellen in. Circular stone walls, a small window beyond the staircase, and he was certain that if he turned around he would see doors leading into three dank, dusty rooms.

He ventured to move, to turn, but he was virtually immobile, held to the stone wall at his back by the very shackles he'd used on the demon female.

It was his dungeon—and yet it was not. His nostrils spread and he inhaled deeply. Empty, fragranceless air.

"Comfortable, I hope."

No, he was definitely not at home. This was the Underworld, and the thing that had just materialized in the room and was floating toward him with commanding purpose was something out of a nightmare. Over ten feet tall with scaly, thin skin the color of blood and eyes the color of snow, Hellen's father came to stand within a foot of him. He was a terrifying creature, a true devil demon, and as much as Erion wanted to attack and kill him, there was another part of him that pinged to life. For in some bizarre and unholy way, he belonged to this creature.

"I am Abbadon," the male said, his voice nearly painful on the ears, like steel grinding against steel. "Ruler of the Underworld."

"So the Devil has a name?" Erion said calmly, covertly pressing against his bindings, testing them. They were impenetrable.

"And you are Erion." Abbadon looked him over, inspected him. "So this is what we get when we put vampire and demon together."

"No. This is what we get." Erion opened his mouth, flashed his razor-sharp fangs.

The demon's lip curled. "I don't like it."

"Good. Then release me." Erion refused to feel fear, trepidation, or curiosity about the one who had given life to all demons. It was too much power to grant this asshole.

Abbadon moved closer, his neck working from side to side like a snake, as he studied Erion. "Show me your demon, Male."

"Show me the *balas*," Erion returned.

The male laughed. "Caring for one's offspring is not a trait of your demon side. I guarantee you."

With such an admonition, Erion could not help but feel sorry for Hellen, having had *that* as a father. Maybe Cruen wasn't the worst parent a child could have . . . He sniffed with disgust. Maybe he and Hellen had more in common than just the demon running through them.

"You will get nothing from me until you tell me where my *balas* is," Erion informed him, relaxing against his bindings in a show of ease.

"Your *balas*," Abbadon repeated with censure. "My daughters care for him. For now." His face split into a terrible grin. "The little demon fought like a hell dog on our journey here. If I didn't find some respect in his temper, I may have been tempted to kill him."

All pretense of calm and ease disintegrated, and Erion roared. Oh, this bastard was begging for it, for his demon blood to spill, for it to run like rancid oil all over the stone floor.

Abbadon laughed, brushed his long, scaly fingertips across Erion's face. "There it is. A fine beast you have. The kind of brutal strength and feral spirit I enjoy."

"Fuck you," Erion snarled.

The demon clucked his forked tongue. "Not me. I need a foothold on the Earth, but if that was not the case, I might be tempted to let you fuck Hellen. Alas, she has been promised to your savior."

The Demon King's callous, contemptible words sent a tornado of fury through Erion. He could no longer pretend to be cavalier. That the male could speak in such a way of his daughter, his blood. There was nothing Erion wanted more than to extinguish him right then and there.

"I want the boy and a one-way ticket back upstairs," he said, his tone dripping with contempt. "Your daughter is no concern of mine."

It took all Erion's will to force out the words. Especially after hearing how her father spoke of her, her future. But he had to think of Ladd first. Hellen had wanted to return home—she'd wanted to return to Cruen.

The strange, scaly ridge that represented Abbadon's brow line had lifted a fraction and he was studying Erion. "You did not think her so uninteresting when you were between her legs, Male."

Erion stilled, his entire body ringing with the blow he'd just been dealt. Clearly, the demon knew about Erion's dungeon and that something had happened between him and Hellen. But how? Had he sent someone to spy? Had he interviewed Erion's staff? No . . . Neither of those theories felt plausible. He could have rescued her if he'd been inside the castle.

Another thought snaked through his mind, one that made his guts twist, made him want to spill the blood of another member of the Demon King's family.

Hellen.

Had she told her father? Had she complained about Erion's savage treatment? Had she bragged about what she'd done with him—what she'd gotten him to do?

Erion sniffed the odorless air. His ire at the idea was only quashed by the fair play reasoning in it. He had stolen an innocent too. Hellen. Could he truly blame her for running home to Daddy and telling him everything? Even if the father in question cared so little for her?

Abbadon was studying him again, an ugly grin playing about his lips. "Yes, I know it all." His grin widened, showing off his thin, pinprick teeth. "Be glad you didn't take her virginity, demon beast. I would have most happily killed the boy . . . after he had watched you die first, of course."

Erion pushed back the horror in that threat. He wouldn't think of Ladd as anything but alive and well. "What do you want?" he asked in a deadly voice.

All humor melted from Abbadon's expression. "You took something that didn't belong to you."

"As did you," Erion reminded him. "As did Cruen."

"Cruen has received punishment."

What did that mean? Erion wondered. Was Cruen dead? Was that part of his nightmare over?

"And you?" Erion said, his gaze locking with the Devil. "What punishment have you been given?"

Abbadon hissed, a sound that resembled a dozen snakes attacking their prey. "An asinine query. Who would dare to punish me?"

"Release me, and I would be more than happy to show you," Erion returned with a thick strain of his own venom.

"Oh, I will release you. Just in time for the festivities."

"No, thanks."

Abbadon's voice lowered. "You will be my guest of honor at the celebration, demon beast, or you will be leaving Hell with a bag of bones over your shoulder." He eased back from Erion, his nostrils flaring with delight. "A child's bones, licked clean."

With a guttural battle cry, Erion dove at him, but didn't get far. "You touch that *balas*, and I will never let you rest for as long as you live."

"I would look forward to seeing you try." He raked Erion with his gaze. "I will need to praise Cruen on his creation. Perhaps you *are* a worthy sample of our worlds' fusing."

Erion wasn't interested in bullshit compliments. "When can I see the boy?"

"Tomorrow eve you will be my honored guest," Abbadon said, ignoring the query. "To witness my creation: the first child of hell conceived."

"The only child I care about is my own."

"And you will see him." Abbadon smiled. "After that glorious event."

"Can't wait," Erion said through gritted teeth.

Abbadon turned to go, though he continued to speak. "Have you no curiosity as to who will be joined together before you, both in union and in body?"

"No." Erion sounded bored. Live sex held no interest for him, but he'd watch, wait. He wanted the boy out without a scratch on him. He wanted to take him home. Wanted him away from this kind of evil, a mad demon who would sell his daughter off to—

Erion's head came up and his fangs descended.

Fuck, no.

No!

Abbadon turned, caught the look on Erion's face, and laughed. "It is a good thing you don't care for my daughter, or this would be a true punishment indeed."

With that, the Demon King evaporated, leaving behind the only scent Erion had caught since he'd been in the Underworld. It was a scent he felt a kinship toward, a scent he would pull into his nostrils, his lungs, and get drunk on.

Misery.

To get Ladd back he would have to witness Hellen not only being bound to Cruen, but having sex with him.

His eyes closed, and he pulled that misery into his lungs to fill himself completely.

There was nothing for it but to accept fate. He would watch. He would endure anything to get to Ladd. He was a good father.

"Alexander Roman. What are you doing here?"

Alex granted his friend and the mother of his true mate a sharp smile as he ascended the porch steps of her cottage.

Celestine Donohue no longer lived in her quaint house in Minnesota. After her run-in with the Order over her son Gray's mating with the *mutore*, Dillon, Cellie had moved into a secure house in the Impure *credenti*. There weren't many who knew of her change of address, and she wished to keep it that way.

"Is it Sara?" she asked, pushing forward in her chair. "The *balas*? Are they all right?"

"Sara's fine," Alexander assured her. He dropped into a chair beside her. "Her *swell* is progressing perfectly."

Relief colored her pale cheeks. "Thank goodness. She is coming to see me at the end of the week. When I saw you, I—"

"Cellie."

"What?"

"We need to talk."

"Something *has* happened. Did they find the boy? Ladd?"

"No. Not yet." His eyes connected with hers and held. "Cruen still holds him."

The quick flicker of fear would have been imperceptible to anyone who didn't know her as Alex did. After all, they had run from their *credenti* together long ago. She had cared for him, mothered him, and he had protected her. As he wanted to do now.

"Then what is it?" she said, concern holding her expression now.

"I never wanted to speak of this again," he said, knowing his tone bordered on disgust. "I wanted to forget what I knew, what I saw. What I believed. But that's become impossible."

Her face had turned ashen. "Alexander ... please don't ..."

"The painting Lucian and I saw at Cruen's hideout—"

"You told Sara and Gray."

"No. As I said, I never wanted to have to say anything."

"Then don't." Her eyes implored him. "My children and I are in such a good place. They know about their pasts now. They don't need any more grand waves knocking them down."

It had been only a week or so ago when he'd listened to Celestine reveal her past to Sara and Gray, and tell them about their father, Jeremy, and his work leading the Impure Resistance and how he'd returned home a changed man. She'd told them how she and Jeremy had kept them hidden from the Order by feeding them blood. That they'd done all of this to keep them safe.

It had been nearly the entire truth.

"Alex, please," she begged, taking his hands in hers. "That was a mistake, a few nights of foolishness in that mad *paven*'s bed." She shook her head, her voice cracking as she continued. "It was over so long ago it matters not. There is no reason they need to know about a mistake that doesn't affect them—that has nothing to do with them."

"Even if it granted them a sibling?"

She closed her eyes, let her head drop to her chest. "There is no sibling."

"I saw the picture of you in *swell* over the *paven*'s mantelpiece, Cellie."

"Oh, gods, Alex. This is so cruel." Her voice broke. "She didn't live. The *balas* didn't live."

"How do you know?"

Her eyes, heavy with tears, lifted to him. "How do I know? Why do you torment me with something so painful? It is unnecessary."

She reminded him so much of Sara in that moment. "I'm sorry, Cellie, but I don't think it is."

"Alex, the *balas* I gave birth to never even took a breath." Her own breath hitched.

He hated to press on—shit, he hated the whole vile subject—but it couldn't be helped anymore.

"After you gave birth, did you see the *balas* at every moment?"

She dropped his hands, and before his eyes, Celestine Donohue broke. Tears streamed down her face and she began to shake. She gripped the porch railing with one hand and pointed her index finger accusingly with the other.

"Why ... why would you torment me in this way?" She moaned softly. "I have only ever wanted to forget that day—that hellish day when I had to say good-bye ..."

Her words, her pain, were like nails being driven into his skin, one tear after the next. But Alexander couldn't relent. If there was even the remotest possibility ...

"Cellie," he said, his voice a mere whisper. "Was Cruen beside you when you birthed the child?"

"Yes!" she shouted, then covered her face with her hands.

"Then you can never be sure of anything."

"Alex ..." she whimpered.

This was his mate's mother, his friend. He stood and gathered her in his arms. She let him; cried softly on his shoulder.

"Cellie, I must know," he whispered. "Did you see the *balas* given over to the sun?"

He felt Celestine grow rigid against him. Then she pulled back. "No." Her eyes clouded as if she'd just remembered something she'd wanted more than anything to forget. "Cruen didn't want me to suffer that. After I named her, he took her from me."

Alexander's chest tightened. "You named her."

Cellie nodded. "Petra." Her eyes lowered. "After Cruen's mother."

Seated at her black stone desk inside the bedchamber that had been hers for as long as she could remember, Hellen uncapped another vial and drank deep. Once again, the familiar coolness of the draft hit her tongue and slithered down her throat in a race to get to all the bits and pieces it had once protected. It was truly the long-awaited thunderstorm in an eternity of field fires, and she smiled in appreciation as she drained the second vial.

Finally, she could breathe again without moaning in desire-filled agony. She could sit down, as she was now, without wishing there was a male beneath her.

She placed the empty vial back in her drawer and locked it with the key she had hidden in her mattress, the key her mother had given her so long ago after hours of explaining what would most likely befall her in the future and how she must secretly care for it. There wasn't a great deal of the potion remaining; it was only her reserve supply. She would need to obtain more before she left with Cruen.

She shifted on the chair. Cruen. Just his name made her snarl. He was not only mating her to gain power, but he had actually abducted an innocent child. In any sane, rational situation, either one of these truths should've made a female promised to him run in the other direction.

But here she was, ready to leave with him when he called for her.

Clearly she was neither sane nor rational.

As the second vial of draft spread through her like cold water inside her veins, she closed her eyes and sighed. The magical potion was attacking every aching muscle, every desperate nerve, every inch that had played host to Erion's wicked, skilled mouth, and yet . . .

She opened her eyes.

It wasn't attacking them fast enough. Or strong enough. It wasn't like before.

Though her body was cooling down, her breathing remained slightly labored. And her mouth filled with saliva at the very thought of a male's kiss. She touched her breasts. They were sensitive, beaded. What was going on?

She slipped her hand down between her legs and felt heat. Panic slowly licked at the edges of her mind. This was impossible. She hadn't just taken one vial; she'd taken two. She should be stone-cold inside. Was it because she'd gone so long without the draft? Her body had to grow accustomed to it again? *Or,* she thought weakly, *has my experience with Erion altered me somehow?*

Erion . . .

She'd promised herself she wasn't going to think of him—for her own good and for his. Her father had met her as she'd fallen into the Underworld, told her he'd taken and housed Erion, warned her to leave the male alone and not go searching for him if she valued his life and the life of his son.

Her father's threats were always promises.

She got up from her desk and grabbed her sweater. She shivered both on the inside and the outside now. Whatever the reason for this change in the draft's power, she had to remain the same Hellen before her family. Her father could never suspect she'd been touched by Erion. She had to protect him and the boy.

The *balas*.

Her sisters were watching over Erion's son, and the agreement was that he would be released into Erion's custody as soon as Hellen's mating ritual to Cruen was over.

As the draft made her stomach curl with momentary

nausea, she left her room and made her way through the tunnels. Their compound sat ten feet below the ground. Hell itself hadn't been deep enough for Abbadon. He'd had his home constructed at the Underworld's lowest point. Hellen had never minded the molelike existence. She and her sisters had always had fun, invented games, and hid from one another, then used magic and projection to find one another again. It had been a good growing period, and frankly all she knew. She'd never yearned for the sunshine she'd experienced aboveground. In fact, she'd never allowed herself to yearn, period.

Until that demon vampire male had touched her.

Looked at her and called her beautiful.

Broke her resolve and made her yearn for more of something she could never have again.

A deep, woeful frown threatened, but she forced herself to smile as she entered a large, rectangular room. Her sisters, Levia and Polly, stood before a wall of glass surrounded by gray stone, laughing and gesturing.

"Is he all right?" Hellen asked as she walked over to stand beside them.

"We have made sure of it," Levia told her.

Polly nodded, her smile broad and appreciative. "He is so sweet, sister. Such a charming boy."

Turning to face the glass, Hellen saw the setup of Ladd's chamber for the first time. It was a good-sized room, and her sisters had clearly designed and furnished it so the boy would feel at home. There were pictures on the pale-blue-painted walls of fierce dragons and bumbling dinosaurs. An armoire stood open in one corner of the room, several pieces of clothing inside, while a small yellow desk sat opposite. The stone floors were covered by brightly colored rugs, and the bed the boy was now sleeping on had coverings that looked new and fresh and young. Toys littered the floor.

"Is he scared?" Hellen asked, her concerned tone obvious.

Levia touched her shoulder. "There are times, but we have comforted him."

"We aren't sure if Father would allow it," Polly added demurely.

"We forgot to ask," Levia said, her gaze flicking downward. "Is that wrong?"

Hellen couldn't help smiling at the pair.

"He did say we could keep watch over the boy," Polly said. "That is the same. Is it not, Hellen?"

"I think you are both good and fine, and he is lucky to have you." Hellen glanced back at the world beyond the glass and sighed. "But he needs to go home."

The boy stirred, rustling his covers.

He needs to go home with his father.

Suddenly the boy sat up and his eyes opened. Sleep weary, he glanced around the room, no doubt wondering where he was. Hellen moved closer to the glass. She was about to ask her sisters something when the boy looked up, straight at the glass—and directly at her. Hellen's breath caught in her throat. She'd never seen the boy before, but as she stared into his beautiful, strong, angled face, she realized just how much of Erion was within him.

Their eyes remained locked on each other until the boy did the strangest thing. He grinned. Wide. At her.

And his eyes—his diamond eyes—flashed with happy recognition.

Hellen stepped back, her brow furrowed and her insides humming. She'd never seen the boy before, and yet he was looking at her as if they were old friends.

"How very odd," Polly remarked.

"Have you ever seen him, sister?" Levia asked, glancing over her shoulder at Hellen.

"No," Hellen breathed, not able to take her eyes off the small version of Erion.

The boy jumped to his feet on the bed and started waving at her.

"Well," Levia said, her voice a thin strand of confusion. "It seems as though he has seen you."

12

"He kept a woman here?"

"Not a woman, exactly. A female . . . something . . ."

Taking a breath, Kate released it slowly in an attempt to remain calm. She and Nicholas had entered the castle gates fifteen minutes ago—courtesy of his matching blood—and while Nicky had followed his nose to the dungeons, Kate had remained in the foyer, interrogating the guards. Though surprised and wary of them at first, the guards inside Erion's home became willing to talk after they'd heard about Ladd's abduction. But they still carried the fear of their master's punishment, and, it seemed, the female who was with him.

"What do you mean?" Kate asked the guard. The blond Impure had been the most helpful of the four who stood sentry in the dim foyer. "A female something?"

"She wasn't like you or Master Erion."

"Was she a vampire? An Impure? A *mutore*?"

The guard shook his head. "She was his prisoner. That is all I know."

Prisoner? What the hell was Erion doing? And why hadn't he let his family know about his plans? Kate knew the *mutore*'s actions had to be related to getting Ladd back . . . but how?

A scent glided into Kate's nostrils, and she turned her attention back to the guard. "Why are you so afraid of this female?" she asked. "Did she hurt you? Did she threaten you? Did she hurt your master—"

"She ate one of the guards," the male blurted out.

There was a soft curse behind her, and the sound of shifting feet on the stone floor. But Kate didn't look away from the male in front of her. She truly hoped he wasn't serious, that whatever he believed or thought he'd seen was a mistake.

"She drained one of them?" Kate prompted. "Killed them? Is that what you mean?"

The male's gaze dropped. "No, that's not what I mean."

Kate's patience was wearing thin. "I don't understand. I need you to be clear. This whole thing is beyond strange. I just want to find the *balas*, and if Erion and this female know anything—"

"They went after the boy."

Kate whirled around. The dark-skinned guard who had been silent as he'd stood sentry beside the front door and who hadn't once glanced at her in all the time she'd been there stared at her intently. His eyes were nearly as dark as his skin, and when he opened his mouth she saw the tips of his snow-white fangs.

"The female Master Erion brought into this house devoured one of our own," he said in a cool, even tone. "She caused the master to kill another whom she believed desired her." He sneered. "She cast her thick scent of arousal into the air to make us all go mad. Finally, the master could take no more and released her."

"Where did she go?" Kate asked him slowly, trying to process his words. This was about Ladd. Had the strange female gone after the *balas*? Did she know where Cruen's compound was? Is that why Erion took her prisoner?

The male lifted his pointed chin. "Master Erion took her. He didn't tell us where, didn't tell us anything. But he has had several meetings with the one who owns the ancient furnishings shop in town. Perhaps he can help you further."

Nicholas walked into the foyer then, his gaze instantly finding and locking with Kate's. She lifted a brow at him.

"Did you hear?" she asked.

He nodded, his eyes grave. "You will fill me in on the details as we travel to Raine's store."

The risk was a great one, and yet she couldn't stop herself. Not after her moment with the boy.

Hellen moved through the tunnels of her father's compound with the ease of one who had run through them or hidden within them every day of her life. This time, however, she was not alone. She followed Eberny. The six-foot-tall male/female hybrid glided along the floor, white robes kissing the stone, gaze watchful, blade in hand. After seeing Ladd, after the connection he'd seem to have with her, Hellen had felt an irrepressible urge to find Erion. She knew he would be worried about the boy, and though the demon male's feelings shouldn't matter to her, when it came to the subject of his child, they did.

"I will keep the guards away for as long as I am able, but if you are caught . . ." Eberny said, rounding a curve in the tunnel and moving down a gentle slope.

"I know," Hellen said, quickening her pace. "I forced you."

"Yes," Eberny agreed. "But how?"

Hellen searched her mind. It was an important question, one that needed just the right answer to be believable. "I threatened to cut out your tongue and eat it?" she offered.

"Yes. Good. He would be furious if I couldn't speak."

"Yes. How would he manage to order his family around if you weren't available to do it for him?" Hellen uttered dryly.

"Do not speak ill of your father, Hellen," Eberny warned.

"Why not?"

They were very deep within the bowels of the compound now, and Eberny slowed and turned to face Hellen. In the light of the lamp Hellen carried, the hybrid's face was pulled into a mask of condescension.

"He is cruel, unfeeling, vile, and hideous."

"Yes," Hellen agreed.

A soft smile broke on Eberny's face. "He is the Devil. How do you expect him to act?"

As a parent. Maybe just once in a while, she thought,

knowing she was reacting like a child. She was a grown demon female now who had made her own decisions based on the choices she had been given. This was the life she'd been dealt. Her gaze shifted to the door a few feet away. But it wasn't the life Erion and Ladd belonged in.

Eberny followed her gaze. "Yes. He is there. But before I open the door, you must give me some evidence to use if your father returns."

Hellen accepted the blade that was shoved into her hand. "Where?"

"My mouth, I believe," said Eberny calmly.

Yes, Hellen mused as she lifted the blade and aimed the tip at her governess's lower lip. A clear message. *Take me to the demon male prisoner, or I won't stop at your mouth.* And Abbadon would believe it. He knew her to be headstrong, impetuous, and, if she ever decided to act on the vile and hidden inheritance her firstborn status had placed within her, capable of being more ruthless than him.

With deft skill, she made a quick and shallow cut in the center on Eberny's lower lip.

"How's that?" she asked, stepping back, watching the blood rise to the surface.

"Stings, thank you."

Hellen laughed softly as she handed back the blade. "I'm sorry."

"No matter." The hybrid turned and moved swiftly toward the door. In a series of strange hand gestures punctuated with softly uttered incantations, the door made a clicking sound and drew open a few inches.

Before Hellen could get past Eberny, the hybrid laid

a hand on her shoulder. Eberny's brown eyes were heavy with magic and with something else Hellen rarely saw in the typically logical, rational demon.

Concern.

"Tell me something," Eberny said softly. "This male is worth your defiance?"

Poised on the tip of Hellen's tongue was the excuse she'd given Eberny earlier when requesting the hybrid's help, and the excuse she'd given herself. She was here to give Erion peace of mind about Ladd, let him know the boy was unharmed and being cared for by her sisters. That was it. That was all. There was nothing more, nothing between them that had caused her to take such a risk. No. She wasn't here to see his face again, scent him. No. She wasn't here to take that scent into her lungs, hear his voice, touch his skin.

That is what she told herself, what she wanted to believe.

Was Erion worth her defiance?

"I don't know," she said. The unsatisfactory and deficient answer made her feel silly, young—but weren't all young, silly demon females risky and foolish when it came to romantic decisions? She was just playing to her demographic. "I need to find out, Eberny."

The hybrid nodded solemnly. "Your father is aboveground. It is not much time to find out anything. But . . ." Eberny's eyes warmed. "You will cut out my tongue if I do not let you pass. Yes?"

Hellen nodded, laughing softly. "You can count on it."

Turning, Eberny grasped the door and opened it wide, allowing Hellen to enter. "You have until the fireflower blooms."

"Got it."

She knew that time of day. It was when everything slowed, the rain ceased in the Fields, the color of their sky lightened to an uncomfortable yellowish hue, and fireflower, whose petals remained locked up tight, suddenly opened and denied the Underworld its luscious scent.

"Demon girl."

Hellen froze just inches past the door. She heard Eberny's retreating footsteps behind her, but what truly stole her breath was the voice that called to her, the low, rough timbre that wrapped around her as she looked about the room.

The room.

Confusion gripped her. How was this possible? What had her father done? And how . . . ?

Hellen turned, rotating slowly like an animal on a spit until she was dizzy from the shock of what was before her and the questions that pinged inside her mind. Stone walls, circular room, three doors, a window . . . Her mouth felt dry, but she swallowed out of reflex. Her father had re-created the very room where she'd been held. Except now . . . Her eyes focused on the male affixed to the wall. He was tall, broad shouldered, and dangerously beautiful, his black hair licking the edges of his hard jawline. It was Erion—Erion, who had his wrists and ankles shackled, who strained against the metal, his gaze feral with rage.

"Look familiar?" he said in a voice that made her insides quiver with fear.

He was more than angry. He sounded betrayed.

She stepped toward him. She didn't give in to fear. "My father did this."

He nodded. "With a little help."

"My father needs no help to torture others." What had Abbadon done to find out this information? Had he gone to Erion's home? Interrogated his guards? Consumed one or more of them whole until they told him everything they knew and had witnessed?

The fireflower doesn't fall far from the fiery ash it grows from, does it? she mused, ashamed.

"The *balas*?" he said, tightly, darkly. "Have you come to tell me about him?"

Her gaze lifted. It had been hovering somewhere between the many waves of muscle on Erion's abdominals and his rock-hard chest. The query he'd just tossed her way still hung in the air unanswered, but the weight of it, the emotional pain of it, filled the room. *Ladd is a lucky child,* she thought. It was obvious that Erion loved him, worried for him, would even kill for him. His diamond gaze fairly bled with the desire to nurture and the pain of separation. It was something she'd never seen in the eyes of her own father.

"He is well," she said, coming to stand within a few inches of him.

Erion's eyes shuttered, and he tensed against his bindings. "You have seen him? You know this firsthand?"

She nodded. *I have seen him,* she thought, *and he has definitely seen me.*

"If they hurt him . . ." Erion's fangs descended.

"They won't," Hellen assured him. "I will make certain of it."

"*You* will protect my son?" he said in a mocking tone.

Her brows slammed together. "Of course."

"Why?

"What do you mean?" she returned hotly. She didn't like this, didn't like how he was looking at her.

He laughed bitterly. "Do you really pretend to care what happens to anyone but yourself?"

She stared back at him, her mouth agape. What a horrific accusation, and unfounded as hell. He had no idea how much she cared about his son, about her sisters, about their futures and their happiness. He had no idea the sacrifices she'd made, and not because she felt obligated or guilty, but because it was the right thing.

"After all, demon girl," he continued, watching her intently, "you are the one who took down my guard in one bite."

Hellen's lip curled as she stepped toward him. "Listen to me, because I won't defend myself on this point again, or any of these jabs you're lobbing at me. You, who took me against my will, kept me prisoner. Whatever I've done to protect myself, keep myself alive—I've *never* hurt your boy. In fact, I'm here right now, risking . . ." She stopped herself, shook her head. "I'm here because of the boy. I only wanted his father to know he was all right."

Erion's lips tightened and he seemed to soften a fraction. "Speaking of fathers. Yours paid me a visit earlier."

She had no doubt. A flash of embarrassment went through her. This male who cared so deeply for his child now knew the truth, knew where and what she had come from.

"Charming, isn't he?" she said.

He sniffed. "He makes an impression."

Regardless of what Erion thought of her, of her father, she'd come here to ease his mind. "He will let the boy go."

"You truly believe he has a grain of decency in him?"

It was a question she couldn't answer. She didn't know what mercy Abbadon possessed or didn't, and she wasn't sure if she wanted to know. They were blood, and she, out of her sisters, was the most similar to him, his heir apparent. If he was pure evil, what did that make her?

"If he does not let Ladd go," Erion said in a chilling voice. "If he hurts the *balas* in any way, he will be destroyed and I will be ruined." He looked away, growled. "I hate not seeing the boy for myself. I hate that he cannot see me, a face he recognizes."

Hellen held her tongue. She wasn't certain what had occurred between her and Ladd earlier, if he'd recognized something in her, but this wasn't the time to discuss it. Right now, if they hurried, she might be able to make Erion's hope a reality.

Maybe even prove to him—and herself—that she wasn't her father's daughter.

She turned, wondering if the room Abbadon had created was truly the mirror image of Erion's dungeon. A bitter laugh escaped her as she caught sight of the treasure she sought. *Daddy thought of everything,* she mused, walking over to where the keys hung temptingly from the very same hook.

"This is truly déjà vu," she said, heading back to Erion and dropping to her haunches at his feet.

"What are you doing?" he demanded just as the familiar click echoed through the fake dungeon's air when the key turned the lock.

She stood, went for one wrist with her ready key. "Freeing you."

"Why?"

With the click of the last lock, she flung the keys at the wall and held out her hand to him.

He just stared at it, his thickly muscled arms slowly lowering to his sides.

"Come with me," she said.

His nostrils flared and he looked as though he'd like to do anything but take her hand. Not because she repelled him, but because she knew he didn't trust her.

"Dammit, Erion," she said, reaching out and grabbing his hand. "I'm trying to do something nice here. I could get in trouble. I could get myself killed, and you too, for that matter."

He grunted and kept his hand in hers, but moved past her. "You, demon girl, are the very definition of trouble."

"And if I wasn't, you'd still be chained to that wall."

"Good point." He flicked his chin toward the door. "What's out there, waiting? Because I know it isn't freedom."

"No. It's not freedom. But it's Ladd."

He growled at her. "It had better be." Then he turned and walked out of the Devil's version of his dungeon.

"I want him out now!"

His breath coming fast, Erion leaned on the glass and pounded his fists like an animal, a madman.

"Stop it, Erion." Hellen sounded panicked as she looked behind her at the two closed doors that led into hallways and tunnels in her father's labyrinth. "It won't break. You can't get to him."

Fuck that! Ladd was inside, on a bed, asleep. *Shit. He had better be asleep,* Erion thought with a snarl. *If they'd drugged him, hurt him—*

"He is sleeping," Hellen hissed, as though she'd heard his thoughts. "My sisters read to him, sang to him until he drifted off."

But Erion couldn't be reached. He was way too pissed, too predatory. He kept on slamming his fists into the glass. His mind had shut down and all that was left were his instincts, which screamed louder than the demon girl. They screamed for him to get to his blood, his child.

"Please, Erion," she begged. "Stop." She grabbed his wrist, held him firmly. "You're going to bring my father's henchmen."

He whirled on her, roared. "Let them come! I will slit the throat of each one in turn."

She didn't back down. Instead her grip on him tightened almost painfully. "And you will get your son killed in the process."

He stared at her, his nostrils flaring.

"You don't want that," she said, her gaze grave. "Right?"

The anger inside him slowly began to flow out, while fear oozed into his veins.

"He's fine," she continued. "As long as he remains in there. My sisters adore him. They dote on him. Nothing will happen to him." He tried to look away, back at the boy, but Hellen grabbed his face and turned him to look at her again. "The magic surrounding this room is impenetrable, Erion—even to me. If someone other than my sisters enters the room, if the boy crosses the threshold—" She hesitated.

"What?" he demanded harshly, grabbing the hand that held his face and crushing it against his palm. "What happens?"

"He's dead."

The reality of what she was saying felt impossible, and Erion wanted to fight against it. But the strain of logic that still worked inside his brain warned him that if he did, he would be risking Ladd's life by attempting to free him. He could not do that—would not do that. Instead he must force himself to cool down, play this game out, follow the Devil's rules as much as he despised them and take what he could get. If he were alone, if he were fighting his own battle for life and freedom, he would be taking a different, far riskier tack. But he would never risk Ladd.

The hand that he was gripping so tightly rotated in his grasp. He tried to release it. But she held fast to him. His gaze shifted back to hers.

"He is well," she said, her face tired, anxious. "He will be ready for you to take him home when the time comes. Just focus on that."

Erion glanced to the right, through the glass to the same figure sleeping on the bed. His growl gentled almost to a purr.

Hellen squeezed his hand. "You don't want him to see you like this. You don't want him to see your fear."

Damn woman. "No," he uttered bitterly.

"Come away, then. Come with me."

"I don't think I like following your lead, Hellen." He said the words and meant them, and yet he left the room with her.

They had come this far through a secret passage that Hellen had admitted to knowing as a child. A place she'd used to hide from her father when he was displeased with her. Erion wondered if that happened more often than not. He didn't like the twist of sympathy he felt for her in that moment and shoved it away.

"Perhaps this was a bad idea. I was trying to help you," she was saying as they ducked their heads and entered a low portion of the tunnel. "Ease your mind. You were so worried."

"Are you looking for a thank-you, Hellen?" he spit out.

"No, of course. But maybe an understanding or, I don't know, a momentary belief that I'm not out to hurt anyone, screw anyone." She made a frustrated sound. "I wanted you to see Ladd, see that he was all right."

As much as he wanted to soften at her words, at her impassioned tone, all he could think about was Ladd, caged and scared and without him.

"Is that what you call all right, Hellen?" he asked. "He is held, jailed like a convict. He is just a *balas*."

"I know. I hate it—hate the monster who . . ."

She broke from her thought, but Erion would not let her get off so easily. "Your lover is that kind of monster."

Hellen whirled on him, her eyes flashing. "Don't call him my lover!"

"Why not?" Erion asked. "Christ! I am to witness that fact firsthand."

"You will not see us wed, Erion. It will be a private ceremony—"

"Private?" he repeated, then broke into bitter laughter. "Not only am I to witness your mating ceremony, demon girl, but I am to watch your lovemaking as well."

"What?" Her face went ashen. "You lie."

"Don't pretend you don't know this," he warned.

She started to back away, her eyes widening with horror. "You lie!"

"I wish I were lying."

Her shoulders hit the stone wall, and she reached back with her palms to steady herself. She looked terrified, and she couldn't seem to stop shaking her head. "I helped you. I risked . . . just to show you that your son was all right, and you say something like this to me."

Erion cooled his verbal attack. His gaze moved over her, his nostrils flared with the scent of fear. There was nothing about her in that moment that even whispered at a deception.

He studied her. Yes, she'd taken a grave risk to show him Ladd and ease his mind. Why? Did she really care? Did she actually have feelings for him that weren't manipulative or false? He fought the strange new layer of hope that moved him and the desire to comfort that went with it as he watched her face crumble with shock and fear.

Her eyes implored him. "Why would you do that? Say something like that? It's disgusting."

"It's true, Hellen. Your father—"

"No." Her voice was hard now, determined. "Even my

father in the most vile and cruel and contemptible state of mind wouldn't—"

"Stop, Hellen!" Erion stalked toward her, his shoulders curled, his lip too. "Christ. He is that vile. He is that cruel. Not just to his beautiful daughter, but to me. I am to sit there and watch while that piece of shit mates with you for life, then mounts you, takes you like . . ." He snarled. "Fuck!"

Hellen's eyes suddenly lost their fight, and her voice dropped to a whisper. "Truly, Erion? And please don't lie to me. My father told you this was his plan?"

Erion didn't know what else to do but nod. "It is to be my punishment for stealing you." Her whimper, her utterly destroyed expression, had him growling with anger. He took her shoulders and squeezed. "And for tasting you."

"What?" She shook her head. "No. He wouldn't know that. He couldn't . . ."

"You told him."

"Never!"

Damned if he didn't want to believe her. "Then how?"

She shook her head. "I don't know. I don't know. But it wasn't me, I swear."

Erion couldn't help himself. He leaned in, pressed his forehead against hers. "Oh, demon girl, I tasted you, the forbidden fruit I couldn't deny myself, and now I will pay with having to watch the one I despise most in the world take the female I . . ." He clamped his mouth closed on the words.

"The female you what?" she asked, her breath fanning his face.

He closed his eyes, so amped up on anger and desire and hate and lust he could barely hold himself back from howling.

"Dammit, Erion," she cried, pressing his face back so she could look him in the eyes again. "The female you what? Say it!" She bit her lip. "Please."

With a ferocious growl, he shoved his thigh between her legs. "The female I want."

"Oh, gods," she whispered. "Oh, Erion . . ."

He lowered his head like he was going to kiss her, then pulled back with a frustrated snarl. "I took you. I stole you away. You belong to me." He ground his hips against her belly. "Do you feel that, Hellen?"

"Yes," she hissed, her chin tipped, her breathing labored. She licked her lips.

"That is the only cock you will ever want, ever need. Mine!"

And to drive his point home, he crashed his mouth against hers and thrust his tongue between her lips in a violent display of unbridled possession.

13

Hellen had given herself more orgasms than she could count, knew much about sex, sexual positions, and parts of the body that responded well to being touched, but she had never truly been kissed in her life. She was sure of it now. In school she had stolen a few pecks from a few brothers of her classmates, and it had been nice, though dry and altogether too quick. But nothing could have prepared her for the feeling of Erion's kiss. He held her tightly, almost protectively, surely possessively, and seemed to make love to her mouth. A sensual drag of the lips, then a breath-stealing, full-bodied kiss, followed by a tug with his teeth.

And then there were his fangs.

She smiled against his mouth as he angled his head and lapped at her lower lip, groaning with a need she felt against her belly.

"Do you laugh at me, demon girl?" he uttered, his tone thick with passion.

She shook her head. "Just want to know what this feels like."

"This feels fucking amazing."

His growl made her laugh again. "No. This." She ran her tongue over one fang, then the other. Smooth, sharp. The muscles between her legs clenched, and she was surprised by the intensity of her desire. Demons weren't supposed to find fangs attractive. Those who knew of the bloodsucker race thought them animals—inferior, undesirable, worse than humans.

Those demons were fools.

"Have you ever bitten anyone?" she whispered against his mouth.

"Only when they deserved it," he growled softly.

She felt the vibration through her chest, and her gaze lifted to meet his. "What do I have to do to deserve it?"

"Keep looking at me like that."

"That's all?" she asked, dark, wicked desire swirling inside her like a storm.

He grinned. "Unfortunately."

She laughed. "How did we get here, Erion?"

"Through that door, demon girl."

"No. Not here in the hallway. Here. You and me and the kisses, and your leg between mine, and me wanting so much more between my legs, and you threatening to bite me, and a feeling that was never supposed to surface . . ."

She stopped, knowing she sounded like a lunatic. She needed to cool this down and regain control of the situation before they were found in each other's arms in the hallway of her father's compound.

"What feeling do you have?" Erion asked, lowering his head and kissing her neck. "Because maybe I have it too."

Hellen closed her eyes and sighed. His mouth. How could something be so soft yet so deadly?

They were in trouble if they continued this. She was in trouble. There was so much at stake here. Her sisters' futures and Ladd's safety.

Placing her hands on Erion's chest, she pushed him away. It wasn't a move of anger or protest, but one of regret and sadness and self-preservation. If she wanted to see things right in the future for those she cared about, she needed to break from his embrace, his hauntingly beautiful eyes, and his mind-shattering kisses.

"I want to take you somewhere," she said, grabbing his hand.

Eyes hooded, mouth heavy and hungry, Erion still wore the look of a male who wanted desperately to fuck, but his body grew tense. "Back to the dungeon? Am I to be punished for feeling your mouth with my own? For wanting what I've already tasted, what belongs to me?" He cursed, ran a hand through his black hair. "Or what, gods help me, should never belong to me?"

Hellen's body trembled at his words. "You're not going back there," she said. "Not yet. Not until you have to."

"Your father." A growl rumbled in his chest.

She shook her head, trying to ignore the heat that surged into her sex when he made that sound. "He's not here. He's gone aboveground. I'll know it when he returns." She tugged at his hand. "Come on. Please. I think you'll like it."

"Yes," he uttered, his eyes moving over her. "That's the problem."

A hot shiver ran through her. From her earlobes

down to the heels of her feet. It was sudden and intense, and with it came a shock of understanding. She hadn't even thought about it before, certainly not while he was kissing her. Her insides were burning up with desire, with longing, and yet she'd taken two vials of cooling draft only an hour or so ago.

Panic flooded her. Had she grown immune to it? Was it an off batch? No, that couldn't be right. She'd felt the cold numbness move through her, reveled in it as it coated the heat inside her. Not fully, but enough.

Erion was watching her, studying her. He looked wary, sexy as the hell she was in both literally and figuratively. *Can one male,* she wondered, *in particular be so powerful?* Had Erion and his claiming touch set her ablaze again? And if so, had he ruined her frigidity forever?

"Second thoughts, demon girl?"

You have no idea, demon male. Maybe it was the heat that was making her reckless. Maybe this was a bad idea—spending more time with him. It would certainly complicate things more for them both.

Her gaze traveled the ripped cords of muscle that were his belly and his chest, and the wide shoulders and thick arms that had wrapped around her in the most exquisite feeling of possession she'd ever experienced, up to his face, his beautiful face with its demon lurking just below the surface.

She had one night left before her mating with Cruen. "No second thoughts," she said, flashing him a smile. "Let's go."

She moved swiftly through the tunnels, her heated

body making her doubly aware of what was around her. It was a strange sensation. She had always been focused, cool in both body and mind, but now she was impassioned, vigilant, strangely impetuous. She couldn't shake the thought that Erion had something to do with this change in her, but when the scent of ash grew heavy in the air around her, she released all thoughts and quickened her pace. She was close. Round a curve, then another. A sudden blast of warm, ashy wind, and she saw it: the archway of light ahead.

"What is it?" Erion called warily behind her.

"Freedom," she called back. "As much as we're going to get anyway."

Hellen paused at the entrance, remaining in the shadow of the archway, Erion beside her. The landscape stretched out for miles, hills of black scorched earth, patches of blooming fireflower, massive crystallized rock that allowed for shade and, as she recalled from childhood, wondrous hiding spaces. It was the most beautiful sight.

For a few seconds, she tracked left to right for any sign of movement or body heat. *Could we be this lucky?* she thought. She detected no one.

She broke into a run and grinned as Erion came up alongside her, his black hair whipping back from his neck. He looked wild, a natural hunter, his demon pushing him as they rounded one massive gold crystal and broke into the pale lemon light of the Underworld.

"Are there guards patrolling the property?" he asked as they jogged up a black-earthed incline.

"Yes, but not here." This was a fairly unused exit from the compound, had been her secret way out of the Underground for years. She'd never even shared it with her sisters.

But even so, Hellen remained cautious, using her senses to feel, smell, even taste anything that might alert her to a problem.

"I love this time of day," she said as they ran side by side. "The scent of the fireflower recedes, and all I can smell is ash."

He laughed.

She glanced over him. "What?"

"Women normally prefer the scent of flowers to the scent of cinders."

"I keep telling you, I'm not a woman."

"No, you're not." His mouth was tipped up at the corners and his eyes filled with sensual, appreciative heat. "You're my demon girl."

She may have actually blushed as they headed down a steep incline. "Not sure I like that name."

"Oh, you like it," he insisted, moving closer to her, his nostrils flaring. "Your body heats up every time I say it."

"You're very arrogant."

"And you're very beautiful."

Without warning, Erion pulled her into the curve of a nearby crystal and had her pressed tightly against his chest as his narrowed gaze moved over the landscape.

"What are you doing?" she demanded, struggling in his grip.

"Quiet," he whispered, his fangs descending and every muscle on his body flexing, preparing for a fight. "I heard something."

"I didn't," she said, hating that their moment was being spoiled, while chastising herself for not being more vigilant. "I don't scent anything either."

For several moments, they remained still and quiet. Then Hellen broke from him, ignored his irritated grunt of protest as she moved through the hollows of the crystal to the other side. She wanted a better view. If there was really something, some*one* out there, she would see him first, take him down quickly.

She gripped the window within the rock and peered out. Suddenly, a smile broke on her features and she started to laugh.

"There had better be some cute, fuzzy creature out there," Erion said blackly as he came up behind her. "Otherwise we have just been made."

"Not cute," she said. "And definitely not fuzzy. Let's go!"

"Hellen!" Erion called after her tersely.

But Hellen was gone, leaping out of the window in the rock and barreling down the other side of the rise. She'd had no idea they were so close. How had she not sensed it?

Ash billowed in the air as she jumped from the hill and landed a few feet below. The long steel trunk that held her equipment winked at her in the pale light, and she hurried over and yanked the top open.

"Dammit, demon," Erion growled, coming up beside her. "Don't make me haul you back to the compound and place you in that false dungeon."

"You wouldn't dare."

He grunted. "Wouldn't I?"

She whirled on him, her bow drawn back. She smiled at him. "Not to worry. I sense no one. Most citizens don't care to go out during the time of ash."

He looked from her to the longbow. "Sexy."

She grinned. "Thank you." Then lowered the bow and tossed it at him.

He caught it with ease. His eyebrow lifted. "Where am I to use this?"

"In there," Hellen said, gesturing to a stretch of land behind him. "What you sensed and heard hides within. Excess magical energy courtesy of my father." She grinned wider. "Ready for some fun, demon?"

He turned to look, and she watched him take in her pride and joy.

"This is the Rain Fields," she said. "The clouds that hang just feet off the ground give hot rain and also give rogue demons a place to hide." She expected curiosity in his expression, perhaps even excitement, but found him looking strained. "What?"

He shook his head.

"Erion, what's wrong?" His face had gone very pale.

"It's not possible," he said, his gaze fixed on her beautiful hunting grounds. "But I swear I've been here before."

The power that surged through Cruen was a welcome friend. It had been so long since he'd felt this strong in mind and in body; he mourned the time he'd lost.

Unfortunately, it would have to be a short memorial.

"It is all you will get until my daughter is with child."

Cruen inhaled deeply, then settled his keen gaze on his benefactor. "No. I don't think so."

Abbadon rose to his full height, his skin a deep and angry red, his eyes piercing. "You dare to speak to me this way?"

They stood outside under the white-tented succulent garden behind Cruen's compound. It was Cruen's feeding ground as well as his place of meditation. He would not have his servants or anyone in his employ seeing him take blood from the Demon King. They would not fear him as they should. Nor would they respect him. Granted, the former was more important to him, but one needed both to rule properly.

Cruen also rose to his full height, nearly ten feet, and when they were eye to eye, he said in a calm yet grave voice, "You want a secure foothold here, I will give it to you. But I have wants, needs—a future I will see. I won't break our bargain, but I won't go into it unprepared."

"You want my power?"

"Yes."

"And yet you insult me."

"I won't bow down to you, Abbadon. I respect you," he added for good measure. "We have an agreement. You continue giving me your blood, and I will give your daughter a *balas*."

"A demon."

"Call it what you will," Cruen said, returning to his natural height and going to sit at the table near his small stream.

Following his example, Abbadon retreated to a more forgiving size and joined him at the table. "Unfortunately, Cruen, that is not quite enough for me."

"Your daughter's demon *swell* is not enough? The child with the perfect magical DNA for you to extract? The DNA that will allow you to remain on Earth indefinitely?" Cruen sniffed. "That is quite a pretty package, unlike your daughter. Truthfully speaking, Abbadon, I don't know many who would agree to take your female. Or have you not looked upon her face as of late?"

The Demon King lifted his chin. "She may not have beauty—"

"She is hideous."

"She is a demon," Abbadon snarled.

"To any vampire, she is ugly, undesirable. I don't say this to be cruel; it is a fact I have accepted. But understand, no one of my rank would take her on. So when you ask me for more—"

"No vampire would take her?" Abbadon repeated, his white eyes glistening with mirth.

"If you feel you must explore that assessment, have at it."

"I don't think that will be necessary. Your former son has already tasted her." He grinned wickedly. "And found her most pleasing."

Cruen stilled. "My son?"

"The *mutore*."

He sat up in his chair, grew a foot taller in his sudden apprehension. "Erion? How would you know such a thing? Where is he?"

The tension was not lost on Abbadon. His grin widened. "I have him contained in Hell."

"You must release him," Cruen said with too much passion. He knew it wasn't wise to show his care, his concern, for the male. Abbadon would use it.

"After taking what didn't belong to him, he must be punished."

"The punishment was the boy. I gave you the boy."

"I claimed the boy," Abbadon said. "You were too weak to fight."

Cruen's jaw tightened. He cared nothing for the *balas*, but Erion was something special to him. He wanted the male home. He had affection for him and wanted to use him and his blood in the new tests he was conducting on an improved Breeding Male gene. But he saw the look on Abbadon's face. His power, his demands with the Demon King only stretched so far. His number-one priority must and should always be himself and getting the blood he needed to sustain his power.

He sat back in his chair and eyed the Devil before him. "How do you plan to punish him?"

"That is the little extra I seek from you, Cruen." His eyes locked with Cruen and held. "He is going to be a witness to your mating ceremony with Hellen."

Is that all? "Fine."

"Your entire mating. Not just the words and the promise of a long life together, but the sexual union. It will be a special and rare treat for him and for my community to witness the conception of my demon child."

As this information took root, Cruen's mouth twisted into a savage expression. "I will not participate."

"If you wish to have my blood and my power, you will." He crossed his arms over his powerful chest and breathed in his triumph. "You will take my daughter before the crowd. And after she has birthed the first child of Hell, if you wish to toss her to your mongrel son, I will not fight you. But until then, this game will be played my way."

*   *   *

Erion's first rogue kill gave him a total hard-on.

Who would have thought it? After an entire life spent serving and protecting Cruen and his interests, never feeling right or real in his own skin, never understanding where he belonged or to whom. As he ran beside Hellen, hunting, his demon fully unleashed and partnering with hers, he was complete.

Maybe that was what he'd felt when he'd looked at the Rain Fields. A connection for his demon side. Whatever it was, he wanted more. A grin touched his lips as he spotted a flash of blue light. Maybe he would bring his son here, let the boy's demon side come out and play. A battle between father and son—

The idea made his insides pulse with dread. What was he thinking? The Underworld was no vacation spot, no matter how much it called to Erion in this moment. Once he got Ladd out of here, they were never coming back.

"There!" Hellen called to him. "Behind you."

Erion rotated, nocking the arrow and drawing back his bow. In less than three seconds, he caught the flash of light between two clouds and released the arrow.

The blue flash cracked under the attack, and Erion growled with victory.

"You!" Hellen called, running toward him, her grin wide. "You were born to do this."

Her words, how she looked at him with both awe and curiosity, made his gut clench. Yes, it felt as if he belonged in here, hunting, killing. And as the demon female's eyes warmed with appreciation, it also felt as though he belonged at her side.

They took off again through the clouds, hunting low,

instincts high. In perfect unison. When she dropped to one knee, he turned and covered her back. When she took out rogue after rogue, he grinned and admired her and congratulated her, and wanted her like he'd never wanted anyone.

He sprinted out in front, and just as he did, the clouds broke around them and hot rain coated their legs from the knees down.

"Erion, to your left!"

He spun, his bow already stretched, and launched an arrow at the blue fire that shot into the air. Another rogue followed, but Hellen was quick to take it out. After the cracks rent the air, they both turned to each other, breathing heavily and grinned.

"Having fun?" she said.

Erion stared at her. She was magnificent, the most beautiful creature he'd ever seen. She was in her full demon state, a proud, capable, sexy warrior, and he wanted her mouth under his, her body under his.

"Oh, shit." Her eyes went wide at something behind his ear, and she bolted toward him, her arrow nocked, her bow drawing back.

Erion didn't have a second to turn and address what was behind him. She yelled, "Get down," and sent the arrow flying as she leaped into the air.

She landed on top of him with a jarring crash. Instantly protective, Erion grabbed her around the waist and flipped her onto her back. His head came up, his fangs came out, and he growled at whatever might be lingering. Then he saw it, the arrow she'd sent. It was for only a second—the tip piercing blue light. Then the arrow dropped and the crackle of dead rogue rent the air.

"I got him, baby. No worries."

Erion looked down at her, tucked beneath his body. She was grinning wickedly up at him, and he broke out laughing.

"We make a good team. Don't you think?" she said.

He placed his arms on either side of her head and lifted himself just enough so she wasn't bearing his weight. "As long as you're around to save my ass, we do."

She pulled her arms free and grabbed his ass. "Oh yeah. Infinitely worth saving."

Erion groaned, his cock swelling, his fingers digging into the ground. "You feel so damn good, demon girl."

Her back against the wet earth, her front snug against him, he leaned down and took what his body, his mind, and his mouth all desired.

It was the worst mistake of his life.

She didn't feel good—she felt electric.

She didn't taste good—she tasted like the sweetest blood.

She didn't belong to Cruen . . .

Shit. He changed the angle of his kiss and consumed her again.

. . . She belonged to him.

14

Accepting the heat that refused to be tamped down or drugged into submission, Hellen moved seductively beneath Erion. She'd never moved that way beneath a male in her life, never known the feeling of long limbs and delicious weight pressing her deeper into the earth as a hungry mouth devoured her. She'd never known the feel of a male's hard cock against her belly or the erotic heat he gave off through his skin. It was completely intoxicating and addictive, and she never wanted him to release her.

As if hearing her thoughts, Erion lifted his head a few inches, concern lighting his diamond gaze. "Am I hurting you?"

"No." She wriggled deeper under him, moaning as the scent of his skin, his sweat, rushed into her nostrils. "No, you feel so good." She reached up and stroked his face with her fingertips. His skin was rough, especially around the mouth. The feel of it made her own skin tighten.

He turned his head, just enough so he could kiss the palm of her hand. "You're so beautiful."

She laughed softly. "I'm really not."

"My eyes do not deceive me, demon girl, nor does my heart—and on this they agree most ardently." Leaning down, he kissed both of her cheeks, then hovered a mere breath away from her mouth. "We may reside in Hell at the moment, but your beauty is heavenly."

No one had ever spoken to her like this. Looked at her the way he did—both hungry and awed. It was so clear in his eyes that he saw her the way no one else did—or ever had, and it made her all the more impatient to touch him and be taken by him.

With a happy grin, she sank her fingers into his hair and tugged him toward her, wanting his lips against hers again. Chuckling, Erion obliged her, fisting his hands in her shirt and taking her mouth in a series of hard, demanding kisses as he slowly circled his hips against her. Heat surged into every cell of Hellen's body, and she responded with a soft growl and a nip to his lower lip. This male didn't ask for what he wanted; he took it. Her mouth, her mind . . . *her.* And she loved it. She'd never believed that there was a being in existence who might be so right for her. Maybe if she had . . .

She growled again. *Do not go there, female, she warned herself. You've chosen your path and it's the right one. This . . . this amazing moment in time will have to serve as a delicious, coveted memory.*

For them both.

She whispered his name, and when his lips parted to

take hers again, she thrust her tongue into his mouth. *Ahhhh*, he tasted good, of spice and heat. Erion growled in response, his hands gripping her flesh through the material of her shirt as he kissed her so deeply, she cried out.

In one smooth movement, he sat up, taking her with him.

"Wrap your legs around me, Hellen," he demanded, his voice silky, erotic. "I want to feel you tight against me, want the heat of your pussy crying out for my cock."

His words inflamed Hellen, and she was quick to straddle him, her sex clenching as he cupped her ass and eased her closer. For one moment, they stilled, staring at each other. It was as if the demons within them required a silent conversation, perhaps even an agreement. The heat off their skin, the heat that raged inside them both, cried out to be released. But was that wise? Hellen licked her dry lips, her breasts tingling beneath her tank, her belly tightening, the hard bud of her clitoris swelling. She wanted him to touch her so badly, make her moan, make her come, make her scream, yet once he did it would be the end of their moment in time—the end of everything good, everything true.

It would be the end of them.

Out of the corner of her eye, Hellen saw a flash. A quick blue flash. But Erion had seen it first. He pressed her even tighter against himself, grabbed his bow from the ground behind her, and before she could manage her next breath, he'd pulled back the arrow and let it fly. Hellen barely heard the crack of the dead rogue over Erion's fierce and highly irritated roar.

She stared down at him, watched with fascination as the feral lionlike features of his demon side surged to the surface and overtook the smooth skin of his vampire.

A hot thrill passed through Hellen, and her nipples and sex hummed with need.

"Cease your play!" he called out in the most terrifying voice she'd ever heard. "The next rogue to interfere will not die without long-lasting torment!"

The Rain Fields fell shockingly quiet. Hellen too. She'd yelled at those little bastards a hundred times, twice when she'd been bleeding, and they'd actually laughed at her before attacking her again.

When Erion's hard, hot gaze returned to her, Hellen shook her head at him and grinned. "Impressive."

He growled at her.

The sound ripped through any shred of clearheaded self-possession that remained within her, leaving only her true demon self. She answered him with a growl of her own, an invitation . . . no, a demand. In that moment, she wanted Erion and his demon more than she wanted her next breath.

Erion's body went rigid beneath hers, and she saw him start to shift, saw him working to return to his vampire form.

"No," she rasped, deeply and painfully impassioned, her nails digging into his shoulders. "Stay in your demon form."

Jaw tight, he shook his head. "I don't wish to scare you, repulse you."

"Repulse me!" The tension within her eased slightly, and she laughed. "That was the sexiest thing I've ever seen. I thought I might come just from your growl alone."

Erion's eyes darkened with lust, and his lion's mouth tipped up at the corners. "Oh, I like that. But you won't come from my growl, demon girl. Not today." He hooked his fingers beneath her tank and lifted it over her head. "Today you'll come from my purr."

Her exposed skin tingled in the soft air of the Rain Fields, and she grinned. Excitement filled her. Anticipation ran wild through her veins, getting lost between her thighs. His hands were on her shoulders and moving down, the rough pads licking at her collarbone. Hellen swallowed, her back arching slightly, knowing where he was going and wishing he'd get there before she died from want.

His gaze followed the movement of his hands, his fingers, his nails as they lightly grazed the skin above her breasts. Saliva pooled in Hellen's mouth, and a moan escaped her lips. He didn't remove her bra but eased the cups down just beneath her breasts, leaving them plump and high and very much exposed.

Erion stared, his lips parted, eyes glazed.

"What's wrong?" she asked, suddenly worried. Was that lust in his expression or repugnance? Did she look different from vampire females?

Then he reached out and grazed one tight lavender nipple with his thumb. "Oh, demon girl," he whispered, his voice harsh with lust. "I think I will die from wanting you."

Relief filled her, and she smiled at his honesty, his desire for her. "Take what you want, then," she said breathlessly. "Anything you want."

One black eyebrow lifted seductively, dangerously. "That was not a request for permission."

Without waiting for her to respond, he dipped his head and slashed his tongue over one beaded nipple.

Hellen cried out softly, her fingers gripping his shoulders, her legs wrapping around him tighter.

"It was a warning."

He grasped both breasts in his hands and took one into his mouth, suckling it deeply. Hellen gasped for air and arched her back further. He kept drawing on her, deep pulls until she moaned and bucked her hips. His tongue, his mouth, was on fire—or maybe she was. She'd never felt such a sensation. It was as if everything he did to her breast directly affected her sex. She was swollen and aching and soaking wet, her clit screaming to be touched.

Erion moved to her other breast, this time flicking the already stiff peak with his tongue so quickly she couldn't keep up. The feeling was so amazing, so frantic—every thread inside her body alert and humming with life.

This is it, she thought incredibly as she rocked her pussy against him, ground herself, her clit, against his stiff cock. She was filled with life.

For the first time in her unimpressive existence.

"Erion!" His name ripped from her throat as she climaxed. A sudden shock of lightning that hit her quick and hard. She moaned over and over into the warm, wet air of the Fields as her muscles, her womb, her pussy, rode the waves of release.

"Oh, my demon girl," Erion whispered against her wet nipple. "You come so pretty, so hard. Every inch of you shakes. And the scent of your cream." He groaned. "You know I have to see it again."

Hellen lifted her chin, her glazed expression making him chuckle. "That's right, beautiful. We're just getting started."

Gentle rain began to fall, the sweet ash scent mixing with the scent of her climax, of the wet heat between her thighs. Erion caught it, his nostrils flaring.

"How hot are you down here?" he whispered, his eyes lusty, hungry as his hand caressed her belly. "Will your cunt burn my hand, Hellen?"

She couldn't speak. It was as if her orgasm had stolen her voice. All that remained within her were moans and sighs and a refusal to think about anything outside of the Rain Fields. Erion slipped a hand beneath the waistband of her pants. She wasn't wearing underwear, and he groaned as he discovered her bare flesh for himself.

"I've thought about being here again," he uttered hoarsely. "Dreamed about it. I love it here. I could spend hours here and be a very happy beast."

Though she had just climaxed, Hellen felt the familiar rush of heat build within her once again, but she also felt the evidence of the act between her thighs. It was slick and plentiful, and she wondered if that would put him off or please him. Suddenly shy, she pulled her sex away from his touch.

Erion reacted instantly, his hand coming around to cup her ass, hold her in place. "What's wrong?"

She whimpered. "I'm so hot, so . . ."

"Wet?" he finished for her.

"Yes."

His hand moved down, his fingers slipping inside her pussy. He groaned. "It's how you will always be when I touch you."

She swallowed. "It's too much."

"No." He eased out of her with a growl. "It will never be enough." He brought his hand up for her to see, his fingers shiny with her arousal. Grinning, he slipped them inside his mouth and suckled.

Heat surged into Hellen's sex as she watched him.

He groaned. "I love your cream, demon girl."

It's too much, she thought as she melted against him. He was too much. Her clit throbbed and her muscles clenched with the need to come again. As the rain fell around them, she felt his hand slip once again inside her jeans, and she closed her eyes.

He entered her with one finger, and she gasped at the sensation. Deliciously impaled, taken, possessed. She wanted more. She squeezed her ass, pressing herself closer to his hand. She heard a soft chuckle as he eased another finger inside her.

"Don't close your eyes, Hellen," he whispered, stroking her slowly, almost gently as his thumb worked her clit. "I need to see you, know you're seeing me when you come."

Her lids fluttered open, and as she pulled air into her lungs, as Erion's slick caresses became deep thrusts, she held his gaze. Within her, her demon snorted and growled and wanted to rise and connect with the male it desired so furiously. Denying it was impossible. With a helpless, wanton cry, Hellen released her demon as she pumped furiously against Erion's thick, ruthless fingers.

"Beautiful," he whispered as the light rain intensified.

Blood roaring in her ears, racing through her veins, Hellen cried out, shattering, splintering, her demon utterly unleashed. Erion continued to stroke her, deep and hungry, his eyes locked with hers as wave upon wave of climax drenched his fingers.

His jaw tight, his eyes flaring with the hunger of a male who wanted to claim what belonged to him, Erion eased his fingers from her slick channel. Hellen wasted no time. With shaky, desperate fingers, she started working her jeans down her hips. Close to feral, Erion growled and attacked, coiling over her like a snake ready to strike. One of his hands shot out to grip the descending waistband of her jeans, and Hellen grinned, thinking he might rip them off her. Every inch of her was trembling, wondering, anticipating. She couldn't wait. She licked her lips as she reached for his zipper.

"Hellen."

The tone of his voice had her stopping, had her looking up into his face, which was a mask of both sexual pain and terror.

Confused, she tried to touch him, get to his skin, but he inched back. "Erion," she whimpered. "I need you, and you need me."

"Shit." He stared down at her, shifting between demon and vampire. "I can't."

It was as if she'd swallowed another vial of draft. A wave of cool insecurity and confusion moved through her. "You don't want to be inside me? You don't want me to touch you?"

He remained poised above her, breathing heavily. "I want it more than anything."

She sighed with relief. "Then let me. You made me feel incredible, Erion. The way you touched me, stroked me, my body was yours. I want to make you feel good."

When she reached for him again, he grabbed her wrist and snarled. "Goddamn it, Hellen! Didn't you hear me? I want it more than anything. *Anything*."

"Oh, Erion," she breathed.

His eyes were wild and raw. "If I touch you, I won't stop until I've taken you fully!" His voice dropped to a deadly whisper. "And if I take you, he'll kill my son."

The words stole not only the desire between them, but the fantasy they'd built over the past few hours. What he'd said was so simple, so awful.

And so true.

Her selfish desire, her burgeoning love, would get Ladd killed. She looked up at him and shook her head. "I'm so sorry, Erion."

"Not as sorry as I am."

Before her eyes, the lionlike demon receded and it was vampire Erion poised above her. They stared at each other, just breathing in and out, one coming down from climax, the other reining in his anger and desire as the rain ceased and the lemon yellow daylight emerged.

Nicholas paced in the kitchen of the SoHo house, his gaze moving from one *mutore* male to the next. "Did you know Erion had purchased a home?"

"No," Helo said simply. "Where is it?"

"He didn't ask you to keep this from me?" Nicholas continued. "From us?"

Lycos sneered. "Who is 'us,' Brother? The Romans?"

Nicholas was amped up and worried about his mate, who seemed slightly despondent when he'd parted ways with her in France. He was anxious to get back, hold her close, fight by her side—fight for Ladd. He just had to get as much information as possible from these *pavens* first.

He stalked over to the wolf vampire and knocked over his cup of blood.

"Hey!"

"I don't have time to play games with you, Lycos," he snarled. "Kate is on her way to meet with the male who might know where Erion has disappeared to—where he's taken this female we seek. Where Ladd might be at this very fucking minute!" He leaned down and got in the wolf *paven*'s face. "I need to know what you know."

Lycos's lip twitched, and he growled softly. "He never told us a goddamn thing."

Nicholas backed up, sighed. He could never tell truth from fiction with Lycos; the *paven* was just a hard-core dick. Had Erion really been that secretive about his new digs?

"You've been to his home?" Phane asked, rounding the kitchen counter, his mismatched eyes concerned.

Now this *mutore* was different, Nicholas mused. The hawklike *paven* was fierce, guarded, but he always seemed to be pretty forthcoming.

Nicholas nodded. "But it's not a home. It's a castle."

Lycos snorted. "No shit? You two really are twins."

"If he has disappeared, we will find him," Phane said, glancing at Helo. "We may be able to scent him."

Helo nodded, then turned to Nicholas. "What about Luca?"

"Already on his way."

"And Alexander and the Brit? Do you want to wait for them?"

Nicholas shook his head. He'd tried several times to contact Alex, but he hadn't replied. "I don't know where they are or when they're coming back, but I don't have time to search for anyone else."

Helo nodded.

"We will leave word with your servant, Evans," Phane said. "Let's go, Ly."

"If they get back in time from wherever the hell they are, maybe they can join us in this fight." With the beasts behind him, Nicholas headed for the door. "If not, we can handle this just fine on our own."

Why didn't Hell have water?

Cold water.

The kind that froze the shit out of your skin and made icicles hang from your dick?

Erion stalked up the hill away from the Rain Fields, his anger and frustration both sexual and situational. He wanted Hellen desperately, wanted her beneath him right now, her legs wrapped around his waist, her sexy green eyes locked with his as he pounded into her.

He wanted to hear her come again.

Twice wasn't enough. Not for him or his demon beast.

"Where are you going?"

His nostrils flared at her voice, coming at his back. He could detect the faint strains of lingering desire, and they made him want to round on her and kiss them away.

Instead he shouted over his shoulder, "Back to the dungeon."

If he wasn't mistaken, he thought he heard her sigh. He knew that sound. Liked it too. It was really hot when he eased a finger inside her and slowly worked her body toward climax.

Fuck.

He broke into a run, his beast roaring to life as he hauled ass toward the archway. As soon as he crossed over the barrier, he slowed. Dropping into a fighting stance, he scoped out every crack and crevice in the tunnel.

"You don't know the way, Erion." She was right behind him.

He stilled, growled. "Then take me there, woman."

"Don't start that again."

"Take me there and tie me up and let me attempt to forget how you smell, how you feel, how you taste." He turned to face her. Her eyes—her goddamn eyes—shimmered with lust and he reached for her, pulled her up in his arms. "And how, to save my *balas*, I must watch you give all those rare and treasured gifts to the most vile creature on earth."

She stared up at him, desire in her eyes but sadness too. She was no longer her full demon self, and that made

Erion mourn. For a moment, they just clung to each other, waiting for an answer to an impossible situation. But nothing came. Finally, Hellen broke from him and took his hand, led him down the tunnel.

They were quiet as they walked, even when they had to duck into another passageway to escape the detection of one of Hellen's father's henchmen. Holding her against him, Erion had forced himself to remain calm. His protective instincts flared when she was near, and ripping apart one of the males who worked for Abbadon might be just the thing to cool his ire.

Or at least satiate his bloodlust.

It was several minutes later when they finally reached the door to the Underworld's dungeon. But Hellen went to stand before it, blocking the way.

"Have you some final parting words to offer, demon girl?" he said bitterly.

"Don't believe I want this."

His gut tightened. "I won't if you don't go through with it."

"If it's not me with Cruen, it will be one of my sisters." She shook her head, her eyes razor sharp in their resoluteness. "I won't let that happen."

"I cannot watch you be the sacrificial lamb!" he roared.

"Then don't."

"What? Close my eyes? I can still hear, still scent." His jaw went tight. "I have no choice."

Her face fell. "I know. Neither do I. We love and protect our own, even at the cost of our own happiness."

He dragged a hand through his hair, paced back and forth in front of the door. "Your father wants what from this union?"

"His foothold on Earth." She added softly, "An heir he believes will have the power to remain in either world for any length of time."

He stopped. "Then let me offer for you. I am vampire. I will give you one."

She blanched, went white as snow. Something crossed her gaze, a sweet, pure unhappiness that had him cursing.

His voice dropped to a prayer. "Say yes."

She shook her head. "Not possible, Erion."

The softness within him fled, and he once again became a vampire beast with his hands tied. "Because I am *mutore*, right?" he spat out bitterly. "It must be that pure asshole's *balas* for Daddy to be happy."

"Partly," she said miserably.

Erion froze, his eyes narrowed. "And the other part?"

She said something, mumbled something.

He reached out, put a finger under her chin, and lifted. He wanted to see her eyes, her mouth. It wasn't a pleasing sight. The former looked grave; the latter trembled. "What did you say?"

Her jaw trembled beneath his fingers. "I can never have a child."

Erion moved quickly, gathering her in his arms, and taking her inside his dungeon. He slammed the door with his boot and set her down to face him. "I don't understand. You said your father wants you to have a child with Cruen, that it will be his chance at a true and lasting foothold on Earth."

Her eyes lost every bit of their brightness. "Cruen will mate with me, thinking I will have a child, but by the time he realizes it's not going to happen, it'll be too late." She turned away and walked past him to the wall where the shackles hung. "I will never allow my father's genes to spread further. The dark magic I inherited from him is so strong, Erion. It is a curse, truly. I'm going to make sure it dies with me. Once Cruen mates with me, he cannot have my sisters. And when I turn up barren, my father will believe this union a failure, the vampire side not strong enough to merge with the demon side."

She turned and found his gaze, gave him a shrug. "He will not embarrass himself or lower himself by trying again with one of his other children."

Erion couldn't believe what she was saying, how she had planned everything. In fact, he wasn't entirely certain she had. "How can you be sure you can't have a *balas*?"

A soft smile touched her mouth. "My mother was an incredible female, honest and strong. She brought me up to be the same way. She knew what I was facing with my father, my future, and when it was decided that I would mate with Cruen, I begged her to help me." Instead of looking sheepish or sad, she lifted her chin and straightened her shoulders in a blatant show of pride. "She was a great proponent of magic, very gifted, and able to keep her talent a secret from my father. She fixed me, used a very strong potion to kill off my ability to have children."

"Oh, Hellen . . ."

Her eyes flared. "Don't pity me."

"That's not what I feel."

"I'm grateful, Erion. You have no idea what is inside me, what should never be unleashed or passed on."

For several seconds, Erion just looked at her. He couldn't speak, could hardly put everything she'd just told him together in his mind. Finally, he turned away, went to the wall, placed his wrists in the shackles, then gave the stone his back. "Your father will return soon. Make sure I am the same prisoner he left."

Silently, Hellen did as he asked, locking both sets of restraints, containing him once again.

When she stood before him, gazed into his eyes, she sighed. "Erion, please don't," she warned. "Your eyes, your demon hovering beneath, it's the worst form of torture."

Utter rage burned inside him, and helplessness gripped his dead soul. He could fight chains and demons, but how did he fight Hellen's conscience? Her selfless ambition? The very thing he understood so well—the very thing that made her his demon girl?

And yet she was his to protect.

"You know I cannot allow him to touch you."

Her eyes went hard, her tone too. "There is no choice here."

"Of course there's a choice. There's always a fucking choice." He laughed bitterly. "After this, after everything we've shared, my demon beast will not sit idly by while another male mounts you. Do you understand?"

"Yes."

"Even if I'm restrained, I will kill myself getting to you."

Her eyes went wide, fearful. "Please, Erion. You would

do anything for your *balas*, your family. Just as I will do anything for my sisters." She grabbed his face with her hands and kissed him, hard and desperate and no doubt for the last time. Then she turned away just as brutally and headed for the door. But when her hand hit the wood, she paused and glanced back. Her demon flashed, but she shook it away, held it back just long enough to say, "Tomorrow eve I will mate with that bastard, and you will take your son and get the hell out of Hell."

15

"You seek a female?"

Alexander nodded, his gaze shifting momentarily to the *veana* on his right. Celestine appeared uncomfortable. For many reasons he imagined, one of which was associating with the Eyes. She didn't trust the street clan who bought and sold information in the vampire world. Hell, Alexander didn't either, but when you've exhausted all other avenues and they are the only ones left, you put aside your mistrust.

At least until they attempted to overcharge you.

"Is this female you seek Impure?" Whistler asked, leaning across the chipped chess table in Washington Square Park. A favored spot for the Eye the Romans frequently used when seeking information.

"She would be Pureblood," Alexander told him quietly, knowing his words—even the mention of the female being alive—were no doubt a knife in Cellie's unbeating heart. "But if she exists, she might not be sure where she belongs."

Whistler tapped his temple with one dirty finger. "A little funny in the head, is she?"

A sound came from Celestine then, a soft groan of ire. Alexander continued quickly, "She may not have been raised among vampires."

"Ah. Well, if she's with humans, she might think herself a little nuts." Whistler glanced over at Celestine and shrugged. "The need for blood and all that." When she hissed at him, the Eye turned back to Alexander. "To help the process along, I'm going to need something of hers. Blanket, clothing, anything from when she was a *balas*. Something I can give to the trackers."

Alex turned to Cellie, and he didn't even have to ask. Her eyes, mournful and hard, told him everything. "As you know, Whistler, we aren't even sure if the female's alive. We have nothing."

It wasn't the answer the Eye had been hoping for, and he sighed. "With no description and no scent to track, it may take some time."

Alex fought the urge to push away from the table and get himself and Cellie out of the moonlit park. He had to make this happen. It wasn't just for Cellie. Shit, it was barely for Cellie. The truth was, his mate, Sara, was in *swell*, months away from giving him a *balas*, nervous and exhausted but happy now that she had her mother in her life full-time. He couldn't stand the fact that he had kept this from her—that he'd actually lied to her.

Whatever he had to do, however much cash he had to part with, he would. Sara could have a sister she knew nothing about, and before she brought their *balas* into the world, she would be given the truth—at the very least the truth about Celestine's pregnancy and relationship with Cruen.

Alex narrowed his gaze on Whistler and thrust a bag of cash at his chest. "This should keep your mouth shut about our request, not to mention help things move along in the search. Don't you think?"

Slipping the money inside his jacket, Whistler gave Alexander a lopsided grin, flashing the tips of his rotting fangs. "Always does, brother. Always does. 'Course, it can't make miracles, but it helps."

"What about blood?"

They both turned to look at Cellie. Her anger and melancholy seemed to have dissipated or at the very least had gone inside to hide. Leaning forward, her eyes pinned on Whistler, she continued, "Could the trackers use the blood of her kin to find her?"

The Eye stared at her. He looked momentarily mystified. "If we had access to that kin, yes."

"Tell anyone of this, and you will die a horrific death." She raised her wrist to her fangs and bit down. As soon as the blood began to flow, she presented her arm to Whistler on the center of the chess table. "Now. Let's see if this changes anything."

Erion rarely slept. From early on in his *balashood*, he'd realized he wasn't very good at it. Whenever he would try, he couldn't seem to shut off his mind. And for a vampire, unplugging mentally was key to allowing one's body to rest and recharge. Granted, Pureblood vampires needed very little rest, but an hour or two a night would assist in creating a powerful body and solid brain function.

For Erion, if he was lucky and lay out on the floor near an open window, there was a chance he'd get in a solid fifteen minutes.

Tonight, however, he was heading into the four-hour mark. And not just that; he was actually dreaming. At first he thought he was awake and back in the Rain Fields with Hellen, but the appearance of the dog who'd followed him home in France caused him to pause and reassess that assumption.

He was running through the Rain Fields, the dog bounding along beside him, barking as Erion took down rogue after rogue. Then Hellen appeared, scooping up the dog in her arms and kissing it, rocking it slowly. His bow at his side, Erion stopped to watch, amazed and content at the sight of Hellen smiling and cooing at the mongrel. Suddenly, everything changed. The sky turned purple and the clouds at their knees broke with hot rain. Hellen looked up, her eyes confused, sad.

"This is the only one we'll ever have, Erion. We must protect him."

Erion tried to move toward her, toward them, but his feet wouldn't budge. He was sinking into the black ash; it swallowed him inch after inch. He called to Hellen, to the mongrel, who whined and wriggled in her arms, but neither responded. He kept on sinking, his legs pinned, the ash up to his waist now.

Hellen's eyes were filled with tears as she watched him, as she pulled the mongrel closer to her breast and whispered in the most haunting of voices, "Your father abandons you to death."

"No!" Erion roared. "Ladd!"

Erion woke with a start, almost relieved to feel his hands and feet bound. He had never dreamed in his life. Not once. Perhaps because he'd never slept long enough to accomplish it. But if this was what he had to look forward to, he'd remain content with the unsatisfying fifteen minutes.

It was then that he realized he was no longer in the dungeon. He was still bound, perhaps even tighter and more restricted than before, but the cage he dwelled in now had no bars or walls and was a hundred times larger than his circular stone prison. It was a theater, arenalike, with seating all the way around. But the seats, which were empty, were more like short benches with plush red fabric and high backs. From his spot in the first row of the balcony, Erion's gaze finally settled on the stage and the primary set piece in the center.

A pallet.

"I designed it myself."

Rage bubbled inside Erion, but he continued to stare at the pallet with its satin gold bedding and solid gold frame.

"Long ago we used this arena for blood sport," Abbadon continued. "I miss those days."

The Demon King sat beside him now, his foul, ancient breath registering in Erion's nostrils.

"Beautiful, isn't it?" he prompted.

"Barbaric."

"Well. As I said, we used it for blood sport, and that is beauty to me."

Erion ripped his gaze from the pallet and directed it to Abbadon. There was no denying it. The Demon King was the most imposing, terrifying being Erion had ever encountered. Besides having skin the color of blood and snowy white eyes that looked right though you and tempted your soul, he oozed the promise of death if crossed. And not a quick death. Even so, Erion could not keep his tongue curbed.

"What can I give you to stop this?" he asked, his tone impressively cool, even to himself.

The Demon King relaxed back on the bench and sighed. "Nothing."

Erion's eyes narrowed. He didn't believe it. Everyone wanted something. Even the Devil. "I would give you the child you require."

His ridge of an eyebrow lifted. "She has told you."

"I would remain here with her. You would have your foothold on Earth and your family at home."

Mirth lit the white eyes of the Demon King.

"I am the better choice," Erion continued, straining at bindings, his tone resolute. "I have vampire and demon blood. A child of both strains might take better inside Hellen's womb." That might have been too much, but he was desperate. Once Hellen stepped on that stage, once Cruen touched her, the beast inside him would attack. Anything and anyone who got in his way—including the red one before him—would feel the wrath he could not possibly control.

Putting Ladd in even graver danger.

Abbadon was studying him, his features, his obvious brawn. And for a moment, Erion believed in the possibility of claiming Hellen as his own—with her father's blessing.

Which just proved him a fool.

"If you were pure, I would perhaps consider it," Abbadon said with deep-seated arrogance. "But you are a mistake, Erion. You are the sad evidence of a broken-down experiment. Something that should have been extinguished long ago." He inhaled deeply, his snakelike nostrils barely flaring. "Not to mention, you are something I would never be able to control."

A rush of electric anger surged within Erion. Not because the bastard in front of him had just called him a mistake. Shit, he knew that. But because Abbadon had denied him. It was over. He'd lost. They'd all lost.

He cocked his head and growled. "And you think you can control Cruen?"

Abbadon grinned broadly, like the most hideous cat imaginable. "I already do."

Erion stilled, his guts twisting. What had Cruen done? What had that mad vampire promised in exchange for filling Hellen's womb?

He watched as Abbadon rose to his feet, a magnificent beast in bloodred. What could Cruen possibly gain for creating this child? A child he would never see? It had to be something vital, impossible to achieve any other way . . .

And Hellen, he thought with icy dread. She was naive to think that her father and Cruen wouldn't make her pay for not producing the one thing they both desired.

"It won't be long now," Abbadon said, rising. "I suggest you sit back, relax, and, when the lights go down, enjoy the show." He smiled. "I know I will."

Erion's demon flashed and he pulled against his bindings, hungry for blood, for the Devil's blood.

"It is a shame," Abbadon said, clicking his forked tongue. "You have much passion, a drive to take and protect. And you think her pleasant to look at."

"She is the most beautiful female I have ever seen." Erion snarled at him. "You are the true beast, Abbadon. The mistake. The one who should have been eliminated at birth."

But the Demon King was gone, his soft rumble of demonic laughter the only thing left in his wake.

Raine stood behind his counter, clutching the wood panel, as he watched the group of vampires file into his shop. He hadn't expected a crowd. In fact, he truly wished he'd never come out as a *mutore* to Nicholas and Erion all those weeks ago. But they'd forced his hand and promised him a possible antidote to the gene that had been granted him at birth—the one that had aged him so rapidly as of late. If he didn't find something to stave off the problem, he would be dead before he saw his children's children born.

As three *paven*s—*mutore*, Raine was pretty sure— drew closer, he heard them bickering back and forth.

"I can't believe him," said one, who looked as though he might be crossed with a wolf shifter. "A castle. What a fucking romantic."

Another, who seemed to have avian blood, reacted coolly to this comment. "We do not own each other's thoughts and choices, Lycos."

"He is family, Phane," the *paven* retorted, leaning

back against an eighteenth-century chaise. "Of course he doesn't have to tell us dick. But he should!"

"I believe he has always wanted what his twin brother possesses," the third *mutore* added. "Castle, mate, *balas*, family . . . We cannot fault him that."

The *paven* was very tall, his hair shaved close to his skull, and under his skin there were pale-striped markings.

They were markings Raine wasn't familiar with.

Just then, a *paven* Raine did recognize walked through the shop, paused between the stand of *mutore*, and entered the conversation. "It seems my true mate is not here. It took too damn long for you bastards to decide to come, and now she's probably returned to this castle you go on about. And for the record, brothers, it matters not what Erion bought or lived in or kept from any of us. He is gone, missing, and so is Ladd. We need to find them." Nicholas turned his attention on Raine. "Where did Erion take the woman?"

The bell over the door jangled furiously and two *paven*s entered, one dark haired, the other pale.

"Sorry about this, folks," called the pale one. "I couldn't stop him. The stupid Brit has a death wish."

The dark one stormed down the aisle, barely looking at the *mutore* or at Nicholas. His eyes were trained on Raine.

"You know Cruen, then?" he demanded in a thick British accent.

Momentarily stunned, Raine glanced from the Brit to Nicholas, then back again. The dark *paven*, though thin, was fierce and formidable like the ones behind him—a true pureblooded vampire, but he was much more than that. He was something that didn't care if it survived, something that lived and fed on hatred.

When Raine didn't answer, the Brit circled the desk and came up on him, assessing him, scenting him.

He bent down, got close to Raine's ear, and whispered one word—but it was the foulest of sounds. "Speak."

"I know him," Raine uttered nervously, glancing up at the *paven* with the utmost caution. "He is my uncle."

The *paven*'s mouth twitched, not into a smile, but into something feral. He turned to Nicholas. "Did you know this?"

His jaw tight, Nicholas nodded.

"And you kept it from me?" His rage, which Raine heartily assumed was very near the surface of his skin at all times, exploded, and he dropped his fangs. "That is not the help I was promised, mate!"

Nicholas didn't flinch. "He cannot get to Cruen, Synjon."

The violent *paven*, Synjon, laughed a frighteningly bitter laugh. "He is family." In one quick stroke, he unsheathed a knife and placed it in front of Raine's nose. "Tell me how you communicate with your dear old uncle."

Terrified, his legs threatening to drop out from underneath him, Raine couldn't stop his mouth from spewing out information. "I don't know. I think of him in my mind, call to him, and sometimes he answers and sometimes not."

"You're a lying sack of shite, *mutore*." He said the last bit with undisguised hatred.

The *paven*s behind him growled low, a warning.

"Back off, Syn."

It wasn't Nicholas who spoke, Raine thought, staring at the blade before his eyes. Maybe the near-albino *paven* . . .

"If you don't tell me where he is, how I can get to him—something, anything—I'm going to cut you into pieces."

"Synjon, back the fuck off."

But Synjon wasn't listening. He seemed incapable of it. In fact, he seemed out of his mind.

Raine started to shake. "I can call to him. Let me try to call to him. I can't take you anywhere. I don't have that power."

"Jesus," someone uttered.

"Brilliant," Synjon said in a soft voice. "Close your eyes and call to him. And I would suggest you call rather loudly. Because if he doesn't come . . . if he doesn't make contact with you—"

"That's enough!" It was Nicholas, and he was coming closer.

Nearly cross-eyed, Raine continued to speak to the blade that was now pressed against his nose. "He may not answer for hours, days. I've already tried once today for a *veana*, who came here and—"

"Shit!" Nicholas rushed forward, jumped over the desk, and punched Synjon hard in the shoulder. The knife clattered to the floor. A terrible growl sounded, and Nicholas shouted orders to the *mutore*. "Hold him! Hold him down, goddamn it!"

Then he shifted his gaze to Raine. As pale as the albino *paven* now, Nicholas's dark eyes flashed with terror. "She was here. Kate. Where did she go?"

Raine's gut twisted. "She is your true mate?"

"Yes. Where did she go? Please tell me she went back to Erion's—"

"She wanted Cruen, just like all of you. She was as demanding as all of you." His voice shook as a few feet away the Brit struggled to get free from the *paven* and *mutore* who held him down. "I tried. I tried, but I couldn't reach him in my mind."

Nicholas grabbed him by the shoulders and howled. "Where is she?"

Shaking, unable to stand, unable to breathe, Raine cried out, "I told her about the cemetery. The way in, the blue fire, the portal they used. The *mutore* and Cruen's bride."

"The portal? The portal to where?"

Raine let the word loose from his aching throat in a screech. "Hell!"

16

"Are you sure you wish to wear this, Hellen dear?"
"I am."

"It's so . . . unattractive."

The deep concern in her sister's voice made Hellen smile. Poor Levia. She was truly desperate to make this a romantic event. Both Levia and Polly knew their sister didn't love Cruen, but in the Demon King's household, love had never been a consideration for a mating union. Granted, they didn't know the particulars of why she'd agreed to mate with Cruen—and they never needed to—but they believed her satisfied with the match.

"It will do just fine," Hellen told her, fastening the buttons of the oversized green gown she'd found among her mother's old things. "Cruen isn't mating me for my fine looks or my clothing choices."

She'd meant the words as a joke to lighten the mood, but Levia didn't look amused. In fact, she appeared slightly embarrassed by her sister's words.

"You are not unappealing, Hellen."

Hellen bit her lip to keep from laughing. "Thank you, Levia."

"But the dress does not help matters."

"It was Mother's."

The female sighed. "I loved Mother, but her sense of style was nearly as singular as yours." She frowned. "Not to mention she was several inches larger than you in both height and width."

All true, Hellen mused, turning toward the mirror the girls had placed in her room earlier. Neither she nor her mother had cared all that much about appearance. They'd had far deeper, far more dangerous worries to plague them. How to find and use one's power, then keep it caged and hidden from Abbadon's keen senses.

Polly burst into her room, making them all turn. She carried an armful of fireflower. "I thought you could hold this."

"Why?" Hellen asked.

"I've heard that in mating ceremonies aboveground, the females carry flowers." Her eyes flashed with romantic fire. "They are blooming now, but perhaps they will close up as you walk toward Cruen."

It was in that moment, the innocent mention of Cruen, that Hellen felt her first true pang of regret-laced panic. She had just finished off a third vial of draft a few minutes ago, and her insides were decently cold and her skin held a calming numbness. Her mind, however, seemed to be refusing the draft's call for oblivion. Images of a dark-eyed, possessive, and caring demon male continued to rise to the surface, and now they were tempting her to run.

"Do you know what you will say?" Polly asked, placing the flowers on Hellen's bed. "Do you know your promises?"

"Yes," Hellen nearly whispered. *To take one mate for life. To give my body, my soul, and my mind. To bring forth the first child of Earth and Hell.*

And perhaps the most important promise of all, Hellen thought as she secured the last button on her mother's gown with shaking hands. *Protect your sisters from the fate you must endure.*

A sudden and sweet giggle punctuated the air. "Do you think the demon will be watching?" Levia asked.

Hellen froze, her back to her sisters. She wouldn't have them see her face, her eyes. No matter how much draft ran through her veins, they would be able to see the misery in her eyes as they spoke of Erion.

"What demon?" Polly asked.

"The one who came into the Underworld with Hellen and me."

"I have not seen this male."

"He is quite fierce. Isn't he, Hellen?" She didn't even wait a beat before continuing. "He is Ladd's father."

Polly gasped, and Hellen could practically see her clutching her skirts and hurrying over to her sister for more information. The rustle of silk confirmed it.

"If Ladd's father is here, why doesn't Abbadon hand over the boy? Let him go home?"

"Father is punishing him."

"For what?"

Levia paused. "He is the one who abducted Hellen from the coach."

"Oh!" she clucked her tongue. "Well, perhaps he deserves punishment. But the boy is innocent. I do not like Father's choices in punishment. They always involve more than the one doing the wrong, it seems."

Hellen's heart squeezed with that truth. Ladd must be freed and safe—Erion too—and she would see to it. No matter how much she wished things could be different.

"He will release them," Levia said lightly, as if she fully believed it—as if she believed her father merciful. "And when he does, perhaps he will allow me to mate with the male. He is part demon, and I find him fascinating."

Hellen's lip curled a fraction, but she caught herself and forced her face to relax.

"The other part of him is vampire, sister." Polly's tone held a decided trace of disgust.

Levia giggled. "Yes, think of it. Fangs."

"I do not wish to think of it," Polly said indignantly. "I would never find a vampire male pleasing."

"Well, I'm not opposed to being bitten. Not if the male doing it looks like the demon male. He is more than pleasing."

Hellen heard a low growl echo throughout the room. For a moment, she thought Erion might be at the door, and her insides battled against the cold draft that fought to repress any and all flashes of heat and excitement. Then, with a heavy heart and a wretched feeling of embarrassment, she realized the predatory, possessive sound had come from her own throat.

Behind her, her sisters had fallen silent. They'd heard her too and were waiting for an explanation. Hellen closed her eyes and slowed her breathing, forcing back the demon that had emerged as her sisters had spoken of Erion. When she finally turned and faced the two curious females, her mask of impassivity was firmly in place.

"I think I'm a little nervous," she said, granting each of them an apologetic smile. "I'd like a moment alone, if you don't mind."

Levia nodded her understanding and grabbed her sister's hand. "Of course. We'll meet you at the entrance to the theater. Father wants us to present you to Cruen."

The Demon King is a true master manipulator. Isn't he? she mused.

When her sisters were gone, Hellen went to stand in front of the mirror once again. Levia was right, of course. The dress was hideous and three sizes too big, but, truly, what did it matter? The one she'd worn in the carriage on the first trip to meet Cruen—the trip that had changed everything—had been destroyed. Much like her hope for a future that didn't involve thinking about the true male she wanted while she continually feigned surprise at her body's inability to produce an heir.

She grabbed the hair band that kept her curls contained on top of her head and yanked it out. The startling red locks spilled down her shoulders, over her breasts. Despite her hair, she was no beauty. Her eyes were too large and set too far apart, and her nose was too long. Her mouth was strange and wrongly built, with a top lip that was fuller than the bottom. She didn't understand how Erion saw her as beautiful when no one else did, including herself. Perhaps he wasn't being sincere, or perhaps he was blind. She smiled at that, seeing him in her mind, and for one brief moment she saw something shift and change in the mirror before her.

It was gone in an instant, much like her smile. But she was certain she'd seen a rosy-cheeked nymphet with a lovely grin and wicked green eyes.

She swallowed and moved closer to the mirror. *Is that it?* she thought, touching the smooth glass. *Am I smiling when he calls me beautiful? And if so, have I truly spent a lifetime with a scowl upon my face?*

Her gaze caught something else in the mirror, something that made every wisp of happiness and hope bleed from her expression. The timepiece on the wall behind her. It was time.

Leaving her child's bedroom behind, Hellen walked out the door. As she traversed the dark corridors like a mole, she recalled the last time she ran the halls. Erion had been beside her, voicing his frustration, his desire. Kissing her. She instantly felt the pressure of heat attempting to penetrate her skin, get into her cold veins, make her remember how it felt to truly desire another being.

Would Erion ever leave her thoughts? Would she have to take double the amount of draft every day to keep the effects of his touch, his taste, his hands on her flesh from reaching her core and her heart?

Her hand ran the length of the damp stone wall as she moved down the tunnel toward her destiny. She'd never thought she'd meet someone like him. Someone who saw her, truly saw her, and wanted her anyway.

If she had . . .

Damn it. She ground her molars. She wasn't going

there. What was done was done, and she would claim her role as a sacrifice with everything she had in her. Her sisters would be saved, so would Ladd, so would Erion—and her father's black soul and nonexistent heart wouldn't stretch any further into the future, but end with her generation.

Her thoughts had carried her not just away in her mind, but to a detour on foot. The theater, where she would give herself to Cruen, was in the north section of the compound. Where she stood now was decidedly east and housed the smallest of prisoners. With a glance around to make sure she wasn't seen, Hellen slipped through the door and went straight up to the glass.

The *balas*, Ladd, was playing with two puppies her sisters had magically conjured for him. He was laughing wildly as they licked his face and tried to seize his toys. Hellen couldn't help but smile at her sisters' manufactured play. They were truly doting on him, teaching him all their favorite tricks and games, making him feel welcome in a most unwelcome circumstance. She leaned closer, trying to scent him, then shook her head at her stupidity.

Erion's child.

He was so beautiful, his features striking like his father's. No doubt he would grow like Erion too, tall and broad, fierce and loving.

The last thought made her stomach clench with pain. And in that moment, the boy chose to glance up. When he caught sight of her, his wild, playful expression turned sweet and knowing. Hellen didn't understand this strange connection he seemed to have with her or the urge inside her to break down the glass and steal him away and hold him in her arms. But his life, her sisters', Erion's too—they all depended on her walking out of this room, out of Ladd's life and his father's, forever.

And so she did. Out the door, into the corridor, and down the hall, dressed in her unattractive mating gown, her hands absent of the flowers her sister had brought her—the fireflower she hoped had closed and released its scent. The fireflower she hoped was dead by the time she returned to get her things and travel home aboveground with her new mate.

The power he had received from Abbadon still soared impressively through his veins.

Cruen stood in the living area of his shacklike hideout, the one located on the grounds of the Long Island *credenti*, and gazed up at the portrait of Celestine. Her belly heavy with their *balas*. Once this dirty business with the demon female was done, and the king had his heir, Cruen could finally have both the power he needed and the female he desired.

His eyes roamed over her. He could finally share their daughter's existence with the mother who believed she'd died upon birth. Cellie would be angry with him at first. But he would help her to understand how important it had been to hide the *balas*, protect the *balas*.

The faint call of the Demon King reached his ears. It wasn't the only one. Raine had been trying to get him to respond for hours. The *mutore* was really getting on his nerves, and if he continued to be such a grand nuisance, Cruen might need to clean house.

With a single thought, Cruen flashed straight into Hell. His feet touched down almost angelically upon the black ash outside the compound and inhaled the foul scent that always permeated the still air in the Underworld. He wanted this over and done. Perhaps he would be lucky enough to have his seed take root the first time around, and he would never have to mount the demon again. Perhaps he would think about Abbadon's suggestion of Erion taking her on. It would clear the path for him to bring Cellie home to live in his house and sleep in his bed full-time.

He entered the compound and walked the hall. His son was here already, waiting to see the *paven* he now despised mate with the female he found himself desiring.

Cruen's lip curled. It was a simple exchange of power—nothing more. He shouldn't care about Erion's feelings in this matter, but there was something deep inside him that did.

A sudden movement to his left had Cruen halting mid-stride and searching the corridor and shadowed curves in the stone for its origin.

He saw nothing.

Scented nothing.

He was about to continue in the direction of the theater, where his mating would be received by the citizens of Hell, when several yards up, he saw a female turn to look at him, then rush off. At first, Cruen thought it was one of Abbadon's other daughters, as both were far better-looking than the plain virgin he was to mate. But as he continued toward the theater, he realized who he'd just seen.

A blip of apprehension gnawed at his mind.

It had to be a mistake.

It was an impossibility for anyone who didn't possess demon blood to get into Hell, and Cruen knew firsthand that Nicholas Roman's true mate, the one who had stood before him at the table of the Order, once a captive in Mondrar, held absolutely no demon blood.

No. He had not just seen Prisoner 626, Kate Everborne, in Hell.

His need for blood was impossible to deny.

Erion hadn't fed in twenty-four hours, and the sting in his belly, the hum in his veins, worked with the unbridled rage inside his mind and muscles to create the perfect recipe for murder.

Still seated in the first-row balcony on the plush bench overlooking the stage, Erion watched as the room filled with spectators. Some appeared almost human in their dress and facial features, but most were decidedly demon. Eyes that glowed jewel-colored fire; skin in various hues. His eyes closed for a moment and he inhaled. *Yes,* he thought on a sigh of wondrous melancholy, *I know that scent.* His cells recognized that scent. It was kin, where the demon side of him had originated.

His muscles jerked as he shifted on the bench—or tried to. He growled, his lids slamming open, his eyes narrowing on his immobile limbs. He was free of the shackles, but his bindings, though invisible, were still in place. The Devil's magic. He wondered in that moment if he'd ever really needed to be shackled to the stone wall in the false dungeon. Could Abbadon have contained him without it? Had it just been a charade or a simple act of mind fuckery, another punishment for taking Hellen? A game.

That male liked to play games. Blood sport, brain sport . . .

And if it was, did he know that Hellen had released his prisoner for a time? Or was his power diminished when he traveled aboveground?

Erion hoped so.

The crowd settled into their seats below him. For a moment he wondered why he was the only spectator in the balcony. Wouldn't Abbadon want his grief, his rage, his desperation to be witnessed and consumed by all the members of Hell? That is, if they knew about him. He lowered his chin, stretched his neck, tried to see if anyone was looking up at him. No one. Every face was turned to the stage.

Was he blocked from their view? Was Abbadon concerned about their reaction to his presence? And if so, why? He was a stranger.

The lights in the theater vanished, taking his questions with them. Erion's guts twisted and his rage flared. This was it. He was to sit here, watch Cruen take Hellen, and silently go mad. For if he moved, roared, or disrupted the event in any way, Erion knew Ladd would be killed.

Suddenly, firelight flashed through the arena. In under a second, a mere breath, hundreds of torches appeared around the stage, making the bed's gold satin sheets and frame glow, and music, strange and haunting, filled the air.

Everything inside Erion, everything that he was made

of, screamed to get free, to attack, to kill. He strained against the magical bands that held him.

His demon refused logic and humanity. It would get to hers.

Whatever the cost.

She belonged to him.

And then Erion saw her. His breath caught in his lungs and remained there while she walked gracefully onto the stage, flanked by her sisters. Her green gown was hideous, unflattering, and several sizes too big, but he knew what riches lay beneath it. His hands fisted, remembering how her skin felt beneath them. Warm, soft, wet, *HIS*.

He propelled himself forward, felt the bindings at his wrists and ankles give just a fraction, and growled with satisfaction. Was it possible? Could the demon within him conquer the Devil's magic? And if it could, would he risk his son's life?

His eyes tracked her, the gown unnoticeable to him now. All he saw was her beautiful face and her flaming red hair, which hung loose in ringlets. Her sisters guided her toward the pallet, then each gave her a kiss on the hand before walking away and leaving her to her fate.

Erion stared at her alone on the stage, willing her to look up, find him. But her eyes never left the formidable bed. Erion snarled as he guessed at her thoughts. It was real now. She would lie back on the gold satin and give herself—

Her head snapped up and he saw all the blood rush from her skin. She'd seen something. Something she feared.

Applause broke out in the theater, and Erion followed her gaze. Cruen appeared on the other side of the stage and as he walked toward Hellen, his lip curled in obvious disgust.

He doesn't want her, Erion realized, his fangs descending.

The bastard found her repellant.

His beautiful, sensual, make-him-weep-with-desire-for-her demon girl.

Hellen watched Cruen advance, her eyes narrowing, and Erion knew she saw the look on his face. He strained again at his bindings, stretching them farther. Erion would see his adopted father die for this, see his blood run for making Hellen cringe with embarrassment.

"Pray hold your applause." It was Abbadon, and Erion's gaze cut to the male who drifted up the steps and onto the stage.

He stood at his tallest, his eyes hard as white crystal, his red skin glistening in the torchlight, making him appear almost reptilian.

A true snake.

"We have come together to witness the mating of vampire and demon. I seek to gain entry and permanent residence in the world above. The fruits of this union between my daughter and her mate will bring a long-denied right to me." He lifted his arms. "For only the child born of both worlds can open the true portal and allow me an infinity to live and walk freely on either plane. It is only then that we as a community can unleash our power on the Earth."

The theater exploded into a near-deafening thunder

of applause. Grinning, Abbadon mouthed a few incantations, and rain began to fall. The torches surrounding the
stage remained lit, and as the Demon King turned to
Cruen and Hellen, who stood several feet apart, eyes on
him, wary and nervous, he did not ask them anything.

"I give you my daughter," he said to Cruen. "Everything she is, everything she has, belongs to you. Do as
you will, treat her as you see fit, but remember"—his
nostrils flared—"the child you conceive is mine."

Erion hadn't realized that he was on his feet, that
he—the full demon—had broken through the magical
bindings, and that he was gripping the balcony railing so
hard, his beast's nails had dug a good three inches into
the wood.

All he had to do was jump, and he could grab her,
take her, run with her.

All he had to do was jump, and Ladd would die.

"The first child of Hell will be conceived before us,
but in the warm rain of our beginnings." He nodded at
Cruen, then slashed his hand in Hellen's direction and
cried out, "Begin the ritual!"

Erion's mind ceased to work, his skin went rigid, and
his muscles flexed against his bones. Before his eyes, the
hideous green mating dress Hellen wore split down the
center and dropped into an emerald pile of silk at her
feet. And when the room erupted in applause at the near
nakedness before them, Erion snapped the wood railing
in two and roared.

17

Gentle rain pelted her naked skin, but Hellen hardly felt it. The triple dose of draft was working too well. Around her, the almost revolutionary crash of applause rent the air, and she stood stock still inside its intensity. For a moment, she believed it to be the only sound she heard—apart from the manic dialogue she had going in her mind regarding her unclothed state and the male beside her who seemed utterly revolted at the sight of her.

But she was wrong.

She heard the roar of a male who refused to be contained by her father's oppressive magic and depraved theatrics.

Her gaze traversed the length of the theater in front of her, skipping over anyone who clapped and seemed delighted at her vulnerability. The roar came again, and she lifted her eyes to the balcony. Standing alone, hands wrapped around a broken railing, Erion looked gloriously vicious. His full demon was displayed: a diamond-eyed, lion-faced monster who flashed his fangs and appeared ready to jump.

The demon inside Hellen screamed for him to do it — come to her, steal her from the eyes of those who cared nothing for her fate. She'd never wanted anything or anyone more than she wanted him in that moment.

But it couldn't be.

If she tried to stop this mating, Ladd's life would be over. Erion's too.

Unless . . .

She shook her head, warm rain splattering the sides of her face. She couldn't go there. She'd sworn to her mother she would never go there. Her eyes implored him as she mouthed the words, *NO. PLEASE.* Then, when her father called for silence and calm, she made a bold choice to move closer to Cruen. She tore her gaze from Erion. She knew he must be brimming with rage, and she didn't want to see it.

"Let's get this over with, demon," Cruen uttered coarsely, turning to look at her. His gaze ran the length of her wet, naked body and returned to her eyes, unimpressed.

Hellen knew she had to spread her legs for this male, but she would never allow him to take her pride or what was left of her self-respect.

On stiff legs, she moved with him toward the bed. "Do you think you are the only one to hold your nose, bloodsucker?" she whispered, sneering at him. "If it is possible, I despise this even more than you."

"Until you breed, we must both endure," he said, removing his shirt and tossing it to the floor.

Hellen sat on the edge of the rain-dampened bed, her hands shaking both out of fear and a need to strangle something.

"Do not keep us waiting," Abbadon instructed perversely. "She is demon. Her body runs on heat. She needs no preparation."

In the back of her mind, Hellen heard the growl—*his* growl—and silently started praying.

Please, Erion. Don't give in to your rage. Think of your son!

Cruen worked the zipper on his pants, a sour look on his face. "Lie back, demon mate," he ordered quietly so the audience could not hear, "and pray do not look at me as I mount you. Your father would not go gently on a male who is unable to remain stiff—no matter what the reason."

"You have no steel in your cock, and I have no cream in my sex," she snarled, turning over on her belly. "Take me this way, so we both may remain oblivious."

It was in that moment—that near death of her soul—that Hellen heard something so impossible, so unjust, she forgot about the male who hovered behind her, ready to take her, ruin her. It was her father, speaking in hushed tones to her sisters from the front row of the theater.

"You will be next, Levia," he said softly, though the utter glee in his voice made the words carry. "Then Polly. Perhaps I will have your mating ceremonies together. That would thrill the crowd. I have never seen them so delightfully agitated. Your males have already been chosen. They are shape-shifters in the world above. I will not stop at a mere vampire/demon union. I will have my power and my influence long reaching."

Hellen flipped to her back and jacked upright on the bed, the force of her movement slamming Cruen backward. He hit the ground hard, right on his ass.

"You stupid demon bitch," Cruen screamed. "How dare you shove me away? I'm doing you a favor. No male in his right mind would fuck you."

The crowd erupted in gasps and chatter over Cruen's continued rant, but Hellen ignored him; he meant nothing to her now, not after what she'd just heard. Their union was no get-out-of-mating-free card. It was only the first of many. How could she have not known, not understood the depths of her father's depravity? How could she have believed he would keep his word? Her gaze narrowed on her father, who sat glaring at her, Levia and Polly bracketing him. This wasn't going to end with her. Even if she had a child, Abbadon had planned all along to use her sisters as broodmares as well. He'd just placated her along the way.

Anger roared inside her, the fierce love for her sisters that knew no bounds, not even murder. She walked to the edge of the stage and pointed at her father's fearsome red face. "I heard everything you said. You will use them too."

His eyes lit with surprise and his forked tongue darted out of his mouth before he hissed, "Return to your mating bed at once."

"I gave up my life for nothing." She shook with the cold knowledge. How long had she been in denial?

"Your life belongs to me," Abbadon returned, sliding

forward on the bench. "Just as your sisters' lives belong to me." His eyes locked with hers. They were so thickly white they seemed to be made of milk. "I may be renting you out to that nearly cockless vampire over there, but make no mistake, female: you will never be free of me."

Behind Hellen, Cruen cursed, while before her, Levia and Polly stared at their father with horror-struck eyes. In the seats, the audience had fallen quiet. And deep in her bones she knew that somewhere above her in the balcony was a demon male who was listening and waiting for his chance to jump.

Perhaps because she was naked, completely exposed to all who looked upon her, Hellen knew she could no longer hide from the unveiled truth. Her assumptions and beliefs had been wrong. No one would benefit from her mating with Cruen—no one but Cruen himself and her lost soul of a father. Abbadon wouldn't give her sisters a reprieve, and she was willing to wager he wouldn't let Erion or his child leave the Underworld alive.

This male was no father. He was an unredeemable monster—she knew because she possessed that monster inside her, and it was calling out to be unleashed.

Abbadon stood; grew to his full, intimidating height; and lashed out at her with his brutal demands. "Get back on that bed and spread your legs, daughter. I will see this done! You have nothing but your womb to recommend you. Fail at this, and you are as good as dead to me."

A sound unlike anything Hellen had ever heard before echoed throughout the room. A terrible, deadly sound that made the citizens of the Underworld cringe and cover their ears.

Hellen looked up just in time to see Erion leap from the balcony like a hungry cat from its perch. He looked large and dark and feral, his fangs flashing and his eyes glowing with rage. Screams and gasps followed his descent, and when he landed with a terrific thud on the aisle floor, the crowd broke to their feet and tried to flee the theater.

Erion was a true demon beast, a male gone mad. He snarled and bared his fangs as he charged toward her. Even her father was momentarily dumbstruck by his ferocity. Anything that crossed his path, he slammed or struck or hoisted out of his way. His eyes were locked on Hellen, and in a matter of moments, he would have her in his grasp.

But the moment never came.

With a spread of his arms and three quickly muttered incantations, Abbadon caused the entire theater and its contents to freeze.

Everyone, that is, but Hellen.

"Can I offer you a glass of blood, Alex?"

"A quick one, if you don't mind," he said, as Celestine retreated into the interior of her home inside the Impure *credenti*.

They'd been back for about fifteen minutes, and in that time Alex had received every one of Nicky's messages. The *paven* was pissed. According to Nicholas, Alexander had been secretive, unreachable, and a straight-up asshole. *Maybe Luca had written that last one,* he thought, heading over to the porch railing. Either way, he felt like shit that he wasn't at his brother's side. Granted, Nicholas had Luca and the *mutore*s working with him, but he wasn't having any luck getting to the *balas*—and Synjon wasn't keen on being a team player.

Alex sighed. He needed to get there, make sure the instability in that *paven* wasn't disrupting the mission. Soon as he downed the cup of blood, he'd flash to France. Whistler was working on finding the *veana* from his end, and he would most assuredly contact Alex if and when he found something promising.

His phone buzzed and he glanced down to check the readout, expecting another text from Nicholas. But the message wasn't from Nicky. His gut tightened.

"Here you go," Cellie called, opening the screen door and heading back out onto the porch. "I warmed it. I remember you like your blood . . ."

The expression on Alexander's face stalled her. She placed the glass on the small table to her left, her hand trembling noticeably.

"What is it?" she asked.

He lifted his BlackBerry. "Whistler."

"No," she breathed. Her eyes went wide and manic and she stumbled forward, dropping the cup. She didn't seem to notice. She shook her head. "It's not possible. It's too soon."

Alex went to her immediately, gathered her in his arms as she'd done with him so many times before. "Oh, Cellie, I'm sorry."

"My blood . . ." she uttered through her tears.

Alex pulled back on his own shock and worry and nodded. "Led them right to her."

*   *   *

Like those around him, Erion had been rendered immobile, and it made him insane to have to watch and listen as the female he wanted to claim faced off with the male he wanted to kill.

"The boy will have to die now," Abbadon said, his eyes locked on Hellen's as he stood between his two motionless daughters. "And you will be to blame."

"You insult me further with your lies, Abbadon." With a heavy sigh, she turned and went over to the bed. She ripped the gold sheet from the top, wrapped it around herself, and returned to the lip of the stage.

A strange shudder went through Erion as he looked at her. It was back—that demon he'd held captive in his dungeon, the hard, unyielding, calculated ball of fire whom Erion had wanted to keep tied up yet desperately wanted to taste.

She regarded the male who had sired her with barely disguised contempt. "The child was dead the moment he stepped foot in the Underworld, wasn't he? Along with Erion."

The devil's mouth twitched.

She stared him down without a flicker of fear. "I won't allow it."

"You won't allow what, exactly?"

"You to hurt either the boy or my demon male."

Heat flared in the Devil's snow-white eyes. "He is yours, is he?"

Erion felt his fangs descend.

Fucking right I am.

He waited for Hellen to look his way, a quick flicker

of a gaze, but she didn't even blink as she nodded at her father.

"In fact," she continued, taking a few steps to her right before halting again. "You won't hurt anyone I care about ever again."

Abbadon laughed. "And who is going to stop me?"

Her voice was so quietly deadly, even Erion's insides flinched. "I am."

Before Erion's eyes and the eyes of everyone who had their heads turned toward the stage in that moment of being frozen, Hellen began to change. Erion had seen her demon before many times, but this was something altogether different. As she grew taller, her skin turned a deep shade of green and her eyes flashed emerald hellfire. But it was the crackle of power that encircled her like lightning that truly stunned him.

This was Hellen of Hell.

This was her father in her.

This was the female Erion had fallen in love with.

"What you fail to understand, Daddy," she said, her voice booming throughout the theater, "is that I agreed to mate this piece of shit behind me not because I was forced to by your highly overrated supremacy, but because I promised my mother I would make sure Levia and Polly were never hurt or controlled or forced to mate, breed, or otherwise by you." She took a breath, shook her head sadly. "I believed you would stop at the first child of Hell. But you got greedy."

"I've had quite enough of this," Abbadon said with a shaky sneer. He'd clearly not expected this, this incredible power within his daughter, but he was not about to give in to it. "Levia will continue in your place. As soon as you are removed from this stage and cast out of the Underworld, she will mate Cruen. She will give me my heir."

He glanced past Hellen and eyed the male behind her, who was still frozen on his ass. "That should appeal to you, vampire. Something you can actually look at while you fuck."

The beast inside Erion broke free in that moment, and though he remained frozen, his roar did not. It echoed long and hard and fierce throughout the theater. He had no patience left either. In fact, it had run out in the balcony.

Abbadon whirled on him, his rage acute and his aim true. "The failed experiment will be the first to leave. It is a world he should have never been allowed to live long enough to see."

He lifted his arms, preparing to send a spell Erion's way, when Hellen screamed and lifted her hands above her head. The room went brilliantly white, a shock to the system, and over the pounding of blood in his ears, Erion heard her cry out a series of words he had never heard before. She circled her hands, then slammed them down to her sides with an audible crash of power.

Electric currents popped in the air, and all eyes that could manage it turned to look at Hellen. But the stag-geringly tall, green-skinned, vicious-looking demon was glaring at her father.

Abbadon was jerking, grunting, his eyes and expression growing more and more confused. His hands went to his body and he started manically groping his torso, his neck, his face. Very slowly, he turned to face Hellen.

"What you feel is the slow coldness of death," she said, her voice no longer a thunder to the ears, but soft and resolute. "It will run through you, seizing your blood, your muscles, and your bone until it takes your breath."

Abbadon looked shocked. "Not possible. You ... How ... ?"

Her shoulders fell a fraction. "I am ashamed to admit it, but I am my father's daughter."

"You don't have this power," he hissed, the breath already abandoning his lungs at a hectic pace.

"I am your firstborn," she said, the words bitter on her tongue. "I have always had the power, the rage, the hate, and the evil inside me. My mother helped me to know it and contain it, then hide it." Her gaze flickered to Erion, but only for the briefest of seconds. "I never wished to access it."

Abbadon's mouth trembled. "Your mother is my greatest torment, and you my greatest disappointment."

His eyes rolled back in his head and his body gave one more shattering jerk before he dropped to the floor of the theater.

The scream that rent the air tore Erion from his immobile state. He raced to Hellen, who was shrinking to her normal height, her skin returning to its pale pink, and pulled her into his arms. She was stiff, her eyes pinned to her father's lifeless body as she shook and moaned.

"Everything is all right, Hellen," he whispered near her ear. "I've got you. It's over."

When she didn't answer, only continued to shake and

moan softly, Erion eased back and tilted her face up to his. *Shit.* Her eyes were unstable as hell, shifting from emerald to milky white and back again.

Fear gripped Erion and he spoke harshly. "Hellen, what is it? What's happening to you?"

"Get the boy," she uttered, her voice changing, lowering to a pitch that was otherworldly. She moaned against it, cursed.

"Tell me what happened," Erion demanded, his gaze moving over every inch of her. "Fuck. Are you hurt?"

For one second, her eyes focused and she looked at him in such a deep panic, Erion's gut twisted.

"Hurry," she whispered. "Please, Erion. They will awaken soon."

"Who?" He looked out at the still frozen crowd. "Them? The ones who sat in their seats and watched that bastard force you into mating?"

The thought made him jerk around, looking for Cruen. The *paven* had been immobile too. Erion had seen it. But now, Erion thought with a sneer, his gaze tracking every inch of the stage, there was no sign of the mad vamp.

Hellen's groan of pain or change—he didn't know— ripped him from his search for Cruen.

"I don't care if any of these bastards wake," he practically snarled, feeling helpless, his rage over what she had done to save him running rampant through his mind and blood. "Tell me what I can do to help you."

"They can't see me," she whispered desperately. "Not like this."

He wasn't sure what she meant. They'd seen her naked, in full demon height and ferocity. Did she mean this pain she was in? Or was this all about the aftereffects of taking down Abbadon?

Shit, did it matter? He wanted her safe, whatever that meant to her. He scooped her up in his arms and took off.

The sounds of her pain, her fear fueled his movement as he ran down the corridors. Every movement, every sound he heard was met with a growl of possessiveness. He would never let anyone hurt this female again after all she'd endured, sacrificed. She was his. She had claimed him in every way that mattered. He owed her his life.

She cried out and jerked in his arms.

"I have you, demon girl," he said, rounding the corner, heading toward the cage of glass that held Ladd. "I'm taking you away. You will never have to see this world again."

"Erion," she whimpered. "I killed my father."

His gut twisted. Abbadon was a monster, something vile and soulless that had glowed in the presence of his daughter's pain and shame. Christ, he'd encouraged it. The male should've been exterminated long ago. But he was also the thing that had given his female life. It was similar to how Erion felt about Cruen; there was hatred and disgust, yet the vampire had saved him from death. Granted, he'd saved him for a purpose—just like Hellen had been born for a purpose, to be used. But there was something in the child's soul they both still clung to; no matter how abused they were, there was still a connection to the one who gave them life.

Erion knew intimately that she would mourn this loss in so many conflicting ways.

"We don't have to speak of it now," he told her, pulling her closer as he quickened his pace.

She looked up at him. "I took his life."

"And you saved mine." Pride exploded with him. "And my son's."

Her eyes clung to his, and he watched her struggle. His mate, the female he would spend a lifetime proving his love to and would care for, would come to understand that the evil she believed was inside her would always be used for good.

"We must get to Ladd," she said, turning her head into his chest and gripping his shoulders as another shudder went through her.

Goddamn it. What is happening to her? Erion prayed it was just shock and fear. Those he could help her with.

"That's where I'm headed," he assured her. "Nothing is holding him now, no magic we cannot break through. No Devil to threaten his life." He growled at a guard as they passed, and the male cowered. "We can take him and get the fuck out of here."

"Yes." She held on to him so tightly. "And my sisters. We can't leave them here."

Erion's skin prickled with tension. "I have more than enough room in my home. Or I will purchase them a home of their own. It can be however they wish — however you wish."

"Thank you."

"I will take care of you, Hellen. Everything is all right."

They reached the room that held Ladd, and Erion burst through the door. But what greeted them on the other side of the stone had Hellen struggling to get free and Erion rushing toward the wall of glass.

"No!" Hellen cried, her eyes wide and fierce as she stared through the glass.

At first, Erion thought he was seeing an illusion. It wasn't possible. "What is she doing . . ."

Hellen's eyes flared white-hot and she finally won her struggle and scrambled from Erion's arms. "She's taking the boy."

Before Erion could stop her, Hellen cast a stream of guttural words at the glass, causing it to shatter and crash to the ground.

Then she leaped through the open frame and attacked.

18

They all converged on the cemetery; two Romans, four *mutores*, and a pissed-off Brit, but all Nicholas wanted was to be the one who was able to make it past the enchantments and into the portal. He couldn't believe Kate had gone into Hell without him. He knew how badly she wanted to find Ladd. He knew her maternal instincts were undeniably strong, and he didn't fault her for that. But they were partners, goddamn it. True fucking mates! She had no right to risk her life without consulting him first—without having him at her back when she did it.

She would feel his wrath.

But he had to get to her first.

A foot in front of him, Lycos reached the gravesite, and without a word made an attempt to cross it and get to the headstone. But after one step in he was thrust back by an invisible force. He cursed, landed on his ass, and muttered, "I'm guessing I don't have demon blood."

"I warned you," Raine said, moving to stand near

Nicholas, who had stopped where Lycos had stood a moment before. "If you would just wait for Cruen to come to me—"

"I'm not waiting for the cockroach to emerge from the dark," Synjon said, coming up beside Raine. "I'm going in with my bloody brilliant headlights on and forcing him out of the crack he's hiding in."

"I hate cockroaches," Nicholas heard Phane mutter to Helo as the pair stood behind them. "Unfortunately, my bird has a real thing for them."

"We all have our vices, bro," Helo returned.

As if he weren't listening to anything but his own stream of consciousness, Synjon barked at the *mutore* beside him. "Take me in."

Raine gaped at him. "I cannot. As the wolf male said, only demons can get through the portals."

"My mate is no demon," Nicholas said, his eyes on the gravestone. "How did she get through?"

"I don't know."

"Can someone without demon blood piggyback on one who has it?" Synjon asked, his gaze shifting to Nicholas.

Nicholas grinned with quick understanding. "My twin brother is part demon, which would mean I have it within me as well."

"That's good enough for me," Synjon agreed, moving closer.

"'Course it is," Lucian uttered, standing a good five feet away from them. "You've got a death wish."

Syn growled at him. "This is none of your affair, Frosty."

"Bullshit," Lucian returned. "None of you know anything for sure. It's like walking outside without knowing if it's night or day. A fucking crapshoot."

"He's right," Raine told them, his tone grave. "Without knowing for sure you could both end up dead. Before you even reach Hell, you could both be nothing but ash."

Synjon shrugged. "We'll see."

Raine turned to Nicholas, his eyes imploring him to think rationally. It was one of the few times in his life where that objective was virtually impossible. Clearly the *mutore* before him had never experienced a mate running straight into danger.

"Perhaps," Raine suggested with conviction, "your mate didn't walk into the hellfire. Perhaps she is back home in New York or at Erion's castle."

"No." He'd already been in contact with both, and Kate wasn't there.

"Sod off, you bloody git," Syn snarled. "We're wasting time."

Continuing undeterred, Raine said, "Perhaps she did try to get into the Underworld. Tried and failed."

A low, foul snarl exited Nicholas's mouth. That thought, that abominable, impossible version of what happened to his mate, would not even be considered.

"Don't listen to this knob head." Synjon moved to Nicholas's side and gave him a questioning look. "Shall we join hands or make this a true piggyback experience?"

"You could be jumping to your death," Raine told him.

"The possibilities are endless."

"Hey, London," Lucian called to Synjon, though he stared hard at Nicholas's back, "that ain't the way."

"Life and death is my way," Syn returned hotly.

"You're being an idiot," Lucian said to Nicholas, then turned to Syn. "And you. Are you seriously going to risk death? Risk leaving Cruen here to live?" Lucian lifted one pale eyebrow.

With an irritated growl, Synjon patted the blade at his hip and eyed Nicholas. "Is your demon blood ready to go?"

"My demon blood wants to leave your sorry British ass behind." Nicholas grabbed the *paven*'s arm and yanked him close. "But unfortunately, I may need backup."

Hellen advanced on the vampire female. "Release him, or I will make you do it." She raised an eyebrow. "And it'll hurt. A lot."

The blond female had thrust Ladd behind her, turned, and was now flashing an impressive set of fangs. Unfortunately, Hellen mused, conjuring up the magic that hummed within her, the vampire female had no idea what stood before her—what was truly protecting the boy. Hellen wasn't so sure either. But she knew that whatever she had unleashed back in the theater, it was impressive and raring to go again.

"Back off, demon," the female said, her tone hard and wary. "I have no fight with you. I just want to take the *balas*."

"It will be a fight to the death if you take that *balas*." She raised her hands. "And I will win."

Erion moved past her to stand between her and the vampire female. "Hellen, wait."

She stared at his concerned expression. "She wants the boy."

"She is his—"

"Guardian," the female provided with deep irritation.

"What?" Hellen stepped to one side and studied the female. Tall, beautiful, with yellow hair, and strong in mind and body. "I don't believe you."

Erion glanced over his shoulder. "Kate, I'm sorry."

"It's all right," she answered.

Jealousy poured through Hellen and she felt her hands curl into fists. Erion knew the female. This blond, beautiful vampire female. Were they lovers?

The growl that erupted from Hellen's throat made both Erion and the female turn to face her.

But it was the boy who spoke.

"She is my Kate." Ladd stepped in front of the female and spread his arms wide. "She takes care of me, like a mother. And she's very good at her job."

The boy's words, his care for the female, had Hellen pulling in a breath. What was happening here? She backed up a foot. She glanced at the female, Kate. Her eyes were wet with tears, but she quickly wiped them away with the back of her hand.

What was this? Was this the boy's mother? The one Erion made the child with?

Ladd eyed her, not with any trace of anger, but as one who was protecting something he loved. "I won't let you hurt her, Hellen."

Shock barreled through her. "You know my name."

He nodded, his eyes flashing with momentary mischief.

Levia or Polly must've told him, she thought. She drew back another foot. "I wouldn't hurt her, Ladd."

But if she has been with Erion, cares for Erion, I may have to get her out of Hell immediately.

Kate got down on her knees and faced the boy. "I think we are all trying to protect you," she told him. "Your friend Hellen didn't know who I was, and she was afraid some crazy lady was stealing you."

"Oh. Well, that makes sense, I guess." He grinned at her. "Sometimes you are crazy."

She laughed. "True, *balas*. Very true."

"Then everything is okay?" he asked, turning to look at Erion.

Erion granted the boy a sturdy nod, then turned to Hellen. "This is my twin brother's mate." He looked at the vampire female, regarded her with a surprised expression. "Kate, how did you get here? You need demon blood to enter Hell. Is Nicholas with you?"

She stood, looked tired and worried. "I waited for Nicky, realized as I stood there that he would have the blood to get through. But he didn't come." She glanced at Hellen. "Something else did, though. A blue specter, a ghost—I don't know how else to describe it—came shooting through the portal. It took one look at me and was headed back in. I panicked. All I could think about was getting to Ladd. I flung myself at the thing, gripped on to its strange mass of light, and I was here."

"It must have been a rogue demon," Hellen said. "They try to get through the portals, cause trouble, but they can't survive long up there. You were very lucky."

She put her hand on Ladd's shoulder. "Yes, I am."

"Hellen!" Levia rushed inside the room, followed by Polly. "There you are. We were so worried. You looked terrifying."

Polly grasped her around the waist. "Oh, Hellen. We didn't know what he was forcing you to do. How you protected us. We thought you wanted the mating, that you felt it was a good match." Tears fell onto her cheeks. "I'm so sorry."

"It's okay," Hellen soothed, her heart breaking for the loss of her sisters' innocence. Damn their father. He could've had what he wanted, had two daughters who feared him but didn't know the absolute truth about him—that he was a loathsome monster who would sell them off as easily as blinking.

"He was going to kill Erion and Ladd." Levia stared at her, horror-struck. "He would've killed you too, Hellen. His own flesh and blood. I saw it on his face. We all saw it."

"I never thought he loved us," Polly said sadly. "I wasn't silly enough to think that, but I believed he had a trace of something good deep within him." Her eyes locked with her sister. "When he spoke to you on that stage, how he treated you, all that he said and did—I realized my beliefs weren't based in truth, but in hope."

"Oh, Polly," Hellen said, shaking her head.

"No, don't. I'm glad you did it. I'm glad you showed your power, and I'm glad he's gone." She looked at the group before her, Erion and Ladd clinging to Kate. "Are you leaving? Going aboveground?"

"Yes," Hellen confirmed.

"Then we're coming with you," Levia said.

Hellen felt a pull inside her, a responsibility to the citizens she was leaving without a leader. To this place she'd always called home. To her mother's memory.

She looked at Erion, Ladd, and her sisters. She wanted to be with them. For once, couldn't she choose what she wanted? Couldn't she be done with the role of perpetual sacrifice?

"Let's go." Erion took Hellen's hand and motioned for her sisters as well as Kate and Ladd to follow.

But it wasn't Hellen who refused the call. It was Ladd.

"I don't want to leave," he said, his lower lip jutting out. "I want to see more of the Underworld."

"Come, Ladd," Kate urged, pulling at his hand.

The boy shook his head and held his ground. "I like it here. I feel good here. Strong. Kate can stay here with us. Right, Erion?"

Shock registered on Erion's face. He looked first at Hellen, then back at Kate. The vampire female looked completely unsure what to do.

Finally, Erion released Hellen's hand and went to the *balas*, knelt down in front of him. "Someday we will return to the Underworld."

The boy's eyes brightened. "Tomorrow?"

"No," Erion said softly. "Not tomorrow. But someday."

Ladd's eyes flickered with frustration. "You promise?"

Erion nodded, then got to his feet and headed for the door, taking Hellen's hand once again. "Ready, demon girl?"

She nodded, smiled with relief. "Let's take the west

corridor. The one you and I took before. Remember? It's the safest." She glanced over her shoulder. "I don't know what we'll encounter with the citizens of Hell. We need to go quickly to the nearest portal."

As they hurried down the corridor, the sound of the crowd leaving the theater hummed through the walls. Hellen led the way with Erion at her side, and all were quiet as they wondered what, if anything, they would encounter or have to fight off to get to the portal.

Time moved rapidly, as it does in anxious times, and when they finally reached the archway leading outside, Hellen forced them to slow down and listen. "I think it's best to try to go through together. We will all touch, hold hands. There is more than enough demon magic here to get us aboveground."

They all nodded their agreement, and Erion squeezed her hand for support.

"See the rock just a few feet away, the dark purple?" she said, pointing. "That is a portal. Take each other's hands. Now. On the count of three, we're going to run for it. I'll be out in front. Levia, Polly, take the rear. There shouldn't be any problems. Just hold on to each other."

No one nodded this time; they were all focused and ready. The countdown was quick, and within seconds, the group charged toward the rock. Out in front, Hellen stretched out her hand, ready to push straight through the rock and sail upward.

But something happened.

Something unexpected and breath-stealingly painful. A force field hit her full on, a smack so strong it sent her flying backward, into the rest of the group.

"Shit!" she uttered, struggling to her feet.

Erion was on her in an instant, checking her for bruises or breaks. "What was that?"

"No idea," she told him. "Levia, you try. Don't run into it, but see if there's something there. Maybe it was just me."

The female nodded and slowly moved toward the rock. Every step she took was calculated. Hellen watched, and in seconds, her sister seemed to bounce off the surface of the air and land a foot backward. Levia turned and shook her head.

"I don't understand," Hellen breathed. "This shouldn't be happening. It's not possible—"

"The portals were your father's, created by his magic."

They all whirled around. Eberny, Abbadon's right hand, stood behind them. The hybrid stared calmly at Hellen. "When he died, the magic died with him, closing all the portals."

"Eberny," Hellen began. The hybrid had worked closely with Abbadon. There was no love or even care, but there was respect for his position in the Underworld, and Hellen wondered what the hybrid thought about the actions taken by his daughter. "Are you going to work against us?"

Hellen waited for the answer, waited to see what emotion, if any, worked within the hybrid's gaze. "Or do you see the reason behind the action I was compelled to take?"

The hybrid didn't say anything for a moment. There seemed to be some consideration of Hellen's words, then a slow nod. "You are firstborn, Hellen. If you wish to open portals to the world above, you must create your own."

Hellen stilled. Levia and Polly turned to look at her, their eyes filled with shock. She felt Erion's gaze on her back, but she continued to address Eberny. "How?"

"I will show you."

"Good. Let's begin."

Eberny didn't move. "It can only be done at the birth of day."

Behind her came muffled gasps and many soft-spoken questions. Hellen shook her head. "We can't stay here."

The hybrid appeared confused. "Why not? It is your home. No matter where you travel or for how long, the Underworld—this compound—is your home."

That statement brought Erion forward. As much as he'd given Hellen space and leadership in finding and traveling the portals, at his core he was her number-one protector.

"The scene in the theater," he said in a rough voice, "what Hellen was forced to do by that male who dared to call himself her father—surely she is an enemy of the people now. We must leave right away. I will not see her or her sisters harmed."

Eberny rarely showed emotion, but Hellen saw a flicker of insult. "We do not think as you do in the upper world. There is no mourning, no anger or resentment for a lost leader. Only the fact that another is needed." She turned back to Hellen. "The compound is secure. I have seen to it. All spectators to your mating have gone."

Hellen couldn't believe what she was hearing. No retaliation? No anger? No justice for their leader?

"There is no other way out of here but the portals?" Erion asked, his tone heavy with concern.

"No," Eberny told him.

Hellen turned to look at him. There was distrust and wariness in his diamond gaze, and she understood it. She felt it too. But what was their alternative? She took his hand. "We must stay for the night."

His jaw worked and his eyes narrowed. "But only for the night."

She nodded.

"Come," Eberny said, loud enough for all to hear. "We have rooms for those who do not live here, food for all, entertainment if anyone wishes it."

"I've had enough entertainment for one day," Erion growled as they followed the hybrid back inside the compound.

"Can we play our flying game, Levia, then conjure the puppies afterward?" Ladd asked. Before the female could answer, he turned to Kate. "Wait till you see the puppies! They're so cute. If we have to go back aboveground, maybe we can take one with us."

"We'll see, Ladd," Kate said softly, her voice a thread of soft worry.

Hellen remained close to Eberny and spoke under her breath. "In the very first call of day."

"Of course," said the hybrid, clearing the archway and heading inside the dark corridors once again. "You will find your power, Hellen, create portals with the deep magic you possess, for all those who wish to leave."

Erion came up alongside them and stated in a very cold voice, "That will be all of us, hybrid."

Eberny said nothing while rounding the corner.

*   *   *

He had been a prisoner here.

Now he was a guest.

Erion left the room where Ladd and Kate were staying and walked down the long hallway toward the corner room that had been assigned to him. The boy was surrounded by females: Kate, Hellen's sisters, and the two pups they'd conjured for him. He was in heaven.

The irony of that thought made his lips thin.

He was glad the *balas* held no fear in the Underworld, and yet it worried him how attached Ladd had become to Hell. It didn't surprise him, because he too felt the pull here; he too felt stronger, clearer, better here than he did aboveground. Clearly it was part of having demon blood. But that didn't mean it was where they belonged.

Once they left this place, once they had a chance to live as a family, everyone would settle. Ladd could have Nicholas and Kate and get to know Erion as a father. Perhaps the boy could even come to care for Hellen.

Hellen.

She had left after the meal, wanting some time to herself. Erion had given it to her. But as time ticked on and his mind conjured thoughts and fears and wants, he couldn't remain closeted for much longer. They were a pair, connected on too many levels to count, and he needed to see her, touch her, hold her against him. He had to make sure she understood how he felt, that she belonged to him, and he would love and care for her always.

The word *love* inside his mind felt strange. He'd never experienced romantic, possessive, needful love. It made him both fearful and anxious. It made him want to rip the door off its hinges and find her, and it made him desperate to kill anything male that might venture to look in her direction.

"Do you need help finding your room?"

He turned and found Polly walking a few feet behind him. "No. Thank you."

She nodded solemnly and was about to walk past him when Erion's next words stopped her.

"But I do need help in finding *her* room."

Polly turned, her amber gaze regarding him coolly. She didn't like him, he could tell, and he wondered why. It couldn't be just that her sister cared for him.

"I believe she is resting," she said haughtily. "I didn't see you eat at mealtime. I'm sure you are hungry. I can have something sent to your room."

He grinned at her meaning. "The only thing I require is blood. Do you have that on tap in the Underworld's kitchens?"

"Absolutely not." She looked utterly repulsed. "So that is why you wish to find my sister? You want her to feed you?"

Just the thought made Erion's body go up in flames, made his cock stiffen and his fangs drop a few millimeters. But Hellen wasn't vampire. He would never ask for or expect such a sacrifice from her. "Not to worry, Polly. I will take care of my needs when we return tomorrow."

She looked relieved.

But Erion was only more determined. "Now, are you going to tell me where her room is, female? Or do I need to use my nose to scent her out?" He lowered his voice. "It shouldn't take long. I know her scent very, very well."

Color stained the demon's cheeks and she stepped

back. She was a pretty female, but nothing compared to
her extraordinary sister.

"I don't think this is the time," she said. "After what's
happened today . . ."

"This is precisely the time," he countered, drawing
closer to her. "She needs the soothing and care and love
of her mate. Don't pretend you didn't hear her claim inside the theatre."

She frowned, her eyes suddenly melancholy. "I heard
many things."

Erion felt pity for the female and all she had learned
about her father and his plans for her, but it was Hellen
who needed him now. "There is nothing to do but move
on and embrace the new challenges of our lives."

She looked down at her shoes.

"Listen, sister—for that is what we are now, whether
you like it or not." Her gaze slowly lifted, and Erion softened. "Hellen and I have chosen each other. We belong
to each other now."

"She might not want to see you."

He laughed softly. "Then she will tell me that herself.
She is anything but coy, yes?"

The female's lips twitched. "You know her."

He nodded. "I know her and I love her. Now take me
to her room."

19

Abbadon was dead.

At her hand.

Hellen paced the floor of her room, stopping every so often to look at the fireflower on her bed. It was still open, still alive.

What was she going to do? Where was she going to live? She was ready to run away with Erion, take her sisters along for the ride, all without a plan in place. She felt so insecure. Erion cared for her; she knew that. But had his feelings changed? Had seeing her end her father's life in such a brutal manner endeared her to him more or made him question if he wanted someone like her in his and his child's life?

Hell, it made her question it. The monster her mother had begged her never to release had protected him and Ladd and her sisters' futures, but it wasn't gentle and benign. It was capable of the darkest acts imaginable. In fact, she wondered if it might actually crave them.

A knock on her door brought her out of her anxiety-ridden question fest, and she immediately crossed the room and opened it wide.

"Hey, demon girl."

Just his deep, magnetic voice made her feel better, made her feel calmer, but the smile he offered made her insides curl with arousal.

Would it always be this way with them? Instant chemistry, instant fire?

Beside him, her sister Polly was attempting to look put out. "He insisted I tell him where your room was."

"And she insisted in following me here," Erion said, leaning against the doorjamb.

Hellen's gaze moved over him covetously. He was so handsome, so wickedly sexy, standing there in his black T-shirt and jeans, his black hair licking the edges of his wide, powerful shoulders. The male made her heart squeeze with wanting. Did it matter that they didn't have a plan aboveground? He wanted her with him. Wasn't that enough? "You can go now." Her eyes remained on Erion. "Thank you for bringing him to me, Polly."

The female grunted, didn't move. "Perhaps you won't be thanking me tomorrow, sister. He is hungry."

"Is he?" Hellen smiled at him.

Erion growled softly, his eyes pinned to hers.

"Yes," Polly said as though she and Hellen were the only ones standing at the door. "And do you know *what* he is hungry for, sister?"

Hellen's breath quickened, her gaze never wavering from his. "I couldn't possibly guess."

"Blood," she said on a horrified gasp.

Heat moved through Hellen at her sister's words, and

she moistened her lips. This male, this incredible demon vampire, wanted her. She saw it in his gaze, in the way he touched her, kissed her, protected and possessed her. While others had only ever found her unsightly, Erion somehow believed her beautiful, desirable—so desirable he wanted not only to claim her but to consume her blood.

Erion's nostrils flared as he inhaled. His expression darkened and he lifted one black eyebrow, scenting her arousal.

Polly continued, completely unaware of what was happening right in front of her. "I told him you would most definitely not be interested in removing your blood and allowing him to consume it."

"That is true," Hellen said, heat now pooling in her belly and threatening to dip lower.

"See there, demon vampire male," Polly said, gesturing to Hellen. "My sister has much more sense than—"

"If he wants my blood," Hellen said in a soft, seductive voice, "he is going to have to take it himself."

That was it. Erion growled, his demon exposed, his fangs too, and pushed his way through the door.

Hellen laughed and backed up. "Good night, Polly. I will see you later."

"Much later," Erion uttered tersely as he closed the door on the female demon's shocked and appalled face.

He wasted no time in coming after her. He yanked the black T-shirt he wore over his head and tossed it aside. As she stared at his wide shoulders and smooth, thickly muscled chest, he flicked open the button of his jeans and sank the zipper.

"You're hungry, Erion?" she said boldly, her hands itching to grip his waist, run her fingers over his hip bones, dip her tongue inside his navel.

He shook his head, his eyes fierce. "Do not play. Do not tease. Do not pretend to give unless you are one hundred percent sure." He kept coming, stalking her until the back of her thighs hit the side of the bed. "Because once I have even a drop of your blood on my tongue, it's over. You will not be able to run without me at your back. You will not be able to sleep without my arms around you. You will not utter a moan of distress that doesn't end in my care or a cry of lust that doesn't begin at my touch." He stopped just inches away and narrowed his gaze on her neck. "Think hard, demon girl. With just one bite, you will belong to me."

Hellen's breath came out in a rush and she stared up at him, panting. His words had pushed her into a place of such deep wanting, she knew she'd never return. She was his. She'd been his since he'd stolen her away, and in doing so had opened her eyes to the truth about herself and her father.

Inside her thin, white silk nightdress, her breasts felt heavy and her nipples ached to be touched. Her belly convulsed with each breath she tried to pull into her lungs. Her legs felt unable to hold her weight, and between her thighs, heat swirled inside her tight, soaking-wet pussy.

Was she sure?

Did she want him?

His hands on her? His mouth on her? His tongue inside her?

His fangs sinking deep and stripping her of the blood that would satisfy his hunger?

He towered over her, his fangs so low they pierced the flesh of his bottom lip. "Am I easing you back on this bed? Am I taking your vein as I take your body?" His nostrils flared. "The answer had better be yes."

"Yes, Erion," she breathed. "Gods, yes."

His satisfied grin made her tremble with anticipation. She'd thought about this moment too many times. Erion taking her completely. She'd never felt the intensity and pleasure of a thick cock pushing into her, but she wanted it—she wanted him.

He pulled off his jeans and threw them in the same direction as his shirt, then grabbed the top of her night-dress and in one clean movement ripped it from neck to knees.

She sucked in a breath as the material slipped off her shoulders and pooled on the floor at her feet. "I would've taken it off for you."

His arm snaked around her and he lifted her onto the bed. "You will never remove your own clothing again," he commanded with a sexy purr. "If I don't ease them over your head with my fingers, rip them from your body with my fists, or bite them off with my fangs, they remain. Understood?"

She nodded, swallowed as he rose over her. She couldn't get over how beautiful he was and how terrifying. Everything about him was large and overpowering, from his shoulders and chest to the thick shaft between his thighs that was so hard it stood tall against his belly.

"You are perfect," she whispered, her eyes meeting

his. "The most beautiful male in the world." She smiled. "And you are mine."

He grinned back at her. "I'm glad you finally understand that."

"And I am yours," she added, her hands going around his neck.

"That too." He growled and leaned down to kiss her. "My good little demon."

"Not so good," she whispered right before his mouth claimed her.

The kiss was anything but soft and slow. They had wanted each other for too long, their need too intense. He took her with ravenous abandon, his tongue plunging inside her mouth to find hers, and once he did, he groaned with possession. She didn't need to hear him say it to know what he was thinking: *MINE*.

And she was.

Wanted to be in every way.

He tore his mouth from hers and dipped his head, brushed his lips across her neck. Hellen sucked air between her teeth with the feeling, every nerve ending on alert, the muscles between her thighs clenching.

"Are you going to bite me now?" she asked breathlessly, wanting him so badly, wanting his fangs inside her—wanting him inside her.

His warm breath caressed her ear. "Not yet, demon girl."

She shivered, then cried out as he raked his fangs ever so lightly up the shell of her ear.

She was going to come, just from his voice, his breath on her skin, the anticipation of his touch.

He eased to one side of her, his hand finding her belly. He stroked her gently, teasing her navel until she felt tears in her eyes.

"Please, Erion," she begged, her hips lifting, straining, to get to him.

His hand stilled on her rib cage. "What is it, my beautiful one? What do you need?"

"Touch me."

He chuckled softly, tracing each rib until his fingers rested just below her right breast. "I am."

She whimpered. "It's too slow. It's torture. I won't be able to hold on."

"You don't have to," he uttered, leaning down, kissing her cheek as his fingers brushed over her breast, his nails raking her stiff nipple lightly. He purred when she cried out. "Come, demon girl. Come for me. It will be the first of many."

He found her ear and licked the shell as he squeezed her breast against his palm, then drifted up to pinch the hard peak.

The sensation went straight to her cunt. "Oh, gods. Erion."

His tongue laved her as he tugged and circled her nipple. Shards of white-hot pleasure assaulted her and she reached down between her legs to touch herself.

"No," he said harshly. "Your cunt belongs to me now."

It was too much for Hellen; his words, his tongue on her ear, his fingers pinching her nipple. Then he bit down gently on her earlobe, and she lost her mind completely. Teeth clenched, hips jutting up, a cry wrenched from her throat and she came so hard it was almost blinding.

"So beautiful," Erion whispered against her ear as his hand moved down her torso, over her belly. "The state of euphoria suits you, demon girl. I intend to keep you there."

Hellen's mind felt heavy and her eyes were unfocused, but her body called to him. She had a feeling it would never stop calling to him.

"Touch me now? Please." She was begging and she didn't care.

He chuckled softly as he lowered his head and kissed her nipple, the one he had pinched and tugged that sent her over the edge. Then he shifted to the other. Hellen arched toward him as her hips continued to lift and lower. Why was he torturing her? And yet even as the thought entered her mind, she brushed it aside. His lips were on her nipple, sucking it into his hot, wet mouth, his tongue flicking the tip as he moved his head up and down. She'd never experienced such a delicious sensation. He was fucking her breast, and she keened and convulsed and felt the rush, the heat, the overwhelming sensation of impending orgasm move over her. She was going to come and the male hadn't even touched her below the waist.

His fangs were descending. She felt it against the flesh of her breast as he sucked her off, as his tongue flicked violently at her tight, aching bud. And then he released her, lifted his head a fraction, and used one sharp fang instead of his tongue. He circled her nipple with the tip, then slowly flicked it back and forth. The slight pain and intense pleasure stole her breath, and once again she climaxed.

She cried out his name and reached for him, took his cock in her hand. He was shockingly stiff and so warm, she smiled. Erion blew a cool breath over her wet breast. And as she rode the waves of climax, as she pumped him slowly and gently and hungrily, somewhere in the back of her mind, she heard him speak.

"I've wanted to possess you from the moment I saw you, Hellen," he said, easing himself out of her grasp and moving down her body. "You taste like heaven. Or, shit, maybe it's Hell. But I want more. I want everything at once. I know you're soaking wet down here, that your cream will drench my fingers and coat my throat. I ache with wanting you." His hand moved between her thighs, his fingers dipping inside her slit to gently circle her clit.

She gasped and whimpered. The feeling was too intense, and she tried to press her ass back into the bed to get away from him, but Erion wasn't having it.

"We're just getting started, demon girl," he whispered against her hip bones as his finger lightly traced her clit. "It's so swollen, so beautiful. It loves to be touched, played with."

"Erion, please," she begged. "I can't . . ."

"How tight are you, Hellen? If I fuck you with my fingers, will you squeeze them tight? Show me what my cock aches to feel."

She fought for breath but lost it again as he slid two fingers inside her.

"Oh, damn," he uttered, his mouth dangerously close to the top of her sex. "That tight grip could kill me. Cream running down my fingers." He inhaled deeply. "I can scent you. I love the way you smell. Oh, fuck it." He left her side and, keeping his fingers inside her, he moved between her legs.

Instinct drove Hellen, and she brought her knees up to her chest. Erion laughed softly. "My demon girl knows what she wants, what her body screams for. You love being licked, don't you, Hellen?" His fingers fucked her slowly as he lowered his head and purred. "Oh, so beautiful. So pink. Every inch of you cries for me. Eating your sweet pussy makes my cock cry too."

He covered her clit with his mouth and drew the bud into his wet heat, suckling it as he'd suckled her swollen tit.

Hellen groaned and fisted the sheets. "Erion, this is torture. Please, I can't think."

He released her clit. "Don't think, demon girl. Just feel. Feel and come."

He rubbed his nose against her, his mouth, then his chin. The roughness of his skin, the pressure of it, was too much for her. She started to cry.

"Let the tears come, Hellen," he whispered. "You deserve them."

He locked on to her clit and sucked it into his mouth. He found a rhythm, thrusting his fingers inside her as he suckled her, as she cried above him and gave in once again to the sweet release of her climax. Erion eased back and just licked her gently as heat barreled through her like a possessed animal.

She was boneless as he moved over her, as his cock slid between her pussy lips and pressed against the entrance to her cunt. But she wanted him still—wanted to be fully and totally and utterly taken by him.

"Your first male, Hellen?"

She watched his face tight with tension and desire, the bands of tension in his neck, the muscles in his arms and chest bunching and flexing.

"Yes," she said breathlessly.

He purred. "And your last, Hellen?"

"Yes!"

"I love you. Fuck, I love you!" He covered her mouth with his and entered her in one deep thrust.

Hellen had never had a male inside her, but there was no pain when Erion sank his cock deep. She was slick and hot and ready for him—more than ready—and all she wanted was for him to claim her body as he had claimed her heart.

She wrapped her legs around him and thrust her hips up, grinding against him, letting him know that she was desperate. His kiss intensified, and as he pleasured her mouth, he slowly fucked her.

Tears pricked at her eyes again. Not because of the heat that surged inside her or the delicious feeling of being completely and totally filled with the male of her dreams—the male she loved—but because, for the first time in her life, she was allowing herself to take without guilt, love without fear, and need without reproach.

Erion tore his lips from hers for a moment and lifted his head so he could stare into her eyes. He had such amazing eyes, so dark and soulful. And they were heavy with desire for her, all of her.

"Your pussy is so tight, demon girl. It sucks me in and refuses to let me go. I don't want to go. I want stay inside you forever."

"Stay," she implored him ardently. "I love you inside me. I want you inside me always."

She moaned and jacked up her hips, and Erion answered with thrust after thrust into her slick pussy. He was impossibly hard, and her clit pulsed with need once again. Would she ever grow tired? Would she ever not need this to breathe, exist?

"You are mine, Hellen," he uttered, moving within her, his thick cock stroking her. "And I am going to mark you now. My seed inside you. But first . . ." He gained in speed, battered her cunt until she saw stars again, until she writhed and cried out and seized and trembled around him.

And then he allowed himself to come too.

It was like an animal's mating—*No, a demon's,* she thought blissfully. His face had changed fully—lionlike, demon eyes, fangs extended—and he snarled and growled and pumped himself into her, making tears escape from her eyes once more.

They were mated.

Well and truly mated.

And she would never give herself to another.

Erion pulled her close but remained buried inside her. His face inches from hers, he nuzzled her nose. "I wish to stay with you, in your bed, sleep with you until the morning, when we leave this place forever."

Her heart seized at his beautiful words. "I want that too."

He grinned, purred.

"You look happy, demon beast," she said, feeling his cock pulse inside her. There was no rest with him.

"I am most happy," he said, his grin widening. "I never expected to feel happiness like this. It's pure and raw."

"Just like you," she whispered, kissing his chin, nipping it with her teeth.

He growled at her. "You are mine, Hellen—you are my unbeating heart, my insides, my family, my future."

She stilled with his words, those raw words. *Family. Future.* She hadn't thought of that. Why hadn't she thought of that? Maybe because she'd wanted him so badly. But a family, children . . . Would he be happy, content with only the one?

"What is it?" he asked, concern in his voice. "Are you all right? Am I hurting you?"

"No, no." Her gaze dropped to his mouth. "You know I can't give you children." She released a breath. "If you wanted more, I would understand." *I'd hate it, perhaps lose my mind over it, but I'd understand.* "If you wanted to find someone who could—"

"Hey." He lifted her chin, forced her to meet his gaze. It darkened even as he stared at her. "Listen to me, and listen well. When I was born and my mother realized I was *mutore*, she tossed me out like trash. I was a bad omen, something broken and unwanted. Something that didn't deserve to be loved." He cupped her face. "Can you give me love, demon girl? And the loyalty of a mate? Because that is what I truly need."

The honesty, the open vulnerability of this male tore at her insides. She leaned in and kissed him. "That I can give you, Erion."

He lapped at her lower lip and whispered, "And I promise it to you as well." He drew back. His eyes deepened and grew in intensity. "I love you, Hellen. I ache with it."

She'd heard him say it right before he'd taken her, and she'd believed him. But like this, wrapped in his arms, satiated and warm and safe, it meant a thousand times more. "I love you too."

He smiled, though a flicker of worry lit his eyes. "You will be all right leaving your home?"

"As long as I'm with you," she said, though she knew it wouldn't be that easy to walk away. "I don't think I belong here anymore. Not after what I've done. No matter what Eberny says, I fear I will be despised."

"You did what you had to do, my love."

"I know." And she did. She had no regrets—only relief that everyone she cared about was safe. "But I am ready to start my life."

"Our life," he amended with a grin. "And we can live anywhere you want. New York, France. Me and you and Ladd."

Her heart sank a fraction. The boy. She wanted the boy to be happy, and she'd seen him that way with the female vampire. "He will want to be with Kate. He clearly adores her, and she him."

"He will. I would never take him from her." His brows came together. "But he is my son, and after witnessing Abbadon's cruelty, I want more than ever to be a good father to him."

"You are a wonderful father," she said with passion, touching his face. "You went into hell to save your son. That makes you a real father."

He grinned proudly. "And you, the way you threatened to attack Kate—that is the act of a loving and overly protective mother."

"No." She drew back, shaking her head. "No. I'm not a mother."

"What do you mean?"

"I fear what is in me now. I have the power of my father in me. I can feel it when I get angry or possessive. It pushes to come out and fight and take without asking and . . ." She shook her head. It was so ugly, this truth, this fear of the unknown that raged inside her blood. "I would die if I hurt a child—"

"Stop, Hellen." His tone was fierce, his eyes too. "No matter what you think you have lurking inside you, you are not your father. You are no devil." He gathered her up in his arms, his mouth a breath away from hers. "You are an angel. My angel."

He kissed her softly, sensuously, convincingly, and as he did, he purred and started to move inside her. "I wish to take you again, but I know you are sore."

"I am demon," she returned, biting at his lower lip. "We don't get sore. We get demanding."

He grinned. "My perfect mate. You demand, my love, and I will give you everything you desire." He pulled out of her and flipped her over onto her belly.

"Wow," she said on a gasp.

His arm tunneled beneath her and he eased her hips back so she was on her hands and knees. "Wow, indeed," he uttered, his voice dark and heavy. "If I wasn't so desperate to get inside you again, I might have to eat you this way. You are so pretty."

He moved over her, his chest against her back, until

she felt the head of his cock. It was so hard he didn't need to guide it. She gasped as he entered her, stretched her.

"I have only just filled you with my seed," he whispered against her ear. "And I already want to give you more. You have the tightest, hottest pussy. It begs me to fuck it, weeps for me to fill it."

One hand brushed past her hip and found her sex. He groaned, and she felt his cock swell further inside her. "Do you know how wet you are, Hellen? It's running down your thighs, soaking your skin, soaking my hand."

She arched her back and pressed against him, ground her ass against him, wanting him deeper, wanting everything as the pressure built inside her once again.

"Hold on, demon girl," he said, his fingers dancing lightly over her clit as his strokes gathered speed. "You're about to come again, and when you do, I'm going to fuck you so hard you won't be able to breathe."

"Yes, Erion! Please!"

He rammed up inside her and froze.

Hellen's breath was caught; she panted as she felt him close to her ear.

"Oh, shit," he whispered, his voice otherworldly. He was demon now. She didn't have to see his face to know it. "I'm hungry, Hellen. I can't hold out any longer. You're mine. Your blood is mine."

Without warning, he bit down hard on her shoulder, and she screamed. His cock swelled again and he started fucking her, slamming inside her so deep, she dropped her head and prayed her legs wouldn't give out beneath her. As he clung to her shoulder with his fangs, pulled on her vein and took her blood into his mouth, Hellen fell over the edge for the fourth time that night. She was utterly gone, hovering somewhere where only madness and heat and mind-blowing climaxes were allowed to exist.

Trying to remain upright, she let him work her over. He was pumping inside her, flicking her clit, and swallowing her life's blood all at the same time. Happiness and pleasure spread through her. In the bed where so many nights had been spent crying and plotting and coming to an understanding about her dismal future, she was being fucked—no, she was being made love to—in every way she'd never dared to imagine.

For the first time in her life, she'd witnessed a happy ending in Hell.

And it was hers.

"Where did you find her?" Alexander asked the moment the door of the Manhattan hotel room opened.

Whistler backed up and allowed them to enter. "Bronx Zoo."

Still living with the shock of such a possibility, Celestine gaped at the male. "What?"

The Eye closed the door and headed past them into the room, took a seat on the couch. It was a generous suite, paid for by Alexander. He hadn't wanted the female brought to his home yet, not until her parentage was confirmed. But he also didn't want her in the park or in some shitty motel.

"She was living near the cages of the animals," Whistler informed them, putting his feet up on the coffee table.

Alexander put a hand on Cellie's and found it trembling. "Why would she do that?"

Whistler shrugged. "You'll have to ask her."

"But you're sure she's . . ." Celestine broke off with a whimper.

"Oh, I'm sure. She carries the blood scent you gave me." He leaned back on the couch, his hands behind his head. "Shall we open her vein and have a closer look?"

"No!" both Celestine and Alexander answered at once.

The Eye chuckled, then turned his head toward an open door to his left.

Out of instinct, Alexander's body shifted into high alert.

"Come here, *veana*," Whistler called.

There was a sound of a soft snarl, then footsteps. "I am not a *veana*."

When she entered the room, Celestine gasped. "Oh, my gods." Her hand went to her mouth, muffling a cry.

Alexander's fighting instincts evaporated, but he couldn't move. Shit, he could barely breathe. He just stared at the wary, snarling female before him. The heavily pregnant female. It was the strangest sensation. Like looking at a different form of his true mate.

"She looks . . ." Celestine uttered, but she couldn't finish the thought.

Alexander did it for her. "Like Sara."

Celestine burst into tears and ran from the hotel room.

*   *   *

Hellen woke with arms wrapped around her.

But they weren't Erion's.

The shock of that knowledge came swiftly and she bucked and slammed her elbow back into the body that carried her through the corridor archway, until it released her onto her feet.

She glanced down at the ash on the ground and at herself. She was wearing a blue robe, not unlike the one her captor was wearing. Her gaze slammed upward and into the serene face that had practically raised her after her mother died. "What are you doing, Eberny? Have you gone completely insane?"

In the dark lavender evening light, the hybrid looked especially foreboding. Eberny nodded. "I apologize."

"For what?" Hellen demanded, her hands on her hips. "Coming into my room unannounced? Taking me from my bed? From my mate's embrace?"

The hybrid's eyes shuttered. "Yes."

Hellen's eyes narrowed. "What's going on? It is still night."

"We must talk."

"And it couldn't wait until morning, when we open the portals?"

"When *you* open the portals," Eberny corrected.

"Me, you—what does it matter?"

"It matters a great deal," Eberny stated, the hybrid's expression graver than usual. "Do you think I have the power to do such a thing?"

Hellen stared at the hybrid, something moving inside her. "I'm guessing no."

"Abbadon was the only one with that power."

"Are you saying I won't be able to manage it either?" Suddenly panicked, Hellen moved past the hybrid and walked over to the massive rock that had once been a portal. "Is that why you brought me out here? To tell me you think we're all stuck in the Underworld—Erion and Ladd. Kate."

"No," said the hybrid calmly. "The others will be able to leave as soon as you open the portal."

Hellen whirled around and hissed. "Eberny, you're starting to piss me off."

"Did you enjoy your night with the demon vampire?"

"Very much," she said in an almost protective way.

"I am glad. You needed to."

"What does that mean?"

Eberny's face remained impassive. "Sex unlocks the final shift, the devil magic you will need to open the portals."

A slow, terrifying vibration started to move through Hellen's blood. "What are you talking about?"

"You are your father's firstborn," the hybrid explained. "And that gives you most of what you require. But not all. Sex is the key, the final step in the fertilization of your true magic."

Hellen attempted to reel in and process what the hybrid was telling her, but it wasn't easy. She had the power—sex with Erion had not only been the best moment of her life, but it was the key to opening the portals. She brightened at the news. "This is good, then, right?"

"Yes," Eberny said, watching her.

But if sex with Erion, with anyone, was the key to unlocking the portals, why wouldn't Eberny have told her before? Hellen wouldn't have wasted a moment. She'd wanted Erion desperately, and he'd wanted her.

Her mouth thinned and the fear-laced vibration was back. "There is more. What is it?"

Eberny regarded her with cool eyes. "Do you know that the citizens of Hell are grateful for what you did, Hellen? Abbadon's cruelty and tyranny was a strain on the society for too long. It is why there was no revolt when you ended his life. They accept you."

Hellen moved away from the rock. Something was growing within her, something other than fear. What was it? Anger ... Violence ... "I don't understand where you're going with this. They know what? Accept what? What are you talking about?"

"I speak of your kind, your demons."

"I have one demon, and he's back in my bed," she snarled, letting the feeling rise to the surface.

"Hellen."

"I want nothing from you, Eberny, nothing from this place."

"This is your home."

Hellen didn't want to hear any more. She'd made up her mind. She turned and headed for the archway.

Eberny followed. "Your mother named you for your birthplace."

"I know. I know the story—"

"Then you know she also named you for the world you would rule someday."

Hellen stopped just inside the arch. She slowly turned to face the hybrid. Eberny no longer wore the usual mask of indifference. Within the hybrid's expression passion and fire now flared, along with a need to force Hellen's hand.

"Why didn't you tell me that sex was the final puzzle piece in opening the portals?" Hellen whispered in a caustic voice. "You knew I was going to sleep with my demon male."

Eberny's gaze flickered with heat. "You might not have if you knew that the very portal you must open to release your lover is the very one you will not be walking through with him."

Hellen's demon emerged and lunged at the hybrid. "Liar!"

Eberny drew back, out into the purple end of night once again. "I took you from your bed, from your one night with your lover, to show you the world you have inherited, the world you will govern."

"I refuse it!" Hellen roared, stalking after Eberny. She would tear the hybrid apart. This is what she feared. This was her father inside her—and right now, it pleased her to call upon it.

But Eberny's eyes weren't filled with fear. They glittered as if Hellen's visceral response was precisely what the hybrid was after. "It is a call you cannot refuse, Hellen. You have a responsibility here. Your mother warned you of this. It is why she begged you not to unleash your monster."

"Do not speak of my mother," Hellen growled, barreling down on the hybrid.

Oh, gods. What don't I know? What didn't she tell me?

"I wanted you to know this now," Eberny continued with slightly less calm than a moment ago. "Perhaps you wish to say good-bye."

"I'm not saying good-bye to anyone but you."

The hybrid's back hit the rock. "You are the new Demon Queen, Hellen."

Hellen coiled over Eberny. "No!"

"Yes, Your Highness. You are the Devil."

20

Erion awoke to warm, soft hands raking up his abdomen and a hot mouth drawing on his cock. Nostrils flaring and his head still heavy from sleep, he glanced down. What he saw made him groan with lust and happiness. Hellen was easing her head back and pressing the tip of her tongue inside the slit in the head of his cock.

"You want me to fuck your pretty mouth, demon girl?" he uttered, his entire body a hot rush of insanity and need. "All the way to the back of your throat."

She moaned, taking him deep as she reached around his hips to grip his ass. She squeezed him hard, so hard her nails dug into his skin and he cursed and thrust his hips forward. He let his head fall back, then thrust into her mouth and quickly withdrew. She moaned, lapped at him with her tongue. Again he thrust into her. But this time, she held tight to his ass and kept him inside her mouth with a deep sucking action.

Erion groaned, his abdomen rippling. Shit. He was going to come. Hot and heavy. And though the thought of releasing inside her sweet mouth made him nearly lose his mind, he wanted inside her in the most desperate way.

In two quick and gentle movements, her mouth was off his cock and he had her sitting astride him. *Damn,* he mused, *if this was how sleeping could turn out, I've just become a fan.*

Then he got a look at her face, and his gut twisted and burned. She wasn't demon, flaring and flashing with lust as she shifted against his groin. She was desperate, worried, anxiety-ridden Hellen, and he grasped her hands and held them tightly.

"What's wrong? Tell me . . ." he demanded, but she cut off his words with a shake of her head.

"I need you," she said breathlessly. "I need all of you. Right now. Please. Inside me."

Erion growled. Gods, he wanted her, wanted to please her and give her what she asked for—his dick was screaming for her wet heat—but her eyes worried him and her fear scent made him insane.

"Hellen . . ."

"Don't, Erion," she begged. "Don't think. Not right now." She pressed against his chest and his hands and lifted her hips. "I need this. I need you. You have no idea how much."

She lowered herself on him, taking his cock all the way, filling her, stretching her. Erion groaned at the feeling of her tight, hot pussy, her lips pressed against his groin. He had already been driven so far by her mouth. There was nothing he could grab on to to take him back to her worry and strain. He was utterly and totally consumed by heat and the raw desire to fuck.

"Yes," she breathed. "Yes, Erion. That's what I want."

She rode him, slow and sensual at first, her hands braced on his chest, kneading his flesh. She was incredible, the most beautiful female he'd ever seen, and she was his. He had her blood inside his veins and on his tongue to prove it.

He gripped her hips and slammed her forward, his feet flexing and his fangs dropping as her cunt squeezed his dick to perfection. Every night he could have her like this. Every morning he could bury his head between her thighs and let her wake to orgasm.

He had love.

Shit, he had so much love.

Her eyes were on him, delving into his depths, and he wondered what she saw inside him or what she was looking for. Did she see how much he loved her?

Then her eyes drifted closed, her lips parted, and her head dropped back.

The sweet honey vice of her cunt suckled him, warned him of the impending quake. Erion felt more precum exit his cock, and he drove into her madly, knowing she was on the verge and desperate to make her scream.

"Come for me, demon girl!"

A cry so pained and erotic ripped from her throat and she shattered around him. Erion felt her muscles contract violently against his shaft, and he couldn't stop himself. The grip was too hot, too tight, her cream drenching him, and he squeezed her hips and slammed her against

him. Hot seed spilled into her cunt, joining the wet heat
of her climax, and as he slowly pumped within her, Hellen collapsed on top of him and wrapped her arms
around his chest. Hearing her pant and whimper, Erion
forgot about the ecstasy raging inside him and just held
her close, demon to demon, male to female.

"Hellen . . . ?"

"I'm all right," she uttered. "Everything's all right."

She was sprawled on his chest, holding him as tightly
as he was holding her, both of them breathing heavily,
both of them coming down from the intensity of climax,
but Erion felt something on his chest; something hot and
wet that worried him.

She didn't want to talk. He knew that. He would respect that. But he would also hold her close and rub her
back and pray that the droplets of hot rain against his
shoulder were only sweat and not a display of a fragile,
pained heart.

Hellen willed the tears away. There was nothing to be
sad or worried about. Eberny's revelations had no impact on her decision. No matter what the hybrid had said
or what names she had claimed belonged to her, Hellen
was not giving up her life for someone again. The Underworld would find a new leader, a devil of its choosing. It
was not going to be her. The only thing she cared about
was breathing and living and the beautiful demon vampire male beneath her.

Erion.

He was her future, her mate. The male she loved.

You could ask him to live here. If what the hybrid said

*is true and you have all the power of Hell, he would be
welcomed as a king, and your sisters as true and honored
princesses. You wouldn't have to give up the home you
love, the Rain Fields, the ash, the fireflowers . . .*

Her eyes moved to the edge of the bed. the fireflower
was still there, still open.

She couldn't ask him that. He had Ladd, needed to be
close to him. He wanted to be a true father to the boy,
and after seeing what a true father actually was, Hellen
would never allow them to be separated again.

*"You aren't like your father. You're not the Devil. You
are my angel."*

She pushed the insecurities and fears from her mind
as Erion's hands continued to brush her back, pet her,
soothe her.

She wasn't the Devil. No matter what Eberny claimed,
Hellen would never accept it. And in the morning she
was going to walk away. No, she was going to run. With
him and with Ladd and her sisters to a new life, and
never look back.

"What's wrong with her?"

Alexander continued to stare at the *veana*. It was
amazing how much she looked like Sara. Though her
eyes were a much lighter shade of blue, her facial structure and hair color were exactly the same.

Was it actually possible that Sara and Gray's sister
stood before him?

"She's upset," Alex told her gently.

"Because of me?"

He toyed with the idea of lying to her but found it

pointless. "Yes. You look like someone she knows, someone close to her."

"Well, I'm sorry for her, but I can't stay here." Her
gaze flickered toward Whistler. "He forced me to come
here, drugged me with something."

Alex's gaze shot to the Eye. "That was not what we
discussed!"

Whistler snorted. "You wanted the *veana* who matched
that blood sample, Roman. You didn't specify how to
bring her in or, more importantly, how not to."

"Get out," Alex snarled. "Get out before I tear you
apart. I've been wanting to for ever so long."

The Eye stumbled toward the door, grabbing his
phone and shoes. "You'll be back, Roman. When you
need something more. Something far more dire than
finding your mate's sister."

The *veana* gasped as the hotel room door burst open
and Whistler walked out.

Alex turned back to face her.

"I don't know who you're looking for or why," the
female said, clutching her pregnant belly. "But I'm not it.
I'm nothing."

The door opened again, but it wasn't Whistler who
walked in and moved past Alex. It was Celestine. She
was together now, calm.

The *veana*'s eyes filled with fear as she watched Cellie
approach. "I need to go," she implored her. "Please."

"Do you know who I am?" Celestine asked her.

The *veana* shook her head. "And I really suck at
guessing." She looked from Cellie to Alex, then back to
Cellie again. "Look, whatever you have planned, under-

stand that I will fight to the death. No one will lay a hand on me or my baby."

"What are you running from?" Cellie asked. "Or who?"

A thread of distrust shimmered in her pale blue eyes. "I'm looking for my father. He's a very powerful vampire who would do great damage to anyone who held me against my will. You would be wise to let me go."

"Your father is a powerful vampire, is he?" Cellie repeated. "And what about your mother?"

A dark shadow claimed that glimmer in a hurry. "I don't have a mother."

Celestine sniffed. "Everyone has a mother, my dear."

"What I mean is, she's not around, not in the picture."

"What happened to her?" Cellie moved a foot closer.

The *veana* didn't like being backed into a corner, and she growled. "That's not really any of your business, is it?"

Seeing how agitated the *veana* was becoming, Cellie stopped and lifted her hands in submission. "I won't play these games any longer. I know your father. I met him a long time ago." The *veana*'s sharp intake of breath didn't slow her. "I was mated, but my male was being held for castration by the Order, the rulers of the vampire breed. It was one of the worst days of my life. I went to a member of the Order, to Cruen. I begged him to release my mate—I said I would do anything he asked. Anything."

The female's blue eyes widened. "You knew my father?"

Celestine nodded. "I'm sure you know where I'm going with this. You're a smart *veana*—I can tell."

The female lifted her chin. "You slept with him to get your mate released."

"Yes."

She frowned. "You found yourself pregnant."

Alex could practically see her mind working, straining to gain information but refusing it at the same time.

"That's right," Cellie said gently.

"Okay." The *veana* looked down, shrugged in a forced way. "I get it. You had a child; you think I'm that child. You came to find me." She shook her head, laughed without humor, and said tightly, "I'll save you the trouble. I'm not interested. Now can I leave?"

Alexander was stunned. He hadn't expected a grand reunion or tears of joy. But this response completely surprised him, and by the look on Cellie's face, she was feeling the same.

"I could be your mother," Cellie said, her gaze pinned to the female.

She shook her head again. "No. I told you. I don't have a mother. I don't want or need a mother. What I need is to get out of here." She started toward the door, her entire body jacked up on nerves and fear.

"There is a male who might come looking for you if he learns of your existence," Alexander called after her, tracking her movement. "He wishes your father dead, and he will stop at nothing to make him pay. Be on your guard. His name is Synjon Wise."

Of all the things that he and Cellie had said to her, this was the one that made her turn white and terror fill her eyes. "No," she whimpered. "You can't let him find me."

Alex looked at Cellie, but the *veana* had her gaze pinned to the young female.

"You can't let him see me," she cried out.

"You may not want a mother, but, honey, you got one," Cellie said, then went to the *veana* and put a hand on her trembling shoulder. "And she's going to help you whether you like it or not."

21

"Do you feel the shift of power within you?" Eberny asked, moving around Hellen as she stood in the very center of the carved-out rock.

"Yes," Hellen said. They had been working since daybreak, the hybrid instructing her with each step as she found her rhythm. "It's as though I'm taking from the rock, from its structure, its strength, pulling it into my blood and sending it back out, farther and farther until I feel the edges of our world and theirs."

"Very good. You are quick," Eberny praised. "You see the barrier in your mind, the hellfire?"

"Yes. But—" She opened her eyes. "Mine is green. My hellfire is different from . . ."

"From Abbadon's, yes. So much of you and what you are made up of is different, Hellen." The hybrid stopped circling her and came to stand before her. "You could do so much good."

They were words she didn't want to hear, refused to hear. "I'm going, Eberny."

The hybrid sighed. "You won't be able to survive up there for any length of time. Why do you think Abbadon was so intent on getting a foothold on Earth? As the Devil, he could remain only for a few of their days at most. He believed the blood, the DNA of vampire/ demon child, would grant him that."

Finding her power, unleashing it, containing it; the work had made her emotions flare. "I'll go for as long as I can."

"Then what?" Eberny demanded, this new ferocity unnerving.

"I don't know." Turmoil, frustration, fury all ran through her. She was trapped, always trapped.

"I do." Eberny turned away, blue robes swishing with the movement. "You will die. And in the meantime, Hell will have no one to rule and govern and inspire."

"I could go and come back," Hellen offered. "Travel back and forth. I can live in both places."

"You don't understand. You don't want to see the truth in this situation."

"I don't turn away from the truth, Eberny!" she cried. "I never have! I'm just trying to find answers, some solution that doesn't involve me getting my fucking heart broken."

There was a moment between them of silence, of sadness; then the hybrid sighed heavily. "If you went above-ground, once you return to Hell you must allow your body to readjust before you could go back."

"How long is that?" Hellen asked greedily. "A day?" Eberny didn't answer.

"A week? What?" Dammit. She was in love. The male

loved her. This had to work—she would make it work. "Why do I have to give up everything?"

"Why do you see it that way?" The hybrid turned around. "This is your home. Without Abbadon, Hell could be a wonderful place for demons."

Through gritted teeth and an aching heart, Hellen implored her to understand. "I want him."

"Keep him."

"He can't stay here. He has a child, a child whose life is up there. Whose family is up there. He wants to be a father to that boy, Eberny." Tears pricked at her eyes. "I can't ask him to walk away from his child. I would be no better than my father."

For one moment, the hybrid appeared sympathetic. "If you go with him and can only stay for a few days at the most, isn't that worse? You will draw him back here with you. He loves you that much. I can see it. He will leave the boy."

Tears fell from her eyes onto her cheeks, and around her, inside her, the hellfire erupted to life.

The hybrid reached out and touched the rock. "You feel the portal's birth?"

Hellen nodded, misery clinging to every inch of her. "It's ready."

"I do not envy your choice, Hellen." The hybrid's eyes burned into hers. "But, then again, I never have."

Hellen shut her eyes tight against the pain, against the tears, and called up the power within her. The pressure started at her feet and grew until it could no longer be contained. Then she sent it out in every direction and waited for the bounce back.

It came instantly, like a fierce, deadly wave of energy, pouring over and through her.

She had done it. Hellen, the Demon Queen, the Devil. Whoever—whatever she was, she had opened the portal.

"Where are they?" Ladd asked.

Leaning down, Erion whispered into the boy's ear, "Keep your eyes open and your arrow ready."

"What color are they again?"

"Blue."

"Oh, there's one." Ladd whirled to the right and sent his arrow flying across the fields. "Did I get it? Did I?"

Erion walked forward and pretended to follow the direction of the arrow that was somewhere deep in a low-hanging cloud by now. "Just missed. But you'll get him next time." When he turned back, Ladd was grinning.

"I love this," he said.

"I am glad, *balas*."

"I feel like I've been here before," he said with a wry grin, then turned back to Erion. "Do we have to go? Leave the Underworld?"

Erion felt a strange pull at the boy's question. Ladd had bonded with Nicholas and Kate, he was like a son to them, and yet he was Erion's blood. He was part demon. Should he know? Should Erion tell him the truth right here, now?

The momentary euphoria of releasing such a closely held secret was tempered by the reality of the pain it would cause Nicholas and Kate. And perhaps even the rejection that might come Erion's way from the son he so badly wanted to love him.

"We will come back," he said, touching the boy's shoulder. "I promise."

"I feel good here," Ladd said, placing another arrow in his bow. "Strong. Why is that?"

Your skin, your cells, your blood—all began here.

The demon inside Erion scratched to get out, tell the boy that his demon was scratching too, but it wasn't the time. "I'm not quite sure."

Ladd pulled back the arrow and tracked the Rain Fields with the tip. "Well, I do miss Uncle Nicky and Uncle Alex and even Uncle Luca."

Erion's mouth twitched. "What of Helo and Phane and Lycos? Do you not miss them?"

"Oh, sure. And baby Lucy and the baby we don't know the name of yet."

Erion chuckled. The boy was singular and funny and good-hearted, and, he thought with a wave of melancholy, someday perhaps even forgiving of the father who hadn't known of his existence.

"Erion?" Ladd said quietly, putting down his bow for a moment and looking at the demon.

"Yes?"

The boy bit his lip. "We will always be together, right?"

"Who, *balas*?"

"You," he hesitated, "and me?"

A great thundering need to run at the child and pick him up, hold him close, perhaps even rock him and say comforting words, rolled through Erion. It was a miracle. The boy liked him, trusted him—he could see it plainly on his determined little face. The boy saw him as something more than Nicholas's fearsome, deadly demon twin.

"You and I will be together for as long as you want," Erion replied. The words felt strange, maybe even sounded strange, but it didn't matter. He had Ladd and he had Hellen, and for the first time in his life, he felt grateful for his existence.

Ladd was grinning. "A promise is a promise."

Erion nodded. "I know. Never fear, *balas*. We will all be together. One family."

"Hi."

Both males whirled around, one with an arrow pointing straight at Hellen's heart.

She smiled at him. "You have good form, Ladd."

Her words were kind and her smile was bright, but Erion knew his mate. Sadness rolled off her skin and pain hovered beneath the surface of that forced smile.

What is wrong? he wondered. Had she been watching them together? Did it bother her to see their affection? Was she mourning the loss of the child she couldn't have?

He went to her and took her hand. He wanted to reassure her that he needed no other *balas*. She and Ladd were everything he could ever want and desire and hope for. His most perfect family.

But before he could say a word, her eyes cleared and she gave them the news they had been waiting for.

"The portal's open," she said. "We can go."

"Oh!" Ladd exclaimed. "Let's go get Kate," he added, springing to his feet. "We're going home!"

Erion squeezed Hellen's hand and smiled. "Home."

They'd been denied access to the Underworld. Over and over they'd tried jumping into the hellfire until Luca and the *mutore* took off and the day started to break.

Now they were waiting out the sun, and it was nearly down. The church basement they huddled within had barely kept the rays from their skin, and both had been burned on their necks and hands. But they refused to leave the portal until they found a way inside.

He wanted his mate and Ladd.

The Brit wanted the vampire prick.

A sudden tremble below them had Synjon jumping to his feet.

"Did you feel that?" he asked, backing up toward the wall.

Nicholas stood too and sidestepped a pencil-thin beam of nearly dying sun. "I did."

"We need to go and see."

"It's barely evening."

"So we get a little singed."

"Again." Nicholas moved to the window and ventured one painful glance out the window. The burn on his cheek hurt like a motherfucker, but it would heal. His mate would see to it. His mate. Gods, he missed Kate. If anything had happened to her, if anyone had hurt her—

"Holy shit!" he exclaimed, inching closer, forgetting about the pain on his cheek or the dimming light.

Synjon was beside him in a second. "What?"

Without answering him, Nicholas broke for the stairs. "Let's go. A few more seconds and the sun will be down. A few more seconds. Burned or not, something has emerged from the portal, and we are going to take it."

Synjon followed. "What the hell did you see out there? Your mate?"

Nicholas reached the top of the stairs and growled. "Cruen."

22

Mornings in Hell normally consisted of a lavender sky, an ashy wind, and the intermittent sound of thunder over the Rain Fields. But on this morning, Hellen's senses were tuned in only to the portal. Making sure it was open and ready to accept travelers. For these were very important travelers, and she wanted to make sure they got home safely.

"I'm going to send you and Ladd through first," Hellen told Kate. "As this is my first time working with a portal of my own design, I want to use caution."

Kate stood beside Ladd, her hand in his. "Of course." Her eyes were bright as she offered Hellen her other hand. "Thank you, Hellen. I know this wasn't easy tapping into the power of the one who went before you. But it'll be good to be aboveground, as you call it, again." She smiled in an almost intimate way. "It's hard to go so long without seeing Nicky. I miss him big-time. No doubt he's worried, and angry."

It was in that moment that Hellen realized what a

good female Kate Everborne was. Hellen had seen the
vampire with Ladd and understood her care and love,
but there was something within her gaze as she shook
Hellen's hand that spoke of hope and a possible friendship.

Hellen had never had a friend other than her sisters.
She wondered what that bond felt like, how it grew, how
it changed over time as one female supported the other.
She imagined it was lovely. But she couldn't mourn the
loss of hope. It was impractical, an emotion that wouldn't
serve her well.

"Remain close together," Hellen told them, pushing
her mind to focus. "And get ready to go home."

She closed her eyes and summoned the power that
hovered—waited—at the very edges of her mind. It instantly responded to her call, humming and purring like
an animal waiting to spring.

"Do you feel it?" Hellen called out, her words echoing inside the rock.

"Yes," Kate said, her voice a vibration now as she
hovered between the two worlds.

"See you soon, Hellen," Ladd called.

The words gripped at her soul, but she forced them
out. The surge of heat and energy blasted through her
and she sent the pair up, into the hellfire and back onto
Earth.

For a moment, she just stood there inside the rock
with her eyes clamped shut. Her breathing was labored,
and she wasn't sure if it was because of the energy she'd
just exerted or the sacrifice she was about to make.

"They're gone."

Erion's voice moved over her like a sweet breeze. How was she going to do this? How was she going to manage this?

Her eyes opened just as Erion caught her up in his arms and kissed her. For a full ten seconds, she let him, even moaned into his warm mouth as she breathed in his scent.

"My female is one powerful demon," he whispered against her lips. "I can't wait to bring you home, beautiful. I can't wait to see you in my bed, your red curls spread out on my pillow."

She drew back her head and died inside.

His diamond eyes held the hope of life and love within them. He grinned, wicked and sexy and yet sweet and true. He was in love with her. Eberny was right. If given the choice, he would tear himself apart, destroy himself, trying to be both Ladd's father and her mate.

She wouldn't allow that.

He pulled out something from behind his back and drew it up between them. Instantly the scent filled the air within the rock. "For you, demon girl."

Tears pricked her eyes, but she warned them to stay back.

"Where did you get this?" she asked, staring at the fireflower in his hand.

"Off your bed," he told her, his nostrils flaring, his gaze pinned to hers. "After you left this morning, it closed and gave off the most incredible scent." He kissed her softly. "It reminded me of you."

The pain that filled her—every inch, every muscle, every bone, and every cell—was nearly debilitating in its strength. She took the flower from him and gripped it tight. She would never let it go, never let it die—she'd use all the magic within her to make it so.

Erion seemed to realize something and he drew back and glanced around. "Where are your sisters? Have you already sent them? Or maybe they've gone themselves."

Her breath took shelter inside her lungs. "They've decided to stay, Erion."

He turned back to face her, his eyes soft with understanding. "I'm so sorry, love."

The tears were hovering inside her chest. They bubbled up like acid, desperate to climb higher—desperate to find release. "It's okay," she managed. "They came to realize that Hell can be a very different place now. It can be a true home for them."

His gaze flickered with sudden tension, and she wondered if she'd said too much.

"You can visit," he said, his arms tightening around her. "They can visit."

Hellen closed her eyes, forced herself to summon the heat within her, then call to the energy around her and demand the power she had claimed. It came quickly on the heels of her last burst of magic, and she was glad.

Do it. Do it now before you change your mind.

"Hellen?" Erion's voice was wary. "Something's not right."

She opened her eyes. They were still inside the rock but surrounded by the blazing light of her pale green hellfire. It was exactly where she wanted them.

Erion's eyes were fierce, panicked. "What is this? What's wrong? Why aren't we moving?"

"I can't go with you, Erion," she choked out.

His face went ashen. "No."

Her lips trembled. "I can't survive there—not for any length of time. A few days at the most."

"That's not true," he uttered blackly, his jaw clenching. "That can't be true."

"It's why Abbadon wanted the child," she told him passionately. "His foothold on Earth. He could never remain long enough to do any real damage."

"Stop this!" he snapped. "Stop talking and take us up through the portal. Take us home, Hellen!"

"I can't go with you, and you can't remain here."

"Demon girl—"

"Ladd needs you," she continued breathlessly. "Go with him, tell him who you are . . ." Her voice broke with emotion. Tears coated her vision. "Tell him what a wonderful, loving father you want to be."

"I love you, Hellen! Christ! Don't do this. I can't exist without you."

She shook her head, her heart pounding, her guts twisting. "There's no choice."

"There's always a choice," he flung back viciously.

"Ladd or me."

He looked horror-struck.

"I can't hold us here for long," she uttered desperately. "You've got to go."

He gripped her tighter, growled at her. "I'm not leaving without you, dammit!"

Tears streamed down her cheeks. "As you said, there's always a choice." She slammed her eyes shut. "And I'm making this one for you."

With everything she had, every last shred of power she possessed, Hellen ripped herself from Erion's arms and sent him up toward the hellfire. The last thing she heard before she returned to the interior of the rock was his roar of betrayal.

Her body heaving, cries wrenching from her throat, she did what she had to do.

She closed the portal on him forever.

For Synjon Wise, Christmas had come early.

The *paven* he had been tracking and whose slow and painful demise he had been fantasizing about nearly every minute of every day for the past seven months was standing on the other side of the room in the *mutore* Erion's very clever dungeon. His legs were shackled, arms too, and the power he had relied on for centuries to defile, maim, use, kill, and scorn seemed completely stripped away.

"Are you looking for revenge, Synjon Wise?" the *paven* sneered, utterly unimpressed with the position he found himself in.

That would change.

Cruen grinned at the lack of response, took it for emotion, lapped at the chance like a dog. "Your *veana*'s death was not my doing. You have only to look up those dungeon stairs for the culprits."

Synjon said nothing. Not even the mention of Juliet could bring emotion to his blood right now. He was too far gone.

Cruen's gaze flickered with confusion. "The Romans. They are to blame. They took her life, her breath. You will not look upon her face again because of their actions."

Peeling himself away from the wall, Syn moved toward the *paven*. His eyes held Cruen's, his mouth relaxed against his fangs, and tension released from his body. He saw it all now, his plan of action. Step-by-step, methodical and attainable.

The shackles clanged like warning bells, and Cruen's expression—his standard, quick arrogance—melted away. Though he showed no fear, there was concern in his gaze.

"There is only one thing I want from you," Synjon said, moving closer.

"What is that?" Cruen uttered.

He coiled over him and whispered in his ear, "Your endless misery."

Cruen chuckled. "Go to hell, *paven*. I've just been. It's lovely this time of year."

Synjon sighed, then in one smooth movement grabbed the *paven*'s ear and sliced off the lobe.

Cruen screamed in pain.

"Don't get your knickers in a twist, old chap," Synjon said coolly. "We're just beginning."

It was glorious to watch the expression on Cruen's face as it shifted from swaggering gleam to horror-filled shock.

Panting, blood dripping from his ear onto the stone floor, Cruen spluttered out, "What do you want?"

"I've already told you," Syn answered, and leaned against the stone wall. "You see, your suffering may bring me back to life. Your slow death could very well be my rebirth. I am compelled to find out."

"You're insane," Cruen said through gritted teeth, his eyes flaring with pain.

"Quite possibly." He brought up his blade again, stained with Cruen's blood. "Shall we try the other ear? Or perhaps a finger?"

Cruen cursed softly, his eyes trained on the blade. "You can't hold me forever. I'm willing to bet that even those bastards upstairs won't allow you to torture me."

Synjon cocked his head. "I'll take that bet. What shall it be?" He pushed away from the wall and walked over to the covered window. He grinned as he gripped the shade. "How about loser takes sun?"

He lifted the metal just an inch. Sunlight streamed through the glass and snaked toward the vampire *paven*.

"And the winner gets to watch him burn," Syn said, as the warm yellow snake attacked its prey.

23

"I have blood for him from Bronwyn," Lycos said, his voice muffled through the door.

"He won't take it," Phane returned. "He won't sustain himself at all."

"He won't do anything that is remotely sensible," Helo added with a frustrated growl. "He can't remain still. He's either working with Gray and the Impures or within one of the Romans' companies. The only one he will truly talk to is that dog he brought back from his castle, and, of course, the boy." He sighed. "Perhaps we should take him back to France. Let him try the portal again."

"It's no use," Phane replied. "He remained there for two days, clawing the ground, using his mind, his blood, his demon to try to contact her, and nothing happened." Phane sniffed. "He needs to forget."

"What he needs is to stop barking at everyone," Lycos said with frustration. "Acting like a total asshole . . ."

The *mutore*'s words died out, and Erion was thankful

for whatever had caused it. His brothers had been hovering outside the door of his weapons hold for more than an hour now. After stocking the Impure *credenti* with more weaponry last night, Erion had wanted to make sure both the Romans' home and the Beasts' had been replenished. The interruption was not a welcome one.

The door clicked open behind him, and he whirled around and growled. So did Mongrel, although the small dog remained in the plush bed the Roman brothers had purchased for him. Such iron balls they had to walk in here without his say-so, Erion mused darkly. Why couldn't they back off? Why couldn't they understand that he wanted nothing and no one to interfere—

But it wasn't his *mutore* brothers who stepped inside and walked over to his table laden with swords and daggers, but Nicholas's mate and Ladd.

Erion grew momentarily confused. "Am I late? I thought we were seeing the movie at seven."

Kate nodded. "We are. We wanted to talk to you."

Erion's skin prickled with tension. He'd heard that phrase a hundred times in the past week, and each time he did, he walked away from the one saying it. But he couldn't do that to Ladd. He would never do that to Ladd. The *balas* meant everything to him. In fact, he was the one bright, shining glimmer of light in Erion's black hole of an existence.

As Mongrel began to snore at his feet, Erion held tight and waited for one of them to speak. To his emotional ruin, it was Ladd. The *balas* stepped forward and eyed the weapons, then lifted his sweet, honest gaze to Erion.

"You miss Hellen?"

Erion's frown deepened, as did the pain in his chest. Just hearing her name gutted him. But he managed to utter a quick, "I do."

Ladd smiled softly. "She is very strong. Like you. And very sad." His eyes locked with Erion's. "Like you."

"I'm sure she is coping well enough," Erion said, gripping the table. After all, she was the one who had sent him away, cut him out of her life —

"No," Ladd said, interrupting Erion's thoughts. "She's not coping. She cries all the time."

Something moved inside Erion, scratched at his mind. "How would you know that?"

The boy licked his lips. "I saw her."

"What?"

"Just two times." He shrugged. "I didn't even think it would work. Levia and Polly told me the game only works in the Underworld. But I wanted to try. I wanted to see if I could . . . see her again."

His muscles growing tense beneath his skin, Erion glanced up at Kate. "What is he saying?"

Kate released a breath and came to stand beside the boy. She put her hand on his shoulder. "It seems that along with charades and how to conjure puppies, Levia and Polly also taught him how to astral project."

Erion stared at the *veana*. "I have no idea what that is."

"It's a game," Ladd began, his eyes lifting to meet Erion's, "a flying game that Hellen and Levia and Polly played when they were my age." He swallowed and bit his lip. "Levia taught me how to concentrate, make my body quiet so my mind could float away. I wasn't very good at it, and Levia and Polly were really strict about where I could go. I managed it only a few times." He looked sheepish. "The first was seeing Hellen walking in the hall. It was so cool. A few minutes later, I woke up, and there she was, looking at me through the glass." He grinned. "I think I scared her a little."

It was like trying to take in an entire novel in one breath. Completely stunned, not sure if he believed what the boy was saying and why it would be relevant now, Erion once again looked to Kate for answers.

She gave him a pitying look. "It seems our *balas* here has managed to project himself into Hell." She smoothed the boy's hair lovingly. "He has seen your female."

Erion's guts twisted. He didn't know what to think or believe, but the tiny fleck of hope that still hovered near his heart blossomed. He dropped to his knees before Ladd and said gently, "You've really seen her? You've seen Hellen?"

The boy nodded. "And she is very sad. Sadder than you."

"Ladd . . ."

"You've got to go to her."

"I can't get back to the Underworld. Whatever it is you've done won't open the portal. I've tried everything."

"Not everything." Ladd smiled with adorable wickedness. "So far I've just watched her hunting in the Rain Fields, but I think I can do more." His grin widened. "I think I know how we can get back home."

"We?" Erion repeated. His eyes lifted, but not to

Ladd. Kate stood there, her eyes swimming in tears, her mouth turned up into a sad but understanding smile.

"He felt it when he was in the Underworld, Erion," she said softly. "He knew something was different about it and about himself."

Dread filled him. "No . . . Kate, it wasn't supposed to be like this."

"He knew he was demon," she said, her eyes imploring him. "And that led to more questions . . . Oh, Erion, I'm sorry. It should've been you who told him the truth. But I can't explain how I felt in that moment. I wanted to deny it, wanted to pretend he belonged to me and only me . . ."

Ladd ran to the *veana* and wrapped his arms around her. "Don't cry, Kate," he told her gently. "I do belong to you. And to Uncle Nicky."

"But you are demon," she said, her gaze lifting. "You are Erion's little demon."

Oh, gods, Erion thought, his lungs tight. The *balas* knew. He knew his true father, where his life had begun. Fear tore at his insides. He was glad his son knew the truth, but what did Ladd feel?

Erion's gaze moved achingly slowly toward the boy. What would he see there? Sadness? Rejection? Need? Hope?

Ladd was holding Kate's hand, but his eyes connected instantly with Erion's. His smile was bright and wide— and happy. "When I was in the Underworld, even with Hellen's mean father, I knew I belonged there. And I knew you did too."

Relief poured through Erion. He loved that Ladd embraced his demon side and saw it in Erion too.

Breaking from Kate, Ladd came toward him. "I brought Kate home to Uncle Nicky. It's where she belongs."

The boy's words concerned him. "You can belong here too," Erion said quickly. "They love you."

For the first time since Ladd had entered the hold, he frowned and his eyes grew heartbreakingly sad. "Don't you love me?"

Erion couldn't stand it any longer. He broke from the table and rushed at his son. He was on his knees, holding Ladd's shoulders. "Of course I do. I love you more than anything."

"Then we can go," Ladd said, "back where we both belong."

His chest felt tight. "Even if this plan of yours works, I can't take you away from them."

"You're not. It's no different from us living in their castle in France or yours, or living at the warehouse here in New York. We're all a flash away."

Erion pulled Ladd into his arms again. "I don't see how this can be done."

"I'll show you, Dad. I'll show you her."

As Erion's mind swelled with hope and possibility, his gaze drifted up to the *veana* who had been a mother to his *balas*, the *veana* who was now holding Mongrel in her arms. Clinging to Ladd, Erion waited, his eyes filled with love and respect and gratitude.

Kate stared down at the two of them, her eyes bright

with tears as she stroked the small dog's fur. "Take him home, Erion. Take your son home."

The rogue crackled and exploded in a blink of blue fire. Hellen stood there, rain soaking her boots, and panted, waiting for the once-familiar thrill of hunting and destroying to come over her. But after a few moments, she knew it wasn't going to happen.

It hadn't happened since the day she'd hunted with Erion.

She wondered if it would ever happen again.

"I believe I am quite a decent shot." Polly approached, her bow at her side.

After many years of trying to get her sister to come on a hunt, the female had finally agreed. Though, Hellen mused, Polly had refused to wear anything other than a gown when she did. It was no surprise that the prim female had ruined three gowns already. Water and ash, mud and the guts of demon rogues. Those were stains that didn't come out easily.

"You have destroyed ten rogues today, and I must be content with one." Hellen forced a smile. It was better that way. Everyone in the Underworld knew she was mourning the loss of her male, and had taken to asking after her feelings far too often.

"It's too bad Levia isn't joining us, but the fireflower garden has become her obsession these days." Polly placed another arrow in her bow. "The demon who falls in love with her had better be an amateur botanist."

Hellen laughed, but it was a tinny sound. "I would like

to see you both have mates who care for you—mates of your own choosing."

"And you." Polly met her gaze with a curious lift of her brow. "You will let go of your memories in time. Won't you? There are many fine demon males who would be on their knees if you claimed yourself ready for a suitor."

Hellen turned away. She didn't want to even entertain such a thought. Memories were the only things keeping her sane. Memories and the fireflower she kept beside her bed. Now if she could just find something to ease the pain. It ran through her blood every second of every day, never letting up. She wondered how Erion was faring. He had her blood inside him. Did it make him miss her more—want her more?

"Ha!"

Polly's exclamation had her looking up. "What is it?"

"That rogue over there. It's been toying with me for the past hour." She started after it, her gown swishing against the rainwater on the ground.

"We'll take it on together. Shall we?" Hellen called, nocking an arrow as she followed.

Polly grunted. "I think we may need to."

But for some strange reason, the rogue didn't attempt to hide from them. In fact, it remained out in the open, near a large white cloud.

"Seems almost friendly now," Polly said, sounding surprised even as she drew back her bow. "This should be a quick kill. Number eleven, and in a gown and pantalets, no less. I'm quite impressive. Don't you think?"

Hellen didn't answer. As she stared at the shock of

blue light, her heart stuttered and she lowered her bow. Something wasn't right. She drew closer. The rogue demon didn't cackle, didn't spit. In fact, Polly was right—it seemed friendly. It seemed . . . She stared hard. Was that a face within the light?

Was that—

"Wait!" Hellen cried out. "Polly, lower your bow. Now!"

Her sister stumbled sideways into a cloud that was pouring down rain. "What? What's wrong?"

Hellen drew even closer, her mouth parted in shock. "That's not a rogue." She wasn't sure what she was saying, what else it could be.

"Looks like one to me," Polly said, wringing out the bottom of her dress, then picking up her bow again. "Come on, I really want it—"

"Hellen? Can you hear me?"

Both females gasped at the soft call that came from the rogue.

"Do rogues speak?" Polly asked nervously.

"No." Hellen moved even closer, was about a foot away when it spoke again.

"Open the portal, Hellen."

Shit. Her heart jumped to her throat and she dropped her bow onto the soaking ground. No. This wasn't possible. The demon rogue was playing with her. Perhaps she hadn't known what they were capable of. Perhaps this was payback for all the times she'd taken out their kind.

"Hellen," he said again. "Will you let us in?"

That voice, Hellen thought, her mind scrambling for

answers, for a clue as to what was happening before her. *That voice.* She knew it. *Who is it? Young and male and—*

Her head shot up. "Ladd?"

There was a squeal from the rogue, and then, "She understands, Dad. I can't hear her, but I can see her. She looks like she knows. I think she said my name."

Amazement washed over Hellen. She didn't know how this was possible, didn't know if she had gone insane or maybe if she was dreaming. But whatever it was, it was incredible and wonderful. She could hear Ladd, and he had called Erion Dad.

"If you can hear me, Hellen," Ladd was saying, as Polly stood stock-still at her side, gaping at what they were witnessing, "Kate and Nicky understand that Dad and I belong there in the Underworld. They want us to be together. And we want to be there with you."

"He's projecting," Polly whispered. "He's done it. I can't wait to tell Levia. Oh, Hellen . . ."

But Hellen couldn't speak. She was too shocked, too amazed.

"We're waiting at the grave," Ladd continued. "Open the portal. Please don't keep us out anymore. We want to come home."

Without another word, Hellen turned around and ran.

"Hellen! Wait!" Polly called after her. "Okay . . . Well, bring Ladd to me. Tell him I missed him. Tell him we can project again, perhaps to Levia's new garden. Tell him I'll summon the puppies—"

It was all she heard. She was out of the Rain Fields now and racing up the incline toward the rock. Happiness surged through her, and she prayed this wasn't a trick or something her mind had conjured to care for her injured heart. Ladd was coming. Erion was coming.

As she neared the rock, she drew on her power. It came sharp and quick, and the instant she was inside, she sent it out in a brilliant burst of green hellfire. Seconds ticked by, her mind raced, her thoughts were hungry and hopeful, and then she felt them, both of them. They were dropping, falling, and in one quaking breath, they both stood before her.

One small and happy and grinning.

One tall and massive and pissed off.

"You are in so much trouble, demon girl."

24

"How does everything look? Is she all right? Is the *balas* well?"

Dr. Leza Franz removed her gloves as she walked away from the bed and deposited them in the trash. "Easy, Alexander. They are both very healthy."

"You're sure?" Alex pressed, following the *veana* as she collected her bag. "I know my mate has told you of my fears regarding this child, so if you are trying to spare me—"

She turned to face him, gave him a very stern look. "Sara is in far better health, both mentally and physically, than you. Especially mentally."

He growled playfully at her.

"Now back up and let me leave," she said. "Call me if you need anything, Sara."

"I will. Thank you, Leza."

When the doctor left the room, Alexander turned and gave his mate, her brother, and Celestine a rare smile. They all huddled around Sara in the bed. He had been a terrified *paven*—so worried he'd be a failure as a father, he hadn't even wanted to try. But now, as his female's belly grew and he felt his *balas* move within her, he couldn't wait. Lucian's child and his would grow up together, a chance he and his brothers hadn't had the luck to experience.

"Alex?"

Cellie was watching him, waiting for him to give her the sign that it was all right to talk with her daughter, tell both Sara and Gray the truth. The complete truth.

He nodded.

"What's going on?" Sara asked warily. "Are you planning something? You guys know I don't get into surprises. They freak me out."

"Whatever it is would be a surprise to me too," Gray chimed in, seated beside his sister on the bed. "I have no idea what's up between them."

Sara and Gray both turned to look at Cellie, who appeared pale and worried but resolute in her desire to come clean.

"Do you both recall the conversation we had outside this house?" she began, her gaze moving from one to the other. "The conversation about your father, your true bloodline?"

"Yes," Gray said, looking slightly uncomfortable. "Not one of my all-time favorite memories."

"No," Cellie remarked. "Mine either."

Sitting up against her pillows, Sara coaxed the *veana* along. "Mom, what's going on? Did something happen?"

"Oh, my dears." Her voice cracked, and she quickly cleared her throat. "Something I never thought I would ever have to tell you. Shouldn't have had to tell you."

Gray cursed. "There's more. Isn't there?"

"Gray . . ." she started.

"I knew it. I knew that wasn't everything."

Stop acting like a whiny child. You're the leader of Impure Resistance, for fuck's sake.

Alexander had said the words in his mind, knowing Gray could hear every word. The Impure male caught his gaze and snarled at him.

Cellie continued, though her eyes weren't connecting with any of them. "When your father was in the Paleo, I thought I'd lose my mind. I couldn't function, I missed him so much, and I feared for his life. I tried everything to get to him. Used every resource." She shook her head. "But I couldn't help him. He was my partner, my friend, the love of my life." When she finally looked up, looked at each one of them in turn, her eyes were wild and desperate. "Ask yourselves: What would I do, how far would I go, to save my true mate?"

Sara glanced at Alexander, who hated the panic he saw in her eyes but remained quiet.

"How far did you go, Mom?" Gray asked, his tone dark.

Cellie looked as though she wanted to melt into the floor. "I went to Cruen."

"Oh, my gods," Sara breathed, put a hand over her mouth.

"I bargained for your father. I gave him what he wanted"—her breath hitched—"and yet Jeremy still returned to me a castrated male."

"What was the bargain?" Gray asked, though the pained look in his eyes said he had a pretty good idea. "What did you give him?"

"Myself," Cellie said in a small voice.

Before another word was spoken, Luca burst through the door, his gaze frantic and pissed off. He found Alex and cursed. "The *veana*'s gone."

"What?" Alex darted a look at Cellie. "When?"

"Bron went to check on her, bring her something to eat, she was gone. We searched everywhere."

"Shit!"

"Oh, gods," Cellie said.

"Why do *veana*s always run from this house?" Lucian remarked.

"Who's gone?" Sara demanded, her now tight, angry gaze on Alex. "Damn it, Alexander! What do you know that I don't? Who was here in my house?"

Alexander hated the stain of his betrayal in her eyes. He had kept something from her and prayed she would come to understand why and forgive him in time.

"Who, Alex?" she repeated tersely.

"Your sister," he rasped.

Everyone within the room turned to Celestine. She looked small and ashamed, and she whimpered as she put her face in her hands. "It was a mistake. She wasn't supposed to have lived." A sob wrenched from her throat. "Cruen and I made a child."

Hellen stared at him, drank him in. It had been only a few days, but it felt as though she hadn't seen him in a year. Dressed in black jeans and a black T-shirt, his dark hair falling to his jaw, his diamond eyes flashing with heat, and his demon resting just below the surface of his skin, he looked dangerous and sexy.

And Hellen wanted to consume him whole.

Ladd was with Levia and Polly in the fireflower garden, bragging about his stellar projecting talents while chasing the puppies one of the females had conjured. Being properly spoiled, he had stated that he was in Heaven in Hell and didn't want to go anywhere else until bedtime. Levia and Polly had begged to keep him, allowing Erion and Hellen the chance to talk.

But looking at him now, Hellen mused, standing beside the mirror in her bedroom, that intense wickedness he wore so well flashing in his eyes, she wanted to do so much more than talk.

Erion, however, was insistent.

"We are back here once again," he said, his tone a perfect key to his mood.

Pissed off.

Hellen stood beside the bed. She hadn't found herself a larger suite, something befitting the ruler of Hell. During their time apart, she hadn't been able to bring herself to move from the room where Erion had made love to her. Lying in her bed at night, she had reveled in the fact that she could still scent him on her bedding, in the air.

She held his gaze and jumped in. "You look angry, Erion."

"Anger doesn't come close to how I feel," he said in a cold voice.

Light from the bedside lamp spilled across the room, casting him in a beautifully strange shadow. "You have to understand why I did it."

"I understand, Hellen. I understand that you made a decision for us—for me—without my approval."

She reacted instantly. "I couldn't have you choosing me over Ladd."

His eyes softened just a hair. "There was your mistake, demon girl. Believing I would."

The shock of his words made Hellen gasp. They were harsh, pointed, and she wanted to run from them. He would've gone anyway? Is that what he was saying? He would've chosen his son over her.

Her shoulders fell. *Yes, of course,* she thought inanely. *That is exactly what he would've done. That is what a good father, a loving father, would do.*

Her eyes lifted. And yet her heart deflated. Maybe that was part of the reason she'd made the decision to send him back through the hellfire without her. She hadn't wanted to hear the truth.

"I can see your mind spinning, demon girl," he said, watching her. "And it's not what you think, what you're creating in that overactive brain I adore so much." He walked over to her. "I love you, Hellen, and I love that *balas*, and I would've found a way to keep us together." His eyes locked with hers. "We would've found a way."

Tears pricked her eyes. "Oh, Erion. I'm sorry."

"You didn't even give us a chance."

Her gaze dropped, swept the floor, her mind searching for answers. "I know." *Oh, gods.* "I know. I think I was afraid of what you'd say, that maybe you didn't love me enough." She hated how vulnerable she felt, how foolish she sounded.

"But it was more than that. Wasn't it?" he said gently. "More than going aboveground, more than your fear I didn't love you?"

"Yes." How did he see her so clearly, when she could barely see herself?

"Tell me, demon girl."

In that moment, Hellen realized what had truly driven her decision to send him back and lock him out. Location and rejection were there and real, but it was more. It was her. It was what Eberny had called her. Who she was—who she'd become the moment she'd ended her father's life. She hadn't wanted Erion to know the truth of what was inside her.

"Hellen . . ."

"I'm the Devil, Erion!"

It wasn't what he expected her to say, and his brows knit together. "What?"

"Not just in some flippant way to express how I feel about myself," she said miserably. "But really and truly. When Abbadon died, I became not just the ruler of Hell, but the carrier of all that is evil and all the power that supports it."

He stared at her for a long time, his gaze moving over every inch of her face as if he was studying it, memorizing it. Finally, he stopped. His eyes connected with hers and he shrugged.

He shrugged.

"You have nothing to say?" she asked, dumbfounded.

"I don't care." He shook his head. "I don't care who you think you are or what you think you're capable of, because I know you. I love you, demon girl. I see what's behind your eyes and in your heart, and it all aches to be good." He reached out and brushed a stray curl away from her face; then he smiled. "We all have evil inside us, but it's the decisions and choices we make, the actions we choose, that make us who we truly are."

"The Devil is evil."

His eyes glittered with love. "Maybe you're a different breed of devil."

Her heart squeezed inside her ribs. "It's a risk, Erion."

He laughed. "Damn right."

Why doesn't he understand this, understand what I am so afraid of? Does he truly see me better than I see myself?

"I have him inside me," she continued, determined to make him understand. "I always have. But I've unleashed it now. When I ended his life, I—"

"When you ended his life, you were able to begin your own," he cut in passionately. "And give your sisters that chance as well."

"It is an ugly creature. This thing inside me." She turned away and laughed bitterly. "The ugliness on the outside is now matched by the ugliness on the inside."

Erion's terrible growl echoed throughout the room, and Hellen snapped back to look at him.

His teeth were bared, his fangs were down, and his eyes blazed with anger. "How dare you say such a thing?"

She drew back, unsure of why he'd reacted so strongly. "I'm sorry, I—"

"I'm taking off your clothes," he said savagely.

"What?"

His voice dropped to a deadly whisper. "If you don't wish for me to rip them from your body, you will lift your arms and hold still."

Shaking slightly, she did as he asked. He made quick

work of her pants and shirt, and when she stood nude before him, he took her hand and led her over to the full-length mirror. Without a word, he whirled her around so her back rested against his broad, rock-hard chest.

"Look at her," he demanded harshly. "Look at the female I love."

Her breath coming quick and uneven, Hellen stared at herself in the mirror. She was naked from head to foot. She had pale skin that liked to turn green from time to time. Her legs were long, her waist trim, her breasts heavy and high, and her face . . .

"Don't you dare turn away," Erion said. "Look at her. She's the most beautiful creature I've ever beheld. Inside and out. She is loved and cherished and desired beyond her wildest imaginings, and if you insult her, you insult me."

Hellen felt that desire press against the rise of her buttocks.

Erion's arms went around her, and his angry, rough expression calmed. "This will be our mating. We will make our promises to each other right now."

She nodded, stared at him in the mirror, her eyes shining with tears, her body trembling with the weight of his ferocity and emotion.

"You will never lock me out again," he said.

"I promise."

"Not from your room, your heart, or your thoughts."

She shook her head. "Never."

His arms squeezed her tighter, closer. "I promise to love you, support you in your rule and care of this land."

His voice broke with emotion. "I will give you my hands to hold when you need friendship, my shoulders when you need to shed tears, my body when you need release and comfort, and my lips to remind you always how beautiful you are."

Tears slipped from her eyes as she held his gaze. "I love you so much, Erion."

Finally, the ire evaporated from his gaze, and it was all softness and heat and happiness. "I love you, demon girl. I am your mate."

"Yes, Erion."

"And you are mine."

"Forever." She broke then, tears streaming down her cheeks. "I was so miserable without you."

He laughed through his own struggle to hold on to his emotions. "I am glad to know I was not alone in such acute misery. Though I hate to think of you hurting. I want you smiling and laughing only." He kissed her shoulder. "Except when I'm touching you."

"Yes," she uttered, a soft smile touching her lips, "Then I will be crying out."

"Moaning for me."

She grinned. "Screaming."

"You are no devil, my love." His hand brushed her face. "Or perhaps you are because you have bewitched me. You have stolen my soul and kept it down here with you, safe and warm and miserable." His eyes clung to hers in the mirror. "I want it back now."

His hand slipped from her face and trailed down her neck. Hellen's breath caught as he ran his fingers over her breast, skimmed across her rib cage to her belly.

"Show me your demon, Hellen," he whispered against her neck as his hand continued its journey.

She smiled and her breath caught as he cupped her sex. "I'll show you mine if you show me yours," she uttered breathlessly.

He chuckled, pressing his cock against her ass as his fingers slipped inside her pussy.

"All in good time, demon girl," he purred, stroking her until she moaned his name, until she bucked against his hand and begged him to take her. "We have all night. We have forever."

Epilogue

The massive hawk shifter touched down outside the gates of the castle and waited patiently for her female passenger to slide from her back.

Seven months pregnant and living in a state of perpetual anxiety, Petra was so grateful, and wrapped her arms around the neck of her best friend. "Thanks, Dani."

"Anytime, Pets," the female shifter replied, her hawk's eyes filled with concern. "And I mean that. I'm so glad you called. We've been so worried about you."

Guilt snaked through Petra's blood and she pulled her coat closer around her, protecting the growing babe. She'd hated these past seven months away from the Rain Forest, away from her mother and father and brothers. Especially in her condition. But the compulsion to find the one who had given her life, protected her, was impossibly strong.

Now that need had increased with the shocking revelation that her birth mother was alive.

She had so many questions, and she hoped the male

who was purported to be inside the castle on the hill before her could answer them.

"Dani, will you tell my family I will come to them soon?" She glanced up at the foreboding landscape she'd found through Celestine and Alexander's whispered conversations. "But please don't reveal my condition. I want to tell them myself."

"Of course," Dani said behind her. "I must get back, Pets. It's nearly dawn and I don't want to be seen. Or shot at."

Petra glanced over her shoulder and smiled at her best friend. "Yes, you have enough holes in your feathers as is."

Dani laughed. "Pinprick little nothings. No one can see them anymore. But you were a cracker shot with a blowgun when we were young."

"It's a wonder we became friends."

"Best friends."

Grinning, Dani didn't wait for a response. She kicked off the ground and sailed beautifully and effortlessly into the air.

Petra watched until she was out of sight, then hurried to the lock at the gate. But to her surprise and her concern, it was drawn open a good two inches. It should never be that easy. *Does Cruen know I'm coming?* she wondered as she hurried up the hill to the door. *But how could that be possible?* She had been searching for him for months. If he could sense her, he would've called for her by now, come and found her.

No, this had to be a mistake, the gate left open by accident.

But when the grand wood door drew back before she even had a chance to knock and the male guard inclined his head and said, "You wish to see Cruen?" she knew her father must have sensed her approach.

As she followed the guard down a long, dimly lit corridor, fear gripped her insides. She'd waited so long, been searching so long . . . she wasn't sure what she expected from him. Would he be glad to see her? Or had he placed her with the shifters for more than just the reasons her adoptive parents had claimed?

The guard came to a stop near another heavy wooden door. He said nothing as he drew it back, just gestured to a flight of stairs that led into a dimly lit space.

A few steps down, her mind warned her to retreat, but where would she go? She was all alone in France. Dani was gone. This is what she'd come to do: talk with her father, know the truth about her birth, and warn him about the male who wished him dead.

But she never got that chance.

Before her foot hit the bottom step, she was swept off her feet and dragged back into the shadows. She tried to fight, to struggle, but the wall of male muscle that had claimed her wouldn't relent.

"Who are you?" he whispered in her ear.

She couldn't speak. She could barely breathe. Her mind swam with questions and fears for the child inside her.

She gasped when she felt a blade at her neck. But oh . . . her senses were going wild. As her mind screamed at her to speak, to scream, her nostrils flared.

She knew that scent.

Oh, gods, she knew that scent.

"Synjon."

The male at her back stiffened. Then after a second or two, lowered the blade.

"Petra?" He grabbed her shoulders and spun her around. "What the hell are you doing here?"

It was dim in the lamplight, but she saw his eyes, sunken and feral though they were, and recognized him as the male she had saved from the sun, the male she had spent one glorious night with.

Her gaze flickered to his right, to a barely conscious figure pinned to the wall. Her skin began to prickle; her belly clenched with pain. It was her father, and he was shackled to the stone. Burns covered his face and neck.

"Oh, my gods," she uttered. "Father? Are you all right?"

"Father?"

It was Syn who spoke, but his voice was different than she remembered, otherworldly and terrifyingly cold. She looked back at him, her gaze imploring him, but she saw nothing of the male she'd known. Only a shell, a hate-filled shell.

"Please, Syn," she begged. "Please let him go."

"Let him go? Cruen?" He burst out laughing. "I will remain here until he's dead."

"Oh, gods—"

"Until I have my revenge."

"No, please—"

Several pairs of footsteps raced down the stairs and into the dungeon. Voices, loud and angry; a warning. Petra felt herself being spun to face the stairs, then yanked back against Synjon, the knife at her throat once again.

"Synjon, stop now!"

"Jesus, what is he doing?"

The room was so dimly lit, Petra could make out only white hair among the crowd.

"Christ, Syn," said another male. "You are out of your fucking mind."

"That's right, Frosty," Synjon said against Petra's ear. "Mad as a hatter."

"Put the knife down," ordered a female voice Petra had never heard before.

"Why should I?" Synjon rasped, his tone pained and bitter.

"Because she's my sister," said the female, softer now, imploring. "Please, Synjon."

Syn gathered Petra tighter around the breasts. "Fuck you all! Juliet was a sister too. She could've been a mother, a mate . . . so much more. This vampire bastard used her." Synjon's voice broke. "Put her in a cage, doped her with drugs, and wanted Frosty here to fuck her until she bred another *balas* he could experiment on."

His words, the ache in his voice, the truth in it, stilled Petra. Her father had done all of that? It wasn't possible.

"He killed the one I loved," Synjon ground out. "Perhaps I should return the favor. Perhaps I should kill the one he loves."

Petra whimpered, whispered to him, "Please don't do this."

"Why?" Suddenly, Synjon lowered his blade and whirled her around to face him again. His eyes were wild and filled with unshed tears. She'd never seen anyone in so much pain. "Why should I let you live, Petra?"

"Because . . . oh, gods, Syn . . ." Her eyes pricked with tears too as she grabbed the edges of her coat, yanked it back, and revealed her swollen belly. "I'm carrying your child."

Don't miss the next novel in the
Mark of the Vampire series,

ETERNAL SIN

Available November 2013
from Signet Eclipse.
Please enjoy this preview.

The hawk shifter flew overhead, circling Petra in the cloudless sky as she stumbled back and forth in front of the mouth of the cave; the same Rain Forest cave she'd pulled a burning, fiercely stubborn Synjon Wise into after he'd tried to follow his lover into the sun seven months ago.

Now it was Petra's turn.

Not to burn, but to feel the constant aftershocks of a misery she couldn't shake.

Tears ran down her cheeks, another great sob exiting her tight throat. She was in so much pain. Unimaginable and inescapable. Her body, her swollen belly, her mind, her heart ...

No. She had no heart. It was silent. An empty, useless organ.

It was a realization that had once filled her with curiosity. She was a vampire. A *veana*. Not a shifter, like her adopted family. Gone were the perpetual feelings of being an outcast among a society who wanted nothing more than to embrace her. Now she had living proof of her own existence. Now her questions could truly be answered.

Who did she belong to? Where were others like her? What could she expect from her life? How long was that life?

He had gifted her with those answers. That male, the *paven* who'd come to the Rain Forest to bury his beloved—and himself if Petra hadn't been there to stop him. Inside the shelter of her tree house so many months ago, Synjon Wise had told her everything, offered her a future. He'd just had to kill someone first.

Vengeance before romance. Love.

But the one he'd had to kill, the one who had murdered his Juliet, well . . . he was Petra's only connection with the outside world. Her only connection to her blood. He was her father.

Cruen.

Another pained cry was wrenched from Petra's lungs, from deep inside, where the ache seemed to emanate from, and she stopped and gripped the cool, moist curve of the cave's entrance.

She heard her mother's voice somewhere behind her. "What can we do?" Not the mother who had given her life, but the one who had raised her. As part of her pride, a cub to be cherished.

The beautiful lion shifter Wen had been the best mother any creature, shifter or vampire, could hope for. Now she nearly wailed in pain at Petra's distress.

"I don't know," said the other female, the one who had brought Petra to the Rain Forest a week before. This was her biological mother, Celestine. A Pureblood vampire who was as desperate to make up for lost time and bond with her daughter as Petra was to push her away.

She didn't need another parent. Especially not one who considered her part in creating Petra a grave mistake.

"You're a vampire, like her," Wen continued, her unsteady voice carrying on the breeze. "Surely you've seen this kind of—"

"Never." Celestine's tone was emphatic, impassioned. Fearful. "Her sister, my daughter, Sara, is also in *swell*, but she is an Impure. She never went through *Meta*. Getting pregnant before you're of age, before you experience your transition, is very rare."

"Do you think that's why she's reacting this way?"

"Emotional surges are predicted in pre-*Meta swell* . . ."

"But not like this."

Celestine paused before saying, "No, not like this. And not this far along. The surges are purported to be very early on in the pregnancy."

"What are we to do?" Wen said, her own throat breaking with emotion. "She's been here a week, and every day—every hour—it grows worse."

Their voices grated on Petra's exposed nerves, searing her mind with agony. Her nails scraped against the rock.

"There must be something we can give her to ease this suffering," Wen continued. "This strange hunger. The pain."

"Blood," said Celestine.

"She won't drink it," Wen returned. "I've tried. She—"

"Stop it!" Petra snarled over her shoulder, tears raining down her cheeks, unstoppable. "Stop talking about me as if I'm not here!"

Both females froze in the glare of the sunlight, their gazes cutting to her immediately. Petra despised the fear and empathy she saw in their eyes. Or maybe their expressions made her feel frustrated . . . or was it desperately sad? She didn't know.

Whimpering, she gripped the underside of her large belly. She couldn't decipher her feelings. There were too many of them. What was wrong with her?

Celestine moved toward her. "You must drink."

"No," Petra growled. *Blood.* Just the thought of it on her tongue, running down her throat, made her gag, made her vicious. She hissed at both of them, pressed back against the mouth of the cave.

Tears in her own eyes now, Wen started rolling up one of her sleeves. "You can have mine, baby. Take all you need. Please, Pets. Please." She bit her lip, the loving childhood nickname swallowed up by a sob of despair. "Seeing you like this . . ."

Overhead the hawk cried, swooping in low over their heads before returning to the sky. Petra glanced up and growled at the bird. She'd told Dani she didn't want to see her, didn't want a ride over the treetops of the Rain Forest, didn't want her looks of sympathy or fear. But her best friend refused to leave, to retreat to her nest.

"Your blood won't stop this, Wen," Celestine said gently. "I'm afraid she needs his."

"The father of the child . . ."

"Yes."

No father, Petra silently screamed. *He was no father.*

He wanted to kill her, the baby ... She turned and ran into the cave. Sobs burst in her chest, scraping her throat. She wanted to get away from them. From everyone. From light, heat, sound. She wanted to search for darkness. Maybe it would claim her.

"Oh, gods," she heard Wen cry. "But that's not possible, is it? After what was done to him. Does he even remember their time together?"

"His memories weren't taken—just his emotions," Celestine said, her voice echoing inside the walls of the cave. "He knows about her and the *balas*. He knows that she carries the grandchild of his enemy. The question is, will he care?"

Petra met the back of the cave. It was dark and wet and cold and rough, but it welcomed her. Breathing heavily, panic and sickness and fear and anger rippling through her, she curled up against it and tried to force every thought, every feeling, every memory from her mind.

But it was impossible.

Along with the staggering emotional and physical pain her body felt, her brain conjured her past. Flipping by, scene after scene, she saw every bit of her childhood in the Rain Forest. She saw the hunts, the shifters, her friends. She saw her work, helping shifters with their early transitions. She saw her brothers.

She saw Synjon.

Once again, she experienced the fear and pain of dragging him inside the cave she huddled within now. She felt his interest in her, both mentally and sexually. She felt his kiss, his touch.

She felt the moment he'd placed a child in her womb.

Tears flooded her cheeks. He was responsible for this, what she was going through. And yet he was completely at peace. She'd hoped for so much more as she'd watched his emotions being bled from his body on the dungeon floor of the *mutore* Erion's castle a week ago.

She'd hoped for the male who'd held her, kissed her, cared for her once upon a time.

Petra swiped at her eyes and whimpered. As she leaned into the cool, hard rock, growing more and more lost, her child weakening along with her body and mind, Synjon Wise was out there in the world somewhere, devoid of care, of concern. His child and the *balas*'s mother the furthest things from his mind.

Within his sprawling penthouse of glass and brick, Synjon Wise sat comfortably at his Bösendorfer, his fingers moving quickly across the keys as he played something complex yet pointless.

The party guests circulated through the six thousand square feet of interior space, leaving the wraparound terraces and 360-degree views of Manhattan to the shard of moon and the cold winter night. It was his third party in seven days. The first being the very night he'd bought the place. The small crowd had been courtesy of his Realtor. Broadway actors, artists, financiers, Pureblood and Impure vampires. He'd never thought much about owning a flat or dipping into the massive wealth he'd accumulated over the years. He'd been far too busy working, spying, following the trail of vengeance . . .

This was so much better.

This was blissful nothingness.

He glanced up from the sheet music he didn't need to read. The dull hum of conversation, the deep thirst of those who continued to empty glass upon glass of Dom Pérignon White Gold, and the females who he'd instructed not to come near him until he ceased playing. It was a far cry from the manic scene in the *mutore*'s dungeon a week ago.

A flash on the terrace snagged his attention even as he continued playing. Three blokes stood on the flagstones, their expressions grave as they headed for the glass doors. Synjon knew them, of course. One far more than the others, and although the memory, the history, he shared with them held a good amount of tension and heaviness, he knew absolutely that they were not his enemies.

Dressed completely in black, and taller, wider, and far more fearsome than any of his guests, the three males entered the Great Room, bringing with them the winter chill. Every set of human eyes widened; every pair of human feet drew back. His fingers still moving over the keys, Synjon tracked the males, waited for them to see him, to scent him. It took no more than a moment before they did, before a pathway was created across the polished stone floor.

Syn continued to play as the Roman brothers moved toward him. They appeared tense. Syn wondered what that felt like.

"Welcome to the party," he said as they came to stand beside him.

The one he knew best, a nearly albino vampire male,

spoke first. "I think our invitation got lost in the mail, Brit Boy."

There was a time Syn would have risen to the male's caustic play. He had no interest now. "You weren't invited, Lucian. In fact, none of you were."

The male turned to his skull-shaved brother, Alexander, and snorted. "Good to know the guy still has some asshole left in him."

Alexander didn't respond. His focus was entirely on Synjon, his tone serious as he spoke. "We have a problem."

"We?" Synjon asked, his fingers moving into Bach's concerto in F minor. He used to despise the piece, but now he felt only the smoothness of the keys against his skin.

Alexander's voice dropped and his eyes narrowed. "The *veana* who carries your child—"

"Petra," Syn supplied, picturing the dark-haired *veana* and feeling . . . nothing.

"Yes," Alexander ground out. "She hasn't gone through her *Meta*. We didn't know that before. When we sent her back . . . And we didn't know a *veana* in *swell* who hadn't gone through her transition would react . . . She's losing her mind, Syn."

Synjon looked up, assessed the male. He couldn't imagine why Alexander was telling him this. "Now that you're here, would you like to stay? Join my guests?"

A growl rumbled in Alexander's chest. "No."

"Perhaps you'd like something to drink."

"Christ," Lucian uttered, leaning against the piano.

"Some*one* to drink, then?" Synjon caught the eye of

one of the humans who enjoyed feeding his vampire guests. She grinned at him.

"We're not here for a party," Nicholas said tersely, moving around the piano to the other side. "Petra is ill, Syn. She can't control her emotions. She's going out of her mind. It happened soon after she returned to the Rain Forest. You have to—"

"Attend to my guests," Synjon said evenly. There was so much to do—select his blood donor and his sexual conquests. He had discriminating tastes. But first, a little Prelude in C-sharp minor. Rachmaninoff used to make him snarl.

Times changed, it seemed.

Arching an eyebrow at the three males, he said, "If you'll excuse me."

"Excuse me?" Lucian repeated, giving Syn a disgusted look. "Whatever happened to 'Get the fuck out of my way, you bleeding tossers'?"

"I don't solve problems with words or threats, Lucian," he said, his voice even. "I take care of them quietly, quickly."

"That's too bad," Lucian muttered.

"We should go, find another way," Nicholas said tightly. "He doesn't give a shit about anything. And it's our fault. We made him that way."

"Cruen made him that way," Alex amended.

"At our request."

Lucian growled, pushed away from the piano. "Another bargain with Cruen."

"It was a good one," Syn remarked, closing in on the final seven-measure coda. "I've never felt better."

"You feel nothing," Lucian returned.

"Oh, I feel quite perfect where it matters—all things physical. I'm not burdened with tedious, irrational emotions. It's all very civilized, really." Rachmaninoff ceased to exist, and Synjon glanced up at Alexander. "I appreciate what was forced upon me."

"Then perhaps we should force you to help Petra." Alexander returned with barely disguised menace. "She needs your blood. Now."

"That's unfortunate for her." Syn jerked his chin in the direction of the Great Room. "As you can see, I am otherwise engaged."

"He's lost," Luca uttered. "Fucking lost."

Synjon stared at the three faces, all twisted into ravaged masks of worry. It suited them: that intensity, those feral, predatory glares. But it held no interest for him. He was rather relaxed, really—though he could use a pint or two, perhaps a quick, hard fuck.

Alexander ground his teeth. "Syn, your child and Petra . . . They could both die without your help. Your blood."

Done with this repetitive, pointless conversation, Synjon uttered a smooth, "Then I suppose they will die," before he returned to the cool, white keys and another song from his past: Nirvana's "Drain You."

Also available from

LAURA WRIGHT

Eternal Kiss
Mark of the Vampire

Raised by the Breed, Nicholas Roman wants to stop the
Eternal Order of Vampires from controlling his life, and
transforming more males from his bloodline for their
vicious reign. Only a beautiful vampire stranger can help
him. But what are her true motives?

Kate Everborne claims she's sheltering Nicholas's long lost
son. If this is true, then who is the mother? And how
endangered are they if indeed he does possess the bloodline so coveted by the Order? These are questions that
with every seductive whisper, every silken touch, draw
Nicholas and Kate intimately closer and nearer still to the
truth. But aroused, too, are Nicholas's fears that this tan-
talizing woman has even more secrets—both dangerous
and provocative—she has yet to share.

"A riveting new series."
—*New York Times* bestselling author Larissa Ione

Available wherever books are sold or at
penguin.com

Also available from

LAURA WRIGHT

Eternal Hunger
Mark of the Vampire

Alexander Roman wants nothing to do with the controlling
rulers of his vampire breed or the family he escaped from a
hundred years ago. But as a new threat to the pureblood
vampires emerges, Alexander's ties to the past are forced
upon him again, and without warning, he finds himself—
disoriented, terrified, and near death—at the door of
a stranger.

Dr. Sara Donohue is dedicated to removing the traumatic
memories of her patients—like those of the stranger at her
front door. But what he tells her of his past is too
astonishing to believe.

As their worlds collide, Sara and Alexander are bound by
something even stronger—as one becomes hunter and the
other prey...

"Dark, delicious, and sinfully good."
—*New York Times* bestselling author Nalini Sin

Available wherever books are sold or at
penguin.com

facebook.com/ProjectParanormalBooks

s0